PENGUIN BOOKS

WEDDING READINGS

Among Eleanor Munro's books are *Originals: American Women Artists*, *Memoir of a Modernist's Daughter*, and *On Glory Roads: A Pilgrim's Book About Pilgrimage*. Her essays and criticism appear in the national and art press, and she lectures widely. She lives in New York City.

Wedding Readings

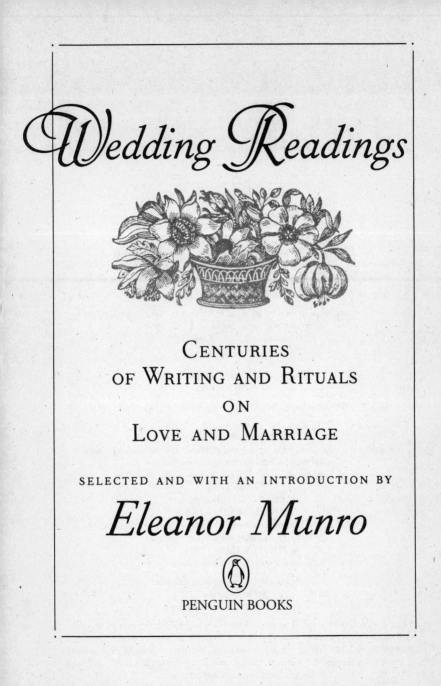

Centuries
of Writing and Rituals
on
Love and Marriage

SELECTED AND WITH AN INTRODUCTION BY

Eleanor Munro

PENGUIN BOOKS

PENGUIN BOOKS
Published by the Penguin Group
Penguin Books USA Inc., 375 Hudson Street, New York, New York 10014, U.S.A.
Penguin Books Ltd, 27 Wrights Lane, London W8 5TZ, England
Penguin Books Australia Ltd, Ringwood, Victoria, Australia
Penguin Books Canada Ltd, 10 Alcorn Avenue, Toronto, Ontario, Canada M4V 3B2
Penguin Books (N.Z.) Ltd, 182–190 Wairau Road, Auckland 10, New Zealand

Penguin Books Ltd, Registered Offices: Harmondsworth, Middlesex, England

First published in the United States of America by Viking Penguin,
a division of Penguin Books USA Inc., 1989
Published in Penguin Books 1996

1 3 5 7 9 10 8 6 4 2

An extension of this copyright page begins on page 259.

THE LIBRARY OF CONGRESS HAS CATALOGUED THE HARDCOVER AS FOLLOWS:
Munro, Eleanor C.
Wedding readings: centuries of writing and rituals on love and marriage/selected
and with an introduction by Eleanor Munro.
p.   cm.
Includes index.
ISBN 0-670-81088-6 (hc.)
ISBN 0 14 00.8879 2 (pbk.)
1. Weddings—Literary collections.   2. Love—Literary collections.
3. Marriage—Literary collections.   I. Title.
PN6071.W4M86   1989
082—dc19   88–40334

Printed in the United States of America
Set in Fournier
Designed by Francesca Belanger

For David and Anath

August 28, 1988

Acknowledgments

Nan Graham of Viking inspired this book. She recognized the need for such a resource. She understood that many couples approaching marriage today want to formalize their hopes within the embrace of ritual both old and modern, traditional and also distinctively personal. And because of the course of much of my own writing so far—about imaginative people's lives and their quest or pilgrimage toward form and meaning in them—she thought I'd find the idea interesting. She was right on both scores. Many people spoke to me about their search for appropriate additions to liturgies of their choice, and a number of clergymen and women did as well. As for me, as I worked my way through the library, I became more and more impressed by the delicacy of their—and my—mission.

The artifices of courtship have changed radically in the past century, but the achievement of a good marriage hasn't been made easier by these upheavals. The challenge for people marrying today is to know what they want from the institution. If their view of it is serious, as most people's is, they'll want to spend time thinking hard about that question. It seems to me that to do so helped along by others from far-flung parts of the world and many past centuries, who've ruminated on the same issues of love, hope, permanence, and related subjects, can't help but be illuminating.

In spite of all that in these days separates us from the language and customs of our forebears, still, as Keats wrote, "some shape of beauty" moves us toward salvaging the essentials in the old ceremonies like those of marriage. The question that confronts people approaching marriage today, then, is: what are the essentials? That question lies at the heart of the contents and organization of this book.

Many poems and prose passages appear in these pages in excerpted form. I owe an explanation of my use of that editorial privilege. In my days as an editor of an art magazine, I learned the effectiveness of details of larger works isolated on a page. At the same time, we understood that to highlight a detail was to do a kind of violence to the complete work, and we always included a small photo of the whole work as a reference. Looking for literary selections appropriate to marriage, I found myself under a constraint. Much writing on love draws power from the dialectic at the heart of human life: the longing for permanence and the absoluteness of passing time. But the marriage ritual, theoretically a timeless sacrament, opposes the literalness of decay. Soundings of realism which give weight to a poem on the page would be horribly inappropriate to the mood of a wedding. So in full if abashed awareness, I offer the light from many of these works without the necessary, more truthful dark. It would have been good to print such poems in full as well, as we used to do with paintings. But the whole works can be found in many places, and I trust readers, once the wedding day is past, to draw on their collective wisdom.

In addition to Nan Graham, others helped shape this book. Graphic designer Francesca Belanger gave it its visual clarity. Ann Bartunek was its expert copy editor. Kate Griggs and Kathryn Harrison, also of Viking, were patient and careful through its changes. For leads, encouragement and other helps, I also thank Georges and Anne Borchardt, Lynn Boillot, Caryn Beth Broitman, William Rossa Cole, the Reverend Jean Curtis, Helen

Handley, Francine Klagsbrun, Stanley Kunitz, the Reverend and Mrs. Edward L. Mark, Pamela Painter, Dawn E. Rickman, Jeannette Rohatyn, David and Catherine Shainberg, Maggie Scarf, Eileen Simpson, William Jay Smith, Carol Southern, the Reverend James E. Thomas, Aileen Ward, Mark Williams, Nancy Dingman Watson, and Peter and Clara Watson.

Thanks too to my extended family—now eight nuclear families and more no doubt on the horizon—who have taught me much about love and forbearance, the twin supports of the married life.

Contents

II. *In Search of Love*

III. *The Processional Begins*

IV. *Eternal Vows in Sacred Space*

V. *The Miracle of the Body*

VI. *The Country of Marriage*

VII. *Morning in Eternal Space*

Wedding Readings

. . . our life reminds me
of a forest in which there is a graceful clearing
and in that opening a house,
an orchard and garden,
comfortable shades, and flowers . . .
The forest is mostly dark, its ways
to be made anew day after day, the dark
richer than the light and more blessed,
provided we stay brave
enough to keep on going in . . .

WENDELL BERRY, from "The Country of Marriage"

Apparently I am going to marry Charles Lindbergh. . . . Don't
wish me happiness—it's gotten beyond that, somehow. Wish
me courage and strength and a sense of humor—I will need
them all. . . .

ANNE MORROW LINDBERGH, from *Bring Me a Unicorn*

. . . when we find ourselves
In the place just right
It will be in the valley
Of love and delight.

from "Simple Gifts,"
a Shaker hymn

*T*he country of marriage, in Wendell Berry's lovely phrase, lies well beyond careless happiness, on the other side of but never out of reach of the valley of delight. A person can drop straight into the place as if by parachute, but the long winding and climbing approach is more interesting. In either case, once there, you have a lot to learn. But when the harvests roll in, they're full and mellow. Each day then breaks like a birthing—no other has been so fresh and new. And night, when it comes, comes easy. Moonlight veils the houses and fields; stars rise, flare, pale, and disappear—to return the next night as if the world had no end.

The ritual which is the gateway into this country or condition is the wedding. In the present day, a wedding has two functions. One is to confirm the bridal couple in their own religious or social heritage against the larger background of cultural history. The other is to address the pair as individuals, leading each one toward an understanding of what it can mean to exchange vows of fidelity and care in this age of radical self-questioning and social change. The ceremony at the gate is one of the "rites of passage," as anthropologists call them, by which people in different parts of the world signal their entry into a new stage of life.

To the wedding formalities, the readings in this book provide a sort of counterpoint. Some of the meditations on the nature of love and union would probably best be read by a couple in private, separately or together. Others should fit gracefully into the proceedings of even the most traditional wedding. Personal additions to the liturgy are allowed today by most Jewish and Christian clergy, who will guide couples in making their choices of readings, assigning them to family members or close friends, and setting them in the proper place in the ceremony.

Included here are passages of scripture and liturgy from various parts of the world, including India and China, as well as secular literature old and new, some of which, in the words of the poet Wallace Stevens, address "the men of the time . . . and the women of the time." In their various voices these writers have sought to describe a mode of feeling which had its origin in our common animal need for protection, warmth, and companionship, but which has evolved over the centuries into something more general and far-reaching. The sensibility these writers have tried to define, which they celebrate and toward which we move in hope and trust as we approach marriage, is experienced as the fundamental orienting principle of a life. In an age of shifting values and emotional inconstancies, of restlessness and faithlessness, the concept of enduring love and the institution which embodies it serves us well.

In a poem about modern poetry, Wallace Stevens makes his way slowly, even gropingly, toward an idea which is only just coming into his mind as he proceeds. "It has to be living," he says, "to learn the/speech of the place.

> . . . [to] speak words that in the ear,
> In the delicatest ear of the mind, repeat,
> Exactly, that which it wants to hear, at the sound
> Of which, an invisible audience listens,
> Not to the play, but to itself, expressed
> In an emotion as of two people, as of two
> Emotions becoming one. . . .

Both the art of modern poetry, as Stevens understands it, and the art of modern marriage entail moving persistently but perhaps not ever quite successfully toward an ideal held in the mind. For a modern person to prepare for marriage in that sense may mean acquiring an understanding of the ideal which will be sturdy enough to survive one's continued failure to achieve it.

The concept of Love as an abstract ideal is credited to the Greek philosopher Plato. Much of the world's literature on romantic and mystical love, including the Jewish and Christian marriage liturgies, take their tone from that source. Perfect Love is a god, Plato proposed, divine, everlasting, and as unattainable by human beings as the stars. In that form, Love has existed in the universe since the beginning of time and will endure forever. On the other hand, there exists also the individual brand of love, which strikes us here on earth like a glint off the sun, making us suffer, pine, rejoice, and, sometimes, marry.

As Plato saw it, the most important thing about Love in the general sense was its power to draw people toward it, to stir in them "a longing for immortality, which in the human consciousness begins with a desire for union." We still don't fully understand what "desire for union" means in terms of human psychology. Perhaps it begins in adolescence with a feeling of nostalgia for the security of infancy. But whenever in later life it surges back, it moves people young and old, in their individual times of readiness, toward marriage or some comparable state of emotional bonding.

The ritual forms by which marriage is inaugurated, those liturgies and the formal postures and actions of the participants, take some of their tone of solemn otherworldliness from Platonic thought as well. These rites come down to us as if out of the clouds, seemingly without connection to everyday language and behavior. In the same way, family histories, often recalled in toasts during wedding festivities, transcend ordinary time. Such summonings of ancestral lines link up the centuries through repeated rhythms of marriage, birth, and death, the "periods of return" of humanity's adventure under the stars. Wound around by these formulations while a wedding unfolds, an individual may feel very small or very important but never alone. The ceremonies, and reminders of long family participation in them, serve to draw young people two by two into the ark of our common heritage. Say the ancient words and you join the generations to live a larger life than your own.

In this sense, marriage is a form of thought and imagination. It is a structure laid around the fruitful period of a lifetime within which otherwise random experiences and years acquire purpose and shape. In that enclosure—in that country—love is twined with the notion of timelessness; awakened sexuality, with trust. The importance in the evolution of human thinking of this double helix of love and timelessness is suggested by the reverence people still feel for the capacity of lifelong fidelity to an ideal or person. The biblical promise "Whither thou goest, I will go . . ." is a pledge which gave the Moabite woman Ruth new awareness of both place and time, for before the promise was made, neither nation nor years had special significance for her, nor had her life a special end. But giving up her homeland to serve her husband's mother, she won respect and love, and a place in the noblest family tree in Western scripture, that of King David. To make a pledge of perpetual loyalty, of the kind marriage entails, is still to lend oneself to the long human quest for moral value.

In antiquity in both Asia and the pagan West, myths of stable (or unstable) bonds between the various gods served as a metaphor for the relationship between elements of the natural world. Sky gods in wedlock with goddesses of the earth, field gods in seasonal marriage with corn and wheat goddesses, represented the enduring if periodically unsettled universe. In ancient Rome, a human male sometimes took on the mantle of a god and was wed to a tree in Diana's sacred grove in the Alban hills, where she reigned as goddess of woodlands and wild animals. Today we accept that that rite symbolized the bond between humanity and the world, on which the continued well-being of each depends. Projecting the image of a marriage bond onto nature, men and women in antiquity humanized the earth at the same time that they magnified their sense of their own place in creation.

The myth of wedlock with the natural world did not pass away. It survives today openly in the wedding rites of Hinduism, a religious community which extends across India, parts of Indonesia and Africa, and into smaller pockets in the West. Bridegroom and bride represent Lord Shiva, creator and destroyer of the world, and his wife, Parvati. They also represent Lord Shiva's shrine-city Benares in India, which is understood to be in perpetual nuptial union with the goddess Ganga, the river Ganges, which flows along its bank. Beyond that, they represent the halves of the cosmos itself: "I am the sky," says the bridegroom to his bride as part of the ritual. "You are the earth. We are sky and earth, united." At the close of their wedding day, the couple stands together under the stars while the husband points out the constellations as they rise, ending with the North Star, to which he makes a ritual prayer:

O Firm one, pillar of the stars, Polestar, how stable you are! As the earth is stable, as the mountains are stable, as the universe is stable, so may this woman my wife be firm and stable in our family.

Then he turns to his wife: "You are united with me. May you live with me for a hundred years! May you be steadfast as that star in your love for me." She acquiesces with the promise to be "ever firmly attached to my husband." Thereafter, husband and wife are each the other's Polestar, and so it may be for married couples wherever they are, whatever their religious orientation.

In the city of Venice for many centuries a comparable rite was performed. The magistrate of the city, the Doge, took on himself the role of bridegroom, throwing a gold ring into the waves of the Adriatic with the words, Desponsamus te, Mare . . . : *We wed thee, O Sea. The rest of the liturgy informed the bride of her perpetual domination by the Venetian Republic. Now that city is no more a political power in itself, and in the West at least the old concept of divinely appointed male authority has faded, but the power of the ritual remains, for it* contained psychological truth. It speaks to us today. It tells us to make our lives a union of structure and emotion. It reminds us that social forms like marriage are drawn out of the universal human well-source of need and desire.

Enduring loyalty is one such structure, which stands like a Venice on the shores of the aimlessness and emptiness which for many people characterize life without it. "I do love thee," said Shakespeare's Othello. "And when I love thee not/Chaos is come again." It is against chaos that many modern writers represented in these pages, like E. M. Forster, W. H. Auden, Wallace Stevens, and others, some of whom were in fact unmarried, others whose marriages were less than satisfying, still described the institution as precious and good.

The symbolism of divine marriage with its apparatus of incantation and magic is still with us. Wedding vows in that sense are spells, invocations not so much to heaven as to a still-unrealized being in oneself who may grow to maturity to fulfill the promise. Often when a wedding takes place in a public place, a small crowd gathers on the sidewalk to wait for the bride. When she comes out the door to stand at the top of the steps, in her white dress with her white veil turned back, she seems more than herself, even a little like a goddess. We are all prone to the illusion. We believe, or want to believe, that a union of two of ourselves, formalized by a wedding, will in some way outlast our lives. Even unbelievers cast themselves forward in marriage through the hope of children, or if not of children, of some other version of the creative old words, to "husband the earth."

So wedding rites and the associations we have with them, like other rites of passage through history, prove that the human family is one, even if its members are as varied as birds in their mating feathers and songs. Whether we identify ourselves as Jewish, Catholic, or Protestant; Hindu, Buddhist, or Moslem; tribal or atheist, we inherit a disposition felt as a lifelong need to shape our thoughts and lives in symbolic terms against the background of the world. Our rites of passage, their formal language and stately pantomimes on the theme of union between humanity and the cosmos, are an answer to this need.

On the other hand, each individual has to find his or her own footing in the ceremony with its architecture of enduring time and moral responsibility. The readings here may provide some guidance. The selections are grouped loosely into sections which follow the narrative course of the event. In the first group are passages by various writers on the theme of psychic change and preparation for a great decision. The next includes meditations on the nature and meaning of love, beginning with Plato's Symposium. Thereafter come selections on the ceremony itself, on the signifance of the "sacred space" where the vows are exchanged, and passages of liturgy, poetry, and prose on related mysteries.

According to ancient myths, sacred space is a site where earth and sky meet, as on a holy mountaintop or in a shrine, temple, or church which has been ritually sanctified. There, according to the myths, time stands still. History dissolves into eternity. The implications of this mystical belief reach out to affect bridal couples today. The Jewish or Christian bride and groom represent the biblical Eve and Adam and later scriptural queens and kings. Bridal couples in the Greek and Russian Orthodox churches wear gold crowns for this reason, as do couples in Indonesia, who represent their own royal and religious ancestors.

In sacred space, every detail of ritual flows from the concept of united earth and heaven. As the wedding day approaches, the site where the ceremony is to be held is ritualistically readied. A garden is planted, watered, and nurtured into bloom. A shrine is cleaned and decorated with flowers, and the instruments of the service, Jewish, Catholic, or Protestant, laid out. In Asia, the shrine is purified by burning herbs and holy oils in it and reciting mantras or magic spells. In a Buddhist shrine, an altar table is set with twin vases of flowers or pine branches, together with a bowl of holy water and prayer beads, and perhaps memorial tablets of both families.

On the wedding day, the bridal couple is prepared to enter the symbolic space. Jewish couples, separately, visit the mikvah or holy bath, whose waters, according to tradition, flow out of the Jordan River to wash away the stains of the world. In Asia, the bride and groom may be rubbed in unguents and spices, ground mustard seed or myrtle, and the palms of their hands and the soles of their feet stained with henna. The bride's hair is arranged and adorned with gold ornaments and flowers.

Finally comes the ceremonial dressing. In Asia, bride and groom wear silks and crowns of royalty and colors taken from nature's palette: red or gold of sunlight, blue of heaven, green of grass. In the West, we reserve only the bridegroom's buttonhole for such unpuritan display, and our brides wear white for angelic unworldliness.

When the couple enters the sanctuary, they stand in ritually prescribed formation, for where they stand represents the center of earth and heaven, the pin of a cosmic compass. A Jewish wedding takes place under a chuppah, or canopy, held upon four poles, which represents the sky of paradise. There the bride first takes her position facing the bridegroom as, in Genesis, Eve was presented to Adam. She then moves to his right to receive the wedding ring on the index finger of her right hand, whose artery, it was once thought, was joined to the heart. In Christian sanctuaries, couples stand before the altar which, architectural necessities permitting, faces east toward sunrise, the direction in which according to old tradition Christ rose to heaven. Standing at her bridegroom's left, the Christian bride receives her ring on her left hand, the heart hand of this tradition.

In Judaism and Christianity, human marriage is said to mirror the union of God and humanity. Western wedding liturgies are filled with expressions of mystical love in which the bridegroom's love for his bride reflects God's for men and women. Committing themselves to fidelity beyond the grave in a ceremony which includes celebration of the Eucharist or Mass, Catholic couples assume symbolic roles referring to God's husbanding of his people and Christ's of his church on earth. Protestant weddings may be shy on mystic symbolism but they include an incomparable rhetoric of instruction to the new family on the responsibilities of humanhood. The language in the revised Book of Common Prayer has entered the bloodstream of the English-speaking world: "Dearly beloved: We have come together in the presence of God to witness and bless the joining together of this man and this woman in Holy Matrimony. . . ." In the Eastern Orthodox Church, by contrast, mood and symbolism count heavily. Bride and bridegroom enter the sanctuary carrying lighted white candles, led by robed priests swinging censers. To the sound of prolonged medieval choral singing, they exchange rings in a ritual betrothal, then don gold crowns for the exchange of vows.

The number seven appears in the liturgies of Judaism, Catholicism, and Hinduism. As with other details of marriage ritual, we have to seek the reason in the past where the roots of belief lie tangled with ancient suppositions about the nature of the world. The number refers to the earth, sun, moon, and four planets visible to the naked eye all apparently locked together in harmonious interrelationship governed by a single law. To speak of "seven" then means to speak of a whole, a cosmic union. Jewish weddings include seven ritual blessings. In the Roman Catholic Church, marriage is one of the seven sacraments. And in the course of their wedding, a Hindu bride and groom take seven steps around a stone or fire on the altar representing the axis of the universe while they pray for seven blessings on their future lives. "We have taken the seven steps," says the groom. "You are mine forever."

The vows in these and other ceremonies bind a couple several ways: subjectively in their own consciousness of the new life they are entering; in a social sense into their community, in which the vows may have legal weight; finally into the fabric of immemorial myth and faith, in which the words are believed to lend stabilizing power to the universe itself.

At the same time all these evolved ideas about marriage hide the simple fact of nature which is the basis for the social ceremony: a man and woman's readiness for monogamous sexual life, their acceptance of adult responsibility. When the groom slips a ring on the bride's finger, he takes possession of her, in the language of symbolism, in the flesh. In Jewish tradition, when the bride and bridegroom share red wine from a goblet, they symbolically take in the fruit of each other's love. So of the nuptial kiss at the end of Christian services and the winding of a newly married couple in flower wreaths and ribbons. So of the flinging of rice and the banging of pot lids at the newlyweds' door: all these are not-so-veiled references to sexual union. In some rural communities and intensely mystical religious sects like the Jewish Hasidim, it is usual to celebrate weddings with sexually charged dances around the bridal couple lifted on high chairs at the center. These exercises may come down the ages and distantly imitate the circling of stars around the axis of the earth, the most glorious image of union the world affords.

Mystics may dance, and nature lovers find wider resonance to their lovemaking at Niagara Falls, but for many young people in the world today a wedding is occasion for somber rites of integration into their nations' history. When the Orthodox Jewish bridegroom crushes a glass under his foot at the end of the ceremony, he metaphorically enacts his union with his bride and, at the same time, recalls the tragedy that still overhangs Jewish national life, the destruction of the Temple. And in Russia today, brides still in white after their bureaucratic weddings make pilgrimage with their husbands to historic places like Lenin's tomb in Red Square in Moscow, the Tomb of the Unknown Soldier of the "Great Fatherland War of 1941–45," or, in the provinces, any statue of Lenin. Reverently they lay down their bouquets on the stones, pose for pictures, and uncork champagne to share with passersby. The legend on the base of the Moscow tomb reads "Your name is unknown but your deed is eternal." The notion of eternality in materialist Soviet Russia is a relic from its Christian past, but reverence for the honored dead is common, and by these actions, couples publicly announce their claim on a larger-than-ordinary life. In a rite even more indicative of the deep meaning of the marriage bond, some hundred couples a year travel to the site of the village of Lidice in Czechoslovakia, destroyed by the Nazis, to be married there and so in some sense carry on its life.

However, the word "eternity" may be too remote and abstract to convey the reality of what most marrying couples today hunger for. All these rites and symbolisms of marriage—the cosmic imagery of the Hindu wedding, the crowns worn by Greek Orthodox brides and bridegrooms, the paradisiacal significance of the Jewish chuppah, the biblical resonances of the Western Christian service, even the angelic white worn by brides in many countries—serve to situate the institution against an expanded background of space, time, myth, and history. Modern couples still long for what their forebears provided the symbolic means of experiencing: a living bond with the world which will outlast their lives.

That longing, and the ideas and images it generates, underlie the final group of readings in this collection, which opens with James Agee's meditation on a house in country-morning sunlight. Call that house "marriage." It stands square and solid on the plains, lit by light from beyond the horizon. So of marriage. It is a monumental, grounded structure in our individual lives as in society. It was built to answer a physical need: to provide shelter and nurture for the fragile offspring of our species. But it reflects these other, less tangible needs.

It was once upon a time imagined that mistletoe in the boughs of an oak tree held the juice of immortality, or Love. The plant was said to bloom on Midsummer Eve. A girl would spread a white cloth under the tree that night, take the flower dust found there and sprinkle it under her pillow to see her future bridegroom in her dream. Good luck, lasting marriage, and long life were conjured for in many such ways in the old days. Girls in rural America spent their years of adolescence stitching quilts to the number eleven, when they'd let be known their readiness for a suitor, then set to work on the twelfth, the Wedding Quilt, which would be done in time for the bridal bed.

We're not so easily charmed into faith today. But there may be mysterious benefit to be had from the kind of meditations I've included in the section "Morning in Eternal Space." These readings lift the curtain on what will be, henceforth, for each couple their landscape of marriage. Oriented in the center of it as if by the Blackfoot prayer to the four directions or the Chinese prayer to the four seasons, they may petition the skies for the kind of simple gifts with which true happiness begins—"calm lake, little wind, little rain . . . moon of good health . . . the year abundant, with millet and rice . . ."—the promise of full harvests for years to come.

All that I've said here applies both to committed members of religious communities and to couples embarking on the kind of secular, or inter-faith, and cross-cultural marriages common in our society today. In all these cases both bride and bridegroom will let widen their mental horizons to make space for the new axis of their joined lives. Then the very process of putting together the ceremony can become a ritual of initiation into a life of examined, shared values. Readings and other personal contri-butions by the couple to one another can be like flags planted at the outermost boundaries of their hopes for the future, while those contributed by the elders may contain modicums of the life-tempered wisdom once handed down, parent to child, by the old ones of the tribe.

Or so the elders hope.

I

The Time Is Come

Hippe, the maiden, has put up her abundant curly hair, brushing it from her perfumed temples, for the time when she must marry is come. Now Artemis, in your loving kindness, grant this girl, who has bidden good-bye to her knucklebones, both husband and children.

Timareta, the daughter of Timaretus, before her wedding, has dedicated to you, Artemis of the lake, her tambourine and her pretty ball, and the net that kept up her hair, and her dolls too and their dresses. Hold your hand over the girl, Artemis, to keep her safe.

Ancient Greek dedications to brides

*ou are considering being married or on the way to that point. Or
your wedding day is already set and you're thinking about the
ceremony, looking for passages of poetry or prose to add to your community's liturgy. In the latter case, you'll already have passed through
a process of inner change, readying yourself for a new stage of life.
While formal wedding ceremonies lead the participants step by step
toward a symbolic rite of full commitment, secular writers have paid
more attention to the tentative, even painful steps of psychic preparation
for the event. The selections which follow contain the thoughts of various
ancient and modern writers on this theme of preparation for a great
decision—a counterpoint to the stately, assured procedures of the ceremony itself.*

Behold, I have set before you an open door, and no man shall close it.

Revelation 3:8 (New English Bible)

God has dressed me with garments of exultation . . . As a bridegroom puts on a priestly diadem, and as a bride adorns herself with her jewels. For, as the earth puts forth her blossoms or bushes in the garden burst into flower, so shall the Lord God make righteousness and praise blossom before all the nations.

Isaiah 61:10–11 (New English Bible)

. . . I saw emptiness under the sun: a lonely man without a friend, without son or brother, toiling endlessly yet never satisfied with his wealth—"For whom," he asks, "am I toiling and denying myself the good things of life?" This too is emptiness, a sorry business. Two are better than one; they receive a good reward for their toil, because, if one fails, the other can help his companion up again; but alas for the man who falls alone with no partner to help him up. And, if two lie side by side, they keep each other warm; but how can one keep warm by himself? If a man is alone, an assailant may overpower him, but two can resist; and a cord of three strands is not quickly snapped.

Ecclesiastes 4:7–13 (New English Bible)

> There be many shapes of mystery,
> And many things God makes to be,
>   past hope or fear,
> And the end men looked for cometh not,
> And a path is there where no one sought.
>   So hath it fallen here.

EURIPIDES

> I got me flowers to straw thy way;
> I got me boughs off many a tree:
> But thou wast up by break of day,
> And brought'st thy sweets along with thee.
>
> The Sunne arising in the East,
> Though he give light, & th' East perfume;
> If they should offer to contest
> With thy arising, they presume.
>
> Can there be any day but this,
> Though many sunnes to shine endeavour?
> We count three hundred, but we misse:
> There is but one, and that one ever.

GEORGE HERBERT, from "Easter"

We're too old to be single. Why shouldn't we both be married instead of sitting through the long winter evenings by our solitary firesides? Why shouldn't we make one fireside of it?

Come, let's be a comfortable couple and take care of each other! How glad we shall be, that we have somebody we are fond of always, to talk to and sit with.

Let's be a comfortable couple. Now do, my dear!

CHARLES DICKENS

> You say, to me-wards your affection's strong;
> Pray love me little, so you love me long.
> Slowly goes farre: The meane is best: Desire
> Grown violent, do's either die, or tire.

ROBERT HERRICK, "Love Me Little, Love Me Long"

. . . the future enters into us . . . in order to transform itself in us long before it happens. And this is why it is so important to be lonely and attentive when one is sad: because the apparently uneventful and stark moment at which our future sets foot in us is so much closer to life than that other noisy and fortuitous point of time at which it happens to us as if from outside. The more still, more patient and more open we are when we are sad, so much the deeper and so much the more unswervingly does the new go into us, so much the better do we make it ours, so much the more will it be *our* destiny, and when on some later day it "happens" (that is, steps forth out of us to others), we shall feel in our inmost selves akin and near to it. And that is necessary. It is necessary—and toward this our development will move gradually—that nothing strange should befall us, but only that which has long belonged to us. We have . . . to realize that that which we call destiny goes forth from within people, not from without into them.

RAINER MARIA RILKE, from Letters to a Young Poet,
translation by M. D. Herter Norton

Understand, I'll slip quietly
away from the noisy crowd
when I see the pale
stars rising, blooming, over the oaks.

I'll pursue solitary pathways
through the pale twilit meadows,
with only this one dream:
You come too.

RAINER MARIA RILKE, from *First Poems*,
translation by M. D. Herter Norton

Oh,
I am thinking
Oh,
I am thinking
I have found
my lover.
Oh,
I think it is so.

Chippewa song

Night is a dead monotonous period under a roof; but in the open world it passes lightly, with its stars and dews and perfumes, and the hours are marked by changes in the face of Nature. What seems a kind of temporal death to people choked between walls and curtains, is only a light and living slumber to the man who sleeps afield. All night long he can hear Nature breathing deeply and freely; even as she takes her rest she turns and smiles; and there is one stirring hour unknown to those who dwell in houses, when a wakeful influence goes abroad over the sleeping hemisphere, and all the outdoor world are on their feet. It is then that the cock first crows, not this time to announce the dawn, but like a cheerful watchman speeding the course of night. Cattle awake on the hillside; sheep break their fast on dewy hillsides, and change to a new lair among the ferns; and houseless men, who have lain down with the fowls, open their dim eyes and behold the beauty of the night.

At what inaudible summons, at what gentle touch of Nature, are all these sleepers thus recalled in the same hour to life? Do the stars rain down an influence, or do we share some thrill of mother earth below our resting bodies? Even shepherds and old country-folk, who are the deepest read in these arcana, have not a guess as to the means or purpose of this nightly resurrection. Towards two in the morning they declare the thing takes place; and neither know nor inquire further. . . .

When that hour came to me among the pines, I wakened thirsty. My tin was standing by me half full of water. I emptied it at a draught; and feeling broad awake after this internal cold aspersion, sat upright to make a cigarette. The stars were clear, coloured, and jewel-like, but not frosty. A faint silvery vapour stood for the Milky Way. All around me the black fir-points stood upright and stock-still. . . . I lay lazily smoking and studying the colour of the sky, as we call the void of space, from where it showed a reddish gray behind the pines to where it showed a glossy blue-black between the stars. . . . And yet even while I was exulting in my solitude I became aware of a strange lack. I wished a companion to lie near me in the starlight, silent and not moving, but ever within touch. For there is a fellowship more quiet even than solitude, and which, rightly understood, is solitude made perfect. And to live out of doors with the woman a man loves is of all lives the most complete and free.

ROBERT LOUIS STEVENSON, from "A Night Among the Pines"

Go seek her out all courteously,
And say I come,
Wind of spices whose song is ever
Epithalamium.
O hurry over the dark lands
And run upon the sea
For seas and land shall not divide us
My love and me.

Now, wind, of your good courtesy
I pray you go,
And come into her little garden
And sing at her window;
Singing: The bridal wind is blowing
For Love is at his noon;
And soon will your true love be with you,
Soon, O soon.

JAMES JOYCE, poem XIII from Chamber Music

[*Mr. Emerson, to Lucy:*] "I used to think I could teach young people the whole of life, but I know better now, and all my teaching has come down to this: beware of muddle. . . . Though life is very glorious, it is difficult. . . . Man has to pick up the use of his functions as he goes along—especially the function of love. . . .

"You must marry, or your life will be wasted. You have gone too far to retreat. I have no time for the tenderness, and the comradeship, and the poetry, and the things that really matter, and *for which* you marry. I know that, with George, you will find them and that you love him. Then be his wife. He is already part of you. Though you fly to Greece, and never see him again, or forget his very name, George will work in your thoughts till you die. It isn't possible to love and to part. You will wish that it was. You can transmute love, ignore it, muddle it, but you can never pull it out of you . . . love is eternal. . . .

"I only wish poets would say this, too: love is of the body; not the body but of the body. Ah! the misery that would be saved if we confessed that! . . . When I think what life is, and how seldom love is answered by love— Marry him; it is one of the moments for which the world was made. . . .

"Now it is all dark. Now Beauty and Passion seem never to have existed. I know. But remember the mountains over Florence, and the view. . . . Yes, we fight for more than Love or Pleasure; there is Truth. Truth counts. Truth does count."

E. M. FORSTER, from *A Room with a View*

The crossing of the threshold is the first step into the sacred zone of the universal source.

JOSEPH CAMPBELL, from *The Hero with a Thousand Faces*

Oh, hasten not this loving act,
Rapture where self and not-self meet:
My life has been the awaiting you,
Your footfall was my own heart's beat.

PAUL VALÉRY

Apparently I am going to marry Charles Lindbergh. It must seem hysterically funny to you as it did to me, when I consider my opinions on marriage. "A safe marriage," "things in common," "liking the same things," "a quiet life," etc., etc. All those things which I am apparently going against. But they seem to have lost their meaning, or have other definitions. Isn't it funny—*why does* one marry, anyway? I didn't expect or want anything like this. . . .

Don't wish me happiness—I don't expect to be happy, but it's gotten beyond that, somehow. Wish me courage and strength and a sense of humor—I will need them all. . . .

ANNE MORROW LINDBERGH, from Bring Me a Unicorn

. . . Really I began the day
Not with a man's wish: "May this day be different";
But with the bird's wish: "May this day
Be the same day, the day of my life."

RANDALL JARRELL, from "A Man Meets a Woman in the Street"

The very earth will disown you
If your soul barter my soul;
In angry tribulation
The waters will tremble and rise.
My world become more beautiful
Since the day you took me to you,

When, under the flowering thorn tree
Together we stood without words,
And love, like the heavy fragrance
Of the flowering thorn tree, pierced us. . . .
The kiss your mouth gives another
Will echo within my ear,

As the deep surrounding caverns
Bring back your words to me.

Even the dust of the highway
Keeps the scent of your footprints.
I track them, and like a deer
Follow you into the mountains.

Clouds will paint over my dwelling
The image of your new love.
Go to her like a thief, crawling
In the boweled earth to kiss her.
When you lift her face you will find
My face disfigured with weeping.

God will not give you the light
Unless you walk by my side.
God will not let you drink
If I do not tremble in the water.
He will not let you sleep
Except in the hollow of my hair.

If you go, you destroy my soul
As you trample the weeds by the roadside.
Hunger and thirst will gnaw you,
Crossing the heights or the plains;
And wherever you are, you will watch
The evenings bleed with my wounds.

When you call another woman
I will issue forth on your tongue,
Even as a taste of salt
Deep in the roots of your throat.
In hating, or singing, in yearning
It is me alone you summon. . . .

Gabriela Mistral, "God Wills It,"
translation by K.G.C.

Will you perhaps consent to be
Now that a little while is still
(Ruth of sweet wind) now that a little while
My mind's continuing and unreleasing wind
Touches this single of your flowers, this one only,
Will you perhaps consent to be
My many-branched, small and dearest tree?

My mind's continuing and unreleasing wind
—The wind which is wild and restless, tired and asleep,
The wind which is tired, wild and still continuing,
The wind which is chill, and warm, wet, soft, in every
    influence,
Lusts for Paris, Crete and Pergamus,
Is suddenly off for Paris and Chicago,
Judaea, San Francisco, the Midi
—May I perhaps return to you
Wet with an Attic dust and chill from Norway
My dear, so-many-branched smallest tree?

Would you perhaps consent to be
The very rack and crucifix of winter, winter's wild
Knife-edged, continuing and unreleasing,
Intent and stripping, ice-caressing wind?
My dear, most dear, so-many-branched tree,
My mind's continuing and unreleasing wind
Touches this single of your flowers, faith in me,
Wide as the—sky!—accepting as the (air)!
—Consent, consent, consent to be
My many-branched, small and dearest tree.

DELMORE SCHWARTZ, "Will you perhaps consent to be"
("méntre il vento, come fa, si tace")

Nothing is plumb, level or square:
   the studs are bowed, the joists
are shaky by nature, no piece fits
   any other piece without a gap
or pinch, and bent nails
   dance all over the surfacing
like maggots. By Christ
   I am no carpenter. I built
the roof for myself, the walls
   for myself, the floors
for myself, and got
   hung up in it myself. I
danced with a purple thumb
   at this house-warming, drunk
with my prime whiskey: rage.
   Oh I spat rage's nails
into the frame-up of my work:
   it held. It settled plumb,
level, solid, square and true
   for that great moment. Then
it screamed and went on through,
   skewing as wrong the other way.
God damned it. This is hell,
   but I planned it, I sawed it,
I nailed it, and I
   will live in it until it kills me.
I can nail my left palm
   to the left-hand cross-piece but
I can't do everything myself.
   I need a hand to nail the right,
a help, a love, a you, a wife.

ALAN DUGAN, "Love Song: I and Thou"

There came you wishing me * * *
And so I said * * *
And then you turned your head
With the greatest beauty

Smiting me mercilessly!
And then you said * * *
So that my heart was made
Into the strangest country . . .

* * * you said, so beauteously,
So that an angel came
To hear that name,
And we caught him tremulously!

José Garcia Villa, from
Have Come, Am Here,
translation by Ben F. Carruthers

As I was walking
        I came upon
chance walking
        the same road upon.

As I sat down
        by chance to move
later
        if and as I might,

light the wood was,
        light and green
and what I saw
        before I had not seen.

It was a lady
    accompanied
by goat men
    leading her.

Her hair held earth.
    Her eyes were dark.
A double flute
    made her move.

"O love,
    where are you
leading
    me now?"

". . . dear beast, you shall not die," said Beauty. "You will live in order to become my husband. From this moment on, I give you my hand and I swear that I shall be yours alone. Alas! I thought that I felt only friendship for you, but the sorrow that I feel now makes me see that I cannot live without you."

Hardly had Beauty spoken these words when she saw the castle blazing with lights—there were fireworks and music and everything to indicate a celebration. None of these wonders held her attention, however; she turned her eyes back toward her dear beast. . . . But to her surprise, the beast had disappeared and at her feet she saw instead a prince handsomer than the god of love, who thanked her for having ended his enchantment. Although this prince deserved all her attention, she could not help asking where the beast was.

"You see him at your feet," the prince told her. "A wicked

The Time Is Come · 31

fairy had condemned me to remain in that shape until a beautiful girl should agree to marry me, and she had forbidden me to reveal my wit and intelligence. You were the only person in the world good enough to let yourself be moved by the goodness of my character, and in offering you my crown, I am only freeing myself of my obligations to you."

Beauty, pleasantly surprised, gave her hand to this handsome prince to help him to rise. They went together to the castle, and Beauty almost died of joy to find in the great hall her father and all her family, transported to the castle by the beautiful lady who had appeared to her in a dream.

"Beauty," said the lady, who was a powerful fairy, "come and receive the reward of your good choice. You have preferred virtue to handsomeness and wit and you deserve to find all these qualities united in one single person. You are going to become a great queen. . . ."

Saying this, the fairy waved her wand, and everyone who was in the hall was transported to the prince's kingdom. His subjects received him with joy, and he married Beauty, who lived with him for a long time in a state of happiness that was perfect because it was based upon virtue.

MADAME LePRINCE DE BEAUMONT, from "Beauty and the Beast," translation by Alfred and Mary Elizabeth David

I have always known
That at last I would
Take this road, but yesterday
I did not know that it would be today.

KENNETH REXROTH, from *One Hundred Poems from the Japanese*

II

In Search of
Love

Did you ever seek God?
No.

What is it that you sought?
I sought love.

And you sought love for what reason?
Those about me, from childhood on, had sought love. I heard
and saw them. I saw them rise and fall on that wave. I closely
overheard and sharply overlooked their joy and grief. I worked
from memory and example.

LOUISE BOGAN, from *Journey Around My Room*

*L*ove is the flame that leads a person from solitude to a state of union, and the wedding is the "ritual of passage" between. For thousands of years, poets and philosophers have tried to define this condition of mind and body and to measure its power to impel a person out of one life into another. A selection of their meditations follows, offering possible additions to traditional Western wedding liturgies.

Some of these passages, like those from the King James translation of 1 Corinthians, are phrased in the lovely old cadences of traditional scripture. Others, like the New English Bible version of Corinthians, address the ancient question in language of plain speech as it is used today by what the poet Wallace Stevens calls "the men of the time . . . and the women of the time." These men and women are ourselves, no less drawn than our ancestors were to the ideals of generosity, permanence, and mutual trust which marriage implies.

Aristophanes: . . . Love is the oldest of the gods, and he is also the source of the greatest benefits to us. . . .

Original human nature was not like the present but different. The sexes were not two as they are now but originally three in number; there was man, woman, and the union of the two. . . . the man was originally the child of the sun, the woman of the earth, and the man-woman of the moon, which is made up of sun and earth. . . . [Now] when one of them meets his other half, the actual half of himself, the pair are lost in an amazement of love and friendship and intimacy. . . . these are the people who pass their whole lives together. . . . The reason is that human nature was originally one and we were a whole, and the desire and pursuit of the whole is called love. . . .

I believe that if our loves were perfectly accomplished, and each one returning to his primeval nature had his original true love, then our race would be happy. . . . [Therefore] we must praise the god Love, who is our greatest benefactor, both leading us in this life back to our own nature, and giving us high hopes for the future, for he promises that if we are pious, he will restore us to our original state, and heal us, and make us happy and blessed.

Agathon: . . . [Love is rather] the youngest of the gods and youthful ever. . . . had Love been in [the old] days, there would have been no . . . violence but peace and sweetness as there is now in heaven, since the rule of Love began. Love is young and also tender. . . . he walks not upon the earth nor yet upon the skulls of men . . . but in the hearts and souls of both gods and men, which are of all things the softest: in them he walks and dwells and makes his home. Not in every soul without exception, for where there is hardness he departs, where there is softness there he dwells . . . he dwells in the place of flowers and scents, there he sits and abides. . . .

His greatest glory is that he can neither do nor suffer wrong to or from any god or any man; . . . all men in all things serve him of their own free will, and where there is voluntary agreement, there, as the laws which are the lords of the city say, is justice. . . .

Of his courage and justice and temperance I have spoken, but I have yet to speak of his wisdom . . . : he is a poet and also the source of poesy in others. . . . at the touch of him every one becomes a poet even though he had no music in him before. . . .

As to the artists, do we not know that he only of them whom love inspires has the light of fame? He whom Love touches not walks in darkness. . . .

[He is] the friend of the good, the wonder of the wise, the amazement of the gods . . . parent of delicacy, luxury, desire, fondness, softness, grace; regardful of the good, regardless of the evil . . . saviour, pilot, comrade, helper . . . leader best and brightest in whose footsteps let every man follow, sweetly singing in his honor and joining in that sweet strain with which love charms the souls of gods and men.

Socrates: . . . [Love] is a great spirit intermediate between the divine and the mortal. . . . He is neither mortal nor immortal but alive and flourishing at one moment when he is in plenty and dead at another moment and again alive. . . . that which is always flowing in is always flowing out, and so he is never in want and never in wealth. . . . Wisdom is a most beautiful thing, and Love is of the beautiful; and therefore Love is also a philosopher or lover of wisdom. . . . love is the love of the everlasting possession of the good. . . . love is of immortality. . . . love begins with the desire of union. . . .

And the true order of going, or being led by another, to the things of love, is to begin from the beauties of earth and mount upwards for the sake of . . . absolute beauty . . . that life above all others which a man should live, in the contemplation of beauty absolute.

. . . of this end human nature will not easily find a helper better than love. And therefore I say that every man ought to honor him, and walk in his ways and exhort others to do the same, and praise the power and spirit of love . . . now and ever.

PLATO, from the *Symposium*, translation by Benjamin Jowett

Though I speak with the tongues of men and of angels, and have not charity, I am become as sounding brass, or a tinkling cymbal.

2   And though I have the gift of prophecy, and understand all mysteries, and all knowledge; and though I have all faith, so that I could remove mountains, and have not charity, I am nothing.

3   And though I bestow all my goods to feed the poor, and though I give my body to be burned, and have not charity, it profiteth me nothing.

4   Charity suffereth long, and is kind; charity envieth not; charity vaunteth not itself, is not puffed up,

5   Doth not behave itself unseemly, seeketh not her own, is not easily provoked, thinketh no evil;

6   Rejoiceth not in iniquity, but rejoiceth in the truth;

7   Beareth all things, believeth all things, hopeth all things, endureth all things.

8   Charity never faileth: but whether there be prophecies, they shall fail; whether there be tongues, they shall cease; whether there be knowledge, it shall vanish away.

9   For we know in part, and we prophesy in part.

10   But when that which is perfect is come, then that which is in part shall be done away.

11   When I was a child, I spake as a child, I understood as a child, I thought as a child: but when I became a man, I put away childish things.

12   For now we see through a glass, darkly; but then face to face: now I know in part; but then shall I know even as also I am known.

13   And now abideth faith, hope, charity, these three; but the greatest of these is charity.

1 Corinthians 13 (King James Version)

Love is patient and kind; love is not jealous or boastful; it is not arrogant or rude. Love does not insist on its own way; it is not irritable or resentful; it does not rejoice at wrong, but rejoices in the right. Love bears all things, believes all things, hopes all things, endures all things. Love never ends.

1 Corinthians 13:4–8a (New English Bible)

All happiness or unhappiness solely depends upon the quality of the object to which we are attached by love. Love for an object eternal and infinite feeds the mind with joy alone, a joy that is free from all sorrow.

BARUCH SPINOZA

Emily Dickinson

611

I see thee better - in the Dark -
I do not need a Light -
The Love of Thee - a Prism be -
Excelling Violet - . . .

What need of Day -
To Those whose Dark - hath so - surpassing Sun -
It deem it be - Continually -
At the Meridian?

917

Love - is anterior to Life -
Posterior - to Death -
Initial of Creation, and
The Exponent of Earth.

1155

Distance - is not the Realm of Fox
Nor by Relay of Bird
Abated - Distance is
Until thyself, Beloved.

from *The Complete Poems*,
edited by Thomas H. Johnson

William Shakespeare

XVIII

Shall I compare thee to a summer's day?
Thou art more lovely and more temperate:
Rough winds do shake the darling buds of May,
And summer's lease hath all too short a date:
Sometimes too hot the eye of heaven shines,
And often is his gold complexion dimm'd,
And every fair from fair sometime declines,
By chance, or nature's changing course, untrim'd,
But thy eternal summer shall not fade,
Nor loose possession of that fair thou ow'st,
Nor shall death brag thou wandr'st in his shade,
When in eternal lines to time thou grow'st,
    So long as men can breathe, or eyes can see,
    So long lives this, and this gives life to thee.

XXX

When to the sessions of sweet silent thought
I summon up remembrance of things past,
I sigh the lack of many a thing I sought,
And with old woes new wail my dear times' waste:
Then can I drown an eye, unus'd to flow,
For precious friends hid in death's dateless night,
And weep afresh love's long since cancell'd woe,
And moan the expense of many a vanish'd sight:
Then can I grieve at grievances foregone,
And heavily from woe to woe tell o'er
The sad account of fore-bemoaned moan,
Which I new pay as if not paid before.
    But if the while I think on thee, dear friend,
    All losses are restor'd and sorrows end.

XXXI

Thy bosom is endeared with all hearts,
Which I by lacking have supposed dead;
And there reigns love and all love's loving parts,
And all those friends which I thought buried.
How many a holy and obsequious tear
Hath dear religious love stolen from mine eye,
As interest of the dead, which now appear,
But things remov'd that hidden in there lie.
Thou art the grave where buried love doth live
Hung with the trophies of my lovers gone
Who all their parts of me to thee did give;
That due of many now is thine alone.
    Their images I loved I view in thee
    And thou, all they, hast all the all of me.

CXVI

Let me not to the marriage of true minds
Admit impediments. Love is not love
Which alters when it alteration finds,
Or bends with the remover to remove:
O, no! it is an ever-fixed mark,
That looks on tempests and is never shaken;
It is the star to every wandering bark,
Whose worth's unknown, although his height be taken.
Love's not Time's fool, though rosy lips and cheeks
Within his bending sickle's compass come;
Love alters not with his brief hours and weeks,
But bears it out even to the edge of doom.
    If this is error, and upon me prov'd,
    I never writ, nor no man ever lov'd.

When in the chronicle of wasted time
I see descriptions of the fairest wights,
And beauty making beautiful old rhyme
In praise of ladies dead and lovely knights,
Then, in the blazon of sweet beauty's best,
Of hand, of foot, of lip, of eye, of brow,
I see their antique pen would have express'd
Even such a beauty as you master now.
So all their praises are but prophecies
Of this our time, all you prefiguring;
And, for they look'd but with divining eyes,
They had not skill enough your worth to sing:
    For we, which now behold these present days,
    Have eyes to wonder, but lack tongues to praise.

SHAKESPEARE, *Sonnets*

The passion which unites the sexes . . . is habitually spoken of as though it were a simple feeling; whereas it is the most compound, and therefore the most powerful, of all the feelings. Added to the purely physical elements of it are first to be noticed those highly complex impressions produced by personal beauty, around which are aggregated a variety of pleasurable ideas, not in themselves amatory, but which have an organised relation to the amatory feeling. With this there is united the complex sentiment which we term affection—a sentiment which, as it can exist between those of the same sex, must be regarded as an independent sentiment, but one which is here greatly exalted.

Then there is the sentiment of admiration, respect, or reverence; in itself one of considerable power, and which, in this relation, becomes in a high degree active. Then comes next the feeling called love of approbation. To be preferred above all the world, and that by one admired beyond all others, is to have the love of approbation gratified in a degree passing every previous experience. . . . Further, the allied emotion of self-esteem comes into play. To have succeeded in gaining such attachment from, and sway over, another, is a proof of power which cannot fail agreeably to excite the *amour propre*. Yet again, the proprietary feeling has its share in the general activity: there is the pleasure of possession; the two belong to each other. Once more, the relation allows of an extended liberty of action. Towards other persons a restrained behaviour is requisite. Round each there is a subtle boundary that may not be crossed—an individuality on which none may trespass. But in this case the barriers are thrown down, and thus the love of unrestrained activity is gratified. Finally, there is an exaltation of the sympathies. Egoistic pleasures of all kinds are doubled by another's sympathetic participation, and the pleasures of another are added to the egoistic pleasures. Thus, round the physical feeling forming the nucleus of the whole, are gathered the feelings produced by personal beauty; that constituting simple attachment, those of reverence, of love of approbation, of self-esteem, of property, of love of freedom, of sympathy. These, all greatly exalted, and severally tending to reflect their excitements on one another, unite to form the mental state we call love. And as each of them is of itself comprehensive of multitudinous states of consciousness, we may say that this passion fuses into one immense aggregate most of the elementary excitations of which we are capable; and that hence results in irresistible power.

HERBERT SPENCER, from *The Principles of Psychology*

It may be asked, is love necessary to man? This is not a matter for reasoning, but for feeling. We deliberate not upon it; we are carried irresistibly towards the conclusion; and we deceive ourselves when we make it a subject for discussion.

Purity (*netteté*) of spirit produces corresponding purity of passion; therefore it is, that a pure and elevated mind loves with intenseness, and has an intense perception of the qualities which excite its ardours.

Who then can doubt that we exist only to love? Disguise it, in fact, as we will, we love without intermission. Where we seem most effectually to shut out love, it lies covert and concealed: we live not a moment exempt from its influence.

Man cannot find his satisfactions within himself only; and, as love is essential to him, he must seek the objects of his affection in external objects. He can find these only in beauty; but as he himself is the fairest being that the hand of God has formed, he must look within himself for a model of those beauties which he seeks elsewhere. . . . Such is the largeness of his heart, that it must be something resembling himself, and approximating to his own qualities. That kind of beauty, therefore, which satisfies man, must not only contribute to his enjoyment, but partake of his own resemblance. It is restricted and fulfilled in the difference of the sexes.

Nature has so impressed this truth upon our minds, that we all find a predisposition towards it; it demands no skill or research for its discovery; we find a void within the bosom, and this it is which fills it. . . .

When a person is in love, he seems to himself wholly changed from what he was before; and he fancies that everybody sees him in the same light. This is a great mistake; but reason being obscured by passion, he cannot be convinced, and goes on still under the delusion. . . .

It has been usual, but without cause, to underrate, and regard, as opposed to reason, the passion of love. Reason and love are, however, consistent with each other. It is a precipitation of mind that thus carries us into partialities and extremes; but it is still reason, and we ought not to wish it to be otherwise. We should, in that case, only prove man to be a very disagreeable machine. Let us not seek to exclude reason from love; for they are inseparable. . . .

It is with love as with the understanding; one person supposes he has as much sense as another, and can love as well as another. But a mind of refinement carries its attachments into the minutest things, and this is not the case with others. It requires, however, a delicate perception to mark this difference.

Under the influence of strong passion the beloved object seems new in every interview. Absence instantaneously creates a void in the heart. But then, the joys of reunion!

Blaise Pascal, from "On the Passion of the Soul,"
translation by George Pearce

The memories of long love
Gather like drifting snow,
Poignant as the mandarin ducks,
who float side by side in sleep.

. . .

Falling from the ridge
Of high Tsukuba,
The Minano River
At last gathers itself,
Like my love, into
A deep, still pool.

Kenneth Rexroth, from *One Hundred
Poems from the Japanese*

John Keats

. . . Ask yourself my love whether you are not very cruel to have so entrammelled me, so destroyed my freedom. Will you confess this in the Letter you must write immediately and do all you can to console me in it—make it rich as a draught of poppies to intoxicate me—write the softest words and kiss them that I may at least touch my lips where yours have been. For myself I know not how to express my devotion to so fair a form: I want a brighter word than bright, a fairer word than fair. I almost wish we were butterflies and liv'd but three summer days—three such days with you I could fill with more delight than fifty common years could ever contain. . . .

[July 8, 1819]

. . . Even when I am not thinking of you I receive your influence and a tenderer nature steeling upon me. All my thoughts, my unhappiest days and nights have I find not at all cured me of my love of Beauty, but made it so intense that I am miserable that you are not with me: or rather breathe in that dull sort of patience that cannot be called Life. I never knew before, what such a love as you have made me feel, was; I did not believe in it; my Fancy was affraid of it, lest it should burn me up. But if you will fully love me, though there may be some fire, 't will not be more than we can bear when moistened and bedewed with Pleasures. . . . I would never see any thing but Pleasure in your eyes, love on your lips, and Happiness in your steps. I would wish to see you among those amusements suitable to your inclinations and spirits; so that our loves might be a delight in the midst of Pleasures agreeable enough, rather than a resource from vexations and cares—But I doubt much, in case of the worst, whether I shall be philosopher enough to follow my own Lessons: if I saw my resolution give you a pain I could not. Why may I not speak of your Beauty, since without that I could never have lov'd you—I cannot conceive any beginning of such love as I have for you but Beauty. There may be a sort of love for which, without the least sneer at it, I have the highest respect, and can admire it in others: but it has not the richness, the bloom, the full form, the enchantment of love after my own heart. So let me speak of you Beauty, though to my own endangering; if you could be so cruel to me as to try elsewhere its Power. You say you are affraid I shall think you do not love me—in saying this you make me ache the more to be near you. . . .

[March 1820]

Sweetest Fanny,

You fear, sometimes, I do not love you so much as you wish? My dear Girl I love you ever and ever and without reserve. The more I have known you the more have I lov'd. In every way—even my jealousies have been agonies of Love, in the hottest fit I ever had I would have died for you. I have vex'd you too much. But for Love! Can I help it? You are always new. The last of your kisses was ever the sweetest; the last smile the brightest; the last movement the gracefullest. When you pass'd my window home yesterday, I was fill'd with as much admiration as if I had then seen you for the first time. You uttered a half complaint once that I only lov'd your Beauty. Have I nothing else then to love in you but that? Do not I see a heart naturally furnish'd with wings imprison itself with me? No ill prospect has been able to turn your thoughts a moment from me. This perhaps should be as much a subject of sorrow as joy—but I will not talk of that. Even if you did not love me I could not help an entire devotion to you: how much more deeply then must I feel for you knowing you love me. My Mind has been the most discontented and restless one that ever was put into a body too small for it. I never felt my Mind repose upon anything with complete and undistracted enjoyment—upon no person but you. When you are in the room my thoughts never fly out of window: you always concentrate my whole senses. The anxiety shown about our Loves in your last note is an immense pleasure to me: however you must not suffer such speculations to molest you any more: nor will I any more believe you can have the least pique against me. . . .

[June 1820]

. . . My head is puzzled this morning, and I scarce know what I shall say though I am full of a hundred things. 'T is certain I would rather be writing to you this morning, notwithstanding the alloy of grief in such an occupation, than enjoy any other pleasure, with health to boot, unconnected with you. Upon my soul I have loved you to the extreme. I wish you could know the Tenderness with which I continually brood over your different aspects of countenance, action and dress. I see you come down in the morning: I see you meet me at the Window—I see every thing over again eternally that I ever have seen. If I get on the pleasant clue I live in a sort of happy misery, if on the unpleasant 'tis miserable misery. You complain of my ill-treating you in word thought and deed—I am sorry,—at times I feel bitterly sorry that I ever made you unhappy—my excuse is that those words have been wrung from me by the sha[r]pness of my feelings. At all events and in any case I have been wrong; could I believe that I did it without any cause, I should be the most sincere of Penitents. I could give way to my repentant feelings now, I could recant all my suspicions, I could mingle with you heart and Soul though absent, were it not for some parts of your Letters. Do you suppose it possible I could ever leave you? You know what I think of myself and what of you.

You know that I should feel how much it was my loss and how little yours. . . . do nothing but love me—if I knew that for certain life and health will in such event be a heaven, and death itself will be less painful. I long to believe in immortality I shall never be ab[le] to bid you an entire farewell. If I am destined to be happy with you here—how short is the longest Life— I wish to believe in immortality—I wish to live with you for ever. . . .

Excerpts of letters to Fanny Brawne

Ah Love! could you and I with Him conspire
To grasp this sorry Scheme of Things entire,
Would not we shatter it to bits—and then
Remold it nearer to the Heart's desire!

EDWARD FITZGERALD, from
The Rubáiyát of Omar Khayyám

. . . Ah, love, let us be true
To one another! for the world, which seems
To lie before us like a land of dreams,
So various, so beautiful, so new,
Hath really neither joy, nor love, nor light,
Nor certitude, nor peace, nor help for pain;
And we are here as on a darkling plain
Swept with confused alarms of struggle and flight
Where ignorant armies clash by night.

MATTHEW ARNOLD, from "Dover Beach"

Ralph Waldo Emerson

Give all to love;
Obey thy heart;
Friends, kindred, days,
Estate, good-fame,
Plans, credit and the Muse,
Nothing refuse.

'Tis a brave master;
Let it have scope:
Follow it utterly,
Hope beyond hope:
High and more high
It dives into noon,
With wing unspent,
Untold intent;
But it is a god,
Knows its own path
And the outlets of the sky.

It was never for the mean;
It requireth courage stout.
Souls above doubt,
Valour unbending.
It will reward,
They shall return
More than they were,
And ever ascending. . . .

from "Give All to Love"

. . . All mankind loves a lover. . . . [Love] is the dawn of civility and grace. . . . Persons are love's world, and the coldest philosopher cannot recount the debt of the young soul wandering here in nature to the power of love . . . though the celestial rapture falling out of heaven seizes only upon those of tender age . . . yet the remembrance of these visions outlasts all other remembrances, and is a wreath of flowers on the oldest brows. . . .

No man ever forgot the visitations of that power to his heart and brain, which created all things new; which was the dawn in him of music, poetry and art; which made the face of nature radiant with purple light; the morning and the night varied enchantments; when a single tone of one voice could make the heart beat, and the most trivial circumstance associated with one form is put in the amber of memory; when we became all eye when one was present; and all memory when one was gone; . . . for the figures, the motions, the words of the beloved object are not like other images written in water, but, as Plutarch said, "enameled in fire." . . .

The passion remakes the world. . . . It makes all things alive and significant. . . . Every bird on the boughs of the trees sings now to his heart and soul. Almost, the notes are articulate. The clouds have faces . . . the trees, the waving grass and the flowers have grown intelligent. . . . Behold the fine madman! He is a palace of sweet sounds and sights . . . he is twice a man . . . he feels the blood of the violet, the clover and the lily in his veins; and he talks with the brook that wets his foot. . . .

The like force has the passion over all his nature. It expands the sentiment; it makes the clown gentle and gives the coward heart. Into the most pitiful and abject it will infuse a heart and courage to defy the world. . . . In giving him to another it still more gives him to himself. He is a new man with new perceptions, new and keener purposes. . . .

Love prays. It makes covenants with Eternal Power . . . the union which is thus affected . . . adds a new value to every atom in nature, for it transmutes every thread throughout the whole web of relation into a golden ray and bathes the soul in a new and sweeter element . . . it is the nature and end of this relation, that [the lovers] should represent the human race to each other. All that is in the world . . . is cunningly wrought into the texture of man, of woman. . . .

The world rolls; the circumstances vary every hour. . . . [The lovers'] once flaming regard is sobered . . . and losing in violence what it gains in extent, it becomes a thorough good understanding. At last [the lovers] discover that all which at first drew them together—those once sacred features, that magical play of charms—had a prospective end, like the scaffolding by which the house was built, and the purification of the intellect and the heart, from year to year, is the real marriage. . . .

Thus we are put in training for a love which knows not sex, nor person, nor partiality but which seeketh virtue and wisdom everywhere, to the end of increasing virtue and wisdom. . . . We are often made to feel that our affections are but tents of a night. . . . But in health, the mind is presently seen again— its overarching vault, bright with galaxies of immutable lights, and the warm loves and fears that swept over us as clouds. . . . But we need not fear that we can lose anything by the progress of the soul. The soul may be trusted to the end. That which is so beautiful and attractive as these relations must be succeeded and supplanted only by what is more beautiful, and so on forever.

from his essay "Love"

. . . he's more myself than I am. Whatever our souls are made of, his and mine are the same. . . . If all else perished and *he* remained, I should still continue to be, and if all else remained, and he were annihilated, the universe would turn to a might stranger. . . . He's always, always in my mind; not as a pleasure to myself, but as my own being.

EMILY BRONTË, from *Wuthering Heights*

. . . our love it was stronger by far than the love
   Of those who were older than we—
   Of many far wiser than we—
And neither the angels in Heaven above,
   Nor the demons down under the sea,
Can ever dissever my soul from the soul
   Of the beautiful Annabel Lee:—

For the moon never beams without bringing me dreams
   Of the beautiful Annabel Lee;
And the stars never rise but I feel the bright eyes
   Of the beautiful Annabel Lee.
And so, all the night-tide, I lie down by the side
Of my darling, my darling, my life and my bride. . . .

EDGAR ALLAN POE, from "Annabel Lee"

. . . our love is a portion of our soul more lasting than the various selves which die successively in us and which would selfishly like to retain this love—a portion of our soul which, regardless of the useful suffering this may cause us, must detach itself from its human objects in order to make clear to us and restore its quality of generality and give this love, an understanding of this love, to all the world, to the universal intelligence, and not first to this woman, then to that, in whom this one and that of our successive selves seek to lose their identity.

MARCEL PROUST, from The Past Recaptured,
translation by Frederick A. Blossom

To love is good; love being difficult. For one human being to love another; that is perhaps the most difficult of all our tasks, the ultimate, the last test and proof, the work for which all other work is but preparation. For this reason [beginners] cannot yet know love: they have to learn it. . . . Learning-time is always a long, secluded time, and so loving, for a long while ahead and far on into life, is—solitude, intensified and deepened loneness for him who loves. . . . it is a high inducement to the individual to ripen, to become something in himself, to become world, to become world for himself for another's sake, it is a great exacting claim upon him, something that chooses him out and calls him to vast things. Only in this sense, as the task of working at themselves ("to hearken and to hammer day and night") might young people use the love that is given them.

RAINER MARIA RILKE, from Letters to a Young Poet,
translation by M. D. Herter Norton

What thou lovest well remains,
  the rest is dross
What thou lov'st well shall not be
  reft from thee
What thou lov'st well is thy true
  heritage. . . .

EZRA POUND, from The Cantos

Be in me as the eternal moods
         of the bleak wind, and not
As transient things are—
         gaiety of flowers.
Have me in the strong loneliness
         of sunless cliffs
And of grey waters.
              Let the gods speak softly of us
In days hereafter,
              The shadowy flowers of Orcus
Remember Thee.

EZRA POUND, "ΔΩΡΙΑ"

Love is a battle. Love is war. Love is growing up.

JAMES BALDWIN, quoted in a statement by
his family to the press after his death

Romantic love is eternally alive; as the self's most urgent quest, as grail of our hopes of happiness, as the untarnished source of the tragic, the exalted, the extreme and the beautiful in modern life. The late twentieth century is the first to open itself up to the promise of love as the focus of universal aspirations. . . .

In the marriage ceremony, that moment when falling in love is replaced by the arduous drama of staying in love, the words "in sickness and in health, for richer, for poorer, till death do us part" set love in the temporal context in which it achieves its meaning. As time begins to elapse, one begins to love the other because they have shared the same experience. . . . Selves may not intertwine; but lives do, and shared memory becomes as much of a bond as the bond of the flesh. . . .

Family love is this dynastic awareness of time, this shared belonging to a chain of generations. . . . we collaborate together to root each other in a dimension of time longer than our own lives.

MICHAEL IGNATIEFF, from "Lodged in the Heart and Memory"

Locate *I*
love you some-
where in

teeth and
eyes, bite
it but

take care not
to hurt, you
want so

much so
little. Words
say everything,

I
love you
again,

then what
is emptiness
for. To

fill, fill.
I heard words
and words full

of holes
aching. Speech
is a mouth.

ROBERT CREELEY,
"The Language"

. . . It has to be living, to learn the speech of the place.
It has to face the men of the time and to meet
The women of the time. It has to think about war
And it has to find what will suffice. It has
To construct a new stage. It has to be on that stage
And, like an insatiable actor, slowly and
With meditation, speak words that in the ear,
In the delicatest ear of the mind, repeat,
Exactly, that which it wants to hear, at the sound
Of which, an invisible audience listens,
Not to the play, but to itself, expressed
In an emotion as of two people, as of two
Emotions becoming one . . .

WALLACE STEVENS, from "Of Modern Poetry"

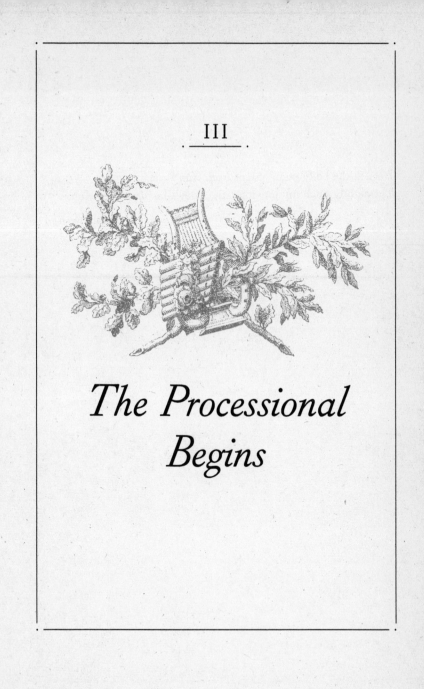

The Processional
Begins

Here in the body pent, absent from Him I roam,
Yet nightly pitch my moving tent, a day's march nearer Home.

from a Moravian hymn

*T*he wedding ceremony is a "ritual of passage" between two distinct worlds: the world of solitude and that of union. To traverse the distance between, as on any voyage, is to experience some anxiety and to pay a price. In the romantic-sounding language of depth psychology, the traveler will be called on to relinquish his or her old self so a new one may be reborn—that is, to exchange certain satisfactions for new and deeper ones. The readings which follow concern the passage across a psychic distance from an old life toward one to come. The Moravian hymn on the facing page expresses the pent-up energy and momentum of the journey, whether it be construed as toward one's heavenly "Home" or toward a new home for life.

Traversing the actual distance from the bride's house to a shrine or to her new home is still an event of extreme gravity today in much of Asia and Islam, where a girl may have been kept in seclusion for days or weeks before the event, then carried in a hooded palanquin to arrive, swathed in veils, before her husband. Even in the West, the start of the bridal processional is a moment of electric tension. In a synagogue, there may sound the shofar, or ram's horn, whose deep melancholy bleat was heard in ancient times in Canaan. A Christian church may fill with the jubilant chords of Mendelssohn's "Wedding March."

Ruth said:
"Intreat me not to leave thee,
      Or to return from following after thee:
For whither thou goest, I will go,
      And where thou lodgest, I will lodge.
Thy people shall be my people,
      And thy God my God.
Where thou diest, will I die,
      And there will I be buried.
The Lord do so to me, and more also,
      If ought but death part thee and me."

Ruth 1:16–17 (King James Version)

I will lead the blind men on their way
And guide them by paths they do not know.
I will turn darkness into light before them
And straighten their twisting roads.

Isaiah 42:16 (New English Bible)

Three nights of [pre]wedding festivities with their music and gaiety expelled my melancholy and kept me from thinking of what was to come. I laughed and was merry along with my friends, so much so that the household interpreted my earlier behaviour as nothing more than the ordinary display of fears common to prospective brides.

On the night of the wedding ceremony, the rapt attention focused upon me, especially by my friends, increased my joy so that I almost leaped with delight while I donned my wedding dress embroidered in thread of silver and gold. I was spellbound by the diamonds and other brilliant jewels that crowned my head and sparkled on my bodice and arms. All of this dazzled me and kept me from thinking of anything else. I was certain I would remain forever in this raiment, the centre of attention and admiration.

Presently, the singing girls appeared to escort me. My attendants supported me while the heavy jewels pressed down on my head and the wedding dress hung heavy on my small frame. I walked between rows of bright candles with rich scents wafting in the air, to the grand salon where I found a throng of women . . . in elegant gowns with jewels glittering on their heads, bosoms and arms. They all turned and looked at me with affection. When I raised my head to ease the heavy tiara back a little I heard a woman's voice whispering, "My daughter, lower your head and eyes." I then sat down on the bridal throne surrounded by flickering candles and decorated with flowers, fancying I was in another world. . . .

Next a dancer appeared and started to perform in front of me. She then made the rounds of the guests dancing in front of the women one at a time. They would take out coins, moisten them with their tongues and paste them on the dancer's forehead and cheeks. . . .

Suddenly, a commotion erupted outside the great hall. The dancer rushed out emitting a string of *zaghrudas*, the tremulous trills hanging in the air after her. To the roll of drums the women hastened out of the room or slipped behind curtains while the eunuch announced the approach of the bridegroom.

In an instant, the delicious dream vanished and stark reality appeared. Faint and crying, I clung to the gown of a relation— the wife of Ahmad Bey Hijazi—who was trying to flee like the others and I pleaded, "Don't abandon me here! Take me with you." My French tutor who was at my side embraced me and cried along with me murmuring, 'Have courage, my daughter, have courage." . . . Then a woman came and lowered a veil of silver thread over my head like a mask concealing the face of a condemned person approaching execution. At that moment, the bridegroom entered the room. After praying two *rakaas* on a mat of red velvet embossed with silver he came to me and, lifting the veil from my face, kissed me on the forehead. He led me by the hand to the bridal throne and took his place beside me. All the while, I was trembling like a branch in a storm. The groom addressed a few words to me but I understood nothing. . . . Finally, my new husband took me by the hand. In my daze I knew not where I was being led.

HUDA SHAARAWI, from *Harem Years: Memoirs of an Egyptian Feminist*,
translation by Margot Badran

The sun-beames in the East are spred,
Leave, leave, faire Bride, your solitary bed,
No more shall you returne to it alone,
It nourseth sadnesse, and your bodies print,
Like to a grave, the yielding downe doth dint;
You and your other you meet there anon;
Put forth, put forth that warme balm-breathing thigh,
Which when next time you in these sheets will smother,
There it must meet another . . .
Come glad from thence, goe gladder than you came,
Today put on perfection and a womans name . . .

The amorous evening starre is rose,
Why then should not our amorous starre inclose
Her selfe in her wish'd bed? . . . all toyl'd beasts
Rest duly; at night all their toyles are dispensed;
But in their beds commenced
Are other labours, and more dainty feasts;
She goes a maid, who, lest she turne the same
To night puts on perfection and a womans name.

Thy virgin's girdle now untie,
And in thy nuptiall bed (love's altar) lye
A pleasing sacrifice; now dispossesse
Thee of these chaines and robes which were put on
T'adorne the day, not thee; for thou, alone,
Like vertue'and truth, art best in nakednesse;
This bed is onely to virginitie
A grave, but, to a better state, a cradle;
Till now thou wast but able
To be what now thou art; then that by thee
No more be said, *I may bee*, but, *I am*,
To night put on perfection and a womans name. . . .

JOHN DONNE, from "Epithalamion Made at Lincoln's Inn"

Grow old along with me!
The best is yet to be,
The last of life, for which the first was made:
Our times are in his hand
Who saith, "A whole I planned,
Youth shows but half; trust God: see all, nor be afraid!" . . .

ROBERT BROWNING, from "Rabbi Ben Ezra"

I have a feeling that my boat
has struck, down there in the depths,
against a great thing.
                              And nothing
happens! Nothing . . . Silence . . . Waves . . .

—Nothing happens? Or has everything happened,
and are we standing now, quietly, in the new life?

JUAN RAMÓN JIMÉNEZ, "Oceans,"
translation by Robert Bly

Here we are . . . on the roads of exodus. Far off in the distance,
the ground lets loose its aromatics. The country behind us winks
out in the blaze of daylight. The stripped earth bares its yellow
bones, graven with unknown ciphers. Where rye once bloomed,
and sorghum, white clay now smokes . . .

Our roads lie elsewhere . . . we move forward into God's
land like a starving tribe . . .

Before us rises the vision of our lives to come . . .

O weather of God, favor us . . .

The adventure is overwhelming, but we plunge toward it . . .

By the seven knit bones of the forehead and the face, let us
go forward, wearing ourselves to the bone, ah! even to the
splintering of the bone! . . .

God's dreams infuse us . . .

God's trickster, evil monkey, keep your distance!

SAINT-JEAN PERSE, from "Drouth,"
translation by E. M.

Walt Whitman

Darest thou now O soul,
Walk out with me toward the unknown region,
Where neither ground is for the feet nor any path to follow?

No map there, nor guide,
Nor voice sounding, nor touch of human hand,
Nor face with blooming flesh, nor lips, nor eyes, are in that
     land.

I know it not O soul,
Nor dost thou, all is a blank before us,
All waits undream'd of in that region, that inaccessible
     land. . . .

from "Darest thou now O soul"

Are you the new person drawn toward me?
To begin with take warning, I am surely far different from what
     you suppose;
Do you suppose you will find in me your ideal?
Do you think it is so easy to have me become your lover?
Do you think the friendship of me would be unalloy'd
     satisfaction?
Do you think I am trusty and faithful?
Do you see no further than this façade, this smooth and tolerant
     manner of me?
Do you suppose yourself advancing on real ground toward a
     real heroic man?
Have you no thought O dreamer that it may be all maya,
     illusion?

"Are you the new person drawn toward me?"

Allons! whoever you are come travel with me!
Traveling with me you find what never tires.
The earth never tires,
The earth is rude, silent, incomprehensible at first, Nature is
    rude and incomprehensible at first,
Be not discouraged, keep on, there are divine things well
    envelop'd,
I swear to you there are divine things more beautiful than words
    can tell.
Allons! we must not stop here,
However sweet these laid-up stores, however convenient this
    dwelling we cannot remain here,
However shelter'd this port and however calm these waters we
    must not anchor here,
However welcome the hospitality that surrounds us we are
    permitted to receive it but a little while.

Allons! the inducements shall be greater,
We will sail pathless and wild seas,
We will go where winds blow, waves dash, and the Yankee
    clipper speeds by under full sail.
Allons! with power, liberty, the earth, the elements,
Health, defiance, gayety, self-esteem, curiosity;
Allons! from all formules! . . .

Camerado, I give you my hand!
I give you my love more precious than money,
I give you myself before preaching or law;
Will you give me yourself? will you come travel with me?
Shall we stick by each other as long as we live?

from "Song of the Open Road"

D. H. Lawrence

Do you think it is easy to change?
Ah, it is very hard to change and be different.
It means passing through the waters of oblivion.

"Change"

Are you willing to be sponged out, erased, cancelled,
made nothing?
Are you willing to be made nothing?
dipped into oblivion?

If not, you will never really change.

The phoenix renews her youth
only when she is burnt, burnt alive, burnt down
to hot and flocculent ash.
Then the small stirring of a new small bub in the nest
with strands of down like floating ash
Shows that she is renewing her youth like the eagle
Immortal bird.

"Phoenix"

Not every man has gentians in his house
in Soft September, at slow, sad Michaelmas.

Bavarian gentians, big and dark, only dark
darkening the day-time torch-like with the smoking blueness
    of Pluto's gloom,
ribbed and torch-like, with their blaze of darkness spread blue
down flattening into points, flattened under the sweep of white
    day

torch-flower of the blue-smoking darkness, Pluto's dark-blue daze,
black lamps from the halls of Dio, burning dark blue,
giving off darkness, blue darkness, as Demeter's pale lamps give off light,
lead me then, lead me the way.

Reach me a gentian, give me a torch!
let me guide myself with the blue, forked torch of this flower
down the darker and darker stairs, where blue is darkened on blueness
even where Persephone goes, just now, from the frosted September
to the sightless realm where darkness is awake upon the dark
and Persephone herself is but a voice
or a darkness invisible enfolded in the deeper dark
of the arms Plutonic, and pierced with the passion of dense gloom,
among the splendour of torches of darkness, shedding darkness on the lost bride and her groom.

"Bavarian Gentians"

God with honour hang your head,
Groom, and grace you, bride, your bed
With lissome scions, sweet scions,
Out of hallowed bodies bred.

Each be other's comfort kind:
Déep, déeper than divined,
Divine charity, dear charity,
Fast you ever, fast bind.

Then let the march tread our ears:
I to him turn with tears
Who to wedlock, his wonder wedlock,
Déals tríumph and immortal years.

GERARD MANLEY HOPKINS,
"At the Wedding March"

We have left the well-tracked beaches of proven facts and experiences. We are adventuring the chartless seas of imagination.

Is the golden fleece that awaits us some kind of new freedom
for growth? And in this new freedom, is there any place for a
relationship? I believe there is . . . an opportunity for the best
relationship of all: not a limited, mutually exclusive one . . .
and not a functional, dependent one . . . but the meeting of two
whole fully developed people as persons. . . .

But this new relationship of persons as persons, this more
human love, this two solitudes conception is not something that
comes easily. . . . It cannot be reached until woman—individually and as a sex—has herself come of age, a maturing process
we are witnessing today. In this undertaking she must work

alone and cannot count on much help from the outsider, eager as he may be in pointing out the way. . . .

Woman must come of age by herself. This is the essence of "coming of age"—to learn how to stand alone. . . . She must find her true center alone. She must become whole. She must, it seems to me, as a prelude to any "two solitudes" relationship, follow the advice of the poet to become "world to oneself for another's sake."

In fact, I wonder if both man and woman must not accomplish this heroic feat. Must not man also become world to himself? Must he not also expand the neglected sides of his personality; the art of inward looking that he has seldom had time for in his active outward-going life; the personal relationships which he has not had as much chance to enjoy; the so-called feminine qualities, aesthetic, emotional, cultural and spiritual, which he has been too rushed to fully develop . . . ?

A good relationship has a pattern like a dance and is built on some of the same rules. The partners do not need to hold on tightly, because they move confidently in the same pattern, intricate but gay and swift and free, like a country dance of Mozart's. To touch heavily would be to arrest the pattern and freeze the movement, to check the endlessly changing beauty of its unfolding. There is no place here for the possessive clutch, the clinging arm, the heavy hand; only the barest touch in passing. Now arm in arm, now face to face, now back to back— it does not matter which. Because they know they are partners moving to the same rhythm, creating a pattern together, and being invisibly nourished by it.

The joy of such a pattern is not only the joy of creation or the joy of participation, it is also the joy of living in the moment. Lightness of touch and living in the moment are intertwined. One cannot dance well unless one is completely in time with the music, not leaning back to the last step or pressing forward to the next one, but poised directly on the present step as it comes. Perfect poise on the beat is what gives good dancing its sense of ease, of timelessness, of the eternal. . . .

ANNE MORROW LINDBERGH, from Gift from the Sea

We were on the pier, you desiring
That I see the Pleiades. I could see
everything but what you wished.

Now I will follow. There is not a single cloud; the stars
appear, even the invisible sister. Show me where to look,
as though they will stay where they are.

Instruct me in the dark.

LOUISE GLÜCK, "Under Taurus"

Corridors of the soul! The soul that is like a young woman!
You clear light
and the brief history
and the joy of a new life . . .

Oh turn and be born again, and walk the road,
and find once more the lost path!. . .

. . . walk through life in dreams
out of love of the hand that leads us.

ANTONIO MACHADO, from "Rebirth,"
translation by Robert Bly

A change is taking place, some painful growth, as in a snake during the shedding of its skin. . . . It is difficult to adjust because I do not know who is adjusting; I am no longer that old person and not yet the new.

. . . With the past evaporated . . . I begin to experience that *now* that is spoken of by the great teachers.

To the repentant thief upon the cross, the soft Jesus of the modern Bible holds out hope of Heaven: "Today thou art with me in Paradise." But in older translations, there is no "today," no suggestion of the future. In the Russian translation, for example, the meaning is "right here now." Thus Jesus declares. "You are in Paradise right now" . . .

We climb onward, toward the sky, and with every step my spirits rise. . . . I begin to smile, infused with a sense of my own foolishness, with an acceptance of the failures of this journey as well as of its wonders, acceptance of all that I might meet upon my path. I know that this transcendence will be fleeting, but while it lasts, I spring along the path as if set free. . . .

PETER MATTHIESSEN, from *The Snow Leopard*

. . . Still, I am prepared for this voyage, and for anything else
    you may care to mention.
Not that I am afraid, but there is very little time left.
You have probably made travel arrangements, and know the
    feeling.
Suddenly, one morning, the little train arrives in the station,
    but oh, so big!

. . . Now we are both setting sail into the purplish evening.
I love it! This cruise can never last long enough for me.
. . . Ribbons are flung, ribbons of cloud

And the sun seems to be coming out. But there have been so
   many false alarms. . . .
No, it's happened! The storm is over. Again the weather is fine
   and clear. . . .

And the voyage? It's on! Listen everybody, the ship is starting,
I can hear its whistle's roar! We have just time enough to make
   it to the dock!

And away they pour, in the sulfurous sunlight,
To the aqua and silver waters where stands the glistening
   white ship
And into the great vessel they flood, a motley and happy crowd
Chanting and pouring down hymns on the surface of the
   ocean. . . .

Pulling, tugging us along with them, by means of streamers,
Golden and silver confetti. Smiling, we laugh and sing with
   the revelers
But are not quite certain that we want to go—the dock is so
   sunny and warm.
That majestic ship will pull up anchor who knows where?

And full of laughter and tears, we sidle once again with the
   other passengers.
The ground is heaving under foot. Is it the ship? It could
   be the dock. . . .
And with a great whoosh all the sails go up. . . .
. . . Into the secretive, vaporous night with all of us!
Into the unknown, the unknown that loves us, the great
   unknown!

JOHN ASHBERY, from "The Skaters"

Henceforth, from the mind,
For your whole joy, must spring
Such joy as you may find
In any earthly thing,
And every time and place
Will take your thought for grace.

Henceforth, from the tongue,
From shallow speech alone,
Comes joy you thought, when young,
Would wring you to the bone,
Would pierce you to the heart
And spoil its stop and star.

Henceforth, from the shell,
Wherein you heard, and wondered
At oceans like a bell
So far from ocean sundered—
A smothered sound that sleeps
Long lost within lost deeps,

Will chime you change and hours,
The shadow of increase,
Will sound you flowers
Born under troubled peace—
Henceforth, henceforth
Will echo sea and earth.

LOUISE BOGAN, "Henceforth, from the Mind"

"Come and play with me," proposed the little prince. "I am so
unhappy."

"I cannot play with you," the fox said. "I am not tamed" . . .

"What does that mean, tame?"

"It is an act too often neglected," said the fox. "It means to establish ties . . . To me, you are still nothing more than a little boy who is just like a hundred thousand other little boys. And I have no need of you. And you, on your part, have no need of me. To you, I am nothing more than a fox like a hundred thousand other foxes. But if you tame me, then we shall need each other. To me, you will be unique in all the world. To you, I shall be unique in all the world . . .

"If you tame me, it will be as if the sun came to shine on my life. I shall know the sound of a step that will be different from all the others. Other steps send me hurrying back underneath the ground. Yours will call me, like music, out of my burrow . . . Think how wonderful that will be when you have tamed me! . . . One only understands the things that one tames . . . If you want a friend, tame me . . . "

"What must I do to tame you?" asked the little prince.

"You must be patient," replied the fox. "First you will sit down at a little distance from me—like that—in the grass. I shall look at you out of the corner of my eye, and you will say nothing. Words are the source of misunderstandings. But you will sit a little closer to me, every day . . . [and you must] come back at the same hour. If, for example, you come at four o'clock in the afternoon, then at three o'clock I shall begin to be happy. I shall feel happier and happier as the hour advances. At four o'clock I shall already be worrying and jumping about. I shall show you how happy I am! But if you come at just any time, I shall never know at what hour my heart is to be ready to greet you . . . One must observe the proper rites."

"What is a rite?" asked the prince.

"They are what make one day different from other days, one hour from other hours . . . "

So the prince tamed the fox . . .

[Then the little prince saw a garden of roses.] "You are not at all like *my* rose," he said. "As yet you are nothing. No one has tamed you, and you have tamed no one. You are like my fox when I first knew him. He was only a fox like a hundred thousand other foxes. But I have made him my friend, and now he is unique in all the world . . .

"You are beautiful, but you are empty," he went on. "One could not die for you. To be sure, an ordinary passerby would think that my rose looked just like you—the rose that belongs to me. But in herself alone she is more important than all the hundreds of you other roses: because it is she that I have watered . . . because it is she that I have sheltered . . . because it is she that I have listened to, when she grumbled, or boasted, or even sometimes when she said nothing. Because she is *my* rose."

And he went back to meet the fox.

"Goodbye," he said.

"Goodbye," said the fox. "And now here is my secret, a very simple secret: it is only with the heart that one can see rightly; what is essential is invisible to the eye . . .

"It is the time you have wasted for your rose that makes your rose so important . . .

"You become responsible, forever, for what you have tamed. You are responsible for your rose."

Antoine de Saint-Exupéry, from *The Little Prince*,
translation by Katherine Woods

IV

*Eternal Vows
in Sacred
Space*

Tonight is a night of *union* and also of scattering of the stars,
for a bride is coming from the sky: the full moon.
The sky is an astrolabe, and the Law is Love.

JALAL AL-DIN RUMI, Persian love poem,
translation by A. J. Arberry

The marriage ceremony itself may be short but it should set the course of the couple's life to come, drawing them into the community in which, like their parents before them, they'll play thereafter a generative role. The event takes place in a sanctuary of sacred space, which is also, in certain religious systems, to be imagined as a place of stopped time. There the celebrant of each religion explains the mysteries and responsibilities of human union, its social, theological, and even metaphysical implications. In Jewish custom, a canopy held over the bridal couple marks the plot as a corner of Eden, a sign of continuity between the world of the Torah and today. In Christian, Hindu, and Buddhist custom, ministers and priests may call down benedictions on the new couple from divine presences beyond the moment. Secular weddings also take place in the presence of symbols and icons—flags, a national seal, accreditation documents of the presiding official (a notary public, a ship's captain), certain features of landscape, and so forth. Even for people whose religious ideas are perfunctory, exchange of wedding vows is no trivial event but should be understood as integrative of life on a deep level.

In fact the human family has evolved countless variations on the rites of union, documented in detail by anthropologists of the nineteenth and early twentieth centuries. I have included short excerpts from two of these standard texts to give an idea of their breadth. Some of this information and some of the liturgical passages included here may strike one as odd. Yet they are all rooted in common traditions of myth and belief, and similar notions resonate through world poetry.

The Marriage of the Gods: At Babylon the imposing sanctuary of Bel rose like a pyramid above the city in a series of eight towers or stories, planted one on the top of the other. On the highest tower, reached by an ascent which wound about all the rest, there stood a spacious temple, and in the temple a great bed, magnificently draped and cushioned, with a golden table beside it. In the temple no image was to be seen, and no human being passed the night there, save a single woman, whom, according to the Chaldean priests, the god chose from among all the women of Babylon. They said that the deity himself came into the temple at night and slept in the great bed; and the woman, as a consort of the god, might have no intercourse with mortal man.

At Thebes in Egypt a woman slept in the temple of Ammon as the consort of the god, and, like the human wife of Bel at Babylon, she was said to have no commerce with a man. . . .

At Athens the god of the vine, Dionysus, was annually married to the Queen, and it appears that the consummation of the divine union, as well as the espousals, was enacted at the ceremony; but whether the part of the god was played by a man or an image we do not know. . . . The object of the marriage can hardly have been any other than that of ensuring the fertility of the vines and other fruit-trees of which Dionysus was the god. Thus both in form and in meaning the ceremony would answer to the nuptials of the King and Queen of May.

In the great mysteries solemnised at Eleusis in the month of September the union of the sky-god Zeus with the corn-goddess Demeter appears to have been represented by the union of the hierophant with the priestess of Demeter, who acted the parts of god and goddess. . . . Thus the custom of marrying gods either to images or to human beings was widespread among the nations of antiquity.

SIR JAMES GEORGE FRAZER,
from *The Golden Bough: A Study in Magic and Religion*

Marriage being the permanent living-together of a man and a woman, what is the essence of a marriage ceremony? It is the "joining together" of a man and a woman; in the words of the English Service, "for this cause shall a man leave his father and mother and shall be joined unto his wife; and they two shall be one flesh." At the other side of the world, these words are pronounced by an elder [of the Malacca Straits] when a marriage is solemnised: "Listen all ye that are present; those that were distant are now brought together; those that were separated are now united." Before marriage, and in many cases also after marriage, the sexes are separated by ideas of sexual taboo; at marriage, they are joined together by the same ideas. Those who were separated are now joined together, those who were mutually taboo, now break the taboo. It is unnecessary to recapitulate the various dangers responsible for the taboo, which lead to the idea that not only all contact of man and woman but the state of marriage itself is harmful and, later, sinful, in fact, forbidden. Hence, the conception that marriage ceremonies prevent this danger and this sin. We have, however, seen cases where the individual in marriage is consciously aware that it is his human partner who is to be feared. In [Ireland] men with guns used to escort the bridal party to church. The guns were fired at intervals over the heads of the bride and bridesmaids. The same practice of firing over the heads of bride and bridegroom on the way to or from the church in which the marriage ceremony is celebrated is found in many parts of Europe. Amongst the Mordvins, as the bridegroom's party sets out for the house of the bride, the best man marches thrice round the party with a drawn sword or scythe, imprecating curses upon ill-wishers. In Nizhegorod the best man walks thrice round the party, against the sun, holding an *ikon*. Then he places himself in front of them, and scratches the ground with a knife, cursing evil spirits and evilly disposed persons. . . .

The practice of throwing rice originated in the idea of giving food to the evil influences to induce them to be propitious and depart, but in many cases it seems to have developed into a systematic method of securing fertility, and on the other hand is regarded by some peoples as an inducement to the soul to stay. In Celebes, for instance, there is a belief that the bridegroom's soul is apt to fly away at marriage, and rice is therefore scattered over him to induce it to remain. . . .

A common class of preliminary ceremonial includes various kinds of purification, the inner meaning of which is to neutralise the mutual dangers of contact. Before the wedding the bridegroom in South Celebes bathes in holy water. The bride is also fumigated. Purification by water forms an integral part of Malay customs at birth, adolescence, marriage, sickness, death, and, in fact, at every critical period in the life of a Malay. The first ceremonies at a wedding consist in fumigating the bride and groom with incense, and then smearing them with "neutralising paste" which averts ill-luck.

Weddings very commonly take place in the evening, or at night, a custom natural enough for its convenience and its obviation of dangers, such as that of the evil eye and those connected with human, and especially with female, shyness and timidity. Amongst the Santals marriages take place at night, and the bride is conveyed to her husband in a basket. Amongst the ancient Romans the bridegroom had to go to his bride in the dark, a custom on which Plutarch speculates in his Roman Questions. Amongst the Zulus it is against etiquette for the bridal party to enter the bridegroom's hut in the daytime. . . .

There are some interesting customs which show both the taboo character of bride and bridegroom, and also an attempt at disguising them by fictitious change of identity. The Malay wedding ceremony, even as carried out by the poorer classes, shows that the contracting parties are treated as royalty, that is to say, as sacred human beings. During the first week of marriage the Syrian pair play at being king and queen; they sit on a throne, and the villagers sing songs. It has been conjectured that *The Song of Songs* is a collection of such songs.

Somewhat similar is the idea underlying the habit of wearing finery or new clothes for a new or important event. On the same plane is the common custom of erecting a "marriage-bower," well known amongst the Hindu peoples, and once common in Spain. In the mining districts of Fife, when a bridal company set out in procession for the kirk, the bride and bride-groom were sometimes "bowered," that is, an arch of green boughs was held over their heads.

Next comes the very interesting custom of substituting a mock bride for the real one. Thus amongst the Beni-Amer, the groom and his friends are often mocked when they come to take the bride, her people substituting a false bride for the true one. The substitute is carefully disguised and allows herself to be taken, and at last when the procession is well outside the village, she reveals herself and runs back laughing. Amongst the Saxons of Transylvania, the bride is concealed with two married women behind a curtain, on the evening of the wedding-day, and the husband has to guess which is his wife, all three try to mislead him. Amongst the Moksha, an old woman dressed up as a bride danced before the company. Amongst the Esthonians, the bride's brother dresses up in women's clothes and personates the bride. In Brittany, the substitutes are first a little girl, then the mistress of the house, and lastly the grandmother.

We now reach the ceremonies which, more than any others, unite the man and the woman. Each of the two parties gives to the other a part of himself and receives from the other a part of him; this part, on the principles of contact, may be, as it is in love-charms, a lock of hair, a piece of clothing, food that has or has not been touched, blood, and the like. This effects union by assimilating the one to the other, so as to produce somewhat of identity of substance. . . .

The commonest of all marriage ceremonies of union is eating and drinking together. This breaks the most important of sexual taboos, that against eating together. The offering of a gift of food, which is part of the biological basis of the custom, is often used as a proposal of marriage. In Halmahera and Borneo a proposal is made by offering *betel* to the girl. She shows her acceptance by receiving it. In Samoa the suitor offers her a basket of bread-fruit; or he asks her parents for her hand. If they are friendly and eat with him, his addresses are sure to be favourably received. In Switzerland, if a youth and a girl fall in love, on the Easter Monday after, they publicly drink together in order to inform the world at large of their love and to warn off others who might wish to approach the girl. . . . In the Duke of York Islands a cocoanut is broken over the heads of the pair, and its milk poured over them. Amongst the Koosa Kaffirs the relatives of the groom hand milk to the bride, reminding her that it is from the cows which belong to the bridegroom. Of this milk she may not drink while the bridegroom is her suitor only, but now she is to drink it, and from this moment the union is indissolubly concluded. The people shout, "She drinks the milk! She hath drunk the milk!" . . .

The survey of marriage suggests many thoughts. For instance, one is struck by the high morality of [early] man. The religious character of early human relations, again, gives a sense of tragedy: man seems to feel that he is treading in slippery places, that he is on the brink of precipices, when really he standeth right. This sensitive attitude would seem to have assisted the natural development of man. . . . Lastly, this desire for security and permanence in a world where only change is permanent has led to certain conceptions of eternal personalities who control and symbolise the marriage tie . . . [for example] the Goddess of Love . . . the Holy Family . . . the eternal feminine . . . the Mystical Rose.

ERNEST CRAWLEY, from *The Mystic Rose: A Study of Primitive Marriage and of Primitive Thought in Its Bearing on Marriage*

Therefore must the bride below have a canopy, all beautiful with decorations prepared for her, in order to honor the Bride above, who comes to be present and participate in the joy of the bride below. For this reason it is necessary that the canopy be as beautiful as possible, and that the Supernal Bride be invited to come and share in the joy.

from "Terumah," in the *Zohar*

The chuppah stands on four poles.
The home has four corners.
The chuppah stands on four poles.

The marriage stands on four legs.
Four points loose the winds
that blow on the walls of the house,

the south wind that brings the warm rain,
the east wind that brings the cold rain,
the north wind that brings the cold sun
and the snow, the long west wind
bringing the weather off the far plains.

Here we live open to the seasons.
Here the winds caress and cuff us
contrary and fierce as bears.
Here the winds are caught and snarling
in the pines, a cat in a net clawing
breaking twigs to fight loose.
Here the winds brush your face
soft in the morning as feathers
that float down from the dove's breast.

Here the moon sails up out of the ocean
dripping like a just washed apple.
Here the sun wakes us like a baby.
Therefore the chuppah has no sides.

It is not a box.
It is not a coffin.
It is not a dead end.
Therefore the chuppah has no walls.
We have made a home together
open to the weather of our time.
We are mills that turn in the winds of struggle
converting fierce energy into bread.

The canopy is the cloth of our table
where we share fruit and vegetables
of our labor, where our care for the earth
comes back and we take its body in ours.

The canopy is the cover of our bed
where our bodies open their portals wide,
where we eat and drink the blood
of our love, where the skin shines red
as a swallowed sunrise and we burn
in one furnace of joy molten as steel
and the dream is fresh and flower.

O my love O my love we dance
under the chuppah standing over us
like an animal on its four legs,
like a table on which we set our love
as a feast, like a tent
under which we work
not safe but no longer solitary
in the searing heat of our time.

MARGE PIERCY, "The Chuppah,"
June 2, 1982, on her marriage to Ira Wood

Blessed are you, Holy One of the Earth, who creates
the fruit of the vine.
Blessed are you, Holy One of the Universe. You
created all things for your Glory.
Blessed are you, Holy One of the World.
Through you mankind lives.
Blessed are you, Holy One of the World. You made
man and woman in your image, after your likeness, that
they might perpetuate life. . . .
Blessed are you, Holy One of All Nature, who makes
Zion rejoice with her children. . . .
Blessed are you, Holy One of the Cosmos, who makes
the bridegroom and bride to rejoice.

Blessed are you, Holy One of All, who created joy
and gladness, bride and bridegroom, mirth and song,
pleasure and delight, love, fellowship, peace
and friendship. . . .

The Hebrew "Seven Blessings"

In the sixteenth century the kabbalists of Safed personified the
Sabbath as a bride and welcomed her every week with fervent
joy. These mystics would go forth to the hills surrounding the
city, robed in white as grooms and would greet the incoming
Sabbath with the chanting of *Lekhah Dodi*—"Come, my friend,
to greet the bride, to receive the presence of the Sabbath." This
well-known hymn, composed by Rabbi Solomon Halevi Alk-
abetz, is still sung at Friday evening services. The celebration
of the Sabbath was considered a wedding feast.

In talmudic days Rabbi Yanni would don his Sabbath clothes
on Friday before evening and say: "Come, O bride, come, O
bride."

PHILIP and HANNA GOODMAN, "The Sabbath as Bride"

Come my beloved, with chorus of praise,
Welcome Bride Sabbath, the Queen of the days . . .
Come in thy joyousness, Crown of thy lord;
Come, bringing peace to the folk of the Word;
Come where the faithful in gladsome accord,
      Hail thee as Sabbath-Bride, Queen of the days.
Come where the faithful are hymning thy praise,
Come as a bride cometh, Queen of the days!

from "Lekhah Dodi," Hebrew hymn to the Sabbath as a bride

Psalms

FROM PSALM 98

O sing unto the Lord a new song; for he hath done marvellous things: . . .

4 Make a joyful noise unto the Lord, all the earth: make a loud noise, and rejoice, and sing praise.

5 Sing unto the Lord with the harp; with the harp, and the voice of a psalm.

6 With trumpets and sound of cornets make a joyful noise before the Lord, the King.

7 Let the sea roar, and the fulness thereof; the world, and they that dwell therein.

8 Let the floods clap their hands: let the hills be joyful together

9 Before the Lord. . . .

PSALM 100

Make a joyful noise unto the Lord, all ye lands.

2 Serve the Lord with gladness: come before his presence with singing.

3 Know ye that the Lord he is God: it is he that hath made us, and not we ourselves; we are his people, and the sheep of his pasture.

4 Enter into his gates with thanksgiving, and into his courts with praise: be thankful unto him, and bless his name.

5 For the Lord is good, his mercy is everlasting, and his truth endureth to all generations.

Bless the Lord, O my soul. O Lord my God, thou art very great; thou art clothed with honour and majesty.

2 Who coverest thyself with light as with a garment: who stretchest out the heavens like a curtain:

3 Who layeth the beams of his chambers in the waters: who maketh the clouds his chariot: who walketh upon the wings of the wind:

4 Who maketh his angels spirits; his ministers a flaming fire:

5 Who laid the foundations of the earth, that it should not be removed for ever.

6 Thou coveredst it with the deep as with a garment: the waters stood above the mountains.

7 At thy rebuke they fled; at the voice of thy thunder they hasted away.

8 They go up by the mountains; they go down by the valleys unto the place which thou hast founded for them.

9 Thou hast set a bound that they may not pass over; that they turn not again to cover the earth.

10 He sendeth the springs into the valleys, which run among the hills.

11 They give drink to every beast of the field: the wild asses quench their thirst.

12 By them shall the fowls of the heaven have their habitation, which sing among the branches.

13 He watereth the hills from his chambers: the earth is satisfied with the fruit of thy works.

14 He causeth the grass to grow for the cattle, and herb for the service of man: that he may bring forth food out of the earth;

15 And wine that maketh glad the heart of man, and oil to

make his face to shine, and bread which strengtheneth man's heart.

16 The trees of the Lord are full of sap; the cedars of Lebanon, which he hath planted;

17 Where the birds make their nests; as for the stork, the fir trees are her house.

18 The high hills are a refuge for the wild goats; and the rocks for the conies.

19 He appointed the moon for seasons: the sun knoweth his going down.

20 Thou makest darkness and it is night: wherein all the beasts of the forest do creep forth.

21 The young lions roar after their prey, and seek their meat from God.

22 The sun ariseth, they gather themselves together, and lay them down in their dens.

23 Man goeth forth unto his work and to his labour until the evening.

24 O Lord, how manifold are thy works! in wisdom hast thou made them all: the earth is full of thy riches.

25 So is this great and wide sea, wherein are things creeping innumerable, both small and great beasts.

26 There go the ships: there is that leviathan, whom thou hast made to play therein.

27 These wait all upon thee; that thou mayest give them their meat in due season.

28 That thou givest them they gather: thou openest thine hand, they are filled with good.

29 Thou hidest thy face, they are troubled: thou takest away their breath, they die, and return to their dust.

30 Thou sendest forth thy spirit, they are created: and thou renewest the face of the earth.

31 The glory of the Lord shall endure for ever: the Lord shall rejoice in his works.

32 He looketh on the earth, and it trembleth: he toucheth the hills, and they smoke.

33 I will sing unto the Lord as long as I live: I will sing praise to my God while I have my being.

34 My meditation of him shall be sweet: I will be glad in the Lord . . .

(King James Version)

Blessed be You, Life-Spirit of the universe,
Who makes a distinction between holy and not yet
    holy,
between light and darkness,
between Shabbat and the six days of the week,
between committed and uncommitted,
between common goals and personal goals,
between love and aloneness.
Blessed be you,
Who distinguishes between what is holy, and what is
    not yet holy.

Hebrew blessing for Sabbath end

Rejoice, O young man, in thy youth,
  And gather the fruit thy joy shall bear,
Thou and the wife of thy youth,
  Turning now to thy dwelling to enter there.

Glorious blessings of God, who is One,
  Shall come united upon thine head;
  Thine house shall be at peace from dread,
Thy foes' uprising be undone.
  Thou shalt lay thee down in a safe retreat;
  Thou shalt rest, and thy sleep be sweet.

In thine honor, my bridegroom, prosper and live;
  Let thy beauty arise and shine forth fierce;
  And the heart of thine enemies God shall pierce,
And the sins of thy youth will He forgive,
  And bless thee in increase and all thou shalt do.
  When thou settest thine hand thereto. . . .

JUDAH HALEVI, from a poem to the bridegroom,
translation by Nina Davis

Thus saith the Lord; Again there shall be heard in this place
. . . The voice of joy, and the voice of gladness, the voice of
the bridegroom, and the voice of the bride, the voice of them
that shall say, Praise the Lord of hosts: for the Lord is good:
for his mercy endureth for ever.

Jeremiah 33:10–11 (King James Version)

Dearly beloved: We have come together in the presence of God
to witness and bless the joining together of this man and this
woman in Holy Matrimony. The bond and covenant of marriage
was established by God in creation, and our Lord Jesus Christ

adorned this manner of life by his presence and first miracle at a wedding in Cana of Galilee. It signifies to us the mystery of the union between Christ and his Church, and Holy Scripture commends it to be honored among all people.

The union of husband and wife in heart, body, and mind is intended by God for their mutual joy; for the help and comfort given one another in prosperity and adversity; and, when it is God's will, for the procreation of children and their nurture in the knowledge and love of the Lord. Therefore marriage is not to be entered into unadvisedly or lightly, but reverently, deliberately, and in accordance with the purposes for which it was instituted by God.

from "The Celebration and Blessing of a Marriage,"
in *The Book of Common Prayer* (Episcopal)

Eternal God, creator and preserver of all life, author of salvation, and giver of all grace: Look with favor upon the world you have made, and for which your Son gave his life, and especially upon this man and this woman whom you make one flesh in Holy Matrimony.

Give them wisdom and devotion in the ordering of their common life, that each may be to the other a strength in need, a counselor in perplexity, a comfort in sorrow, and a companion in joy.

Grant that their wills may be so knit together in your will, and their spirits in your Spirit, that they may grow in love and peace with you and one another all the days of their life.

Give them grace, when they hurt each other, to recognize and acknowledge their fault, and to seek each other's forgiveness and yours.

Make their life together a sign of Christ's love to this sinful and broken world, that unity may overcome estrangement, forgiveness heal guilt, and joy conquer despair.

Bestow on them, if it is your will, the gift and heritage of children, and the grace to bring them up to know you, to love you, and to serve you.

Give them such fulfillment of their mutual affection that they may reach out in love and concern for others.

Grant that all married persons who have witnessed these vows may find their lives strengthened and their loyalties confirmed.

Grant that the bonds of our common humanity, by which all your children are united one to another, and the living to the dead, may be so transformed by your grace, that your will may be done on earth as it is in heaven; where, O Father, with your Son and the Holy Spirit, you live and reign in perfect unity, now and for ever.

from *The Book of Common Prayer*

The maiden is the daughter of light . . .
Delightful is the sight of her,
Radiant with shining beauty.
Her garments are like spring flowers,
And a scent of sweet fragrance is diffused from them . . .
Truth rests upon her head.
By the movements of her feet, she shows forth joy . . .
Her two hands make signs and secret patterns, describing the
dance of the blessed aeons.
Her fingers open the gates of the city.
Her chamber is full of light . . .
Her bridesmaids are seven,
Who dance before her.

Twelve are they who serve her
And are subject to her,
Gazing toward the bridegroom
That by the sight of him they may be enlightened;
And forever be with him in eternal joy.
Bride and groom shall be at that marriage . . .
And both shall be in joy and exultation.
And thus they glorified and praised, with the living Spirit,
The Father of Truth and the Mother of Wisdom.

from the apocryphal Acts of Thomas, translation by R. McL. Wilson

Husbands, love your wives as you love your own bodies. In loving his wife a man loves himself. For no one ever hated his own body: on the contrary, he provides and cares for it; and thus it is that a man shall leave his father and mother and shall be joined to his wife and the two shall become one flesh.

It is a great truth that is hidden here . . .

Ephesians 4:25–32 (New English Bible)

Have you not read that he who made them from the beginning made them male and female, and said, "For this reason a man shall leave his father and mother and be joined to his wife, and the two shall become one"? So they are no longer two but one. What therefore God has joined together, let no man put asunder.

Matthew 19:4–6 (New English Bible)

Beloved, let us love one another; for love is of God, and he who loves is born of God and knows God. He who does not love does not know God; for God is love. . . . Beloved, if God so loved us, we also ought to love one another. No man has ever seen God; if we love one another, God abides in us and his love is perfected in us.

1 John 4:7–12 (New English Bible)

Put on then, as God's chosen ones, holy and beloved, compassion, kindness, lowliness, meekness, and patience, forbearing one another and, if one has a complaint against another, forgiving each other; as the Lord has forgiven you, so you also must forgive. And above all these put on love, which binds everything together in perfect harmony. And let peace rule in your hearts . . . And be thankful. Let love dwell in you richly, as you teach and admonish one another in all wisdom . . .

Colossians 3:12–17 (New English Bible)

Be thou magnified, O bridegroom, like Abraham, and blessed like Isaac, and increase like Jacob, walking in peace and living in righteousness . . .

And thou, O bride, be magnified like Sarah, and rejoice like Rebecca, and increase like Rachel, being glad in thy husband and keeping the bounds of the law . . .

from the Greek Orthodox marriage service

We thank thee, O Lord God almighty, who art before the ages, master of the universe, who didst adorn the heavens by thy word, and didst lay the foundations of the earth and all that is therein; who didst gather together those things which were separate into union, and didst make the twain one. Now again, our Master, we beseech thee, may thy servants be worthy of the mark of the sign of thy Word through the bond of betrothal, their love for one another inviolable through the firm sureness of their union. Build them, O Lord, upon the foundation of thy holy Church, that they may walk in accordance with the bond of the word which they have vowed one to another; for thou art the bond of their love, and the ordainer of the law of their union. Thou who hast brought about the oneness, by the union of the twain by thy words, complete, O Lord, the ordinance of thine only-begotten Son Jesus Christ our Lord, through whom and together with the all-Holy Spirit be praise to thee now and always.

from the Coptic Orthodox marriage service

We have taken the seven steps. You have become mine forever. Yes, we have become partners. I have become yours. Hereafter, I cannot live without you. Do not live without me. Let us share the joys. We are word and meaning, united. You are thought and I am sound.

May the nights be honey-sweet for us; may the mornings be honey-sweet for us; may the earth be honey-sweet for us; may the heavens be honey-sweet for us.

May the plants be honey-sweet for us; may the sun be all honey for us; may the cows yield us honey-sweet milk!

As the heavens are stable, as the earth is stable, as the mountains are stable, as the whole universe is stable, so may our union be permanently settled.

from the Hindu marriage ritual of "Seven Steps"

O Lord Fire, First Created Being! Be thou the over-lord and give food and drink to this household. O Lord Fire, who reigns in richness and vitality over all the worlds, come take your proper seat in this home! Accept the offerings made here, protect the one who makes them, be our protector on this day, O you who see into the hearts of all created beings!

Hindu wedding prayer

Nothing happens without a cause. The union of this man and woman has not come about accidentally but is the foreordained result of many past lives. This tie can therefore not be broken or dissolved.

In the future, happy occasions will come as surely as the morning. Difficult times will come as surely as night. When things go joyously, meditate according to the Buddhist tradition. When things go badly, meditate. Meditation in the manner of the Compassionate Buddha will guide your life.

To say the words "love and compassion" is easy. But to accept that love and compassion are built upon patience and perseverance is not easy. Your marriage will be firm and lasting if you remember this.

Buddhist marriage homily

Wash your hearts and souls clean of dust in the water of Wisdom so you won't have regrets. Isn't it always the case that Love is the essence? Apart from Love, everything passes away.

The way to heaven is in your heart. Open and lift the wings of Love! When Love's wings are strong, you need no ladder.

Though the world be thorns, a lover's heart is a bower of roses.

Though heaven's wheel be mired down, lovers' lives go
forward.
Let other people be downcast, the lover is blissful and sprightly.
Invite a lover into each dark corner. The lover is bright as a
hundred thousand candles!
Even if a lover seems to be alone, the secret Beloved is nearby.

The wind of ignorance has died down; the wind of love has
risen. The heart puts forth roses, eglantine and basil,
watered by the rain of generosity.

The time-span of *union* is eternity.
This life is a jar, and in it, *union* is the pure wine.
If we aren't togther, of what use is the jar?

The moment I heard my first love story I began seeking you,
not realizing the search was useless.
Lovers don't meet somewhere along the way.
They're in one another's souls from the beginning.

You are the sea, I am a fish . . .

I am a crystal goblet in my Love's hand.
Look into my eyes if you don't believe me.

> JALAL AL-DIN RUMI, Persian love poem,
> adapted from the translation by A. J. Arberry

Julia, I bring
To thee this ring,
    Made for thy finger fit;
To show by this
That our love is
    Or should be, like to it.

Loose though it be,
The joint is free;
    So, when love's yoke is on,
It must not gall,
Nor fret at all,
    With hard oppression.

But it must play,
Still either way,
    And be, too, such a yoke
As not too wide
To overslide,
    Or be so straight to choke.

So we who bear
This beam, must rear
    Ourselves to such a height
As that the stay
Of either may
    Create the burthen light.

And as this round
Is nowhere found
    To flaw, or else to sever,
So let our love
As endless prove,
    And pure as gold forever.

ROBERT HERRICK, "To Julia"

Go little ring to that same sweet
That hath my heart in her domain . . .

GEOFFREY CHAUCER

An Unconventional Family

SANDRA LIPSITZ BEM

Yale University Press   New Haven & London

Published with assistance from the foundation established in memory of Amasa Stone
Mather of the Class of 1907, Yale College.

Designed by Rebecca Gibb.
Printed in the United States of America.

Library of Congress Cataloging-in-Publication Data
Bem, Sandra L.
An unconventional family / Sandra Lipsitz Bem.
p.   cm.
ISBN 0-300-07424-7 (alk. paper)
1. Sex role.   2. Family.   3. Communication in the family.   4. Man-woman
relationships.   5. Feminism.   6. Equality.   I. Title.
HQ1075.B455   1998
305.3—dc21
97-47696
CIP
A catalogue record for this book is available from the British Library.

The paper in this book meets the guidelines for permanence and durability of the
Committee on Production Guidelines for Book Longevity of the Council on Library
Resources.

10 9 8 7 6 5 4 3 2 1

Contents

Acknowledgments

No memoir is ever about the author's life alone. For giving me permission to write about them, I thank my husband of many years with whom I am no longer partnered, Daryl Bem; my children, Emily and Jeremy Bem; my sister, Bev Lipsitz; my sister- and brother-in-law, Robyn and Barry Bem (who will always be my as-if siblings, whether legally or otherwise); and my cousin, Jack Tombosky. My mother and father are no longer living; neither are Daryl's parents.

I also thank Daryl, Emily, and Jeremy for contributing their own voices to this memoir: Emily and Jeremy, in lengthy interviews that comprise the bulk of chapter 8, and Daryl, in a brief essay that appears as an epilogue. Their voices enrich the book immeasurably.

Many others have also enriched this book. Jill Ker Conway, Mark Freeman, Charles Grench, Carolyn Heilbrun, and Barbara Risman graciously read early drafts and provided constructive criticism from the perspective of either not knowing me at all or not knowing me well. Karen Gilovich, Mary Katzenstein, Sally McConnell-Ginet, and Beth Povinelli provided constructive criticism too, but from the perspective of knowing me all too well.

Finally, I thank my editor at Yale University Press, Gladys Topkis, to whom I was graciously referred by Mary Roth Walsh. Gladys told me frankly in June 1996 that she had read parts I and II of my manuscript on the train from New Haven to Manhattan, and she had loved them so much that she had almost called me from Grand Central Station to tell me so. But then she read the final part, she said, and here I unfortunately turn into an "ordinary" person doing the same kind of intellectual and emotional self-exploration that everybody does who has ever been divorced or separated. If this was what I really wanted to write about, she continued, she had no interest in publishing the book. On the other hand, if I would be willing to grapple seriously, and in retrospect, with the question of what Daryl's and my experience has to say about the prospects for both egalitarian marriage and gender-liberated child-rearing, then she would be very interested indeed. One hears on occasion about the rare editor who is able to redirect an author when she has lost her way. For me, Gladys has been that rarity.

Prologue

Like many feminist scholars, I live my life with little separation between the personal, the professional, and the political. My theory and my practice are thus inextricably intertwined.

In the final five pages of *The Lenses of Gender,* which is my major theoretical work to date, I argued that in order to interrupt the social reproduction of male power, we need to dismantle not only androcentrism and biological essentialism but also gender polarization and compulsory heterosexuality. In other words, we need to sever all the culturally constructed connections that currently exist in our society between what sex a person is and virtually every other aspect of human experience, including modes of dress, social roles, and even ways of expressing emotion and experiencing sexual desire. We need to cut back the male-female distinction to a narrow—if critically important—aspect having to do primarily with reproduction.

With complete gender depolarization, I suggested, the biology of sex would become a minimal presence in human social life. This does not mean that males and females would merely be more free to be masculine, feminine, or androgynous, heterosexual, homosexual, or bisexual, than they are now. It means that the distinction between male and female would no longer be the dimension around which the culture is organized. Hence the very concepts of masculinity, femininity, and androgyny, heterosexuality, homosexuality, and bisexuality, would be as absent from the cultural consciousness as the concepts of a "hetero-eye-colored" eroticism, a "homo-eye-colored" eroticism, and a "bi-eye-colored" eroticism are now.

Consistent with this argument, I ended *The Lenses of Gender* by calling not just for a revolution in our social institutions and cultural discourses but also for a psychological revolution:

> Simply put, this psychological revolution would have us all begin to view the biological fact of being male or female in much the same way that we now view the biological fact of being *human*. Rather than seeing our sex as so authentically who we are that it needs to be elaborated, or so tenuous that it needs to be bolstered, or so limiting that it needs to be traded in for another model, we would instead view our sex as so completely given by nature, so capable of exerting its influence automatically, and so limited in its sphere of influence to those domains where it really does matter biologically, that it could be safely tucked away in the backs of our minds and left to its own devices. In other words, biological sex would no longer be at the core of individual identity and sexuality.

If *The Lenses of Gender* is the statement of my theory, *An Unconventional Family* is the statement of my practice. More specifically, it is an autobiographical account of an attempt by a woman and a man to function as truly egalitarian partners and parents and also to raise children in accordance with gender-liberated, antihomophobic, and sex-positive feminist ideals.

Since Daryl Bem and I first designed our own form of egalitarian marriage out of romantic necessity one night in 1965, many other feminist couples have experimented with egalitarian relationships and feminist child-rearing. But few have so consciously incorporated into their child-rearing practices what I think of as an inoculation against both the sex-negativity and the homophobia of our culture. And fewer still have shared the details of their daily lives as exuberantly as Daryl and I did in public lectures in the 1960s and 1970s in order to provide at least one concrete example of an alternative to the traditional heterosexual family. To a certain extent, this autobiographical account is simultaneously both a personal history of our own past and a social history of a moment in feminism's past. But it is a look into feminism's future as well, because our children, Emily and Jeremy, currently aged twenty-four and twenty-one, also speak in this book, and they (and others like them) speak in the voice of the future.

The first official issue of *Ms.* magazine, published in 1972, included an interview with Daryl and me entitled "A Marriage of Equals." Although I still agree with most of what we said there, I did make one false prediction. "Relationships with best friends are more stable," I said. "They have more in common than do two people who had a spark of infatuation for one another when they were eighteen. I believe we are unlikely to get divorced. When people check back in twenty-five years, I hope they'll find I was right."

Well, I was right technically, in that Daryl and I are not legally divorced. But we did split up about four years ago, and both of us became involved in relationships with people of our own sex. Although I'm sure there are those who would like to know more both about why we split up and what our lives are like now, that is not the story this book tells. But there are two related points I would like to make. First, even though Daryl and I are no longer "close-coupled," our lives are still deeply intertwined, and we still serve as important emotional anchors for each other in the aloneness of the cosmos. Put somewhat differently, we are still family. Second, I still think of myself as having more or less the same sexual orientation I always said I had. To quote once again from *The Lenses of Gender,* this time from the preface,

although I have lived monogamously with a man I love for over twenty-seven years, I am not now and never have been a "heterosexual." But neither have I ever been a "lesbian" or a "bisexual." What I am—and have been for as long as I can remember—is someone whose sexuality and gender have never seemed to mesh with the available cultural categories.... [By this] I mean that the sex-of-partner dimension ... seems irrelevant to my own particular pattern of erotic attractions and sexual experiences. Although some of the (very few) individuals to whom I have been attracted ... have been men and some have been women, what those individuals have in common has nothing to do with either their biological sex or mine—from which I conclude, not that I am attracted to both sexes, but that my sexuality is organized around dimensions other than sex.

In her 1995 book *Vice Versa,* Marjorie Garber makes the very wise argument that for people who have already had serious and meaningful heterosexual relationships, like Daryl and me, the unidimensional and exclusionary concept of "always gay" misleadingly suggests that one's earlier life was nothing but a sham, whereas the much more fluid concept of bisexuality restores "both to them and the people they have loved the full, complex, and often contradictory stories of their lives." Garber also reconceptualizes bisexuality "not as just another sexual orientation but ... [as] a sexuality that undoes sexual orientation as a category, a sexuality that threatens and even challenges the easy binaries of straight and gay, queer and 'het,' and even ... male and female." For both theoretical and personal reasons, I appreciate Garber's notion of bisexuality as "a category that defies and defeats categorization . . . an identity that is . . . *not* an identity." Perhaps someday I will apply the category to myself. Alternatively, I may come to define myself more and more as a lesbian.

As a culture, we are much more aware today than we were thirty years ago that both individuals and families come in a diversity of forms—and that is all to the good. But we are also having to fight more against organized right-wing forces that seek to reestablish the traditional patriarchal heterosexual family as the only real family. And this, in turn, makes it that much more urgent for long-lived alternatives to the traditional heterosexual family—like the one that Daryl and I built together—to become a part of the written record because, as Carolyn Heilbrun says in *Writing a Woman's Life:* "Lives do not serve as models; only stories do that."

PART 1

Coming Together

CHAPTER ONE

Courtship

In February 1965, I was a twenty-year-old senior psychology major at Carnegie Institute of Technology in Pittsburgh. For months, my roommate, Hedda, had been urging me to take a course from the young new psychology professor, Daryl Bem. She had been doing a research project under his supervision and thought him both brilliant and good-looking. I couldn't yet judge his brilliance, but I had seen him once, and he had reminded me of a pigeon because of the way his head jutted forward.

Unfortunately, this brilliant professor wasn't offering any undergraduate courses during my last semester in college, so I built up my courage and asked if he would direct me in an independent reading course in social psychology, which was his specialty. Another second-semester senior had recently made the same request, so he created a seminar and set us to work reading his doctoral dissertation. The three of us met once a week in his office.

I don't remember those early meetings at all. In fact, all I remember about that whole month of February is the story Daryl and I later came to tell about the events leading to our first date. Each of us was becoming romantically interested in the other, the story goes, but we were both afraid to express that interest directly because of my being a student and his being a professor. So we each started counting the number of times the other person seemed to be pulling us into unnecessary conversation, and when the number of times I did the pulling reached seven—the seventh being "Would it be all right if I called you by your first name?"—Daryl decided he could safely move a step closer toward a date without worrying that he might be misreading me.

One day in late February, the phone rang in my apartment. Hedda answered. It was Daryl Bem. Would she and I like to come to dinner at his apartment that Wednesday night, March 3? He was also inviting another senior psychology major, along with the psychology graduate student who was her fiancé. I knew instantly that this dinner was designed as a message to me, so of course I said yes. Hedda also said yes, but she had no idea why the invitation had come when it did. (Bear in mind, by the way, that this was all happening at a time when feminists hadn't even invented the term *sexism* yet, let alone the term *sexual harassment*. It is thus to Daryl's credit that he not only waited for a clear signal from me before asking me out; once we started dating, he also arranged for one of his colleagues to grade my work.)

Emboldened by my having said yes to his dinner invitation, Daryl made another move. As I was walking by his office on the day of the dinner, he called me in and said, "Sandy, I have tickets to the drama department play for opening night tomorrow. I hate opening nights. Would you like to go?" Thrilled, I accepted.

But as I walked out the door and down the hall, the words, "I hate opening nights. Would you like to go?" began to reverberate in my head. "Wait a minute," I said to myself. "Did I just get invited on a date? Or was I being offered two unwanted tickets for a play?" I had no idea but wasn't going to make a fool of myself by asking.

Off I thus went with Hedda to dinner at Daryl's apartment, hoping to find some clue. Thirty years later, all I remember about that dinner is that Daryl served lamb chops with garlic and didn't mention the play even once. Not knowing what else to do, I hung around his office much of the next day, hoping the answer would magically emerge. It finally did when a graduate-student friend of Daryl's asked if he and I would like to have dinner with him and his date before the four of us all went to the play.

The following day, I told a friend that, as absurd as it sounded, I believed that I was going to marry Daryl. Our interaction was so free of male-female game-playing and role-playing, I said, that I loved being with him, and I couldn't imagine that many other men existed who were like him. Exactly what Daryl and I had talked about until two or three in the morning I don't remember any longer. But we had talked honestly, openly, and straightforwardly, as if we were already best friends, and the fact that he was male and I was female had not seemed to be part of our chemistry. I loved that.

My being female had played a role during one moment, however, and I remember it because I would later have to rescind what I had said to Daryl. As we were waiting for the play to begin, he had posed the following question as a way of making small talk. "Sandy," he had said, "you obviously take your academic work very seriously and mean to have a career. How do you see yourself coordinating career and marriage?" If this question had been posed to me a couple of years after that, in the late 1960s, I would have thought that the person asking it needed his feminist consciousness raised. So my reply probably would have run something like: "Gee, Daryl, that's an interesting question. But why are you addressing it to me instead of to yourself? How do *you* plan to coordinate career and marriage? Or do you think that's something only women need to worry about?"

But it was only 1965, and my own feminist consciousness hadn't emerged yet. True, Simone de Beauvoir had already written *The Second Sex* and Betty Friedan, *The Feminine Mystique,* but I hadn't read those books, and I doubt I knew what they were about. And not only that: I wasn't expecting to get married, at least not in the near future. Not many boys had ever been romantically interested in me, and although that bothered me, I had come to envision a more or less satisfying life lived alone, with a rocking chair and a cat, until maybe age thirty-five, when I would perhaps meet some interesting but similarly lonely man, and, as I often put it at the time, "out of companionship would slowly grow love."

But it was only the beginning of our first date, and I didn't want to go into this whole sad story, so instead I just said: "Well, I do always want to work, but my husband's career will always come first, and if my career advances a little more slowly as a result, that will be okay, but I do always (I mean always) expect to work." Not exactly a conventional answer for a young woman at the time, but definitely not what I would have said if I had taken the question more seriously.

The topic didn't come up again until a month or so later—when Daryl and I seemed to be deciding to get married at the beginning of that summer. It's impossible to recapture what had happened in that one month to cause two such staid and unromantic characters to make such an impulsive and seemingly romantic decision. But we had spent virtually every waking moment together and many sleeping ones as well; we had already planned a fabulously unconventional wedding ceremony; and at some point, the frame of our conversation about getting married simply shifted from "if" to "when."

Having slid into this decision, however, I suddenly remembered what I had said to Daryl that first night at the play, and I knew it wasn't true. I also knew that there was no way I would be willing to do what I presumed a good wife was supposed to do for her husband: namely, wash his floors, darn his socks, cook his meals, raise his children, and, most important in the academic world, move from one town to another as he got progressively better jobs. Much as I loved Daryl by then, I thus told him I couldn't marry him after all.

I have no way of knowing what would have happened next if Daryl had said, "Too bad, 'cause I love you too, but OK, if that's the way it is, then good-bye." Maybe I would have married him anyway (although I doubt it). But Daryl didn't say that. Instead, he paused, talked briefly about how the thought of losing me upset him, and then went (as he always does) directly into problem-solving mode. In other words, he raised the question of whether we might be able to construct some less traditional form of marriage that would be more acceptable to me.

The conversation immediately shifted, as did our moods. Rather than talking sadly about ending our relationship, we began to talk excitedly about how to design an egalitarian marriage. The details of daily life seemed trivial once we began to think about them nontraditionally. We would wash the floors only when our shoes started to stick to them, and then we would wash them together. We would each buy three weeks' worth of underwear so we wouldn't have to do laundry very often, either, and we would do that together as well. No one would darn socks; that was just a rhetorical example. We would take turns cooking dinner every other night; we would do the grocery shopping together because we both thought it was kind of fun; and so on. None of this produced any emotional conflict in either of us, and we couldn't understand why we hadn't thought of it sooner.

The emotional tone shifted a bit when we turned to career mobility. Daryl was a rising young star in social psychology, and he very much wanted to move to California, not so much for professional reasons as for the weather. I, in contrast, hadn't even gone to graduate school yet, though I was looking forward to starting the Ph.D. program at the University of Michigan in the fall. Although most people in that era would have thought that I, as both the woman and the younger person, should have been willing to shift my plans for graduate school to the University of Pittsburgh so that Daryl and I could be together, my view was different. As I saw it, Daryl had already had an excellent educational foundation for his career, and I deserved the same.

So I still wanted to go to the University of Michigan even if we got married, and I also wanted Daryl to understand fully that, if he married me, he would no longer be able to respond to job offers as a free agent. Nor would I, of course, but what's new about that for a woman? This loss of total independence gave Daryl a moment's pause as he saw his dream of moving to California drifting away, but he quickly recovered, and we excitedly moved on to framing an egalitarian philosophy.

Each of us would be willing to make career sacrifices for the sake of the other person, we said, but we would *both* make those sacrifices rather than just me making them. We would make these sacrifices, we said, because it was more important to both of us that we be together than for either of us to have the best possible job. On the other hand, if and when the time ever came that we no longer felt this way, we would get a divorce. Finally, if and when we had children (I was not sure I wanted to have any), our children would not be any more my responsibility than Daryl's; hence I would never give up my career to stay home with them, and we would share equally in their care. We were very clear that none of this implied that we saw our careers as the most important things in our lives. Quite the contrary. As long as everything between us was equal, our relationship was more important than our careers; otherwise, we wouldn't be getting married. By the same token, if we decided to have children, they too would be more important than our careers; otherwise, we wouldn't choose to have them.

Having formulated this new egalitarian philosophy, both of us now felt free to move ahead with our marriage plans and also to share those plans with the people around us. But were we in for a series of surprises.

The first surprise was how much interest, and sometimes even hostility, our plans for egalitarianism evoked in others. When told that Daryl and I would be living apart when I went to graduate school at Michigan in the fall—and that Daryl would also try to take a leave from Carnegie Tech for a year and get a temporary teaching position at Michigan so that he could be with me during part of my graduate education—even the most accepting of our friends and acquaintances were so stunned that they wanted to talk to us for hours about both the personal details and the cultural implications of what we were planning. In retrospect, this interest should not have been surprising. Although neither of us yet had a political consciousness with respect to feminism, both the women's liberation movement and the concept of sexism were about to be born. Hence, for the people around us, we were the harbingers of the feminist revolution that would soon envelop the country.

The second surprise was how my Jewish family—or, more accurately, how my mother and her family—reacted not to our unconventional marriage plans but to our unconventional wedding plans. Earlier that winter, Daryl had been to a Quaker wedding where, in accordance with Quaker custom, the bride and groom had "married themselves" in the presence of the congregation. We liked this idea so much that we designed a whole ceremony around it. Unfortunately, the ceremony wasn't Jewish, and my mother's family couldn't accept that. Had Daryl himself not been Jewish, they would surely have found him unsatisfactory, but at least they would have understood our reasons for a non-Jewish wedding. As it was, however, they could make no sense of our plans, and so they tried every avenue of persuasion to change our minds. It was a battle they never had a chance of winning, but they didn't know that—so we were all in for several weeks of emotional frenzy.

Amid the crying and the screaming, the main thing my mother seemed to say was that if her father were still alive, he would drop dead before permitting this wedding to take place. My Uncle Arnold was even more creative. If we went through with this wedding, he said, our children (should they ever be born) would all grow up to be Catholics. But it was my maternal grandmother (bless her heart) who took the most memorable tack of all. "Sandy," my Boby said, "go ahead and have whatever wedding you want, it's fine with me. But listen, I want you to have a Jewish wedding, too, and I've already talked to the rabbi, and he says you won't have to say a single word. All you have to do is stand there, silent, in front of him, while Daryl puts a ring on your finger. That's all Jewish law requires." My budding feminist consciousness was not persuaded.

Having exhausted all of her family resources (which included her two sisters and one brother, their spouses, and my grandmother), my mother turned next to a rabbi who was the father of my closest friend since seventh grade. He repeated much of what my aunts and uncles had already said. This plan of ours was wrong, immoral, and sacrilegious; it would also harm us and our children irreparably.

Sometime during all this trauma and anguish, my mother began to have abdominal pains and was put into the hospital for tests. (Her problem turned out to be gas.) I think it was while my mother was in the hospital that she and her siblings cooked up their theory of how I, their beloved A+ student educated from ages three to eleven at Hillel Academy, could possibly be making this monstrous decision. The theory centered on Daryl and his lifelong interest in magic. As a child, Daryl had spent hours practicing card tricks and other sleights of hand, but sometime during adolescence, he had turned to mental magic, and at age twenty-six, he could now captivate huge audiences for hours with demonstrations of ESP. Grasping for straws, my family reached the conclusion that Daryl, like Svengali, had hypnotized me.

Not knowing how else to end this endless carrying-on, I finally took to my typewriter like the good professor I was going to become and tried to explain to my family, once and for all, what I was doing and why I was doing it. The letter in its entirety read as follows:

Wednesday, April 21, 1965

Dear Family,

On June 6, 1965, Daryl and I are getting married. It is to be a strange ceremony, to be sure, the essence of which can be described by the following words: We, Daryl J. Bem and Sandra R. Lipsitz, Unite Ourselves in Marriage.

I have never before, during the course of my adult life, felt the need to justify my actions to anyone but myself, and I do not feel that need now. I am an intelligent, educated young woman, well aware of my strengths as well as my weaknesses. I have a great deal of confidence in my ability to choose among all possible alternatives that one which is most appropriate for me in any given situation at any given time, and so I do not now feel a need to consult with any or all of you about any facet of my present decision. That is not the purpose of this letter.

Rather, I have a desire to present to you certain evidence which I feel is relevant since you now seem to be making some kind of judgment about me, about Daryl, and about our wedding. Let me say before I go on any further that your judgment will have no influence whatsoever on our wedding plans. If that influence is your major concern, you need read no farther. If, on the other hand, you feel a concern for or a curiosity about me, please read on. In my opinion, you scarcely know me, and I now am offering you the opportunity to find out who I am.

I plan to be married in the Carnegie Tech chapel. No officiator will be present nor will any mention be made of religion. Because I am an agnostic, that is, because I can find no valid evidence to prove either that God exists or does not exist, I would consider it totally unethical to be married according to Jewish custom. Because Daryl and I have ourselves made the decision to marry, and because the state of Pennsylvania declares it perfectly legal that we perform the marriage ceremony without an official, we find the presence of such a person superfluous.

These, I believe, are the two major points about my wedding that you question. Let me assure you all that Daryl and I have thoroughly examined the question of legality, and our ceremony differs not at all from any other more conventional one. We are not bound by the law to be married by anyone other than ourselves.

Because the bounds of legality are the only limits which I can accept as meaningful, I do not feel obligated to be married according to any pattern traditionally established as proper by you or by anyone else. So long as I am fulfilling the requirements of the government of this country, that is, so long as my marriage is legal, then I feel I have performed all those things which I must do.

I believe I have now reached the point at which we truly disagree. You feel that you have the right to dictate the form of my wedding. In a broader sense, then, you feel that you have the right to dictate the course of my life, to impose your values upon me and upon my future husband, to assert that you are right and that we are wrong. I deny you that right. At the very most, you can say that our values differ from yours, that you find our values unusual, that you find us odd, that you would never choose to live according to our values. In addition, however, you say that we are wrong. Neither Daryl nor I would ever be so pretentious as to judge any personal set of values which dictates only the behavior of its possessor as right or wrong, nor would either of us attempt to impose our values upon anyone else. If you care to make evaluative judgments about my behavior, that is your prerogative, but do not attempt to impose your values upon either of us. I am not bound to them any more than you are bound to mine.

I have several things of a less formal and more personal nature to say to you all. I would like to describe our wedding ceremony as it has been planned thus far.

The ceremony, more appropriately named an exchange of rings than a wedding, will take place in silence, or, more accurately, no one will speak. Music will be playing from beginning to end. Daryl and I will walk down the aisle together. I will not wear a wedding gown or a veil because I do not care to appear any more pure or bride-like or innocent than I do on any other day. I will not be given away by my father because I am not being delivered from one protected state into another. Rather, I have decided, with total understanding of the consequences of my actions, to live my entire life side by side, as an equal, with a marriage partner of my own choosing.

The following events will take place during the ceremony:

a) Daryl and I will exchange rings and kiss.

b) We shall drink from a single glass of wine, to be brought to us by our sisters, which Daryl will then crush, thereby signifying that no one else will ever share that particular drink with us or that segment of our common life which it represents.

c) We shall sign our marriage certificate.

d) Every guest shall sign his name to a scroll which we have designed, thereby sharing with us the total meaning of our marriage ceremony. We will keep that scroll as a symbol of the happiness of our friends for us on our wedding day.

You have all been told by this time, I think, that Daryl and I have decided not to invite the family to our wedding. Let me state definitely that the final guest list has not yet been made up. All we have decided upon are the criteria which we plan to use in making such a list:

a) That either one or both of us truly wants that person present.

b) That that person be sincerely happy for us.

c) That that person be able to accept the form of our marriage as totally right for us and be able, without hesitation, to sign his name as a witness to our marriage.

As far as I am concerned, I would like very much to hear that you are very happy for me. You see, I believe that Daryl and I are perfect for one another. Our likes, our dislikes, our values ... all coincide. Our marriage ceremony is a true expression of everything that we are. We'd like very much to be congratulated by all of you, to be wished luck and happiness in our marriage, even if you don't approve of our ceremony. We shall be quite happy with or without you, but, if given complete freedom, we'd prefer a family which accepts us rather than one which rejects us.

Let me extend to you all an invitation to the reception following our marriage ceremony. It will take place in the Highlander Room in Skibo. If, in addition, any of you would like to attend the wedding, simply express that desire, and we would be very happy to have you come, so long as there is enough room in the chapel. So long as you are truly able to accept us and to be happy for us as we are, then we should be delighted to have you. I hope that a few of you will be able to make the decision to come.

If you choose not to come to the wedding but to come only to the reception, neither Daryl nor I will be at all insulted. You have as much right to your convictions as we have to ours, and we have no intention of challenging or even questioning that right. My only hope is that in denying the ceremony, you do not deny me.

Daryl and I have given much thought to our wedding. Its form is not open to discussion. I hope you will be able to separate your feelings about the ceremony from your feelings about me and about my husband.

The denial of one need not lead automatically to the denial of the other. In fact, I hope that some of you may even come to like the ceremony....

Please feel free to call us, to wish us luck, to ask any questions about plans which you, as my family, might like to know. In other words, feel free to love us, but don't try to destroy us or any of our plans. Your attempts will all be unsuccessful and will lead only to unnecessary anguish for you and for us.

I would like to say one more thing. Boby, please understand that what I am doing is right for me. I'm a big girl now, and I must base my decisions on my own values. I hope that you in particular will be able, in the end, to accept my marriage. You're a smart woman and you know that the marriage is far more important than the ceremony. I can guarantee you a good marriage.

Well folks, you've seen me as you never have before. My plans won't change, and I don't care to argue them any more. You can accept me or not, but understand—it is you who are doing the accepting and rejecting.

I hope to see you at the reception. If you would like to come to the wedding, please let me know. Be sure, if you choose to come, that you will be able to smile inside and to sign your name without hesitation to our scroll. Whether or not you can decide to come to the wedding, though, I hope you can be happy about my coming marriage and that you can express that happiness to me and to Daryl.

As ever,
with love,
Sandy

Thankfully, this letter ended my family's attempts to change our plans.

But then came the day when Daryl and I had to get our official marriage license. I was still about six weeks shy of my twenty-first birthday, which meant, ironically, that I needed one of my parents to give permission in writing in order to get a marriage license. Convinced that she had lost the battle over the ceremony and having no objection to Daryl himself, my mother agreed to go to a notary with us to sign the relevant form. But when we went to pick her up, her emotions got the better of her and she said she couldn't do it after all. We told her in no uncertain terms that both the ceremony and our openly living together would happen on June 6 even if the legalities couldn't be completed until June 22, when I would turn twenty-one, but she wouldn't (or couldn't) budge.

At that moment, I knew our strategy had to shift. "Forget my mother," I said to Daryl. "We have to get to my father as quickly as possible because if she speaks to him first, he won't sign, either." So we dashed to the downtown post office where my father was a mail clerk, caught him as he came out the door at the end of his workday, drove him to the notary's office, commandeered a woman off the street to witness his signature, and thereby avoided the two weeks of "living in sin" that we had used unsuccessfully to threaten my mother into signing the form.

By the time of the wedding, everyone in my mother's family had been invited to the ceremony, but only my Boby had honored our request for a reply. Daryl and I had inadvertently scheduled the wedding on Shevuoth, a Jewish holiday when weddings are not allowed to take place, and my grandmother quickly latched onto this as a legitimate excuse for not attending. In other words, she used the conflict with traditional observance to sidestep the more explosive question of whether she could bring herself to accept the non-Jewishness of our ceremony.

My mother, on the other hand, never did find a way to resolve the conflict, so when the time came for her to leave the house for the wedding, she couldn't do it. Not knowing in advance that my mother wouldn't be there, her two sisters came with their husbands in order to support her emotionally. As they sat there waiting for her, her sister Jane became so distraught that, when Daryl and I finally started down the aisle, she ran blindly from the room, almost knocking us down as she ran, and then wandered through the streets in a daze for several hours.

In a rare moment of independence from my mother, my father came to the wedding without her and sat in the front row with my fourteen-year-old sister, Bev. Everyone else in his family came as well, including my father's brother, his wife, and their children. A few adult cousins from my mother's side of the family came, too, including my cousin Jack, whom I had grown up with, but there were no young cousins from my mother's family. The ceremony was considered too provocative for them.

Daryl's family reacted differently. Although Daryl's mother would later become concerned about various aspects of our unconventional marriage (which never bothered my mother at all), when told about our wedding plans, she began reminiscing about how she and Daryl's father had wanted to get married on horseback but had buckled under to family pressures. Hence she thought it delicious that we were going to have exactly the wedding we wanted and had only one request: if we wanted to have the wedding in early June, before various friends would be leaving Pittsburgh for the summer, could we please have it on Sunday, June 6, because she was in a bowling tournament in their hometown of Denver the following Sunday? Of course we said yes, and thus it came to pass that the wedding was scheduled on Shevuoth.

Present at the ceremony were four people from Daryl's family, who all watched the goings-on in my family with disbelief. These included his mother, his father, and his fourteen-year-old sister, Robyn, who had already become fast friends with my sister, Bev, when she visited Daryl by herself during spring break. His sixteen-year-old cousin Marlyn also came, because she and her parents so much wanted her to experience this wonderfully interesting and innovative wedding ceremony. Daryl's brother, Barry, then twenty-three, couldn't be present because he was in his last two months as a Peace Corps volunteer in Colombia.

My family's craziness notwithstanding, the wedding was lovely. Some sixty friends and family attended the ceremony, we all ate sponge cake with frozen raspberries and drank champagne, and the whole affair cost me and Daryl only a few gray hairs and $120.

I could end the story of our courtship here, but I want to describe the next day, Monday, June 7, when I graduated from college.

Although I had been far too involved in my wedding plans to give any thought in advance to my graduation, almost everyone in my mother's family surprised me by showing up for my commencement. In a fit of pique, I wouldn't go near them. "How dare they treat my wedding as a tragedy," I said to myself, "and then expect to joyously share my graduation the very next day?" So I stayed near Daryl's family and, after a while, my mother and her relatives all left.

It took only an hour or so before I felt guilty. Daryl and I then quickly went to my grandmother's house, where I was sure my mother's family would have gathered. I no longer remember who was there in addition to my mother and my grandmother, but we took them all out for lunch and thereby began the process of reconciliation. In time, the anger dissipated on all sides and the relationships healed, except for the relationship between me and my Uncle Arnold. I made several overtures over the years, but he responded to none of them. Eventually Daryl and I began to joke that if he ever sent us a wedding present, we would send it back. But no present ever came.

CHAPTER TWO

Why Daryl?

Why did I marry Daryl in particular? There are many reasons, I'm sure, but the deepest is that I had lived my entire life on the edge of a certain kind of chaos, both internally and externally. Daryl enabled me to separate from that chaos—and ultimately even to rescue both my sister and my parents from it—which is exactly what I had been struggling to do on my own for as long as I can remember.

The kind of chaos I'm talking about is hard to describe because nothing was blatantly wrong with either my family or my life. Yes, we did live in a government-subsidized housing project until I was eight years old, but there were no drugs being sold in the hallways, no bullets flying in the streets. And even in my own family, no one was ever unemployed, no one was alcoholic, no one was sexually abused or physically battered; everyone was basically healthy, and we always had enough to eat. All those good things notwithstanding, however, chaos could erupt at any moment, and only I could hold it at bay.

Memory: My father is driving me home from a visit to his parents' house. We are about halfway up a steep cobblestone hill. I know for certain I'm under eight because of the route we're taking to get home. I'm fairly certain I'm not yet six because I don't think my sister has been born. My father says: "I made Mummy an ice-cream soda with too much foam in it. She got mad and started talking about a divorce, so be really good when you get home."

Memory: I'm lying in bed, listening to my parents negotiate their sleeping arrangements for the night. I could be almost any age because this happened again and again, but I picture myself in the house where we lived after we left the projects, so maybe I'm eight or nine or ten. My mother is watching television, and my father wants her to come to bed. "C'mon, Lil," he says, "don't sleep on the couch again. Please, please, come to bed." But she won't budge. "Leave me alone," she says, "I'm watching television. Maybe I'll come later." Sometimes my father just goes to bed at that point, but often he comes to me, tears running down his face, crying, "She won't come to bed, Sandy. She won't even talk to me. Do something. Go talk to her. You're the only one who can get her to do anything. Do something." I don't remember if I do anything or not. I don't remember if I get my mother to go to bed or not. I just remember my father's suffering and the plaintive "Do something, Sandy; you're the only one who can do anything."

Memory: My mother is yelling at my father. My father is sweating, looking the other way, wiping his forehead, desperate to get out of the room and off the hook. "But Pete," she is shouting, "you left here with $45 and now you have only $14. What happened to it all? Where is it? Did you lose it? Where have you been? What have you been doing? We need that money. Pete, we need that money." "Shush, Lil, please, shush; I don't know, Lil, I don't know. What do you think? I drank it up or something? I don't know what I did with it. I bought gas, I got a quart of milk, I picked up a newspaper. I don't know what happened to it. I didn't do anything wrong. Stop yelling at me. Please. I didn't do anything wrong. Please, stop yelling at me."

Memory: Of a recurring dream throughout my early childhood. My family is in the divorce court. The judge says to me, "Sandy, who do you want to live with after the divorce, your mother or your father?" I sit straight up in my chair, calm and serious. "Neither," I say. "If they don't love each other enough to stay together, then they can't love me very much, either. I'll go to an orphanage." This makes my parents feel guilty. They get back together, and we all live happily ever after.

Memory: I'm at home with my mother. I don't know if anyone else is home or not. We've had another one of our rip-roaring fights. In my college autobiography, which I wrote for a psychology course when I was nineteen years old and a junior at Carnegie Tech, I said that I provoked these fights because I was angry at my mother for picking on my father. "She was the active one in the fights with my father," I wrote. "He was passive, taking it all, even apologizing later, and then crying to me. I fought with my mother constantly. I became stubborn and spiteful. If left alone, I would do everything expected of me and more. But if she told me to do the slightest thing, I would scream at her and refuse to do it."

Although I have no reason to doubt my earlier analysis, I don't remember all this anger at my mother. What I remember are the fights and their aftermath. First we would just be screaming at each other, but after a while she would lose control and start to throw things — glasses, dishes, ashtrays, books, food, knives, whatever was at hand. She didn't throw these things *at* me, but she threw them everywhere else: at the walls, at the windows, onto the countertops, wherever. Then, as I wrote in my college autobiography, "she would sit down in a chair, exhausted, and cry. Guilty and ashamed, I would go over to her, sit on the floor in front of her, and beg her to forgive me or punish me or something. She would look at me, say that she wasn't angry at me, that forgiving me would be silly because 'Saying that you're sorry doesn't change anything. The damage has been done.' Physically exhausted, she would fall asleep. I would begin picking up all the broken glass, trying to create a home out of a farce, crying all the while. Then I would go upstairs and cry and blame myself and beat my head against the wall over and over again for punishment."

Memory: We are at a Thanksgiving dinner at my Aunt Jane's house with everyone in my mother's family. It is time to go home. I am about eleven. My sister, Bev, who has a history of temper tantrums, is about five. She doesn't want to go home yet. The adults get her coat on her somehow, but she refuses to let them zip it or fasten it. She just stands there defiantly, holding its front edges tightly in her fists. Usually I would have been the one to get Bev to cooperate, but this time I am standing on the sidelines with everyone else for some reason, watching in horror as my mother or maybe my Aunt Jane (I can't remember who) begins banging Bev's hands with a high-heeled shoe, over and over, trying to get her to let go of her coat so that they can close it.

Memory: I am in the eighth grade and have just had another fight with my mother. This time, however, the loss of emotional control is mine, not hers. As I described it in my college autobiography, when the fight was over,

I went upstairs and I looked in the mirror and I hated myself and them and our home and our family and the whole farce that we represented. I picked up my hairbrush and I threw it at the mirror with all my might, causing it to shatter into a million little pieces. I fell on the floor and cried. My parents came running upstairs. They were shocked, but they didn't do anything to me. They didn't even ask me why I had done it. I got up and walked out. My hands and face were cut a little, but I just walked around the streets for hours, thinking and crying and remembering everything that had ever happened to me. I hated my parents, but even more, I hated myself for that explosion. I should have been able to control myself, I thought. Something changed that day.... I learned to control every emotional response that could have been elicited from me, fearful that it might have gotten out of hand the way it did with the mirror.

Memory: I am in the tenth grade. I have some kind of fight with Bev, who is now nine. She goes upstairs, climbs onto a second-story window ledge, and although to this day I don't know for certain whether she jumped or slipped (she says she jumped), down she fell to the pavement below—and I was the one who saw her go by the dining-room window. (Miraculously, this fall crushed just one small bone in Bev's back, and she suffered no permanent ill effects.)

Memory: It is August 1964. I have recently turned twenty. Bev is thirteen. My mother's father has just died. Bev and I are walking together to the funeral home, and as we walk, we must be talking about the horror of living in our family. I say to her (and thirty years later, having never discussed it in the interim, she remembers not only what I said but where we were standing when I said it): "Bev, I make you one promise. When I leave for good, I will try to find a way to take you with me."

During childhood and adolescence, everyone develops a set of psychological defenses and interpersonal strategies for dealing with the environment, a way of seeing the self in relation to the world that helps to allay anxiety, a way of being that helps the person adapt to her social context. At approximately age fifty, in therapy, I finally began to distance myself enough from my own defenses and strategies to ask what they cost me and whether I still need them enough in my adult environment to hold onto them as a way of life. Even when I was twenty, however, it was clear to me what those defenses and strategies were.

Quite simply, I perceived myself and defined my identity in direct opposition to how I saw my family. If they were irrational, incompetent, irresponsible, and lacking in emotional control, then I would be rational in all things, competent, responsible for both myself and others, and in control of my emotions at all times. If they were passive, dependent, and unable to deal with life's problems in an adult fashion, then I would be an active agent in the world, not only solving my own problems but helping those around me to solve theirs.

This stance comes through clearly in my college autobiography:

I am highly organized and rational. . . . I perform well all that which I seriously undertake. . . . I require of myself that I ultimately be successful. . . . I see no reason ultimately for failure. . . . I am quite responsible and dependable on the whole, and I expect myself to be so. . . . I cannot accept weakness very easily. I feel I can overcome it, and I always try to make the effort to do so. . . . I believe it is up to me, and to no one else, to ensure that I attain my goals. . . . I must control those impulses within me which might hinder me in doing what I truly want to do, in attaining my real goals. . . . My frame of reference as to proper conduct consists almost entirely of myself. . . . I am highly critical of myself. When I fail at anything, I can blame no one but myself.

This supercompetence and denial of weakness worked for me on many levels from early childhood through college. Most important, I was extremely successful in school, thereby laying the groundwork for an academic career. And I was able to do much of what my family—especially my sister—needed me to do, both emotionally and practically, including such mundane things as selecting furniture for our living room when my mother threw away what we owned but then couldn't manage emotionally to shop for anything new.

But as much as this stance may have enabled me to do what I needed to do, it was driven by insecurity. As I wrote in my college autobiography,

I believe that the major source of much of my development was the desperate insecurity I felt as a result of my parents' relationship, the guilt I felt considering myself as much of the cause of their poor relationship, and the consequent taking upon myself the entire burden and responsibility of building a secure foundation. This was the way I could handle my fear. . . . With every passing day, I grew more and more dependent on myself for security. It could not come from my family. . . . I believe that all my successes . . . are a direct attempt to cope with my inner fear and insecurity, to deny that any such insecurity really exists. . . . I must more or less succeed in all that I do for failure could come to mean total elimination of my emotional supports.

When I was very young, another source of security I managed to stand on was religion. As I wrote in my college autobiography, "I could always depend on God. He would never get emotional and throw things around. . . . My relationship with God was quite personal."

But my personal competence and my relationship with God were never enough to eliminate my insecurity. I'm sure that's why, as a child, I spent so much time regularly neatening up not only my own drawers but everyone else's as well. I'm sure that's also why, as an adolescent, I frequently walked for hours on end, first pounding the pavements and then gradually slowing down and lightening my step as my tension began to dissipate.

Whenever I was especially anxious or upset, this intense walking was one of the ways I sometimes managed to avoid what I described in my college autobiography as "an emotional upheaval." At such times, I wrote, "I begin to feel very empty, very alone, very anxious to do something about the situation, but unable to come up with a satisfactory solution. On occasion, I sit up all night, thinking, thinking, thinking. I cannot necessarily solve it at the time; yet I cannot accept the idea that it is just going to pass unresolved. I must try and try to find the answer. I analyze and I rip apart and I analyze. I come to school the next day with my hair pulled back, wearing my sweatshirt and Levis, with my fingernails bitten, and with my stomach bloated from all the food I have shoveled into it. I am at that time an emotional wreck, and I dislike myself intensely."

This susceptibility to emotional upheaval, I wrote, is

the main aspect of my personality which I cannot tolerate. . . . Try as I do to overcome it, upset as I am that I have not totally overcome it, embarrassed and guilty and ashamed as I am that it ever happened as frequently as it once did, weekly, and that it still happens on occasion, nevertheless, I cannot totally overcome it. I must sometimes not eat for an entire week beyond the barest essentials in order to offset the weight gain of the one little binge. . . . I try all sorts of other release mechanisms. I walk for hours. I clean the basement, hosing the walls, scrubbing the floors, painting the pipes. I sit down and write one of my term papers, not due for another two months. I must control the urge to eat because there may not be a stopping point, at least not before the point of a quite upset stomach. This eating is the only weakness which I have had so difficult a time in learning to control, but it, too, is slowly being overcome.

Clearly, I was a young woman in a great deal of pain, but, as I said in the last sentence of my college autobiography, I was "equipped to cope with problems." And not only that; I was also committed to escaping into another world someday, taking my sister with me if possible.

I had already been escaping from my family for short periods for as far back as I can remember. Beginning at age three, I spent long weekdays at Hillel Academy and many weekends sleeping overnight at one or the other of my grandparents' houses. I have few memories, and almost no happy ones, of life at home with my parents and sister, but I vividly remember the time spent at my grandparents', and in my mind's eye, it is suffused with a golden glow.

My father's parents (whom I called Grandma and Grandpa) lived above a small grocery store, which they owned. In the bedroom were a big bed and a folding rollaway bed. To my knowledge, no one else ever slept in the rollaway but me: it was mine. At night we would open it up and I would go to sleep in it. In the morning, my grandfather would get up early to open the store, and I would crawl into bed with my grandmother, sleep a while longer, and then happily laze with her in bed while she read her Yiddish newspaper, the *Daily Forward.* Then we'd go downstairs and eat breakfast together while we listened to soap operas on the radio. *One Man's Family* and *Stella Dallas* are the two I particularly remember. If it was really cold in the house (and it often was, as they did not have central heating), we would turn on the oven to low, and I would put my feet inside to warm them up a bit.

Over the years we did many everyday chores together. We did laundry in an old-fashioned washing machine in the kitchen that had a double-wringer on the top; you pushed the clothes between the rollers (making sure you kept your fingers safe), and the rollers squeezed the water out. I washed and set my grandmother's hair; it was thin and wispy but she liked the way I curled it. One year we cleaned all the wallpaper in the house by rubbing it with some pink stuff that had the consistency of Play-Doh.

When lunchtime came, we would fix a meal for my grandfather, and then either my grandmother or I would go into the hallway between the kitchen and the dining room and stomp on the floor as hard as we could. This was the signal to my grandfather that his lunch was ready and he should come upstairs to eat. The two of them would then pass on the stairs as she went down to mind the store in his absence.

I also spent lots of time in the store with my grandfather. He didn't talk much, but he let me do whatever I wanted. I sold (and ate) candy, I made change for people, I practiced using the long-handled grabber-gismo to get things off the higher shelves, and I spent hours and hours arranging things. For some reason, I loved arranging all the little cigarette packages and especially the comic books, which I liked to put into one big pile but with the different comics turned at 90-degree angles to one another so you could easily see where one comic book ended and the next began. In the back of the store was a walk-in cooler. Whenever I felt like it, I would go inside and take out a big roll of bologna (which we called jumbo), my grandfather would cut some slices for me on his huge electric slicer, and I would make a sandwich for myself. If there were no customers in the store, my grandfather would sometimes sit on his wooden milk crate and play catch with me. We didn't do this often, though. It was more fun to play with all the things on the shelves.

I don't know how often I slept at my grandparents', but until my grandmother died and the house and store were sold when I was eleven, I'm pretty sure I slept there at least one weekend a month.

I also liked staying with my mother's parents (Boby and Grand-daddy), but the feeling was a little different there because I never liked my Granddaddy. He was a stern, humorless German who was idolized by his children, but I never could (and still can't) see why. My Boby was another story. She and I were great companions. We played card games (especially canasta), we watched soap operas on television, and we laughed together, although I no longer remember about what.

One of our favorite activities, especially in the summer, was going out for ice-cream cones late at night. We waited until 11:30 and then walked the six blocks or so to Isaly's, which closed at midnight. She always got something called Whitehouse, which was vanilla with cherries in it. I always got toasted almond fudge. On Friday nights we sometimes went to visit an old aunt and uncle of hers. The aunt was bedridden, and my Boby liked to cheer her up.

The sleeping arrangements at my Boby's were more variable than at my Grandma's. Boby rented out two rooms, almost always to students at the mortuary school a few blocks away. If a bedroom was vacant, I slept there, but if both rooms were rented (as they usually were), then I slept between my grandparents in their bed. Wherever I slept, though, in the morning I would get into bed with just my Boby and cuddle. In between the cuddles, I would peek at my Boby's breasts (which we called titties). They were huge and were always flopping out of her nightgown, which made us both laugh. Lucky for me that both my grandfathers were early risers.

In all the time I spent with my grandmothers, I don't think either of them talked to me in a supportive or concerned way about the dysfunctional aspects of my family, and I also don't think I ever turned to them for that kind of help. In fact, when they did talk to me about my family, I usually found it distressing rather than helpful because, as I wrote in my college autobiography, "my mother's parents [would] talk about my father, how dumb he was, how lazy, how weak . . . [and] my father's parents [would] talk about my mother and her family, how they didn't think my father was good enough for her." In the larger scheme of things, though, this sniping was trivial. I loved being with my grandmothers, not only because I was happy when I was with them but because they provided me with respite from my life at home.

When I got older, I found other worlds to escape to. There was, for example, the home of my friend Barbara Landy, another of those places suffused with a golden glow in my memory. And then, beginning the summer after I graduated from high school, there were overnight camps where I lived and worked every summer until I married Daryl. These summers away from home were a salvation because, even during my first three years in college, I still had to live with my family during the school year.

By my second summer away from home, these months at camp were accepted as a matter of course, but going away the first summer required a struggle. My cousin Jack and I had both just graduated from high school, and he had somehow gotten a job at Camp B'nai B'rith, which was several hundred miles away in northeastern Pennsylvania. I, in contrast, had nothing in particular to do, so I was thrilled when he called me long-distance to say that, if I could manage to get to the camp by the next day, I could have a job as an assistant counselor. If I couldn't get a ride, I was to take a series of two or three buses and someone from the camp would pick me up at the final stop. Not to worry, I said, I'll be there.

My mother's reaction was different. "You can't go," she said. "We don't know anything about the camp, you'd have to travel alone on a bus at night, and anyway we need you here." I didn't have time to fight with her. I called Greyhound, found out the schedule and fare, arranged for a friend to drive me to the bus station, and packed my things, probably while my mother cried and screamed.

We had a similar scene that Christmas when I was invited to spend a week in Boston at the home of a girlfriend I had met during my first semester in college. Once again my mother said no because it might be snowing, in which case the bus ride would be too dangerous. Once again, I didn't fight her about it. My friend and I found someone to drive us to the bus station and off we went.

These efforts to escape from my family in small ways prefigure the larger struggle that would begin during my junior year in college and end, a year later, with my marriage to Daryl.

The struggle began with my attempt to transfer to another college from Carnegie Tech. I had gone to Tech originally because I couldn't afford to live anywhere other than home, and I also had a scholarship to pay for my tuition there. But unfortunately, Tech's Margaret Morrison Carnegie College for Women, where I was a student, was intellectually unstimulating from the moment I arrived.

Near the end of my junior year I thus decided to try to transfer. I no longer remember how I thought I would pay for college away from home, but I sent transfer applications to a number of schools and was ultimately accepted at Indiana University with both a scholarship and the promise of a job in the psychology department for the following September. In the end, however, this attempt to break free was a disaster.

I was spending the summer happily working at a camp away from home, but in Pittsburgh, my mother was suddenly having to grapple with the discovery that her father was seriously ill. She immediately called me back from camp to consult with her and the doctor about my grandfather's condition. Apart from that one consultation, however, I was not required (thankfully) to have any further involvement in my family's medical decision-making, which included a trip to the Mayo Clinic at the beginning of August. My grandfather died shortly thereafter.

For my mother, the timing couldn't have been worse. Within a few days, she lost her father, whom she idolized, for eternity. She also lost me, her firstborn daughter, upon whom she depended emotionally for so many things, when I left for Indiana.

The shock hadn't yet hit my mother by the day my father and I left Pittsburgh to drive to Indiana, probably because she and her family were still spending all their time sitting shivah at my grandmother's house. But a few weeks later, when I telephoned home, my father started crying and said that my mother had not been able to get out of bed since the end of the shivah period, that all she talked about was how she had lost not only her father but me as well, and would

I please, please think about transferring back to Carnegie Tech and coming home.

Psychologically, I had no choice. For my mother's sake alone, I had to say yes, I would come home, but the truth is (and I knew it at the time) that I wasn't saying yes only to satisfy my mother's (and my father's) needs. In a weak moment, I was also saying yes to satisfy my own needs because, as much as I wanted to escape from my family, my first few weeks at Indiana had been very lonely. I had never lived away from home before except during the summers, I was terribly shy, I was living in a single room surrounded by sorority girls with whom I had nothing in common, I didn't know how to go about building a life on a college campus, and there was my father on the phone, begging me to give up the fight for the sake of my mother's sanity. So many pressures pushing me back to Pittsburgh. Who knows whether or how I ultimately would have coped with college away from home had the needs at home not made it so easy to give up?

The moment my father and I got off the phone, he and my mother started driving to Indiana to pick me up, and I set in motion the bureaucratic process necessary to withdraw from Indiana and reinstate myself at Carnegie Tech. Luckily, I could still have my scholarship, so the decision to return to Tech was not going to cost me anything financially. Luckily I could also still catch up with my coursework so the decision would not delay my graduation.

But as we started the drive home, in the quiet of the car I began to think about what a decision to return to Pittsburgh, to Carnegie Tech, and to my family was going to cost me psychologically. And as I thought about this, I became more and more distressed by the fact that I was taking the easy way out of a difficult and necessary transition for myself. So I turned to my parents and said: "I can't do this. It's wrong for me to go home. I'm not getting a good enough education at Carnegie Tech. I have to make a go of my life at Indiana.

Mother, you'll just have to find a way to manage at home without me. Dad, turn the car around. I'm staying at Indiana after all. It's the right thing for me to do. Mom, you'll just have to learn to manage without me. Dad, turn the car around now." My father obligingly turned the car around. But at the same moment, my mother started screaming and crying and shrieking in panic and pain.

What happened then is a bit of a blur. I think, on my instruction, that my father turned the car around several times, as I tried to come to terms with the conflicting pressures inside me. Finally, with the car heading toward Indiana and my mother still shrieking, I knew what had to be done, and I also knew that I had to be the one to do it. "Pull over to the side and change places with me," I said to my father. "We will now turn around for the last time and go home, but I have to be the one to turn the car around." My mother stopped shrieking, I turned the car around one final time, and we drove home.

The only specific thing I remember about my first six weeks back in Pittsburgh was a conversation I had with Professor Bob Morgan, for whose class I had written my college autobiography the previous semester. I told him in detail about how and why I came back, emphasizing my needing to be at the wheel myself when the die was cast. He told me (almost in passing, it seemed at the time) about a fellow student named Hedda Bluestone who was illegally living on her own in an apartment even though, at the time, female undergraduates were allowed to live only in a dormitory or at home.

A lot must have been going on inside me during those six weeks, however, because there came an evening in mid-October when my Boby was having dinner with my family and some kind of altercation broke out. I don't think it involved me, but I went upstairs and packed my things. When my father drove my grandmother home that night, I went with her and never again slept in my parents' house. No one fussed much at my leaving because, having just lost her husband, my grandmother was in even greater need than my mother.

I lived with my Boby for about five weeks, until Thanksgiving. She was still renting two bedrooms to mortuary students, so she and I slept in the same bed the whole time I was there. I remember this period as a little lonely and a little sad, but wonderfully calm. I had coffee with my Boby in the mornings and then walked to Carnegie Tech, often not returning until late at night. Occasionally she cooked dinner for the two of us; veal chop smothered in onions was her favorite.

At some point I had lunch with Hedda Bluestone and asked whether she might like to have a roommate. I had found a part-time job at the Jewish Community Center that paid $75 a month. If we lived really cheaply, I could afford both rent and food. Hedda was delighted. I moved into her one-room apartment over Thanksgiving break, and after Christmas we found a bigger place, where we lived for the rest of our senior year. In February of that year I met Daryl and in June I married him.

And so back to the central question of this chapter: Why did I marry Daryl in particular? For that matter, why did he marry me? And why did we seem so right for each other? The answer to all this lies in not just what I was like in 1965 but what he was like as well.

Simply put, Daryl was exactly the opposite of my family and hence everything that I then wanted to be. That is to say, he was competent, responsible, rational, and emotionally stable. Even when I told him I couldn't marry him, his distress barely distracted him for more than a moment before he went directly into problem-solving mode and, together, we resolved the dilemma. This pattern was replicated again and again during our courtship. Something he did would bug me during the day. I would stew about it until maybe 1 A.M., call him to discuss it, and within an hour or so he would see my point of view (I was very persuasive), and everything would be settled. No one would yell. No one would throw things. There would be no hullabaloo. Everything would just be worked out.

The rock-solid emotional stability and rationality that Daryl seemed to have at his core was not only what I sought for myself and hence found appealing in him. Even more important, it provided me with the secure foundation that my family had never been able to give me and that I had always needed so desperately. Maybe I would have ultimately managed to climb out of the emotional abyss that my family had created and build a good and satisfying life, maybe even a life as a college professor, if I had never met and married Daryl. But when I was twenty years old, Daryl's way of being in the world was a lifeline for me and I latched onto it.

Daryl grabbed onto me, too, but his reasons were different. Whereas he gave me the rationality and solidity that my life had lacked up to that point, I gave him the emotionality and intensity that his had lacked.

When Daryl and I met, he was twenty-six years old and worried about whether he could ever fall in love. As an undergraduate at Reed College, he said, he had followed the "neurotic pattern" of attaching himself each year to a new girlfriend whom he could "show around Portland, Oregon." In other words, he had had unequal relationships that bored him by the end of the year. By the time he was in graduate school, his girlfriends were much stronger and more secure, he said, but they were still more enamored of him than he was of them.

I was something new for him. Insecure underneath, absolutely, but not afraid to push and probe and challenge my intimates when something didn't seem right to me, and certainly not afraid of arousing people's emotions, at least not people like Daryl, who was not about to lose control in the way that my mother always did. Part of what was happening to Daryl in those 1 A.M. phone calls was that I was waking him up, not just from sleep, but from the repression of his own emotionality.

This dynamic between us became most obvious when I was offered a summer job at the University of Michigan by the professor who would be my graduate adviser when I entered the Ph.D. program in the fall. Daryl and I had not yet decided to marry, but I thought I should still ask him how he felt about my going. When I did, he instantly stepped into his most comfortable role in life: a combination of neutral or rational observer, problem-solver, and helper. In other words, he started asking me what I saw as the pros and cons of my various options. I listened in disbelief. "Daryl," I finally said, "I know how to make decisions. I'm not asking you for that kind of help. I can make decisions perfectly well on my own. What I asked was how *you would feel* about my going away to Michigan for the summer. Am I important enough to you, and is this relationship important enough to you, that you would want me to stay here? Because, if I leave in June, chances are that our relationship will come to an end, so could you please stop talking like someone who is not involved in the decision and tell me how you feel about the idea of my leaving in June. Because if it doesn't make any difference to you whether I go or stay, then I'll go." Had I been all intensity, had my emotions seemed out of control, I'm sure Daryl would never have come near me. But given my background context of rationality and self-discipline, my insistence that Daryl acknowledge his own emotions began to awaken something in him that he had never before experienced.

It's not that Daryl had no enthusiasms. He loved music, magic, and science. He loved making up limericks and telling jokes. But he came from a cheerful and orderly family, albeit a loving one, where intense emotionality was almost completely suppressed. Just listen to one of his mother's favorite stories about how she and his father handled the situation when Daryl and his brother, Barry, started bickering, as siblings do. The parents staged an argument between themselves, something their kids had never observed before. Then, when the kids became upset by the argument, the parents drew the obvious conclusion for them: Yes, arguing is upsetting, and that's why we don't do it and why you shouldn't do it, either. It's stupid and completely unnecessary.

The year after we got married, Daryl, Barry, and I spent a week-end together in New York, where we saw a play called *The Subject Was Roses,* which was about a family in distress. It had a lot of ten-sion in it, a lot of hollering, and a lot of anger. I liked the play, as I recall, but it didn't have a profound impact on me. Daryl, in con-trast, was shaking when the play was over. Well, I didn't make Daryl shake, although I'm sure a weekend with my family would have. But I did put him back in touch with his own emotionality, and that was as irresistible for him as his intellectual competence, rationality, stability, and sense of humor were for me.

And then, of course, there was our shared discomfort with— and rejection of—conventional male and female roles. In part, this gender nonconformity reflected our family backgrounds. Although Daryl's family and mine couldn't have been more different emotion-ally, in both families the mother was dominant and the father had not a macho bone in his body. Deep in our psyches, it thus felt com-fortable and normal for the woman in a heterosexual relationship to have many strong preferences and for the man to be accommo-dating.

This model of a dominant mother and an accommodating father was much more positive in Daryl's family than in mine. Daryl's father, Darwin, was a quiet and gentle soul who, it was always lov-ingly said, never graduated out of Walt Disney movies. He owned a small manufacturing company, started by his father in 1906, which made trophies, badges, ribbons, and other novelties given out as prizes at events like the county fair. Although his wife and children sometimes joked that he was never able to deal adequately with conflicts among his employees because they never wanted to upset him and so never told him about their difficulties, he was viewed by friends and family alike as a competent and compassionate human being.

Daryl's mother, Sylvia, may have griped occasionally about how easy it was for people to take advantage of her husband's good nature, but it was clear to everyone, including his children, that his good nature, his gentleness, and his kindness were precisely what Sylvia most loved about him. The one accommodation they all knew they had to make to him, however, was to save any gossiping until after he went to bed. If he heard them telling juicy stories, he would invariably say that if you don't have anything nice to say about a person, you shouldn't say anything at all, and that put a damper on their fun.

Sylvia, in contrast, not only liked to have things just so; she was good at getting her way. From the time I first met her, she bragged that even though she was always a homemaker and hence not "liberated" in the modern sense of that term, once evening came and she put her children to bed at 7 P.M. or whenever, her time was her own and her children dared not disturb her. She also boasted that her kids were so well trained that no one who visited after 7 P.M. would have known she had children because they knew better than to leave their toys lying around. How she managed this level of control has always been a mystery to me, but two stories of her child-rearing have stuck in my mind.

In the first, two- or three-year-old Barry tried to argue that he didn't need to take his afternoon nap any longer. Sylvia let him skip the nap, but when dinnertime came and he got tired, she wouldn't let him fall asleep, nor would she let him go to bed until his regular bedtime or maybe later. He learned his lesson, she was fond of saying, and he never resisted his nap again.

In the other story, ten- or eleven-year-old Daryl tried to persuade his mother to let him have a big birthday party. "OK," she allegedly said, "we can arrange that. We can invite all the kids from your class at school, and they can run through the house and break all your toys and make a big mess. Or I can invite your favorite cousin, Stephanie, to come to the park with us, and the two of you can ride on the boats, and I can make spice cake and whatever else you'd like to eat, and we can all have a wonderful time together. Whichever you prefer." As was so often the case in the Bem household, Daryl ended up "preferring" exactly what Sylvia wanted him to prefer, although, from his own point of view, he had absolute freedom of choice and no sense of having been manipulated. Daryl was the most naive of the three children in this regard. Barry and Robyn both claim to have seen through their mother's manipulation at a much earlier age and hence resisted her control to a greater extent.

Sylvia's ability to control her world showed up in many ways. Some of my favorite examples come from bowling, which was central to Sylvia's life for fifty years. It's not just that she bowled at least three nights a week and bragged that she never missed a night, not even for a meeting with a teacher or a child's performance. She was also instrumental in bringing serious women's bowling to Denver at a time when a bowling alley wasn't considered a proper place for a lady to be.

This was all before I knew her, of course. Even later, however, she was still the organizer of a traveling league that bowled in a different town each week, and she always giggled a little when she told us that no one in the league quite understood how it came to be that, at the height of the winter snows, the league always seemed to be bowling in the vicinity of Sylvia's house. Not long before her death, Sylvia was inducted into the Bowling Hall of Fame, not for her bowling ability but for her leadership in women's bowling.

In the more than twenty years that I knew Sylvia and Darwin as a couple, I never saw them in serious conflict. To a great extent, this was because Darwin wouldn't engage in conflict. At the most fundamental level, both he and Sylvia knew that Sylvia ruled the roost, albeit in a way that did not demean the husband she loved and respected. So whenever possible, he just did whatever Sylvia wanted him to do, and if she scolded him because he didn't get home from work on time or he had to make a last-minute delivery of some trophies on their way to a concert or he forgot to do some errand he had promised to do, he would just smile sheepishly, shrug his shoulders, and move on. I don't think his blood pressure even went up.

In the eyes of Darwin and Sylvia, and—this is important—in the eyes of Daryl as well, Darwin and Sylvia had the perfect relationship and the perfect marriage. In other words, Daryl grew up with his parents' rendition of a dominant mother and an accommodating father as his image of the ideal relationship between husband and wife.

I, of course, did not idealize my parents' relationship in the way that Daryl idealized his. In fact, as I wrote in my college autobiography, for a brief period my "goal" was "to live someday in a vine-covered cottage with a husband I could love by serving, a husband who would be my master for the rest of my life. Thus would I vindicate my father."

I did have one relationship in college with a bit of this dynamic, but I was never enough of a masochist to like the experience. Even more important, as much as I may have hated my parents' rendition of the dominant mother and the accommodating father, the fact is that I still internalized that model. I still identified with my mother's dominance even as I despised both my father's weakness and the way my mother demeaned him.

Yet, there were many things that I admired about my mother. It's true, as I've already suggested, that she was often passive, helpless, depressed, emotionally out of control, frustrated with my father, and overdependent on me. But she was also intelligent (and proud of it), committed to education, and terribly disappointed that she never realized her childhood dream to go to college and then become an interpreter at the United Nations. She was also a believer in the need for every woman to be able to support herself and was outspoken in her extended family about her thoughts and feelings. She was completely honest about being an indifferent housekeeper but a perfectionist in her full-time job as an executive secretary who could type over ninety words a minute on a manual typewriter. And she also had a beautiful soprano voice.

Although I couldn't abide living with my mother and hated the way she treated my father, I thus identified with many aspects of who she was. In fact, when my Boby and I used to take those late-night walks to get ice-cream cones, we would pass an uncurtained bank window through which we could see a secretary's private office much like my mother's. When I was ten years old, I thought that when I grew up, I wanted a job and an office just like the one in the window and just like my mother's, an office with my own desk and my own telephone. In contrast, I did not want a job anything like my father's as a postal clerk sorting parcels. Not only did he not have a desk or a telephone, but he had to wear a uniform, his job required little in the way of skill or knowledge, and he came home from work every day dirty and sweaty.

I appreciate my father's manual labor a lot more now than I did then, but as a child, I completely identified with my mother's intelligence and professional skill, and I still do. I also identified with her commitment to full-time work—and, as much as we needed the money, she never once suggested that she kept her job for the money alone. Most important, I identified with the way my mother took herself and her work seriously—and never devalued herself or her work in relation to men and their work.

The reversal of traditional gender roles in both of our parents' relationships easily found its way into the relationship Daryl and I had as well. Consider the story, for example, of our wedding rings. We had gone to a jeweler in downtown Pittsburgh about a month ahead of time with our own design for a pair of rings. We said that we wanted two identical gold bands, Florentined, and with three small diamond chips a few millimeters apart in each one. We were to pick up the rings a week before the wedding.

But when we went back to get them, we were horrified to discover that our rings didn't look anything alike. The jeweler's explanation was that when the diamond chips we had chosen were placed in a ring small enough to fit my finger, the two outside diamonds ended up so far to each side that they weren't visible. The jeweler hadn't known, he said, whether to substitute smaller chips in my ring or cluster the larger chips closer together. Since most people like diamonds, he used the larger chips in both rings. If that was unsatisfactory, he said he would happily redo my ring at no extra cost. Of course he couldn't possibly redo it in time for the wedding, but he could lend us two other rings to use instead.

Daryl and I both disliked my ring from the instant we saw it, and we were both unhappy that we couldn't be married with our own rings. We swallowed hard, took the substitute rings he offered us, and left the building. As we walked to the car, however, I was getting more and more steamed up. "For Christ's sake," I said to Daryl, "why didn't he call and ask us whether to use the smaller or the larger chips? And since he's the one who made the wrong decision, why do we have to pay for it by not having our own rings at our wedding? I don't want to get married with these stupid other rings. I want our own rings. We ordered them in plenty of time. The wedding is still a week away. How long could it take to make one new ring from scratch?"

Daryl agreed with me and was willing to come along if I wanted to take on the jeweler, but he had no desire to confront the jeweler himself. That was fine with me: I liked the idea of having Daryl for moral support, but I also liked the idea of standing up for my own rights. So back we marched to the jeweler's shop, I said what I had to say, and the jeweler agreed to make me a new ring in time for the wedding.

For both Daryl and me, this interaction was ideal. I got to insist on what I wanted and get what I deserved, but I didn't have to stand alone when I did it. Daryl got what he wanted as well, but he didn't have to engage in direct conflict with anyone.

As important as it was that both Daryl and I had parents whose gender roles were counter to the norm, our shared gender nonconformity went far beyond our vision of the husband-wife relationship. For both of us, the sense of being a gender misfit was at the core of our identity. I don't mean to suggest by this that it distressed either of us—quite the contrary. If anything, we were both kind of proud of our gender nonconformity, and that shared pride was something else that pulled us together.

Daryl's difference from other boys (more specifically, his being what kids call a "sissy") was apparent by kindergarten, when he was already being chased home from school by bullies so regularly that his family moved to another neighborhood. After the move, Daryl was never bullied again, but he continued to have no conventional male interests except intellectual ones like math and science. He thus became very much like a certain stereotype of an intellectual man: all head and no body. I mean by this that he participated in no athletics of any kind, nor did he develop any interest in watching sports as a spectator, and all of his hobbies, including piano and magic, were sedentary. Perhaps because of all this (or perhaps not), his way of moving his body was sufficiently unmasculine that my mother asked me, soon after meeting him and with concern in her voice, whether he wasn't perhaps just a tad effeminate.

In fact, Daryl had told me in one of our earliest conversations that he was primarily what he then called "homoerotic." He did not mean, he said, that he wasn't attracted to me. I had caught his eye the first time he saw me, perhaps because he had always loved things that were "transistorized"; hence my compact four-foot-nine-inch body really appealed to him. What he meant by "homoerotic," he continued, was that it was much more likely to be random male bodies on the street that caught his attention rather than random female bodies. Daryl's "homoeroticism" made so little difference to me that I never worried about it. I just thought of it as yet another aspect of our shared gender nonconformity, which I valued.

My own gender nonconformity was also apparent by kindergarten, but it didn't get me into trouble, at least not with other kids. Perhaps this was because from ages three to eleven I was in a class of only three girls (myself included) and nine boys. I don't ever remember wishing I were a boy instead of a girl, but during those early years at Hillel Academy, I situated myself among the boys and was accepted as a member of that group. Like them, I never wore dresses to school, even though I repeatedly got into trouble with the principal for this flaunting of the rules. (For some reason, beginning in first grade I capitulated on picture day, so all my school pictures —except my much-beloved kindergarten picture—show me wearing a dress, as I never did on any other day.) I played football, baseball, and especially dodgeball on the playground. Even more than the boys, I also picked on the one early-maturing girl in our class, at least once swinging my notebook at her in a way that whipped her dress up in the air and exposed her underpants. "On account of this misbehavior," I wrote in my college autobiography, "I, Hillel's most prized student, was almost suspended . . . and I gloried in it."

My first conscious realization that I was a gender misfit came in the fifth grade. I had a crush on a boy in my class, and whenever I was behind him, I would try to kiss him on the back of his head. On one of these occasions, he turned around and said something that

I now consider a wonderful example of how compulsory hetero-sexuality imprisons us in rigid gender roles. "I could really like you, Sandy," he said, "but I can't like another boy."

When I switched from Hillel Academy to the public junior high in my neighborhood at age eleven, I gave up most of my tomboyism in order to fit in, but I never did use makeup very much, and even now, in my fifties, the idea of wearing really feminine clothing still makes me feel as if I would be in drag.

Both Daryl's gender nonconformity and mine have always seemed part of an even more general independence or aloofness from cultural norms, and this was yet another aspect of our psychological makeup that drew us together. In Daryl's case, this willingness to stand apart from the crowd was probably imbibed along with his mother's milk, because one of his mother's most often repeated stories was how much she had enjoyed shocking the neighbors by regularly riding a boy's bicycle with baby Daryl seated on a pillow that was somehow wedged onto the bar between the handlebars and the seat.

Daryl himself didn't talk so much about shocking people, but he did always manage to remain separate from the crowd and yet special in some way. In high school, for example, he was always the one who played the piano at parties, and he was also the only nice Jewish boy in his high school who declined an invitation to join AZA (the youth affiliate of the American Zionist Organization), preferring to hang out either by himself or with his one buddy, Dick Smith, who was a tap dancer.

Sometime in high school, of course, he also began teaching himself to do those ESP shows. Whether you believed he really had ESP or just thought him an extraordinarily impressive entertainer, this definitely put him in a category by himself. Finally, in graduate school, he avoided becoming a part of the social psychology community and instead linked up with the youngest and brashest professor on the faculty, Harlan Lane, a fervent believer in the not-very-popular radical behaviorism of B. F. Skinner. Adopting this radical behaviorism for himself, Daryl then used it as the basis for a theoretical challenge to Leon Festinger's cognitive dissonance theory, which was the dominant creed in social psychology at the time, and thereby made a name for himself in his field.

By 1965, when Daryl and I met and married, my own willingness to stand apart from the culture and the crowd had probably shown up most clearly during my second year in college, when I decided to resign in protest from the sorority I had joined the previous semester. After wanting so much to be in a sorority during high school, I was thrilled to be invited to join one in college during my freshman year. But after sitting through just one "cut" session during which my sorority sisters dissected the new crop of women applicants— after having talked to them for all of five minutes maximum—I was so disgusted that I wrote a formal letter of resignation in which I critiqued the sorority system as a whole. (I wish I had that document along with the others I did save.)

It would be disingenuous, however, to represent either Daryl's independence from the crowd or mine in purely positive terms because, for both of us, that independence derived from a deep and complicated ambivalence about people in general and about our peers in particular, from a sense that others could easily constitute a threat to our security.

I've already told the story of Daryl's being threatened by his peers when he was chased home from kindergarten. For me, the paradigmatic peer-threat story happened not long after my family moved out of the projects and into our own house, when I was eight or nine or ten. As the only kid who didn't go to the public school, I was pretty much excluded from all the neighborhood groups and hence spent most of my play time as I had always done, either alone or with my grandmothers or my cousin Jack. One startling summer day, however, out of the blue, I was invited to play hide-and-seek with the whole gang. I don't remember how I felt when I got this invitation, but I vividly remember how I felt when I learned it had all been part of a thoroughly successful plot to humiliate me by getting me into an isolated spot, surrounding me, and pulling down my pants for all to see.

By the time Daryl and I were adults, we weren't worried any longer about being chased home by bullies or having our pants pulled down, but we both felt sufficiently different from other people that there was something wonderfully warm and safe about the prospect of constructing a tight little cocoon around just the two of us. It was also empowering to join forces and thereby multiply the strength of our defenses. Together, we would not only be safe; we would also be in a position to show the world both how special we two were and how special feminism was as an ideology and a way of life. We thus bonded almost instantaneously and felt that we were the perfect couple.

PART 2

Writing Our Own Script

CHAPTER THREE

Community of Family

When I met and married Daryl at age twenty, I entered what I now think of as the second act in the drama of my life. It was a long second act, lasting almost thirty years, and one I will never regret because, in the context of that relationship, I was able to do the most unexpected and even magical things, beginning with rescuing my sister, Bev, and then slowly building a whole new community of family.

Like my own life, Bev's life began to change immediately after Daryl and I got married. Within days, she left Pittsburgh to spend three weeks in Denver with Daryl's sister, Robyn, who was as much a tomboy as she was. And then, in midsummer, on a late-night walk through Schenley Park with Daryl, I concocted the beginning of the rescue operation.

"Daryl," I said, "we're going to be living apart for much of this year anyway." I was going off to Ann Arbor for graduate school, and he had to stay in Pittsburgh because of his job. "How about if Bev comes with me?"

I'm sure we must have worried aloud that night about how Bev's presence in Ann Arbor might jeopardize our relationship; how could we not have worried about that? Also, I think I remember an anxious tone in the conversation even if I don't remember all of its content. By the end of the conversation, however, we had both become so invested in the project of rescuing Bev that the decision was easy. Of course we would invite her to Ann Arbor, and of course she would accept.

I wish I remembered the conversation in which I told my parents we were taking Bev away, but I have no memory of it. I wish my mother were still alive so I could ask her to reflect back on what it felt like to have us say the things we must have said and do the things we clearly did. I have this vague recollection of my mother's saying at some point (but I don't remember when) that she wished we had talked to her before talking to Bev. But of course we had talked to Bev first on purpose, because we knew that if Bev had already been invited and already wanted to go, my parents would be unable to intervene without risking . . . what? The temper tantrum to end all temper tantrums, I guess.

Bev and I moved into a one-bedroom apartment in an old house on East William Street in Ann Arbor at the beginning of the fall semester. She rode her bike every day to high school, and I started taking classes and doing research in the psychology department at the University of Michigan. We lived together, even sleeping together in the same double bed, five days a week, and then on the weekends, either Daryl drove to Ann Arbor to be with me (with Bev moving to the couch to sleep), or we drove to Pittsburgh so that I could be with him.

Even though Bev had been a troubled child and was still a troubled adolescent, things went well until the end of January, when

Daryl rearranged his teaching schedule so that he could be in Ann Arbor five days every week, from late Tuesday night until dinnertime on Sunday. At that point things stopped going smoothly.

First Bev started to have temper tantrums on Tuesday evenings, and then she started having trouble going to school. In the beginning, she just didn't get out of bed when her alarm rang, so either she was late or she missed the entire day. But then she missed the next day, too, and then another and another—until eventually she wasn't going to school at all, and we didn't know what to do about it.

Once again, the details are gone from my memory. I think I spent hours talking to her about her resentment at having to share me with Daryl, and maybe that helped. Did I ever tell my parents what was happening? I don't know, but I doubt it. At what point did the school guidance office get involved? I don't remember that, either.

The only thing I remember clearly is the day Bev finally went back to school. Both Daryl and I went with her. We took her straight to an appointment at the guidance office, where the counselor was understanding and Bev was courageous. She went directly from there to her next class, and life began anew. There were aftereffects, of course. For example, I don't think either Daryl or I ever took it for granted again that she would get up and go to school when her alarm rang, which meant that our stomachs filled with acid each and every morning. But she did get up and go, and I was proud of her for that.

Of course there were still problems. Daryl and I had little time alone together, and the time we did have was often spent discussing how to deal with Bev. And Bev herself, we began to feel, had benefited about as much from living with us as she was likely to.

She had already begun, for example, to perform many of the routines of daily life that other kids take for granted but that she had always avoided, like taking baths and putting on deodorant and brushing her teeth. I now realize that her avoidance of these activities must have been driven by some kind of deep anxiety. At the time, however, I didn't think much about the emotional aspects. I just made up my own teaching techniques, based on Skinnerian principles, to get her to do what needed to be done. For example, just as you can start teaching a child to tie her own shoelaces by doing everything for her except the last step in the process and then gradually doing less and less until she is finally doing all of it by herself, so I started teaching Bev to run her own bath by doing everything except turning off the water. Then I did everything except turning off the water and putting the stopper in, and so on, until finally she was doing it all by herself.

Years later, I wondered aloud to my own therapist how it could have happened that no one, including Daryl and me, ever thought to take Bev to a therapist. She said that therapy wasn't all that common then, but I think it was also my own arrogance. I had watched my parents mishandle Bev for as long as I could remember, giving her whatever she wanted in order to avoid her temper tantrums and thereby reinforcing her use of outbursts to get what she wanted. They required nothing of her in the way of daily hygiene, like brushing her teeth, lest that requirement itself produce a temper tantrum, and thereby gave her no grounding in discipline—or *self*-discipline. What they had mistaught her, I believed, I would reteach her, and to a great extent I did. But surely she should have seen a professional therapist who could have dealt with the emotions underlying her behavioral problems. At the time, I didn't even think of it.

In any case, by April or May, Bev was taking care of her daily needs, she was attending school pretty regularly, and she was moderately happy. But she still hadn't made any friends, which she clearly wanted and needed. She was finally able to make those friends the following year, when she began to attend a boarding school in Massachusetts.

The course of Bev's life would be bumpier than mine for many years. But now, in her late forties and still living in Portland, Oregon, where she went to college, she has a master's degree, a job she likes very much, a home she owns, and a deep and satisfying love relationship with a woman named Roz that has endured for over twenty years. Bev has struggled long and hard to construct and reconstruct her life, just as I have my own life, but Daryl and I did shift her path a bit when she was fourteen years old. Even if that had been the only magic to come out of our relationship, as it is written in the Passover Haggadah, *Dayenu.* It would have been enough.

As it turned out, however, Bev wasn't the only person in our family who used our home as a place to regroup and begin again. In the early 1970s, when we were living in California, Daryl's brother, Barry, spent a month with us after he resigned from his job in the foreign service. Later that year, my cousin Jack spent a month with us in the aftermath of a business failure and, not long after that, Daryl's sister, Robyn, lived with us for many months when she was breaking up with her first husband.

This use of our home and our hospitality by family was not limited to periods of crisis or transition. Especially after we moved to California in 1970, our home was also the place where all the Bems gathered at least once a year. Many of these family gatherings, especially the early ones, included my sister. In a typical year, Daryl's parents, Sylvia and Darwin, would stay with us for two weeks in December, Robyn for a shorter period of time, and Barry for the shortest time of all.

No matter when in December the Jewish holiday of Chanukah fell, our Chanukah gift exchange took place on the first night after Barry's arrival. Often he didn't arrive until the day after Christmas, so our kids had to wait forever for their gifts. They never minded because they loved our Chanukah ritual, as did I.

We began by lighting all the candles in the Menorah and eating homemade latkes, salad, and applesauce. We then adjourned to the living room where we would each gather up (or, in later years, the kids would gather up for us) all the gifts that had our name on them. We then went around the family circle as many times as necessary, with each person opening one present on every turn and with everyone else looking on and oohing and aahing as we did so.

I think everyone in the family liked this ritual. I know our children did, but I think I liked it most of all. The reason is obvious: as a child, I remember getting only one gift from my parents, a little bottle of perfume sitting in a miniature gold rocking chair with a Styrofoam head over the cap decorated with a face. My father bought it for me after a family argument to make me feel better.

In contrast, I bought my mother and father presents on every imaginable occasion—every birthday, every anniversary, every Chanukah. A pair of socks, a paperback book, a pair of stockings—it didn't matter, they always got something. So these Jewish Norman Rockwell Chanukah evenings, complete with wrapping paper and a fire in the fireplace, were an experience I had never known and always wanted, a symbol, as it were, of a happy family.

Until I met and married Daryl, the only truly happy times I had with my family were at the seders we all went to on the first and second nights of Passover—one night at my Boby's house with my mother's extended family, the other night at my other grandmother's house with just my grandparents. Reliably, dependably, consistently. And never any fighting. Just hours and hours of reading from the Passover Haggadah, eating traditional Passover fare, and then singing one Hebrew song after another, with my mother's joyful soprano voice rising high above the others.

Amazingly enough, once I was married and the trauma of my wedding had begun to recede, Daryl and I were gradually able to make even my mother's family a part of our family community. By and large, this took place during the two and a half years that Daryl and I lived together in Pittsburgh before we moved to California.

Part of that time I was still a Ph.D. student at the University of Michigan, but in absentia, writing my doctoral dissertation while living in Pittsburgh so that Daryl could live where he taught. The rest of that time I, like Daryl, was a faculty member at Carnegie-Mellon University (as Carnegie Tech had been renamed).

Daryl often joked about the fact that during his adolescence he was much better at interacting with "little old ladies" like his music teachers than with young women his own age. Hence the mothers of the girls he went out with always liked him a whole lot better than his dates did. This facility with much older women may have been a problem for Daryl during his adolescence, but it was a boon when the time came to reconstruct our relationships with my extended family.

Consider the most important little old lady of all, my Boby. She may have been unhappy about the kind of wedding we had, but she loved going to hear the Pittsburgh Symphony with us on Sunday afternoons. She loved having us visit her for tea each week on our way home from work. She loved coming to our house for dinner and having me wash and set her hair before we drove her home. Above all else, she loved having us cheer her up and make her laugh.

One such occasion was particularly memorable. Daryl and I had stopped by after work to see if she wanted to come home with us for dinner. She did want to come, she said, but in an hour or so the host of a certain radio show was going to select someone from the telephone book, call the person's number, and give him or her $10,000 for knowing the show's phrase of the day, which she did. She thus couldn't come to our house for dinner, she said, because what if they called her? She would lose all that money.

Without hesitating for a moment, Daryl whipped his wallet out of his pocket and wrote a check to her in the amount of $10,000. "Come to dinner," he said. "If they call you and you're not home, you won't lose any money. Your friends who are listening to the show will tell you they selected your name, and, if that happens, you can cash my check." We never knew if my Boby really thought Daryl had $10,000 in the bank (he didn't) or just got caught up in the ridiculosity of the whole situation, but she burst out laughing, got in the car, and very carefully tucked Daryl's check into one of the special compartments in her handbag.

There aren't any funny stories to tell about how Daryl gradually won over my mother's two sisters. But my Aunt Beadie, the mother of my cousin Jack, worked as a secretary in the modern languages department at Carnegie-Mellon, and Daryl began to drop into her office pretty regularly, and basically to flirt with her, even when I was still living in Ann Arbor. We had less contact with my Aunt Jane, the sister who almost knocked us down at our wedding by running blindly from the room. But one night when we were at her house for some family event, she took me by the hand, led me into another room, opened a drawer, and took out a tightly folded little packet of paper. Tearfully she put the packet into my hand and closed my hand around it, looking at me meaningfully all the while but never saying a word. She then took me back to rejoin the others and never spoke to me, or to anyone else as far as I know, then or later, about this silent little ritual. What she put into my hand that night was her own dittoed copy of the letter about my wedding plans that I had sent to my mother's whole family in order to end their meddling. Returning that letter was her way of undoing the rupture in the family that my wedding had produced.

A few nights before Daryl and I moved to California in the summer of 1970, we had an informal dinner on our patio for my extended family, to clean out the freezer and simultaneously celebrate my parents' twenty-ninth anniversary. Virtually every one of my relatives who should have been at our wedding was at that dinner, except my Uncle Arnold, who turned down every invitation I extended to him. For me, that dinner symbolized the reclamation of my extended family. Not that we saw any of these people very frequently over the years or even talked to them much by telephone, but after what we had all put each other through, it felt good to have even that momentary sense of community.

As for my parents, their lives took a turn for the better, and so did my relationship with them, almost from the moment Bev came to live with me in Ann Arbor. Not too long afterward, for example, I started to hear a lot about this great two-for-one coupon book that was enabling them to try a lot of new restaurants. My Aunt Beadie and Uncle Joe had bought a coupon book as well, so eating out had became a social occasion.

And then, the day when my parents finally sold their house, one of my mother's lifelong dreams came true. All my life, I remember her saying she wanted to live "on a streetcar line" so she wouldn't have to rely on my father or anyone else to drive her places. (She never considered learning how to drive herself; the very thought of it made her too nervous.) She also said she wanted to live in an apartment on the top floor of a public library so she could always be certain of having a book to read.

My mother never got to live above a library, but in the late 1960s, the city of Pittsburgh did decide to build a new public library at the busiest intersection in the part of the city where my parents lived, an intersection with a very large array of public transportation, including streetcars. Not only that: my mother found a small apartment in a modest building just half a block away.

The character of this apartment building was almost as important to my mother as its location. She had started looking for an apartment as soon as she heard that the library was going to be built, but, as she put it, the apartment buildings in the neighborhood were all so ritzy and the people who lived in them all had such fancy clothes that just riding in the elevator with them made her feel inferior. It was thus a special day when she found an apartment building where she didn't feel out of place, even if she were seen in the hallway with her hair in pincurls.

After Daryl and I moved to California, my parents came to visit us in the sunshine for two weeks every year. They usually came in March, when the climate contrast with Pittsburgh was the greatest. My sister always came down from Portland for part of these visits, and one year my Boby came as well.

We never had any serious tension during these visits. Daryl and I went to work almost every day, leaving my parents alone to sleep late, have a leisurely breakfast, walk over to the Stanford University swimming club and sit by the pool and read, or do whatever else might give them pleasure. On weekends and occasional days off from work, we were tour guides for them (and for ourselves), going to San Francisco, Carmel, Sausalito, Tahoe, Monterey, or wherever else any of us felt like going.

My parents were wonderfully good sports on these sightseeing days. No matter how ethnic the restaurant, how hilly the terrain, how splashy the boat ride, they cheerfully chugged along and had what I think of as the second-best time of their lives.

The best time of their lives (or at least of their life together) began in 1974, when Emily was born and they moved to California. This period began painfully, with the death of my Boby in February. Poor Boby had a stroke while alone in her house, and no one found her until a day or so later, when her children finally realized that she hadn't spoken to any of them on the telephone for a while. When they finally got to her, she was lying on the floor in the bedroom, still conscious and able to say a few words, but unable to move. Her house was only a block from the hospital so the ambulance arrived almost immediately, but the next time they saw her, she was in a coma from which she never emerged. She died about five weeks later. And just two weeks after that, Emily Jennifer Lipsitz Bem was born in Stanford.

I talked to my mother frequently about my Boby's condition during the weeks she was in a coma, and I also thought about how horrible it must have been for her to be lying on that bedroom floor, hour after hour, knowing she was probably going to die there but unable to do anything to help herself. At the same time, I was in my last weeks of pregnancy and looking forward with great anticipation to giving birth. I just didn't want the baby to come too soon because I was lecturing twice a week to a class of some three hundred undergraduates, hoping against hope that I would make it through the quarter.

It is customary for Jews to name their children after relatives who are no longer living. In the context of American assimilation, only the Hebrew name given to the child usually matches the namesake exactly; the English name merely begins with the same letter or sound. Although I wish that my Boby could have lived to know my children and that they could have known her, it is fitting in many ways that my firstborn was named after my two beloved grandmothers: Emily (in Hebrew, Esther) for Esther Sobel Lehman, my Boby; Jennifer (in Hebrew, Zisel) for Jenny Weisberg Lipsitz, my Grandma.

When Emily was a few days old, my mother came for a visit. Unlike many grandmothers, she had no sense of being an expert in matters related to child-rearing, so she wasn't inclined to criticize anything about our handling of our new baby. Quite the contrary: she tended to assume (not necessarily correctly) that we knew more about how to take care of an infant than she did, so she relaxed, sat back, and left the driving to us.

And then something magical happened. She fell in love with her granddaughter, or maybe she just fell in love with being a grandmother. I'm not sure there's much of a difference. But whatever happened, she began almost immediately to radiate a new kind of happiness. This happiness is detectable even in a black-and-white photograph Bev took of her while she was watching me and Daryl give Emily one of her first baths. It is striking in a home movie of her and Emily playing together on the floor when Emily was about eighteen months old.

In the film footage, Emily and my mother are playing a game organized around the tension between Emily's loving to suck her thumb and my mother's thinking that Emily shouldn't suck her thumb. With her bright red cheeks just inches away from my mother's face, Emily puts her thumb in her mouth but with her fingers extended and her mouth wide open, which isn't her actual thumb-sucking position but merely a symbol of it. Looking almost as excited as Emily, my mother makes disapproving sounds ("uh, uh, uh," she keeps saying) and reaches toward Emily's hand, as if to pull it out. The two of them enact this little dance for fifteen seconds or so until the tension reaches a peak, and then my mother does pull Emily's thumb out of her mouth, with both of them giggling. Finally, Emily falls down onto the floor or into my mother's lap in a fit of hysterical laughter.

But as soon as the tension dies down, which only takes a matter of seconds, the game begins again. Back goes Emily's naughty thumb into her mouth. Out reaches my mother's threatening hand. The tension mounts. The thumb is pulled out. Emily gets hysterical. The tension dissipates. And then they begin again. This repeating round lasts for three minutes exactly, the full length of time available on a single roll of the sound-movie film I was using. In real life, it could go on for nearly fifteen minutes.

Every time I watch this scene, it takes my breath away because the woman with my daughter was someone I had never seen before. I suspect it was also someone my mother had never seen before.

Watching how happy my mother was, Daryl and I began to think that maybe my parents should move permanently to Stanford, where they could be part of their grandchildren's daily lives and ours as well. The question was: How to bring this move about?

We felt certain that my father would be thrilled at the prospect of retiring from the Pittsburgh post office and moving to sunny California, so we weren't particularly worried about convincing him. We also felt certain that my mother would be incapable of actively deciding to relocate. If such a move were to be made, my mother would thus have to slide into it fairly passively. With this in mind, we began to encourage my mother to see what kind of job she could find in the area without committing herself in advance to making a permanent move. She found this idea appealing because it gave her an excuse to stay for a longer visit with her granddaughter and it also kept her options open.

It didn't take long before she was offered a full-time position as a private secretary to a Stanford University chemistry professor, at which point we all went to see what kind of apartment she could afford. We found one that was perfectly nice but not too fancy, with a swimming pool, just five short, nonhilly blocks from the Palo Alto Library. At this point she had no trouble making the decision. She just called my father on the phone and told him to get himself out there.

With the help of various relatives, my father retired, sold or gave away much of what they had in their apartment, loaded up the car, and drove west. My mother didn't even go back to Pittsburgh to settle her affairs. She just started her new job on Monday morning, and that was that. A year or so later, she switched from working for the chemistry professor to working for a sociology professor. Not only was the sociology professor's writing more meaningful to her; he was also Jewish, and that made her even more comfortable in her new environment. When my father arrived, he too started looking for a job and found one as a part-time mailroom clerk in a private corporation.

That the years after my parents moved to California were the happiest in their (our) life together is true in the sense that we all had lots of good times together: playing with Emily and then later also with Jeremy (who was born exactly two years and nine months after Emily), walking in the woods, eating out, going to the zoo or the beach or San Francisco, spending time with Bev at least three or four times a year. But there was a dark side to this period as well, because only seven months after my Boby died and six months after my mother came to California for the birth of her granddaughter, she discovered that she had advanced breast cancer. She died just three years later, when Emily was not quite four and Jeremy was not even one year old.

Although these years were filled with anguish and pain, as well as pleasure and happiness, my mother spent this time, and died, exactly the way she wanted to. Like the fatalist she was, she didn't seem to mind that death was coming, and hence she did little to try to extend the span of her life. She permitted the doctors to do a mastectomy and some local radiation, but she permitted no chemotherapy, no spinal tap—indeed, no invasive testing of any kind. By the time she died, she had been suffering for months from devastating headaches (the cancer had spread to her brain), but she took nothing more than aspirin for them and stoically went to work every day until the night of her death. When I called her boss the next morning to explain why she wouldn't be at work, he was shocked. He knew that she sometimes had headaches but had no idea that she was seriously ill.

I think I spoke to my mother on the telephone an instant before she died. I had called around dinnertime to see how she was. She had been napping on the sofa, she said, and would have something to eat as soon as my father got back from the store. She said this in a voice so completely devoid of energy that I was overwhelmed with guilt for having made her get up to answer the telephone. I apologized, told her to go back to sleep, and hung up. A short time later, the phone rang. It was my father. He had returned from the store to find my mother dead on the floor by the phone. Apparently she had said good-bye to me and collapsed on the spot.

My mother was only sixty years old when she died, and not many of her dreams had come true, but at least her final years (and my final years with her) included moments of joy we had never experienced before.

After my mother's death, my father, my sister, and I all went back to Pittsburgh with her body for the funeral. My father remained in Pittsburgh for about a month, but when he returned to California, he was clearly ready to begin a new life. In what for him was an unusually direct and thoughtful conversation, he told me not long after his return that he hoped I wouldn't see him as being disrespectful to my mother, but during those long nights when he could hear her moaning because of her headaches, he kept himself going by promising himself that when she finally died, he would put the past behind him and look for someone else.

And so he did. Much as it hurt and angered my mother's siblings, he never initiated any further contact with them, not even when he went to Pittsburgh to visit his brother. Even more to the point, he started exploring every over-forty singles group in the Palo Alto area. Within weeks, he discovered that as a reasonably healthy and normal man of sixty-four, he could afford to be picky. So when the first woman he took out for dinner wouldn't kiss him good-night, he dropped her. I tried to talk to him at that point about the value of friendship, but he wasn't interested.

Apparently he found what he wanted because, shortly after dropping that woman, he met Rita, and he married Rita just seven months after my mother died, in July 1978. Although I was ever so slightly ambivalent about my father's being able to replace my mother so quickly, my overriding reaction was one of relief: Thank God I will not have to be responsible for him. I felt some of that same relief when my father died in 1996, but I also felt enormous warmth toward Rita, because my father's eighteen years with her (and with her daughter Janice, who lived with them and was his best buddy) had clearly been the happiest of his life.

Just a few weeks after my father and Rita got married, Daryl, the kids, and I all moved from California to Ithaca, New York, so his new family never became an integral part of our lives—although for a year or so, they did become an integral part of Bev's life when they briefly moved to Portland to be closer to Rita's other daughter. I have to give Rita credit because, as far as we could see, she was completely accepting of Bev's relationship with Roz (many heterosexual women of her age would not have been), and she regularly invited Bev, Roz, and Roz's young son, Ben, for dinner on Friday nights.

It wasn't only family that Daryl and I incorporated into our family community. Two other members were our two daytime babysitters: Margie Daniels, who took care of our kids in California from the time Emily was three months old until the day we moved to Ithaca four years later; and Pat Van Order, who started working for us as soon as we got to Ithaca and stayed on for some seven years. Margie had school-age kids of her own, so she liked to leave on the dot at five, but the boundary around our family was so permeable that when Pat was babysitting for our kids, she usually ate dinner with us two or three nights a week.

Various other family and friends became a part of our family community over the years as well, including Emily's and Jeremy's friends who, at every age, treated our house as a kind of community center. During the earlier years, this meant that we always seemed to have half a dozen creative and rambunctious, if lovable, troublemakers running around making noise. In later years, I learned to tell how many extra people had slept in the house overnight by counting the number of shoes in the back hall and dividing by two.

Some people would have surely hated having so little privacy, so few personal and family boundaries, but I loved living in such a large and loving social community. Like some 1950s mom, albeit one with a full-time academic career and an egalitarian husband, I loved making hot chocolate for them all, watching them have a good time together, and becoming someone that not only my own children but even some of my children's friends felt comfortable talking to about important things.

Given my desire for the family I never had as a child but always wanted, it will come as no surprise that I eagerly became the family photographer and to this day savor the many photographs and movies I took, especially when Emily and Jeremy were young. Both the kids and I particularly treasure an audiotape I made of each of them at two or three years old. In Emily's case, I taped hours and hours of her conversation and then edited it down to a pithy thirty-five minutes. I didn't have time to be so elaborate with Jeremy, but it is definitely a kick to hear him reading *Frog and Toad* aloud to Daryl when he was only three. (Both our children were very early readers.)

One moment from our life together captures the best of what we felt like as a family. When Emily had just started sixth grade and Jeremy had just started fourth, I arranged for all of us to spend an early September weekend at a lodge in the Adirondack Mountains. It was going to be a long drive in bad weather, so we picked up the kids from school a little early and got to the lodge just in time to eat before the dining room closed for the night. Then the storm knocked out all the electricity, which meant that our cottage was both dark and cold for the rest of the night.

For the next couple of hours, from dinnertime to bedtime, we cuddled together under the blankets and listened to Daryl make up

Nancy Drew stories. Nancy Drew was then Emily's favorite story-book character, and Daryl had the girl-detective genre completely mastered. But every now and then, he would start to fall asleep in mid-sentence. We could tell this was happening because he would gradually begin to fade, like a tape running at a slower and slower speed, and then his words would start to get a little garbled and his breathing a little snorey—until one or the other of the kids would poke him, and he would almost unconsciously wind back up and be off and running again.

CHAPTER FOUR

Egalitarian Partnering

As much as I may have loved being scrunched under a blanket with my family and making hot chocolate and wrapping Chanukah presents, the life that Daryl and I created together, for nine years without children and for twenty years with children, was never a traditional one. From the start, we were gender pioneers, inventing first an egalitarian form of marriage for ourselves, and, later, a gender-liberated, antihomophobic, and sex-positive way of rearing our children. We invented these new family forms because the existing forms provided by our social world would not allow us to live the lives we wanted to live or be the people we thought ourselves to be.

Because of the particular historical moment in which we were doing all this, people around us found the new family forms we were creating and the feminist ideology underlying them both provocative and useful. As quickly as we invented these forms, we were called upon to speak about them in public. Our private lives were thereby transformed into the subject of public feminist discourse, we became the role models at the center of that discourse, and people we had never met began to build their lives around the models we had initially invented for our own personal needs.

This transformation of our private practice into public discourse happened so fast that I now remember more about the lectures we gave on egalitarian marriage and gender-liberated child-rearing than I do about the experiences on which those lectures were based. But whether it's the lived experience I remember or the stories we told hungry audiences, the gender-pioneering that Daryl and I did together was productive not only for us personally but also for the two political struggles that have most engaged us over the years: the struggle for the equality of women and the struggle for the equality of lesbians and gay men.

I've already talked about the moment in our courtship when we first began to frame our egalitarian philosophy. It was only about eighteen months later, in the fall of 1966, when the first formal request came for a lecture on the topic. The lecture was to be given to a Carnegie-Mellon honors seminar for senior women entitled "The Role of the Educated Woman in American Society." This request contained two ironies. First, I had avoided this seminar during my own senior year because I thought it would be too traditional. Second, the invitation to lecture came to Daryl, the male professor, rather than to me, the female graduate student, or to us, the egalitarian couple.

I'm embarrassed to admit that we let Daryl give this first lecture on egalitarianism by himself. And not only that: he did most of the work preparing it. I'm not sure what we were thinking: maybe that he was the more experienced teacher.

It is testimony both to the traditionalism of the times and to our own naïveté as feminists that the first newspaper clipping in my egalitarian lecture files should contain a photograph of Daryl alone with a caption that reads: "Dr. Daryl Bem tells women: Assert yourself." Daryl gave just one more solo lecture about egalitarianism, at the First Governor's Conference on the Status of Women in the State of Delaware in April 1967.

I don't have a clipping about it or even a precise date, but I remember the first time we spoke about egalitarianism together in a formal setting. It was in 1967, and it wasn't technically a lecture but a Sunday morning sermon at a Unitarian church in Pittsburgh. The congregation was very open about what it considered a sermon: the only requirement was that we include a few quotations from the Bible. We thus began our lecture that Sunday morning (and most of our lectures thereafter) with the following words:

In the beginning God created the heaven and the earth. . . . And God said let us make man in our image, after our likeness; and let him have dominion over the fish of the sea, and over the fowl of the air, and over the cattle, and over all the earth. . . . And the rib, which the Lord God had taken from man, made he a woman and brought her unto the man. . . . And the Lord God said unto the woman, What is this that thou has done? And the woman said, The serpent beguiled me, and I did eat. . . . Unto the woman God said, I will greatly multiply thy sorrow and thy conception; in sorrow thou shalt bring forth children; and thy desire shall be to thy husband, and he shall rule over thee. (Genesis 1–3)

There is a moral to that story, we went on to say, which Paul spells out even more clearly:

For a man . . . is the image and glory of God; but the woman is the glory of the man. For the man is not of the woman, but the woman of the man. Neither was the man created for the woman, but the woman for the man. (I Corinthians 11)

Let the woman learn in silence with all subjection. But I suffer not a woman to teach, nor to usurp authority over the man, but to be in silence. For Adam was first formed and then Eve. And Adam was not deceived, but the woman, being deceived, was in the transgression. Notwithstanding, she shall be saved in childbearing, if they continue in faith and charity and holiness with sobriety. (I Timothy 2)

Of course, we didn't want anyone to assume that only Christians have this rich heritage of ideology about women, so we next asked the congregation to consider the morning prayer of the Orthodox Jew: "Blessed art Thou, oh Lord our God, King of the Universe, that I was not born a gentile. Blessed art Thou, oh Lord our God, King of the Universe, that I was not born a slave. Blessed art Thou, oh Lord our God, King of the Universe, that I was not born a woman."

Finally, we asked the congregation to consider a quotation from the Koran, the sacred text of Islam: "Men are superior to women on account of the qualities in which God has given them preeminence."

Having thereby fulfilled our obligation to sermonize, we introduced the theme of our lecture, which was entitled "Training the Woman to Know Her Place: The Power of an Unconscious Ideology." Because they think they sense a decline in feminine "faith, charity, and holiness with sobriety," we said, "many people today jump to the conclusion that the ideology expressed in these passages is a relic of the past. Not so. It has simply been obscured by an egalitarian veneer, and the same ideology has now become unconscious. That is, we remain unaware of it because alternative beliefs and attitudes about women have gone unimagined. We are very much like the fish who is unaware that its environment is wet. After all, what else could it be? Such is the nature of all unconscious ideologies in a society. Such, in particular, is the nature of America's ideology about women."

In the two years Daryl and I lived in Pittsburgh after giving this first joint lecture, we gave evolving versions of it to many groups, both small and large, but the pace of our invitations picked up dramatically when we moved to California in the fall of 1970. I have newspaper clippings for only a fraction of our lectures, but even so, I was surprised in retrospect to see how many lectures we gave during a short period of time and how much coverage these lectures received in the local papers. Here, for example, are the headlines from just the clippings I happen to have in my files:

"Sharing the Chores: An Egalitarian Marriage" (*San Francisco Chronicle,* March 1971), based on a lecture at Mills College;

"How to Stay Equal in Marriage" (*Oakland Tribune,* March 1971), based on the same lecture;

"Wife and Husband Professorial Team: Their Target—Inequality of Women" (*Stanford Observer,* May 1971), a joint profile on the occasion of our appointment as full-time faculty members at Stanford University after having been visiting professors there for one year;

"An Egalitarian Marriage and How It Works" (*Los Angeles Times,* February 1972), a profile of us written in anticipation of a talk to be given at a Stanford University conference;

"Drs. Bem Discuss Concept of Egalitarian Marriage" (*San Jose State University Spartan Daily,* April 1972), based on a lecture given during Women's Week at the university;

"Modern Ms. in for Rude Awakening" (*San Jose News,* April 1972), based on the same lecture;

"Psychology Team Examines Sex Roles" (*Sacramento Beaver,* April 1972), based on a lecture given at a symposium at American River College;

"Stanford Psychologists Will Be 'Status of Women' Speakers" (*Fresno Bee,* April 1972), in anticipation of a lecture to be given at Fresno State College;

"Fifty-fifty Partnership Includes Lecture Dais" (*Hayward Daily*

Review, November 1972), in anticipation of a talk to be given at Canyon High School for members of the Castro Valley community. This Hayward article was by far the most interesting clipping in my files because it described exactly how we had come to be invited:

> Drs. Bem were invited because some ... AAUW [American Association of University Women] members had been kept waiting for their share-the-ride companions a few months ago in San Francisco. Branch members had piled into cars to attend a series of seminars at the Jack Tar Hotel, agreeing to meet at a predesignated time for the return home. One group waited so long for their co-passengers, they decided to see what detained them. They were located in the lecture hall with others in the audience, too fascinated by the animated give-and-take between listeners and lecturers to tear themselves away. The second contingent, impressed with the proceedings, joined the crowd. Among them were members of the program committee of Hayward AAUW who—on the spot—invited the Drs. Bem for a Nov. 15 appearance on this side of the bay.... They suggest husbands accompany their wives to the meeting.

It wasn't only older folks who were this excited by what we had to say. College students too were so hungry for the brand of feminism we were preaching that, for a brief period during 1972, we allowed a booking agency specializing in college audiences to arrange our speaking engagements. That venture didn't last long, however, because it generated too many invitations. Also, the agency couldn't consistently arrange the only two things we cared about: that the podium be low enough for me to be seen over it and that we be scheduled into a two- to three-hour time slot so that the audience would have plenty of opportunity to ask questions.

Of all the documents in my personal archives from this period, three best convey how provocative and productive our ideas and our lives were for a certain segment of the population.

The first document is a five-part series from the *Stanford Daily,* dated October 25-29, 1971, that reproduced the entire text of our hour-long "Training the Woman" lecture. As well as I recall the campus fascination with feminism during the 1970s (including the hundreds of small consciousness-raising groups set up by the Stanford Women's Center), it is difficult for me to conjure up the mindset that led the editors of the student newspaper to devote so much space to our lecture.

The second document is the interview with us entitled "A Marriage of Equals" that I quoted in the preface and that appeared in the first regular issue of *Ms.* magazine in July 1972. An earlier "preview" issue had appeared in the spring and had sold out in eight days. This first issue of *Ms.* has some classic pieces in it, including "Body Hair: The Last Frontier" by Harriet Lyons and Rebecca Rosenblatt; "The Value of Housework: For Love or Money?" by Ann Crittenden Scott; "Lesbian Love and Sexuality" by Del Martin and Phyllis Lyon; "Women and Madness" by Phyllis Chesler; and an interview entitled "The Radicalization of Simone de Beauvoir" by French feminist Alice Schwartzer, in which de Beauvoir discusses why and how the radicalism of the women's liberation movement had finally persuaded her to call herself a feminist rather than just a socialist. The interview with us was written by another French feminist, Claude Servan-Schreiber, who also published a French translation in *Elle* magazine. Looking back at this issue of *Ms.* now, I cannot help but be impressed by the vibrancy and radicalism of our feminist voices.

But what most captured my attention twenty-five years later was the gender-bending job advertisement immediately opposite the magazine's contents page—because Daryl and I had played a role in the historical process producing that ad. In bold type at the top of the page, a headline reads: "The phone company wants more installers like Alana MacFarlane." Alana MacFarlane, the text goes on to say, is a twenty-year-old from San Rafael, California, who was one of

AT&T's first female telephone installers. But "she won't be the last," because AT&T now has a policy that there are "no all-male or all-female jobs at the phone company." Alongside the text, trim, cheery, and attractive Alana MacFarlane herself appears, at full length and in full color, suspended from the top of a telephone pole with her feet firmly planted on two rungs of the pole and the rest of her held comfortably at a forty-five-degree angle by a strap around her waist.

This ad was one of the by-products of a lawsuit brought by the Equal Employment Opportunity Commission against AT&T for race and sex discrimination. Daryl and I had become involved in the suit because the EEOC asked us to gather some specific data to counter AT&T's claim that the reason women and men then had such different, and differently paying, jobs at AT&T was that women and men simply don't have the same job preferences.

Accordingly, we did a study in the early 1970s showing that the way a job is advertised dramatically affects the number of women and men who are interested in it. The study included four telephone jobs, each advertised to three groups of people in three ways: the traditional gender-biased way, a gender-neutral way, and a gender-reversed (or gender-bending) way.

When Daryl and I were being cross-examined at the hearings before the Federal Communications Commission, AT&T's attorneys tried to have our study thrown out because, they argued, not only were all our gender-bender ads ridiculous; the one for female pole-climbers even made "unsubstantiated health claims" (it read in part: "We're Looking for Outdoor Women! Do you like fresh air and exercise? If sitting behind a desk isn't for you, stay slim and trim as a linewoman working in the great outdoors for Pacific Telephone"). It was thus especially delicious to see how closely AT&T's own gender-bender ads were modeled after the ads we used in our study.

AT&T did not create these ads out of the goodness of its heart, of course. At the conclusion of the hearings, the FCC found AT&T

guilty of both sex and race discrimination, and AT&T was forced to change its ways. In a letter written to us when the case had just been settled, William H. Brown, III, chairman of the EEOC, described the settlement as follows:

The agreement which we reached with AT&T was a milestone in the history of civil rights. In addition to an unprecedented back pay award and greatly increased job mobility for women and minorities throughout the Bell system, the companies are committed to recruit and hire or promote females until they hold at least 38% of the inside craft jobs and 19% of the outside craft jobs. Males will have to be recruited and hired into at least 10% of the operator jobs and 25% of the other clerical jobs. In the long run, this means that about 100,000 or more persons will be in jobs traditionally held by the opposite sex. These commitments go well beyond any current or previous programs by any company and they have been obtained largely because of your work. . . . Since AT&T's principal justification for its sex-segregation of jobs was lack of interest by females, your experiment provided the spearhead of our argument on that issue.

This experiment on men's and women's interest in telephone jobs was not the first we had done on how advertising aids and abets sex discrimination. In fact, the EEOC had contacted us because we had gathered analogous data in the late 1960s for a lawsuit filed by the National Organization for Women against the *Pittsburgh Press* for its policy of segregating its help-wanted columns into "Male Help Wanted" and "Female Help Wanted." That case went to the U.S. Supreme Court, which finally upheld the decisions of the lower courts when it ruled against the newspaper in June 1973. A few years later, we were involved in yet another such lawsuit, this one brought by the League of Women Voters against the U.S. Department of Labor because of its failure to set goals and timetables for hiring women in the construction industry, even though it was setting such goals and timetables for people of color. In all three cases, the excuse given by the defendant was the same: women and men have different job preferences, and that difference allegedly justifies whatever discriminatory practice was the target of the lawsuit.

The third document in my personal archive that I want to single out is an oddly disturbing little coloring book entitled "Up or Down with Women's Liberation." On its bright pink cover is a line drawing of the most revolutionary little schoolmarm I have ever seen. With her hair pulled back in a bun, her oddly shaped spectacles accentuating the pointiness of her chin, and her breasts hanging down asymmetrically under her shapeless shirt and sweater, she stands serenely, a lighted match held proudly in one hand and a burning bra in the other. She is (we are later told by the child-narrator) Ms. Marian, the librarian, whom "Daddy calls . . . a 'women's libber.' She says she hates men [but] she loves books. Color her well-read."

Not too many people in this coloring book come off as well as Ms. Marian. Mommy, for example, went to college "once upon a time. . . . Now she is just a housewife. Color her drab." Daddy's secretary "is very smart. But she plays dumb. Why? She wants to keep her job. Why? Color her shrinking violet." Baby sister "loves dolls. Color her forever pink. Put her into a mold. Label her 'female.' " Big brother "is lucky; color him golden boy. He gets everything. He gets to ride a motorcycle. He gets to go surfing. . . . He gets to go to Vietnam."

And then, of course, there's Daddy, whom "Marian calls . . . an 'm.c.p.' " (which means, we are told in a footnote, male chauvinist pig). And Daddy's pigginess shows up on page after page, as, for example, when he says, "Nature made men and women to be different" or that he likes our neighbor Bonnie because "she is a 'real female' " or that "it was 'just like a woman' . . . [when] Mommy hurt the car." If that were not enough, there is also the time he calls the petition that Mommy signs in favor of the Equal Rights Amendment "the 'scarlet' letter." And the time he promises Mommy he'll clean up the kitchen while she goes to a meeting, but: "Here is how the kitchen looked when Mommy came home. . . . Color it the same." Worst of all, perhaps, there's the time he was supposed to be taking care of the baby: "Color baby's bottom brown. Where's Daddy? He is hiding somewhere in the picture. Find him and color him yellow."

On the last page of this coloring book, the feminist ideology that has thus far been personified only by Ms. Marian gets a new personification. Picture two heterosexual couples sitting across from one another on two sofas. On the sofa closest to us are Daddy and Mommy. They have their backs to us, but we can see their profiles so we know exactly what they are feeling. Daddy, his back stiff as a board, is tense, silent, and angry. Mommy, leaning forward enthusiastically with a big open smile on her face, is happy and excited. On the other sofa, facing both them and us, are a young, placid, pleasant-looking woman and man who are barely distinguishable from each other because they have the same round face, the same Beatles-style haircut, and the same shirt and necktie. Who are these people?

These are the Bem-Bems,
Tweedle-he and Tweedle-she.
He works three days. She works three days.
He keeps house three days. She keeps house three days.
On the seventh day, they rest.
Mommy thinks it's a super deal.
What does Daddy think?
What do *you* think?

The coloring book has a 1972 copyright date and a legend on the back saying that proceeds go to AAUW fellowships. An address for ordering additional copies is in Costa Mesa, California, which is consistent with my feeling that it was especially in California that we were taken up as role models.

But why was what we were doing and saying so meaningful to so many people?

The answer to this question has to begin with at least a brief description of the times. When we began lecturing together in 1967, the word *sexism* had not yet been invented, let alone terms like sexual harassment, acquaintance rape, or wife battering. Hence we frequently found ourselves saying during a lecture that "the ideology about women we're trying to describe is a kind of . . . [pause, drop your voice into a hushed whisper to emphasize the enormity of what you're about to say, and then say it slooooowly and deliberately] . . . *sexual racism.*"

And not only was there no concept of sexism. Middle-class people were not open to the idea of providing child care outside the child's own home. As hard as this may be to believe, on those few early occasions when we tried to talk about day care, even our college audiences branded it as "communist." For several years, the only way we could even introduce the idea of good but not mother-provided child care was thus to say, "Mary Poppins would not have answered an ad for cleaning lady."

By the time we moved to California, the political landscape had changed dramatically, and the desire for both personal and social change was palpable. But how were people to think about this change? Even more important, how were they to live their lives in this new age?

Enter the Doctors Bem. Or, more accurately, enter an auditorium in which the Doctors Bem will, in a mere two or three hours, answer all those questions for you on both a personal and a theoretical level—and give you lots of laughs along the way. Of course, we might also motivate you to dramatically alter the way you are living your life, but if truth be told, that is part of the reason you (especially if you are a woman) have come to hear us—which is why, of course, that article in the *Hayward Daily Review* had suggested that "husbands accompany their wives to the meeting."

In the first hour of the evening, the Bems deliver a written lecture, taking turns at the microphone, each speaking for about five minutes before turning the microphone over to the other. Although we did not speak extemporaneously, no one found the lecture boring because it had been written and rewritten to be both persuasive and stimulating. Also, we thought of ourselves as a kind of Broadway show. Hence our role throughout the evening, even when we were reading aloud, was to deliver the best performance we could. During the lecture, this meant reading "with expression." During the question-and-answer session, it meant telling tried-and-true stories, anecdotes, jokes, and even statistics as if they were only now being thought of for the first time.

The lecture began with a series of religious provocations, but it moved quickly to the question of why women are so "homogenized" in American society. Why is it so difficult to predict what a newborn baby boy will be doing some twenty-five years later, especially if he is white and middle class, but so easy to predict what a newborn baby girl will be doing?

Time studies have shown that she will spend the equivalent of a full working day, 7.1 hours, in preparing meals, cleaning house, laundering, mending, shopping, and doing other household errands. . . . Even an I.Q. in the genius range does not guarantee that a woman's unique potential will find expression. . . . Talent, education, ability, interests, motivation: all are irrelevant. In our society, being female uniquely qualifies an individual for domestic work—either by itself or in conjunction with typing, teaching, nursing, or (most often) unskilled labor.

It is true, we conceded, that most women have several hours of leisure time every day.

And it is here, we are often told, that each woman can express her unique identity. Thus, politically interested women can join the League of Women Voters. Women with humane interests can become part-time Gray Ladies. Women who love music can raise money for the symphony. Protestant women play canasta; Jewish women play mah-jongg; brighter women of all denominations and faculty wives play bridge.

But politically interested *men* serve in legislatures. *Men* with humane interests become physicians or clinical psychologists. *Men* who love music play in the symphony. In other words, why should a woman's unique identity determine only the periphery of her life rather than its central core?

Why? Why nurse rather than physician, secretary rather than executive, stewardess rather than pilot? Why faculty wife rather than faculty? Why doctor's mother rather than doctor?

Although I wouldn't answer this question in exactly the same way today, at the time, Daryl and I said it had three basic answers: (1) discrimination; (2) sex-role conditioning (as opposed to biology); and (3) the presumed incompatibility of family and career. I'm going to skip right past numbers one and two and move directly to number three because the first two sections of our lecture now seem particularly out of date. Also, as we said at the time: "If we were to ask the average American woman why she is not pursuing a full-time career, she would probably not say that discrimination had discouraged her; nor would she be likely to recognize the pervasive effects of her own sex-role conditioning. What she probably would say is that a career, no matter how desirable, is simply incompatible with the role of wife and mother."

Agreeing with this conclusion about the *traditional* role of wife and mother—and always restricting our comments to heterosexual couples (which was itself a sign of the times)—we began at this point to undermine this family-career incompatibility by posing the possibility of an alternative family form. The traditional conception of the husband-wife relationship is now being challenged, we said, not so much because of the widespread discontent surfacing among older married women, but because it violates two of the most basic values of today's college-age generation. These values concern personal growth, on the one hand, and interpersonal relationships, on the other. The first of these emphasizes individuality and self-fulfillment; the second stresses openness, honesty, and equality in all human relationships.

Because they saw the traditional male-female relationship as incompatible with these basic values, young people of the time were experimenting with alternatives to the traditional marriage pattern. Although a few were testing out ideas like communal living, most seemed to be searching for satisfactory modifications of the husband-wife relationship, either in or out of the context of marriage, with an increasing number even planning fully egalitarian relationships very much like that described in the following passage, which was read by Daryl:

Both my wife and I earned Ph.D. degrees in our respective disciplines. I turned down a superior job offer in Oregon and accepted a slightly less desirable position in New York where my wife would have more opportunities for part-time work in her specialty. Although I would have preferred to live in a suburb, we purchased a home near my wife's job so that she could have an office at home where she would be when the children returned from school. Because my wife earns a good salary, she can easily afford to pay a housekeeper to do her major household chores. My wife and I share all other tasks around the house equally. For example, she cooks the meals, but I do the laundry for her and help her with many of her other household tasks.

Without questioning the basic happiness of such a marriage or its appropriateness for many couples, Daryl continued, we can legitimately ask if such a marriage is, in fact, an instance of interpersonal equality. Have all the hidden assumptions about the woman's "natural" role really been exorcised? There is a simple test. If the marriage is truly egalitarian, then it should retain the same flavor and tone even if the roles of husband and wife were reversed, as when I, Sandy, read the description:

Both my husband and I earned Ph.D. degrees in our respective disciplines. I turned down a superior job offer in Oregon and accepted a slightly less desirable position in New York where my husband would have more opportunities for part-time work in his specialty. Although I would have preferred to live in a suburb, we purchased a home near my husband's job so that he could have an office at home where he would be when the children returned from school. Because my husband earns a good salary, he can easily afford to pay a housekeeper to do his major household chores. My husband and I share all other tasks around the house equally. For example, he cooks the meals, but I do the laundry for him and help him with many of his other household tasks.

Somehow it sounds different, we went on to say, and yet only the pronouns have been changed to protect the powerful! (In the early years of giving this lecture, by the way, and even later if the audience was fairly traditional, the first of these two paragraphs was heard as so completely egalitarian as to seem utopian. Hence no one laughed until the trick was revealed in the second paragraph. In later years, the laughter would begin during the first paragraph.)

After talking just a bit more about what true egalitarianism would look like, we switched gears and tried to undermine the family-career incompatibility from another direction. More specifically, we began to challenge the long-standing notion that children inevitably suffer when their mother works outside the home.

For example, we made some fun of Dr. Spock, who wrote in a

1963 article for the *Ladies' Home Journal* that any woman who finds full-time motherhood unfulfilling is showing "a residue of difficult relationships in her own childhood." If a vacation doesn't solve the problem, she is probably having emotional difficulties, which can be relieved "through regular counseling in a family social agency, or if severe, through psychiatric treatment. . . . Any mother of a pre-school child who is considering a job should discuss the issues with a social worker before making her decision." The message here is clear, we said: If you don't feel that your two-year-old is a stimulating full-time companion, you are probably neurotic. But the truly important point, we went on to say, is that

maternal employment in and of itself does not seem to have any negative effects on the children; and part-time work actually seems to benefit the children. Children of working mothers are no more likely than children of nonworking mothers to be delinquent or nervous or withdrawn or anti-social; they are no more likely to show neurotic symptoms; they are no more likely to perform poorly in school; and they are no more likely to feel deprived of their mother's love. Daughters of working mothers are more likely to want to work themselves, and, when asked to name the one woman in the world that they most admire, daughters of working mothers are more likely to name their own mothers! This is the one finding that we wish every working woman in America could hear, because the other thing that is true of almost every working mother is that she *thinks* she is hurting her children and she feels guilty. In fact, research has shown that the worst mothers are those who would like to work but stay home out of a sense of duty. The major conclusion from all the research is really this: What matters is the quality of a mother's relationship with her children, not the time of day it happens to be administered. This con-clusion should come as no surprise; successful fathers have been dem-onstrating it for years. Some fathers are great, some fathers stink, and they're all at work at least eight hours a day.

At this point in the lecture, we made a strong statement about the need for child-care centers, reiterating a point we had already made a number of times: Like all the other reforms then advocated by the feminist movement (including the Equal Rights Amendment, equal pay for equal work, and even the equal sharing of household responsibilities by husband and wife), child-care centers are not merely for the benefit of middle-class women who wish to pursue professional careers. They are an absolute necessity for the millions of working mothers already in the paid labor force who work outside the home because they cannot afford not to and who currently have no choice but to make do with whatever child care they can put together, no matter how inadequate those arrangements might be.

We ended our lecture by returning to the theme of egalitarianism. A truly egalitarian marriage, we said, embraces a division of labor that satisfies what we like to call "the roommate test": "That is, the labor is divided just as it is when two men or two women room together in college or set up a bachelor apartment together. Errands and domestic chores are assigned by preference, agreement, flipping a coin, alternated, given to hired help, or—perhaps most often the case—simply left undone."

It is significant, we went on to say, that today's young people, so many of whom live precisely this way prior to marriage, find this kind of arrangement within marriage so foreign to their thinking. Consider an analogy:

Suppose that a white male college student decided to room or set up a bachelor apartment with a black male friend. Surely the typical white student would not blithely assume that his black roommate was to handle all the domestic chores. Nor would his conscience allow him to do so even in the unlikely event that his roommate would say: "No, that's okay. I like doing housework. I'd be happy to do it." We suspect that the typical white student would still not be comfortable if he took advantage of this offer because he and America have finally realized that he would be taking advantage of the fact that such a roommate had been socialized by our society to be "happy" with such obvious inequity. But change this hypothetical black roommate to a female marriage partner, and somehow the student's conscience goes to sleep. At most it is quickly tranquilized by the comforting thought that "she is happiest when she is ironing for her loved one." Such is the power of an unconscious ideology.

Of course, it may well be that she *is* happiest when she is ironing for her loved one. Such, indeed, is the power of an unconscious ideology.

At this point, there was usually thunderous applause. When it died down, I would introduce the question-and-answer session by saying that people in the audience should feel free to ask any question that came into their minds, whether intellectual, political, or personal. They needn't worry about censoring themselves. If they happened to ask a question that was too personal, we would simply decline to answer it. That was unlikely to happen, I said. "After all, we have been asked questions as personal as 'Who's on top?' And we answered it. The answer is: We alternate." This little joke reliably produced uproarious laughter and was a good transition to the question-and-answer period, which sometimes lasted a full two hours.

I wish I had a tape recording of at least one long question-and-answer session so I could try to re-create what it felt like to be there. I cannot remember how people worded the questions they asked us; instead, I can only infer these questions from my memory of the little monologues Daryl and I used to give in response. As often as not, we both responded to every question. (As luck would have it, the wealth of experience we thereby accumulated in responding to questions in tandem was enormously useful when we later had to testify at the AT&T hearings I mentioned earlier. The AT&T attorneys quickly agreed to our request that we be cross-examined together because they thought we would trip each other up. In fact, we were able to work off each other very well. The first person to respond would simply do the best she or he could, and then the second person would elaborate—but without contradicting—and frequently smash the essential point home.)

Following our formal lecture, what people most wanted to hear about was us. Who were we? Where did we come from? How did we manage to escape the sex-role conditioning that seemed to be imprisoning almost everyone else in traditional gender roles? How did we live our egalitarian philosophy on a day-to-day basis? How did we make decisions, large and small? How did we decide who would do what? Did we find it hard to be egalitarian? Did we think we could continue being egalitarian after we had children? Or, in later years, how had we managed to remain egalitarian even after the children were born?

People also wanted to know whether and how they themselves could become egalitarian. If they were young (and female), this meant, among other things: Where could they find men like Daryl to be egalitarian with? If they were older, this meant, among other things: Could they change the gender relations within their existing marriages, and if so, how?

I'll skip over the answers to who we were because I've already said a lot about that. But I haven't said much about how we lived our egalitarianism.

Before our kids were born, day-to-day living was so easy for us that it hardly seems worth describing. What is there to do, after all, when there are no children? And was there really a time when we didn't have children? It's hard to recapture.

But, as we suggested in our lectures, like congenial (if a tad over-organized) roommates, we divided up the chores in a way that felt comfortable to both of us and then changed the system whenever one or the other of us expressed a desire to do so. For example, for a little while we took turns cooking dinner every other night, and we also had the cook be the dishwasher so that she or he would be motivated to dirty fewer pots and pans. Later we decided it was silly for the same person to have to cook and clean, so we started having one of us cook and the other clean up, still alternating every other day. The one rule that never changed, however, was that you couldn't buy your way out of cooking, so if we went out for dinner, your cooking night just got postponed to the next day.

What other chores were there to do? Cleaning the house? We always had a cleaning person come at least every two weeks to do the heavier cleaning, and on a daily basis, we pretty much picked up after ourselves—although Daryl did like to joke that, from time to time, he wished I would put my clothes away more regularly. Once, he used to say, he got so frustrated with my lack of fastidiousness that he took all my clothes out of the closet and hung them on various doorknobs. I allegedly didn't notice, so he eventually put them all back in the closet. This story is apocryphal, but its point was supposed to be that our division of labor sometimes boiled down to a meshing of our neuroses. In other words, since Daryl cared more about having the house neat, he sometimes cleaned up more, and since I cared more about what we ate (Daryl would have been happy to eat hamburger every night), I sometimes cooked dinner more.

Other chores? Grocery shopping? We usually did that together. Paying bills? We alternated, but on an extended and unspecified rotation. In other words, I did it for several years, but then one day, when Daryl was mumbling about where our money went, I handed him the checkbook and said, "Here, you do this for a while and you'll see." Figuring out our income taxes? I think Daryl did it for the first few years because he already knew how, and then I wanted to learn so I did it for a while, and then we traded on and off with no

particular pattern—until one year when Daryl made a huge mistake
in favor of the government and then we started using an accoun-
tant. (This is obviously egalitarianism for the sort-of-rich.)

None of this daily division-of-labor stuff generated any conflict
or tension for us. For a long time, we thus couldn't figure out why it
was such a problem for other people, and I'm not sure we ever did
figure it out. We suggested during the q-and-a, however, that some
kind of power struggle must be going on because, when you don't
have children, there just isn't all that much labor to do every day;
hence, the fuss must be about something else.

We also didn't have much conflict about decisions, neither big
ones like which car or house to buy nor little ones like whether to
go to a movie that night and which movie to see if we did go. We
sometimes joked that this was because we always did whatever the
person with the stronger preference wanted to do, and that person
was always Sandy. That's not entirely fair, however, because neither
of us was particularly invested in getting our own way or in control-
ling the other person; we both wanted both of us to be happy, and
not that many decisions mattered much to either of us, so reaching
an agreement wasn't hard. (This is obviously also egalitarianism for
the sort-of-passive.)

The one time we did have a truly stupid fuss, it was over the most
trivial amount of money, and I was the jerk. In true form, however,
we regrouped immediately so as to try to avoid such fusses in the
future. We were still living in Pittsburgh, so maybe the year was
1967. We were wandering through stores with no particular goal in
mind on a Saturday afternoon, and Daryl found a little white digi-
tal clock he wanted to buy for all of twenty dollars. We could easily
afford the twenty dollars, and I knew that, but I am much less of a
consumer than Daryl is, and for some reason on this particular day
I balked. Daryl, knowing I was being ridiculous, persisted.

Many couples who both have jobs keep their earnings separate so they each have their own money to spend, but Daryl and I combined our money from the beginning and neither of us wanted to change that, so we briefly put our money into two separate accounts, which Daryl labeled the "fun fund" and the "funeral fund." (Guess whose desires were said to be mapped onto which fund.) Into the fun fund went any money we got in addition to our regular salaries, and this money could be spent on complete frivolity and without the consent of the other person. We may even have shifted some salary money into this fund from time to time. Into the funeral fund went everything else. The two funds were more symbolic than real. Once they had served their purpose of getting me to accept the fact that Daryl was always going to be more of a consumer than I was— and that was okay because he wasn't going to do anything truly irrational—the two funds were gradually merged.

Life got more complicated, of course, after our kids were born because there was lots more to do, and we couldn't just bail out if we felt like it and leave the chores for tomorrow. Like it or not, the baby had to be fed, diapered, bathed, rocked back to sleep in the middle of the night, and so on.

And not only was there more to do. There was also that nagging little fear that maybe other people would turn out to be right. Maybe children would put an end to our egalitarianism, not so much because we wouldn't be able to divide the labor equally but because I, Sandy, would be so full of raging maternal hormones that I would develop a whole new set of desires. This had been predicted as early as the first summer of our marriage, when a faculty wife at Carnegie-Mellon told me that she, too, had always planned to have a full-time career—she was a physician—but that from the moment she saw her first child, her whole motivational structure changed, and she was sure that mine would change as well.

Being quick on my feet (and just a tad defensive), I asked her whether she already had a child-care person lined up that she had to let go when she changed her mind. No, no, she said, to my relief, she hadn't hired anyone yet; she had always planned to stay home with the baby full-time for at least a little while. I say "to my relief" because I had no intention of ever taking care of a baby full-time (I assumed that Daryl and I would each be doing half-time), and her admission reassured me a little.

But reassured or not, I (we) did still worry, and that worry led us, as usual, to innovate. We may not be able to control my hormones, we said, or the fact that I'm the one who will carry the baby for nine months, but insofar as it is biologically possible, we can arrange for Daryl to participate in all aspects of babydom—and not just from the moment of birth but from the moment of conception. Although the obstetrician surely thought us a little odd, Daryl came with me to every one of my prenatal checkups, which meant that when I first got to hear the baby's heartbeat through an amplified stethoscope at nine weeks, so did he. And who knows if he would have been as attached to that newborn baby if he hadn't heard her heartbeat so early? He was also present at the baby's shower some seven months later, which meant that he too got to sit in the circle and squeal with unrestrained delight as tiny little sleepers and stuffed animals and storybooks were passed around. And, especially given that he was raised as a male, who knows if he would have had as much delight with the baby herself if he hadn't been socialized by this experience before she was born?

Then, of course, there was the issue of breast-feeding. Almost any child-care book will tell you that breast-feeding creates a special bond between mother and child. Well, I certainly wanted to bond with my child and bond pretty intensely at that, but I also wanted Daryl to feel just as close to the baby. Did that mean, I wondered, that I shouldn't breast-feed? That would be a shame because I'd be missing out on an interesting experience for myself and one that would also be good for the baby, if only because breast milk passes on the mother's immunities. Alternatively, I thought, maybe we could both bond more or less equally if I breast-fed part-time, and Daryl bottle-fed the rest of the time. We asked the pediatrician if we could split the feeding this way, and he said yes, as long as we waited to bottle-feed for three weeks because, by then, my milk would be fully established.

By the time the three weeks were up, however, we were both already so bonded to the baby, and without Daryl's having done any feeding at all, that we decided to stay with the breast-feeding except when it was inconvenient. How did Daryl establish such a close tie to our new daughter?

Babies are such dependent little creatures and they need you to do so many things for them. They also get so distressed at times, and when they do, it feels so good to be able to make them feel better. And it's funny: even though you come home from the hospital feeling as if you don't know the first thing about how to take care of a baby—how to get its shirt on and off, for example, without breaking its arms; how to diaper it without leaving a gap so big that everything spills out anyway; how to pacify it when it gets upset and you've already fed it—after just a few days of having complete responsibility for the baby (assuming, of course, that the baby is not especially irritable and that you are financially secure enough to have a reasonable living situation), you suddenly discover that you're an expert. Maybe two or three days before, the hospital nurse could pacify your baby better than you could, but now it feels as if no one in the world knows better than you how to pacify her best; no one who knows better than you how to get her to burp all her gas out or how vigorously to rock her when she's having trouble falling asleep. This may all be illusion, of course, but it's the stuff of which bonding with babies is made. So how did Daryl bond with Emily in those first three weeks? He did everything the baby needed and more, except for breast-feeding, and he did the other things many, many times.

I guess I should make clear that, just like that faculty wife who scared me some ten years earlier, Daryl and I didn't hire a babysitter in advance of our first baby's birth, in part because we didn't want an expert around to make us feel incompetent. Instead, we arranged our teaching schedules so that each of us could be home for half of every working day. Emily herself made our life easier by having the good sense to be born during the last week of winter-quarter classes, so that we both had three full weeks during which we could stay home even more than half-time. We finally did hire a daytime babysitter, Margie Daniels, when Emily was three months old. Margie continued to take care of both of our children during the day (and to do lots of other things that stay-at-home mothers usually do as well) until we finally left California in 1978 to teach at Cornell University in Ithaca, New York, when Emily was four and a half and Jeremy was almost two.

I want to describe three vivid memories from our earliest parenting days because they speak to Daryl's bonding with Emily and also to our daily practice of egalitarianism. The first memory is purely visual. I see Daryl sitting in a chair and reading, standing in the kitchen and washing the dishes, playing the piano, watching television, or doing any number of other things, with little Emily sleeping on his chest in a corduroy Snugli securely attached to his body with straps around his neck and waist. The second memory is still vaguely distressing after twenty years. Daryl is cutting Emily's tiny fingernails for the first time in her life. His hand slips, he cuts the tiniest bit of her skin, she shrieks in pain, and tears instantly come to our eyes. We, her parents, with all our best intentions, have inadvertently injured her. We silently ask ourselves: How many more times, and in what other ways, will we do this during the course of her life?

The third memory involves the middle-of-the-night feedings. Most parents of newborns take the view—and it is, in many ways, a sensible view to take—that during the weeks or months when the

baby is not yet sleeping through the night, at least one parent should
be able to sleep undisturbed; and if the mother is breast-feeding,
that parent would presumably be the father. I took a different view.
Egalitarianism doesn't end at bedtime, I said. If I don't get to sleep
through the night, neither should Daryl. But this little joke makes
it sound as if I actually remember how and why we devised our
middle-of-the-night routine when all I really remember is the routine itself.

Wet and hungry, Emily would wake up and cry. Daryl—who was
used to getting up in the night to pee (in contrast, I rarely got up
to pee even when I was pregnant)—would get up, go into Emily's
room, put a clean diaper on her, and bring her into our bed for
me to feed her. Still three-quarters asleep, I would prop myself up
just enough to get her on my nipple, open my eyes now and then
to see how she was doing, shift her to my other nipple when some
signal I've long since forgotten told me to do so, and then mumble
to Daryl that she was finished when she seemed to be full. I would
then sink back into oblivion while Daryl changed her diaper again
and rocked her in the rocking chair until she fell asleep. Then he
would put her in her crib and go back to sleep himself. It's true that
I did the feeding, but I'd be willing to bet that, during the night
anyway, it was Daryl who did the bonding.

Our division of labor during the daytime hours was a little more
reasonable. As usual, we alternated, first on a daily basis and then on
a weekly basis, being on duty, so to speak, as the parent in charge.
Being on duty meant being responsible for doing everything the
baby needed and also for remembering that it needed to be done. It
also meant being responsible for making decisions about the child.
Could Emily have two cookies tonight instead of one? Did she have
to eat her vegetables in order to have her dessert? If you were the
parent on duty, the decision was up to you. In contrast, being off
duty meant that at any given moment, you could do for the baby or

not, play with the baby or not, and even help the parent who was on duty or not, depending on your whim at the moment. In conventional terms, when you were the on-duty parent, you were like the mother, and when you were the off-duty parent, you were like the father or perhaps the grandparent.

By the time our kids were two or three years old, they were fully aware of this on-duty/off-duty distinction, probably because the off-duty parent would so often use it—in a loving and laughing way, of course—as an excuse for not doing something the child wanted done. What? You want me to come into the bathroom and keep you company while you poop. Ask your dad, it's his turn. What? You want to turn your bedroom into a giant labyrinth made of cardboard boxes and you want me to help you build it and you want to start right now. Ask your mom, it's her turn.

Eventually we posted a sign on a kitchen cabinet announcing who the parent-on-duty was. At first there was just one sign, for Emily, drawn by Daryl, who is not by any stretch of the imagination an artist. On one side of the sign was a childlike drawing of Mommy, complete with glasses, earrings, and breast markers, that said MOMMY'S TURN at the top in thick black letters. On the other side was an equally sophisticated drawing of Daddy that said DADDY'S TURN at the top. Daddy had shorter hair than Mommy and also had no glasses, no earrings, and no breast markers. He did, however, have a little line jutting out from his crotch that signified a penis, but I think this was an embellishment added later by one of the kids. Mommy's very red lips may have also been a kid embellishment. As I recall, Emily flipped the sign every Sunday night.

The sign situation got more complicated when Jeremy reached age two or three, because he then wanted a special sign for himself. And so he drew one, which we thumbtacked onto the cabinet next to Emily's sign. Like the sign Daryl had made, Jeremy's sign had a drawing of Mommy on one side and a drawing of Daddy on the other. Unlike Daryl's sign, however, Jeremy's sign said at the top: MOMMY'S TURN [or DADDY'S TURN] TO PUT ME TO BED, which tells us what aspect of our turn-taking was then salient to Jeremy and perhaps to Emily as well.

Our audiences loved hearing everything we were willing to tell them about who we were and how we lived our egalitarianism, but as I've said, they also wanted to hear about whether and how they themselves could become egalitarian. In retrospect, I see one part of what we said on this topic as nitty-gritty on-the-ground strategizing and the other part (to borrow a term from the 1990s) as empowerment. And though I don't want to underestimate the usefulness of the strategies we offered them, I now think it was probably the empowerment that made our message so compelling, especially to the women in our audiences.

More than anything else, the empowerment part of our discussion emphasized that women must be prepared to take themselves seriously and must also expect to be taken seriously by their husbands and boyfriends. Put somewhat differently, women must begin to see their own activities, projects, preferences, goals, careers—whatever it is that they do and desire—as no less important and no less deserving of special consideration than those of the men in their lives. They must also understand that, on this critical issue of whether a woman's desires are to be given as much consideration as her partner's, she and her partner cannot agree to disagree. If they do, they will have already violated the fundamental criterion of egalitarianism, which is that neither person has a right to continuing priority over the other person for any reason. It doesn't matter if one person is stronger than the other, or taller or richer or smarter or more educated or more professional or more highly paid or more valued by the culture at large—or simply male. The essence of an egalitarian relationship is that both individuals are equally entitled to be taken seriously in every decision, every conflict, every interaction.

If we lived in a social world where women and men were equal, no more would have to be said about egalitarianism. "Equal entitlement for everyone" would suffice. But because we live in a world that is male-dominated, the fact is that egalitarianism requires the woman (and ultimately the couple) to take power and privilege away from the man that the culture (and perhaps even the man himself) feels is rightfully his and give it instead to her. In the eyes of the outside world, this will frequently make the woman look like a selfish bitch and the man like a damn fool or a wimp, but there's no way around it. The culture has given men in general and husbands in particular far more than their fair share of power and privilege, and the only way for a couple to be egalitarian is to shift some of that from the husband to the wife.

This relocation of power and privilege will frequently require the couple to resist even our most rational-looking cultural values, we said. Consider, for example, the not uncommon scenario in which a husband gets a job offer in another city where he can advance in his career and earn thousands more dollars per year. In a culture that values money, power, ambition, social status, professionalism, and men, it's hard not to be seduced into believing that the couple should just pick up and move, even if the wife would prefer to stay where they are. Unless they truly need or want the money, however, this apparently rational inclination to go where the better job is must be resisted, as must any tendency to give special consideration to the partner with the better job. In a sexist society, after all, it will almost always be the husband who is in the better career position, and the sexism that positions women and men unequally in the economic structure will thereby reproduce itself in the dynamics of the relationship.

Of course, not all men will be willing to give up power and privilege. A woman who takes herself seriously must thus be prepared for the possibility that the man who is currently her partner might not be willing to give up these advantages, in which case her only alternatives are to find a different man or to give up the idea of having a man altogether.

There is no need to be so pessimistic from the outset, however. Once a woman makes it clear that a shift to egalitarianism is what she really wants, the best men will willingly work with her to make it happen (including, if she's lucky, the man who is her partner), and still other men will change when and if she finally convinces them — and not necessarily with words alone — that they are not entitled to any extra measure of privilege. And not only that: they also have no choice about whether to give it up.

So much for empowerment. Let's move now to the nitty-gritty of strategy.

In the 1970s, women in long-term relationships with men (whether married or not) wanted to talk a lot about how to make the transition from a traditional division of labor to a more egalitarian division. As many of these women described the problem, it wasn't so much that the men in their lives wouldn't agree to do the work. It was, rather, that the men didn't do it soon enough or well enough or independently enough to satisfy the women. Hence everyone ended up feeling as bad as they had before, if not worse.

Although we had never made such a transition ourselves, we had a number of strategic suggestions. Here are a few of them:

One: Make a list together of who is to do what.

Two: Let the person who is responsible for doing a chore also get to judge whether the chore has been adequately performed. In other words, we said to the women in particular, don't think you can give up merely the doing of a chore. Realize that you must also be willing to give up control over how the chore is done.

Three: Let the person who is responsible for doing a chore also be responsible for remembering that the chore must be done in the first place. In other words, we again said to the women in particular, don't take on the role of always reminding the men in your lives what they have to do. It won't hurt the floor to be dirty. Within limits, it won't even hurt the baby to be hungry. And if you find it hard just to sit there while your partner isn't doing what you think he ought to be doing, then don't just sit there. Leave the room or, better yet, leave the house for a while. Chances are the baby will have been fed by the time you get back.

Four: Think about this responsibility for remembering what has to be done and for planning ahead (which we called the "executive" or "administrative" function) as one of the main things that has to be shared equally by the two of you. So don't think of yourselves as just having to divide up the physical work of chore-doing. Think of yourselves as also having to divide up the mental work of chore-remembering.

Five: If the man in your life completely refuses to cooperate in this project, make a list of the chores you are unilaterally defining as his rather than yours, and then stop doing them. You will surely precipitate a crisis, but sometimes it is only through revolution that change occurs.

I want to end this discussion of Daryl's and my egalitarianism as both lived experience and public performance with two of my most vivid memories from our days on the lecture circuit.

During one of our question-and-answer sessions, a middle-aged man raised his hand and said: "I found your presentation here tonight completely convincing, and I totally agree with you. But I'm curious: What is your opinion of the women's liberation movement?"

On another occasion, a middle-aged woman came to the podium at the end of a very long evening to speak to us in person. "I heard you a couple of years ago," she said, "and I came up afterwards to tell you that I didn't know what to do because my husband wouldn't let me go back to school, he wouldn't let me learn to drive, and he almost wouldn't let me come to your lecture. Well, I just want to tell you that I drove here tonight in my own car, I'm well on my way to getting my bachelor's degree, and this person here beside me is my new husband."

CHAPTER FIVE

Feminist Child-Rearing

Shortly before Emily was born, in 1974, I put an end to our public lecturing on egalitarianism and to interviews about our lives because I didn't want our children to become local celebrities, as we had become. Daryl and I did continue lecturing on egalitarianism in my undergraduate course on gender, however, and within a few years, I developed a second lecture for that course based on our lives, this one on the feminist child-rearing practices we had developed.

Until the 1990s, I rarely gave this lecture outside my class. As early as the mid-1980s, however, I did incorporate parts of it into my scholarly writing, and Daryl also wrote about it in his textbook on introductory psychology. As much as I may have once intended to protect my children's privacy, by the mid-1990s, the story Daryl and I told most often—about what happened to Jeremy the day he wore barrettes to nursery school—had become so well known that a feminist legal scholar used it (with my permission) as both the title and the prologue of a law review article on gender-specific dress requirements in the workplace.

I'll tell the barrettes story a little later. I mention it now only to highlight the fact that, although we were much less public about our feminist child-rearing than about our egalitarianism, here too we quickly transformed our private feminist practice into public feminist discourse. Hence I remember more about how I analyzed my life in public than how I lived my life on a daily basis.

I began thinking about feminist child-rearing in the late 1960s, when I read an influential article by the developmental psychologist Lawrence Kohlberg, in which he suggested that young children are rigidly gender-stereotyped in their thinking and acting not because of the way they are raised but because of their "cognitive-developmental stage." It is not our gender-stereotyped culture, in other words, that convinces our children (and especially our boys) to eschew anything and everything associated with the other sex, including toys, clothes, colors, and even people. No, this idea emerges naturally and inevitably from the child's own immature mind. No need to worry, though. With age and maturity will come a more advanced cognitive-developmental stage and hence a more flexible way of seeing both the self and the world.

"I don't believe this for a second," I thought to myself. It may be difficult to raise a gender-liberated child, but it is surely not impossible. And even the reason it's difficult is not primarily because of any cognitive limitation on the part of the child. It's because the child is situated in a culture that distinguishes ubiquitously on the basis of sex from the moment of birth. Given that social reality, moreover, it ought to be possible for even young children to be gender-liberated if we can inoculate them early enough and effectively enough against the culture.

Note the medical metaphor here. The culture's sex-and-gender system is like a bacterium that will infect you unless you are given a vaccination in advance to build up your resistance and perhaps even make you immune. Without such an inoculation, we can try to heal you once you have become infected, but an ounce of prevention is worth a pound of cure.

How are children to be protected against the culture's sex-and-gender system? I always describe inoculating our own children in two distinct phases.

During the first phase, our goal was to enable Emily and Jeremy to learn about both male-female difference and the body without simultaneously learning any cultural stereotypes about males and females or any cultural stigmas about the body. Put somewhat differently, our goal was to retard their gender education while simultaneously advancing their sex education.

To retard their gender education, Daryl and I did everything we could for as long as we could to eliminate any and all correlations between a person's sex and other aspects of life. For example, we took turns cooking the meals, driving the car, bathing the baby, and so on, so that our own parental example would not teach a correlation between sex and behavior. This was easy for us because we already had such well-developed habits of egalitarian turn-taking. In addition, we tried to arrange for both our children to have traditionally male and traditionally female experiences—including, for example, playing with both dolls and trucks, wearing both pink and blue clothing, and having both male and female playmates. This turned out to be easy, too, perhaps because of our kids' temperaments. Insofar as possible, we also arranged for them to see nontraditional gender models outside the home.

I remember telling my class I was so determined to expose our children to nontraditional models that when Emily was very young, I drove her past a particular construction site every day because a female construction worker was a member of the crew there. I never let on that it was always the same site and the same woman we were seeing because I wanted there to be a time in her life when Emily didn't even think of such women as unusual. More important, we never allowed there to be a time in our children's lives when they didn't know that some people had partners of their own sex and other people had partners of the other sex. This was both extremely easy and extremely important in our family because so many of our closest relatives were either lesbians or gay men. I'll say more about this a little later.

Another way we retarded our children's gender education was to monitor—even to censor—books and television. I had no qualms about limiting television to three hours a week because, in addition to being filled with gender stereotypes, it also kills children's brain cells (metaphorically speaking) by addicting them (again, metaphorically speaking) to a state of passivity. Books, in contrast, I hated even the thought of monitoring because I love books and wanted our children to love them, too. The problem is that if young children are allowed to sample freely from the world of children's literature, they will almost certainly be indoctrinated with the idea that girls and boys are not only different from each other but, even worse, that boys are more important. What else can one conclude, after all, when there are approximately ten boys in these stories for every girl and almost a hundred "boy" animals for every "girl" animal? (I'm not exaggerating.) Or when the few females who are in these books almost always stay indoors and at home—no matter what their age or species—while the males go outdoors and have adventures. Or, perhaps worst of all, when the females are so unable to affect their own environments that when good things happen to them, those things just fall out of the sky, whereas when good things happen to males, their own efforts have usually played a part in making them occur.

Not only did we censor books with traditional messages like these. For a time, we restricted our children's access even to feminist books like *William's Doll*. After all, for a child who doesn't yet know about the American cultural taboo with respect to boys and dolls, even a book that argues that it's all right for boys to have dolls is teaching a gender stereotype in the very process of trying to counter it.

To compensate for all this censorship, I worked hard to locate as many books as I could that were free of gender stereotypes. Ironically, this may have been easier in the 1970s than it is today because of the many small feminist collectives that specialized in producing such books then. And although I have no artistic talent, I was handy with my whiteout and magic markers, which I used liberally to transform one main character after another from male to female by changing the character's name, by changing the pronouns, and even by drawing long hair (and, if age-appropriate, the outline of breasts) onto the character's picture. Nor did I limit my doctoring to the main characters. I frequently changed even background characters who appeared in the illustrations from male to female because, if I didn't, the main character would be living in a world disproportionately populated by males.

The only time I remember this getting me into trouble was when I bought my children a Curious George book and decided to change the tall man in a yellow hat into a tall woman in a yellow hat. Never having heard of Curious George, I didn't know it was a series, and I also didn't know how very, very often the tall man would reappear. So, after making him a woman in the first book, I let her revert to a man in the rest of the books, thereby giving our children their first encounter with an implicit sex-change operation. They, bless their gender-liberated hearts, never seemed to notice.

When reading books aloud to our children, we also chose our pronouns carefully in order not to imply that all characters not wearing a dress or a pink hair ribbon must necessarily be male: "And what is this little piggy doing? Why, he or she seems to be building a bridge." Jeremy, in particular, seemed to hear this pronoun phrase as a single word because, for many years, he used the he-or-she form exclusively in almost all third-person contexts. If I asked Jeremy to tell me what Emily or Dad or some character in a book was doing, Jeremy would typically say that "heorshe" was doing whatever he or she was doing. I had thus unwittingly introduced a gender-nonspecific (but not neuter) third-person pronoun into the English language.

So much for retarding our children's gender education. To advance their sex education, we taught them about the body as early as we could. That is, we provided a clear and unambiguous bodily definition of what sex is. A boy, we said again and again, is someone with a penis and testicles; a girl is someone with a vagina, a clitoris, and a uterus; and whether you're a boy or a girl, a man or a woman, shouldn't matter unless and until you want to make a baby. Consistent with this premise, I also refused to provide a simple answer when the kids asked me in the supermarket or the park or wherever whether someone was a boy or a girl, a man or a lady. Instead I said (quietly, so as not to draw attention to myself) that I couldn't really tell without seeing under the person's clothes. When this answer began to be unsatisfactory, I complicated things a bit by conceding, for example, that since the person was wearing a dress, we might guess that he or she was a girl because, in this country, girls are the ones who more often wear dresses. As always, however, I concluded that one cannot know for certain without seeing under the person's clothes.

I was not the only person my children talked to, of course, and they were not dummies, so eventually they came to understand that I was playing a kind of game with them, and then we began to play the game together. One time I remember in particular, Emily brought me a magazine with a male face on the cover and teasingly said to me, "Look, Mom, it's a boy head." Knowing it was a game,

I immediately started laughing and said to her, "What do you mean it's a boy head? I don't see any penis on that head. How can it be a boy head if it doesn't have a penis?" Then she started laughing too. But even if everyone treated these interactions playfully, the game had a serious subtext: an important distinction must be made between an attribute that is merely correlated with sex and an attribute that is definitional of sex. Attributes that are merely correlated with sex, like clothing and hairstyle, don't really matter; only your genitalia define you as male or female.

Both the liberation that can come from having a narrow bodily definition of sex and the imprisonment that can come from not having such a definition are strikingly illustrated by what happened to Jeremy on the day he decided to wear barrettes to nursery school. When Jeremy came to me that morning and asked me to put barrettes in his hair, the first thought that came into my mind was: "Hmmm. I wonder if Jeremy knows that barrettes are 'just for girls.'" The next thought was the script I imagined the good liberal parent would now begin to read from. "Jeremy," this good liberal script would say, "you're certainly welcome to wear these barrettes to nursery school if you want to. It's fine with me. But there's something I need to tell you to help you make your decision. Even though our family thinks boys and girls should be able to do anything they want as long as it doesn't hurt anybody or break anything, a lot of other people still have the old-fashioned idea that some things are just for girls and other things are just for boys, and (can you believe it?!) barrettes are actually one of the things these people think of as just for girls. Now just because that's what some people think about barrettes doesn't mean you shouldn't wear them. But you probably should know ahead of time that if you do wear them, you might get teased a bit."

I myself said none of this, however, because I had vowed long before, never, in the domain of sex and gender, to be the carrier of the culture to my children. So with barrettes in his hair, off Jeremy went to nursery school.

When Jeremy came home that day, I was dying to find out what, if anything, had happened, but I didn't want to ask because I didn't want to make a big deal of it. I waited and waited for Jeremy to bring it up spontaneously. But he never did, not that day, not the next day, not for a long time. Then I forgot about it until one of his teachers asked me at a parent-teacher get-together if Jeremy had ever described what happened on the day he wore barrettes to nursery school. Several times that day, another little boy had asserted that Jeremy must be a girl, not a boy, because "only girls wear barrettes." After repeatedly insisting that "Wearing barrettes doesn't matter; I have a penis and testicles," Jeremy finally pulled down his pants to make his point more convincingly. The other boy was not impressed. He simply said, "Everybody has a penis; only girls wear barrettes."

But I didn't try to "teach the body" only to provide our children with a stereotype-free definition of male and female. I also tried to teach the body as a stigma-free foundation for sexuality.

Consistent with this goal, there was much nudity in our home on the part of both children and adults alike, and Daryl and I also carried out many of our bodily functions in the children's presence. In everyday language, this not only included peeing and pooping but even putting tampons in and taking them out. Making women's bleeding visible to both Emily and Jeremy at the earliest possible age was important, as I saw it, because just as I wanted them to know about the difference between males and females, and also about the existence of gay people, *before* they had the opportunity to learn any relevant cultural stereotypes or stigmas, so too I wanted them to learn about menstruation *before* they learned any cultural notions about women's bodies being polluted or women's blood being "yucky."

I apparently forgot to tell them one important fact about women's bleeding, however, or perhaps they were too young to assimilate it when I did tell them. At around age four, one of the kids (I now forget which one) revealed during a chat we were having while I was putting in a tampon that he or she thought I bled not just a few days every month but every day of every month. Perhaps this child was using peeing or pooping as the model here for bleeding. In any case, whichever child it was didn't seem particularly relieved to learn that women's bleeding was periodic rather than continuous. He or she just took in the information, which surely came with some further clarification about how babies are made.

The question of how babies are made quickly brings us to the topic of heterosexual intercourse, and that too was an aspect of the body we began to teach our children very early. For example, I clearly remember taking a bath with Emily when I was visibly pregnant with Jeremy (which would make Emily two), and I know we talked during that bath, and not for the first time, about the man's penis being inside the woman's vagina and squirting "seeds" which join up with the woman's egg, and about the baby's then growing from that seed-and-egg combination and eventually coming out head-first through the woman's vagina, just as the baby growing inside me would eventually do. (In retrospect, the one aspect of this discussion that baffles me is why I called sperm "seeds" when I called everything else by its technical name.)

Emily was always interested in these discussions, and she listened carefully and learned the facts exceedingly well, but we discovered when she was about five that in this domain, too, there was a funny misunderstanding. Not long after we moved to Ithaca, the four of us went to Toronto for a few days, where one of the highlights (in addition to riding the subway) was getting to see an animated documentary about birth control that was part of a special exhibition for children at the Ontario Science Museum. I can't quite visualize the two characters in this documentary anymore, but I know they were some kind of schematic male and female figures, complete with genitalia and internal physiology.

The animated cartoon showed a series of separate but similar sequences in which the male and the female joined together in the middle of the screen after moving toward one another from their starting points at opposite ends of the screen. In the first sequence, they were both clothed and, when they got together, they kissed. In all the remaining sequences, they were both nude; we could see that the male's penis was erect, and we could also see that the male's penis was inside the female's vagina when the two of them got together. We could see whatever other things made sense during any given sequence as well—for example, sperm coming out of the penis and going into the vagina, an egg coming out of the Fallopian tube and traveling down into the uterus, the sperm and egg meeting and becoming a fetus, and ultimately a baby growing and emerging from the vagina.

In the first nude sequence, no form of birth control was used; hence the joining of male and female produced a baby. In the remaining sequences, one or another form of birth control was used, and the point of each sequence was to show exactly how each particular form of birth control served as a barrier to reproduction. In the condom sequence, for example, the sperm was shown getting trapped inside the condom and never making it into the vagina. In the diaphragm sequence, the sperm was shown getting into the vagina but never making it into the uterus.

All four of us seemed to be enjoying the movie while we were watching it, but as soon as it was over, it became apparent that there was something about it Emily didn't understand. Daryl and I were having a hard time deciphering exactly what she didn't understand because she seemed able to answer every question we thought to ask her. Slowly, however, it became clear. I understand how to make a baby, she was essentially saying, and I also understand all the ways of stopping a baby from being made. But why, she kept asking, would people do those things to stop a baby from being made? At first we took her to be asking why people wouldn't want a baby, given that babies are so neat to have around, so we tried to answer that question, but that wasn't it. What she was asking, it turned out, was why people who didn't want to make a baby would ever put their penises and vaginas together in the first place. For her, in other words, birth control made no sense because heterosexual intercourse was about baby-making and nothing more. Clearly we had failed to communicate that heterosexual intercourse feels good and so people do it even when they don't want to make a baby. Once we explained that, Emily wasn't confused any longer.

If I had somehow misrepresented heterosexual intercourse as exclusively about baby-making, one of the reasons may have been that I wanted our children's understanding of love and sex (as opposed to their understanding of reproduction) to be fully grounded in the premise that there is nothing intrinsically special about heterosexuality as compared to homosexuality. I think Emily's learning about the pleasures of heterosexual intercourse did raise this issue for her because, as I recall, it was shortly after we saw the birth control movie that Emily asked me outright what my sister Bev and her partner, Roz, do together for love and pleasure. (I don't think she and I actually used the phrase "love and pleasure.") I replied that they do all the same things Dad and I do—except have a penis in a vagina. In other words, they hug and kiss and rub their bodies together and giggle. I don't recall if I also said (I hope I did) that they rub on each other's clitoris. I might have said so because Emily and I had already talked about how good it feels to rub on one's own clitoris, but I don't remember if I ever talked that explicitly to either of our children about nonreproductive sex between any two people, whether heterosexual or homosexual.

I remember another time when I did something embarrassing because Emily asked me to do it. Emily was probably about two years old, and we were sitting on the bathroom floor drying ourselves and talking after having taken a bath together. As was often the case when we were both nude, the talk turned to the body. Emily expressed a desire to look at her vagina and clitoris (which she called her "little toris"), and then at mine, in the mirror. After we did that for a while, we sang a little, still sitting on the floor in the nude, and then Emily started asking for kisses, as she did very often. Kiss my ear, she would say, and I would. Kiss my nose, and I would. Kiss my knee . . . kiss my shoulder . . . and so on through a whole array of body parts, including, on this particular day: kiss my vagina.

Whoops, I thought to myself. This is a request I didn't anticipate, and it is definitely making me a little anxious. But, I continued in my private monologue, I don't really think there's anything wrong with the request, and I don't want Emily to think there's anything wrong with it either. So maybe I'll just go ahead and grant her request because, if I don't, I will be communicating that her genitals need to be treated as a special and untouchable part of her body in a way I've never done before and I don't really want to do yet. Someday, that will probably be necessary, but it's not the base assumption I want to build on.

So I gave her a quick little peck on her vagina, and we moved on. She never asked me to kiss her vagina again, so it's possible that my giving her just a quick little peck rather than a great big nuzzle communicated indirectly that I wasn't so keen on this.

In the end, what I found most interesting about the whole experience was that I told virtually no one about it, and I feel some trepidation about making it public even now. This is not because I think I did anything wrong; I don't think that. Nor is it because I think sex between adults and children is perfectly acceptable; I don't think that, either. What I do think is that in our current cultural frenzy over child sexual abuse and pornography, we have gone way too far in the moralistic and puritanical direction of thinking all touching, all sensuality, and even all nudity is inherently wrong if it involves children. And that assumption is completely antithetical to how we raised our children.

When we lived in the warmish climate of northern California, Emily and Jeremy ran around nude almost all the time, both indoors and out, and I took dozens of photographs and movies of them, both nude and not nude, because I loved watching them play, and I loved trying to capture that play on film. But in the very years when I was taking these nude photographs for fun, serious professional photographers were being accused of trafficking in child pornography when they tried to publish or exhibit their own versions of such photographs as art. This is wrong. The child's nude body is not inherently pornographic nor is touching the child's nude body inherently abusive.

On a lighter note: Because our children were nude so much of the time when they were young, toilet training was a snap. When they began to pee or poop, they could immediately see it coming out, as could I. They thus learned very easily to rush to the toilet as soon as it started coming, and it wasn't much longer before they learned to anticipate its coming.

A colleague of mine told me years ago that she, too, had been open about nudity in the home when her children were young, but when her oldest son reached puberty, she said, she began to detect a leer in his eye whenever he saw her nude, and that embarrassed her, so she brought the nudity to an end. She thought I would probably need to do the same. I had no way of knowing exactly what the texture of the nudity was in her household, but I found it hard to believe that the adults in my household would suddenly find it embarrassing to be seen in the nude by either Emily or Jeremy. Maybe the kids would become embarrassed at some point, I speculated, but even that seemed unlikely given years and years of the kind of casual nudity we all experienced on a daily basis. As it turned out, I was right. Although there was a brief period during his early adolescence when Jeremy declined to be seen in the nude, the rest of us pretty much continued as we had before, with the exception of taking baths together, which we did gradually stop sometime around puberty. Eventually even Jeremy got over his embarrassment and there we all were again, doing whatever we happened to be doing in whatever state of undress.

By advancing our children's sex education and retarding their gender education, Daryl and I enabled them to learn their earliest lessons about sex and sexual difference without simultaneously learning the many cultural stereotypes and stigmas that typically accompany these lessons. But how were we to keep them from sliding over to the enemy side, so to speak, as they gradually began to hear the voice of the dominant culture? How, in other words, to keep them from forsaking these early lessons when they later began to realize, as they inevitably would, that their parents' beliefs about sex and sexual difference were different from those of most other people? This question brings me to the second phase of the children's inoculation process.

During this second phase, our overarching goal was to make our children skeptical of whatever conventional cultural messages about sex and gender they might be exposed to, whether from television, from books, from movies, from other people, or from anywhere else. More specifically, our goal was to provide them with the kind of critical feminist lens or framework that would predispose them to "read" the culture's conventional messages in an unconventional way. How did we go about trying to provide them with such a framework? In retrospect, four things we did seem particularly important.

The first thing we did—though I'm not sure we understood its relevance to our feminist goals when we did it—was to emphasize the theme of difference and diversity long before it was relevant to sex and gender. "Why are some of our friends not allowed to play in the nude, but we are?" our children would ask when they were young. "Why do other families say grace before meals but we don't? Why do we have to wear seat belts in the car when other kids don't have to? Why can cousin so-and-so drink Pepsi with dinner but we have to drink milk?" To these questions and dozens like them, our answer was always the same: Different people believe different things, and because they believe different things, they make up different rules for their children.

Few of these early diversity conversations focused on sex or gender. Nevertheless, they provided our kids with the underlying premise that different—and even contradictory—beliefs are the rule rather than the exception in a pluralistic society. This premise served as an excellent foundation for what we would later say about difference and diversity when our conversations turned to sex and gender, as they did when the kids started asking questions like: Why is some boy in Emily's nursery-school class not allowed to dress up in a princess costume for Halloween? Or, why is some girl in Jeremy's kindergarten class not allowed to sleep overnight in Jeremy's bedroom?

The second thing we did was to provide Emily and Jeremy with a nongendered way of reframing the many conventional messages about male-female difference that they began to hear when they were three or four or five years old. These messages came in many variations, but they all boiled down to the same idea: Boys and girls are different from each other in innumerable ways, as are women and men. We always responded with a script something like the following: Yes, it's true, some girls don't like to play baseball. But you know what? Other girls like to play baseball a lot (including, for example, your Aunt Bev and Melissa who lives across the street), and some boys don't like to play baseball at all (including your dad and Melissa's brother Billy). As soon as our children began to mouth the conventional cultural stereotypes about male-female difference, we extended our earlier discussions of difference and diversity by telling them that it's not males and females who are different from each other. It's people who are different from each other.

The third thing we did was to help them to understand that all cultural messages about sex and gender (indeed, all cultural messages about everything) are created, whether now or in the distant past, by particular human beings with particular beliefs and biases. The appropriate stance to take toward such messages is thus not to assume that they are either true or relevant to your own personal life but to assume instead that they merely convey information about the beliefs and biases of their creators.

Perhaps the most obvious example of my trying to teach this stance occurred when I sat down to read to Emily from her first book of fairy tales. An older relative had given her this book when she was four years old, and although I knew it would expose her to many gender stereotypes she had never seen before, I didn't want to hold back from reading it because I thought that would indirectly and inappropriately be a criticism of the gift-giver. Besides, I thought Emily would probably enjoy the fairy tales immensely, just as I had when I was a child. Once again the challenge was how to get her own "reading" of the fairy tales to subvert the culture's messages about males and females rather than support them.

I gave Emily a little feminist lecture before I started to read. "The fairy tales in this book," I said, "are wonderfully exciting, and I think you'll like them a lot, but you need to understand before we read them that they were written a *long looooong* time ago by people who had some very peculiar ideas about girls and boys. In particular, the people who wrote these fairy tales seemed to think that the only thing that matters about girls is whether they're beautiful or not beautiful, and the other thing they seem to think about girls is that they are the kind of people who always get themselves into trouble and then need to be saved by boys, who—according to these fairy-tale writers anyway—are naturally brave and smart. Now, I haven't read these particular fairy tales yet, but I did read a lot of other fairy tales when I was little, and I'm willing to bet that if you listen really carefully, you'll hear lots and lots of stories where a brave, wise boy rescues a beautiful girl, but what you won't ever hear is even one story where a brave, wise girl rescues a beautiful boy."

Emily loved the fairy tales, just as I thought she would, but after each one, she giggled with glee about how I had been right. "There's another one, Mom," she would say. "Aren't the people who made up these stories silly?"

Several years ago, a feminist colleague of mine was lamenting a question her preschool daughter had asked after watching *Mr. Rogers' Neighborhood* on television. "Why are kings royaler than queens?" her daughter had wanted to know. The question had troubled my colleague because she couldn't figure out how to use her daughter's question as a springboard for a feminist lesson. I knew immediately what I would say, but then I began to wonder what my kids would say, so I asked them (they were then maybe eleven and fourteen), and they both said basically the same thing: "Your friend should tell her daughter to think about who writes the script for *Mr. Rogers' Neighborhood.* If King Friday is more royal than Queen Sarah, it's not because kings *are* more royal than queens. It's because Mr. Rogers *thinks* kings are more royal than queens."

All this talk about difference and diversity is fine as far as it goes, but from a feminist perspective, not all beliefs and biases are equally valid. At some point, we also needed to convey to our children that the view of women and men represented by fairy tales, by the mass media, and by sexist and homophobic people of all ages everywhere is not only different or even "old-fashioned." It is plain and simply wrong. Accordingly, the fourth thing we did to provide our children with a critical feminist framework was to teach them about sexism and homophobia.

I distinctly remember how I introduced the concept of sexism to Emily because she immediately custom-fit my lesson to her own needs. I'm not sure why I chose the particular moment I did. Probably Emily had been quoting some classmate at nursery school who said that either Emily or some other girl couldn't do this activity or that because of her sex. Whatever the catalyst, I then read Emily a children's book I had been saving for just this occasion. The book was *Girls Can Be Anything,* by Norma Klein. The main characters are two kindergartners named Marina and Adam. Marina and Adam love to pretend that they are grown-up workers in a grown-up work environment. One day they're flying an airplane, another day they're staffing a hospital, a third day they're running a country. The plot has a certain redundancy. Both Marina and Adam want to pilot the airplane, but Adam says "girls can't be pilots . . . they have to be stewardesses"; both Marina and Adam want to be doctors, but Adam says "girls are always nurses"; and so on. I think you get the message. Luckily, Marina not only has feminist parents. She also has an abundance of extremely accomplished female relatives. Thus, when she complains to her parents at dinner about whatever sexist stereotype Adam asserted that day, her parents not only reply that of course girls can be pilots or doctors. They also remind her that one or another of her aunts is either a famous jet pilot who just logged her millionth mile (see her picture on the front page of the *New York Times*) or a famous heart surgeon who just performed her millionth heart transplant. I'm exaggerating a bit, but not much.

After we read this book together, Emily, then age four, spontaneously began to call anyone who said anything the least bit gender-stereotyped an "Adam Sobel," in the most contemptuous voice she could muster. Clearly Adam Sobelness (also known as sexism) was a concept she was ready for.

I don't remember exactly how I began to teach our children about homophobia, but I can reconstruct the general outline of what happened. Remember that they always knew that my sister, Bev, and Roz were partners. At some point, I think one of them said something to me about Bev and Roz being married, and I think I said in reply that they would be married if they could be, but they were only "like married" because of evil laws that prevented people of the same sex who loved each other from getting married. I think I may have told them at the same time that there used to be other evil laws that didn't allow people of different races to marry.

It used to be that when I lectured to my class about how we raised our children, the story that produced the strongest reactions, both positive and negative, was about Jeremy and his barrettes. But now that I have talked to my class on a few occasions about how we dealt with adolescent sexuality, I realize it is here that we have been the most radical. We weren't trying to be radical, mind you. We were merely trying to treat our children's developing sexuality as healthy and natural. But if Dr. Joycelyn Elders can be forced to resign as Surgeon General of the United States because she dared to say in public that the schools should treat masturbation as a natural part of sexuality, no wonder my students think us so radical—because we, of course, considered Dr. Elders one of the few sane voices coming out of our government on the subject of sexuality.

In American public-school health classes, sex (especially adolescent sex) is typically categorized as one of the triumvirate of vicious vices, along with alcohol and drugs. I, however, think it should be categorized instead as one of the many developmental tasks—along with walking, talking, reading, writing, crossing streets, and driving—that need to be mastered on the way to maturity.

In keeping with this view, I stocked our children's bookshelves with every educational book on sex and birth control that I could find, even before they reached puberty. And not only our children, but our children's friends, devoured these books. Their favorite, as I recall, and mine as well, was *Our Bodies, Ourselves,* written primarily for adult women by the Boston Women's Health Book Collective. (Impressed with my own cleverness, I tried stocking their bookshelves a few years later with college guidebooks. It didn't work as well.) But this isn't the radical part.

Even more in keeping with the view that learning to be sexual with other people is a developmental task, I made the decision early on that it would be no more appropriate to expect our children to take their first sexual steps alone in a drunken fraternity party or the backseat of a car than to expect them to take their first street-crossing steps alone in the middle of Broadway. Especially for a young woman, heterosexual sex in particular can be so risky an enterprise that it seems negligent for parents to do what our cultural norms seem to tell them to do: that is, to treat adolescent sexuality as so taboo that their children are forced not only to keep it secret from them but also to do it in places where they have no safety net. No wonder so many young women have unwanted pregnancies, and no wonder so many more young women have sexual things done to them against their will.

Maybe what we did as the parents of two adolescents could only be done in a very large house, but we not only assumed that Emily and Jeremy would begin to experiment sexually. We also told them that, if and when they began to do so, it would be fine with us (indeed, we would prefer it) if they did so in the relative privacy—and safety—of their own third-floor bedrooms, and with us at home downstairs to serve as a behind-the-scenes (and, we hoped, a never-to-be-called-on) support system. Part of our thinking here was that a young woman in particular would be much more confident and assertive on her own home territory (especially knowing that she has supportive parents downstairs) than she would be in most of the other situations where sex usually happens, and hence she would be much less likely to relinquish all control of the sexual encounter to the boy. This explicit treatment of our children's own home as a safe space for sexual experimentation is the radical part of what we did.

I recently learned that at Cornell University, where Daryl and I are still on the faculty, only the fraternities but not the sororities are allowed to serve alcohol at their parties. One consequence of this double standard is that most of the big weekend parties, and much of the heterosexual sex that undergraduate women later describe as unwanted, takes place on the boys' home territory rather than the girls'. Perhaps if the girls got to party in their own sorority houses, whatever heterosexual sex was going to happen would be more likely to happen in the girl's bedroom rather than the boy's, and with her so-called sisters outside the door rather than his so-called brothers. And perhaps, under those circumstances, we wouldn't have as much unwanted sex, or even date rape, on the campus as we do now.

We did one more thing consistent with my view of adolescent sexuality as a learning process, and that was to give our children the same feminist critique of how our culture defines sex that I had been giving my undergraduates for years. "What does it mean," I ask my undergraduates, "when a heterosexual couple says 'We had sex last night' or even 'we made love'?" They all agree. It means *both* that the man's penis was in the woman's vagina (or possibly, given that it's the 1990s, in the woman's mouth) *and* that the man had an orgasm. The woman may have had an orgasm, too, but even if she didn't, the couple would still say "we had sex." On the other hand, if the man didn't have an orgasm, the couple would probably not say they had sex. Instead, they would say (if they said anything at all) that they had "just fooled around." Well, I say in reply, no wonder the statistics show so many more men than women having orgasms during heterosexual sex. "Having heterosexual sex" means vaginally stimulating the man's penis until he reaches orgasm. It doesn't mean stimulating the woman's clitoris (or any other part of her body, for that matter) until she reaches orgasm. This may be fine for baby-making, but as a definition of sex or pleasure outside the context of procreation, it is completely male-centered. Not only does it all but ignore the woman's clitoris and thereby make the woman's orgasm unlikely. It also puts the woman at risk for pregnancy even though there are plenty of other satisfying sexual things to do that would not put her at such risk. The bottom line in this little lecture is that rather than continuing to think about penis-in-vagina heterosexual intercourse as the only real (or grown-up) sexual act and everything else as just peripheral, both my students—and my adolescent children—might want to begin thinking about penis-in-vagina intercourse as but one possibility (and not necessarily the best possibility) among many sexual options.

This feminist fantasy has several implications. First, there is no longer any preset script for the sexual encounter, no preset goal or target toward which all sexual activity is directed. Second, it redefines sex as a playful pleasuring of the body and the sexual encounter as an open-ended interaction that needs to be custom-choreographed by every new set of participants (and even, to some extent, on every occasion). It implies that the participants in a sexual encounter always need to figure out *together* both what they want (and don't want) to do and what they want (and don't want) done to them in order to both give and receive bodily pleasure.

As I see it, this redefinition is especially important for heterosexual women because it gives them much more opportunity than they now have to tailor their sexual experiences to their own needs and desires. It is also especially important for adolescents because it enables them to be as passionately and orgasmically sexual as they wish to be but without necessarily incurring either the risks associated with penis-in-vagina intercourse or the feeling that, if they're not having penis-in-vagina intercourse, they are somehow missing out on "the real thing."

During most of Emily's and Jeremy's public school years, Daryl was heavily involved in the local chapter of Planned Parenthood, serving several times as either president or vice president. Family conversation at the dinner table thus regularly drifted to sex-related topics—for example, whether Planned Parenthood should begin an abortion service and, if so, whether they should use laminaria to help open the cervix; how to handle the antiabortion protests when they did start their abortion service; whether they could do anonymous AIDS testing or merely confidential AIDS testing; how much training the staff would need before it could begin giving Norplant as a birth control method; what strategies to use to persuade the Ithaca elementary schools to let the local Planned Parenthood redesign their sex education programs, and, once the school system agreed, how exactly to shape the curriculum. One dinner conversation I particularly remember happened the day Planned Parenthood was giving out free condoms. Daryl brought a few home for the kids to see. After dinner was over, the kids immediately put them to good use: they rounded up all the other neighborhood kids and had a rip-roaring water balloon fight. In our household, talking about sex (and our culture's conservative politics with respect to sex) was thus as free and easy an activity, and also as daily an activity, as talking about television or sports might be in another household.

By the time Emily and Jeremy reached middle school, there was yet another reason why both sex and the cultural politics of sex were so frequently discussed in our household: All of Daryl's and my siblings had turned out to be gay. The kids had always known about my sister, Bev, as I've already mentioned. Both they and we learned about Daryl's sister, Robyn, almost as soon as she fell in love with her first female lover, after two unhappy marriages. We waited until they were in middle school, however, to tell them about Daryl's brother, Barry, because he never did come out to his mother or father, and we didn't want the kids to have to keep that kind of secret from their grandparents until they seemed mature enough emotionally to handle the responsibility.

When I first made the decision to inoculate our children against our culture's rampantly conservative sex and gender politics, I had no way of knowing that not only their aunts and their uncle, but even their mother and father would later turn out to be gay. Lucky for everyone involved that I was probably one of the most gay-positive married women with children in the history of the world. Of course, most families have at least one member who turns out to be gay, so it is not just our children who would be well served by an inoculation against homophobia.

Up to now, this discussion of our feminist child-rearing has made little or no distinction between raising a daughter and raising a son. That's not surprising, given that my vision of utopia has always been so genderless. But now I want to talk about what special challenges I thought we would face in each case, how we tried to deal with those challenges, and what some of our children's lived experiences were in the outside world insofar as they related to being either the male or the female child from a fanatically feminist home. I'll begin with Emily because she came first.

I remember conceptualizing only one special challenge when I thought about raising a daughter, and that was how to keep her as big and as strong and as loud and as confident and as assertive and as full of her own needs and desires as she was on the day she was born. How, in other words, to keep her from shrinking her sense of self into the conventional confines of a girl rather than a kid, a woman rather than a person, a selfless giver-upper of *both* arms on those connected airport seats rather than a tenacious fighter for her fair share of all the resources life has to offer.

When we first moved to Ithaca in 1978, we placed an ad in the local newspaper for a daytime babysitter and interviewed four applicants in person after ruling out many more on the basis of a telephone interview. One of these applicants aroused so much emotion in me that I vividly remember the interview to this day. She had interacted warmly with both Emily, then age four, and Jeremy, age one, and they both seemed to like her, as did Daryl and I. She was also bright, energetic, confident, college-educated, experienced with children, and full of great ideas for creative activities. But, she said before she left our house, she did believe in limits more than we seemed to, and she thought she should tell us that. For example, although she too thought that kids should have free access to the use of pots and pans as toys, she would want to make only one of the kitchen cabinets available to them and keep the others off limits. Also she said she thought Emily in particular needed a little more "taming."

No way, I thought to myself: that is exactly the opposite of what Emily needs, given that she is a girl and that the outside world tames girls all too much already. Better she should stay a little undertamed. Better she should get to live, at least for a while, in an underregulated world where the default assumption is yes, you can, unless someone has a good reason why you can't, a world where—as we always told our kids—you can do anything you want as long as it doesn't hurt anybody or break anything. So if tonight you want to sleep in your clothes rather than in your pajamas or on the floor instead of in the bed, why not? And if tomorrow you want to play outside in the nude, that's fine, too. You will just have to learn someday that the next-door neighbors want you to have at least your underpants on when you cross their property line, but there's plenty of time to learn that when that time comes. And if the experience in the meanwhile of getting to live in a less fettered world fosters a certain antiauthoritarian intolerance of bureaucracy and convention, so much the better as far as I'm concerned.

This example of playing outdoors in the nude should bring to mind all the things I said earlier about wanting to "teach the body" in as stigma-free a way as I could. And I'm sure I emphasized this as much as I did in part because our first-born child was a girl, and I felt that a girl in our society would especially need to be inoculated against the ubiquitous cultural message that there is something fundamentally wrong with the female body in its natural form. Why else, after all, would we women have to watch our weight so meticulously, shave our legs and underarms, douse ourselves in perfume, cover ourselves with makeup, augment or diminish our breasts, curl or straighten our hair, and so on ad nauseam? So when Emily asked for the first time, at about age three, why some very made-up woman in a restaurant had "all that stuff" on her face, all I could say, and I think I said it with a perfectly straight face, was that the woman wanted to look like a clown. As outrageous as this now sounds to me, the reason I said it was that I didn't want Emily, at such a tender age, to have to conceptualize the wearing of all that makeup as a necessary part of being a grown-up woman.

The underlying issue here isn't just makeup, of course. I wanted to enable Emily to think of a woman's body—and her own body in particular—in ways that had nothing to do with adornment and everything to do with the power and strength and confidence of her own physicality. So although she wasn't the kind of physically precocious kid who crawled and climbed and pushed and pulled and grabbed faster and harder than other kids, I fostered Emily's physical development in every way I could, from tossing her up in the air when she was an infant to roughhousing with her when she was a toddler to sending her to the trampolines and swinging rings and balancing beams of "kindergym" when she was a preschooler to encouraging her to participate in every kind of team sport when she was in school. I still have the team photographs to show how well she mastered the stance and swagger of all those sports, even if she didn't excel at the game itself. But I'm not being fair here; she mastered much more than that, as I realized the first time I saw her confidently spike a soccer ball with her head.

Thanks to Title IX's encouragement of women's athletics in the public schools, lots of other girls were learning to spike those balls as well. But to my surprise, few girls in Emily's social group were allowed the independent mobility in the outside world that I thought was at least as important for a girl as for a boy. I didn't notice this difference in kindergarten, when Emily asked for blanket permission to be allowed to walk home from school instead of taking the school bus whenever she felt like it rather than having to ask for a note at breakfast if she wanted to walk on that particular day. But by the time middle school rolled around, it was clear that few of her girlfriends wanted or got the freedom of movement that Emily took for granted.

When Emily was in eighth grade and Jeremy was in sixth, Daryl and I spent a year at Harvard, during which time the four of us lived in Lexington, a historically famous, very white, upper-middle-class town. What I found most interesting about that town was that although the sixth-grade boys Jeremy knew all liked, on occasion, to take the subway into Cambridge and hang around Harvard Square, the eighth-grade girls Emily knew all preferred to take the local bus to Burlington Mall. I don't know if these girls would have been allowed to take the train into Cambridge or Boston if they had wanted to, but I do know that in the whole year we were there, Emily could get only one of her friends to take the "T" with her, and that friend was a boy. Part of what was going on here, I think, is that the families of most of Emily's girlfriends had moved to a town like Lexington in the first place because they wanted to protect their children—

especially their daughters—from what they saw as the evils of the big city. By the eighth grade, those daughters had internalized their parents' anxieties.

The parental anxieties that truly took me by surprise, however, were the ones I saw in safe and peaceful Ithaca, New York, where a not insignificant number of Emily's girlfriends, even at high-school age, were still so closely monitored that they didn't even have the freedom to walk to the downtown area known as the Commons after school without getting special permission ahead of time from their parents. Nor were they encouraged to get around independently by traveling on city buses. In contrast, I wanted Emily to be making her own decisions about where, when, and with whom to do things and go places, so she entered high school with one and only one after-school rule: that she be home by 5:30. As often as not, she came home much earlier—and with a gang of male and female friends.

When Emily was five years old, her kindergarten teacher told us that she functioned as a kind of bridge between the girls in the class and the boys, who would otherwise not have been playing with one another so productively. I doubt that Emily was still playing the same role in high school, but she did still have at least as many male friends as female friends, just as she had in kindergarten and nursery school. I don't know whether her ability to get on so well with boys had anything to do with her experience in rough-and-tumble physicality, because the boys she was friendly with were rarely the roughest. But whatever the reason, I was glad that, at every age, she constructed both a self and a social world big enough to incorporate both sexes.

When you're raising children, you never know in advance what impact your child-rearing practices will have on them. Even in retrospect, it's rarely clear which things would be worth doing again and which would be better never repeated. So it was gratifying when

Emily managed to escape from a group of muggers at Mardi Gras in New Orleans at age twenty-one, in part, she later told me, because of something I had drummed into her head when she was in nursery school.

The original occasion was probably a time when some little tyke had taken a toy away from Emily that she wasn't finished playing with, or maybe had teased her or pushed her or hit her. What I told her to do if anything like this should happen again, as it surely would, was "Yell NO in as big and loud a voice as you can make, and that kid will know you mean business and leave you alone." We practiced that loud NO together in a game of making our voices as big and as loud as we could.

I know that when I taught Emily that lesson, I was hoping somewhere in the back of my mind that it would help her to raise holy hell—and to scare the bejesus out of some boy—if she ever found herself anywhere near a situation of acquaintance rape. So I was pleased when she told me that when she and two friends were surrounded and accosted by a group of teenagers in a kind of tunnel at Mardi Gras, the first thing that came to her mind was my telling her to yell NO as loud as she could. She embellished the NO to fit the circumstances as she did it: she yelled, she punched, she pushed, and she broke free. Her two friends got a little more roughed up than she did, and one also had some money stolen, but luckily no weapons were used and no one was seriously injured.

If I were surrounded and accosted by those teenage muggers, would I have managed to do what Emily did? I don't know the answer to that question any more than I know whether I could learn to spike a soccer ball with my head. But I'm glad my daughter can do those things, and I know she might not have been able to do them had she been more "tamed."

Let's move on now to Jeremy.

Time and time again during the past twenty years, I have heard feminist mothers worry aloud about the same three things related to their sons:

How to deal with the "boys will be boys" phenomenon when they are young. In other words, what to do about their seemingly universal predilection for aggressive play with other boys, for meanness toward girls, and for guns.

How to prevent them from turning into *men* (said contemptuously) when they are older. Among other things, this seems to mean: how to keep them from becoming closed off emotionally, from thinking they know more than everyone else does, and from believing that they are naturally entitled to more rights and benefits than the women around them.

How to continue loving your sons even if you can't prevent them from becoming stereotypical boys and men. And/or as a variation on this, how to keep respecting yourself as a feminist if you do continue loving them.

I didn't worry about any of these issues when I discovered that my second child was a boy, perhaps because I thought Daryl was a perfectly OK kind of man and so Jeremy probably would be too, especially given the kind of household he would grow up in. As it turned out, I never did have to deal with the "boys will be boys" phenomenon. I know there's a belief in our society that a predilection for guns, trucks, action figures, war toys, aggressive play with other boys, and meanness toward girls is all but inevitable in boys, but it's not true. Whether because of their biology or their environment or some combination of the two, not every little boy likes this kind of macho stuff, and Jeremy was one of those little boys who didn't, as was his father before him and his Uncle Barry and his cousin Jack and, now that I think about it, probably also his Grandpa Darwin and maybe even his Grandpa Pete.

I remember one picture book Jeremy particularly liked me to read to him when he was one or two years old. It was about a lonely little bear who wandered around on her birthday looking for a friend to play with, but every friend she went looking for was either not at home or already busy—as we, the readers, learned with every disappointed turn of another page. Jeremy loved having me read this book to him, but after a few readings, he would let me read it in only one particular way. I had to skip past all the many sad pages, which were probably 90 percent of the book, and read only the final two or three happy pages, in which the little bear comes back home and discovers to her joy that the reason none of her friends could play with her that day was that they were all at her house preparing a surprise birthday party for her.

In retrospect, it is not surprising to me that the little boy who felt such deep empathy for this little bear would have only female friends during his preschool and early elementary school years. Nor is it surprising to me, especially given his family background, that in the fourth grade, this boy would also be the only male in his elementary school who chose to spend every Tuesday afternoon for six weeks in an afterschool class where he learned to make his own teddy bear from scratch. Finally, it is not surprising to me that the teddy bear he made in that class, whose name is Loysha, still keeps him company wherever he lives.

But it would be misleading to represent Jeremy as just an empathic little boy surrounded by girls and teddy bears, because such a portrait fails to include what is perhaps most distinctive about Jeremy, namely, that he has an extraordinary interest in and an extraordinary aptitude for mathematics. It may be testimony to Jeremy's empathy that after a few readings of the lonely little bear book, he wanted me to read only the happy ending, but it is even greater testimony to his mathematical mind that this was one of the few stories in which he showed any interest at all. In most other books, he just wanted me to turn the pages so we could read the page numbers together. By the time he was three or four, something he occasionally liked to do himself was to open one of our Great Books of the Western World volumes, turn to the table of contents, note that the chapter numbered Roman numeral I was supposed to begin on page 4, turn to page 4 to see that Chapter I really did begin there, turn back to the table of contents, note that chapter II was supposed to begin on page 67, turn to page 67, and so on through the entire volume.

Even when Jeremy was as young as two or three years old, he thus spent most of his waking hours playing with neither girls nor teddy bears. Instead, he played inside his own head, and frequently on the computer, with abstract symbol systems. And when people asked me how such a little pipsqueak could deal with such abstractions, I used to say: "For other children and even for you and me, numbers may be abstractions. But for Jeremy, numbers are his friends."

For a fanatical feminist mother like myself, Jeremy's mathematical giftedness could have been a nightmare. After all, mathematics is a field in which few American women have yet entered the highest levels, and that gender disparity could have easily made Jeremy even more disrespectful of women's intelligence than most boys and men are. And not only that, from the time he was three or four years old, Jeremy has been so praised, so rewarded, and so generally fussed over for his mathematical brilliance that he could have even more easily developed the kind of intellectual male arrogance that treats not just women but everyone who is not an intellectual peer as subhuman.

But ironically enough, Jeremy's mathematicality seems to have made him less arrogant than other males in our male-dominated society. I think there are at least two reasons for this. First, mathematics has passionately engaged Jeremy's mind from the time he was two years old, and it has also given him as secure a sense of who he is in the world as any individual could possibly need. In his whole life, Jeremy has thus never had either the time or the psychological motivation to tear other people down in order to build himself up. Second, as much as Daryl and I tried to nurture Jeremy's aptitude for mathematics, from the time he was very young, we tried to make him sensitive to the inadequacy other people might feel because of his mathematical aptitude. I think we did a decent job teaching him this lesson. But who knows? Given his empathy for that little bear, maybe he would have figured it out by himself.

I said earlier that I never worried much about the issues that other feminist mothers of boys seemed to worry about, and it was just as well because those issues never did become problems for me. Something I did worry about, however, was that if Jeremy spent so much of his time inside his own head solving math problems, then he might not hear, let alone assimilate, the many feminist messages I was always sending him. As it turned out, I needn't have worried about that, either. Although it is true that Jeremy's receptors to the outside world were turned off a lot of the time, nevertheless, the feminist messages in our household were so pervasive and, *as a boy,* his own gender nonconformity (including, for example, making his own teddy bear) bumped up against the outside world enough of the time that he himself became a passionate and outspoken feminist by the time he was in elementary school. I say *as a boy* because I think nontraditional girls in our society now have so much freedom to cross the gender boundary (by playing sports, for example, or wearing pants and having short hair) that they are not nearly so likely as nontraditional boys to discover on the basis of their own experience that the world of gender is still a prison.

But as a boy, Jeremy couldn't help discovering this. Consider the moment, for example, when even I, his fanatical feminist mother, who had vowed never to serve as the carrier of the culture's gender system to her children, ended up serving not only as a carrier of the culture but as a prison guard. It was during a sabbatical year in California when Jeremy asked if he could please wear the one pink, ruffly, ankle-length dress that Emily had ever owned (which she had now outgrown) to his first-grade class in an elementary school where we were completely unknown to the teachers, the principal, and the other parents.

"Oh no," I said to myself. "How in the world am I going to deal with this? Maybe if I were home in Ithaca, I could find a way to say yes, but I don't feel like dealing with whatever the fallout might be in an unfamiliar place, and I'm pretty sure there will be fallout." So I tucked my tail between my legs and mouthed the good liberal script. In other words, I told Jeremy that he couldn't wear Emily's long, pink, ruffly dress to school because it could produce too big a problem for us all. If he wanted to wear it at home, he could do that anytime he liked. I think Jeremy did wear the dress once or twice as a nightgown, but neither that nor anything else could have compensated for what Jeremy and I both lost that day, which was our innocence.

I, of course, was not the only person in Jeremy's childhood who ever tried to keep him from straying into female territory, and, in time, Jeremy learned to resist these border guards, one and all. He wasn't quite ready to resist in the second grade when he got teased for wearing Strawberry Shortcake sneakers to school, so after a while he gave them up. But when he asked the salesperson for powder-blue sneakers in the fourth grade and the salesperson said he couldn't have them because they came only in girls' sizes, Jeremy insisted that the salesman bring those shoes for him to try on. Finally, when he bought himself a bright pink backpack in the fifth grade and his peers teased him so much that even I finally said I would be willing to buy him a new backpack if the teasing was becoming intolerable, he said, "No way, Mom, and it's not because I care all that much about what color my backpack is. It's because those sexist kids should not be able to dictate what color backpack I can and cannot wear." I couldn't have said it better myself.

CHAPTER SIX

My Unorthodox Career

In *Writing a Woman's Life,* Carolyn Heilbrun argues that, although scholars of Virginia Woolf have been angrily critical of Woolf's husband, Leonard, and appropriately so, for making the particular medical decisions about her that he did and in the way that he did, "marrying Leonard was the wisest thing Virginia did. . . . He made her writing life possible." Nigel Nicolson, whom Heilbrun quotes, takes a similar view: "[Virginia] deeply respected [Leonard's] . . . judgment on what meant most to her, her writing; and he, lacking the flight of soaring imagination and recognizing that she possessed it, shielded her, watched her fluctuating health, nurtured her genius, and with instinctive understanding left her alone in a room of her own, while he remained always available in the common room between them."

I hesitate to begin this chapter with these quotations because I do not want even one reader to think that I see either genius in my own

137

work or a lack of imagination in Daryl's. I do not. But the quotations still resonate deeply for me, because, by being always available to me and supportive of me and by also seeing in me an unconventional creativity, Daryl may have made possible not only my writing life but my whole unorthodox career.

When I was nineteen years old and a junior in college, Bob Morgan, the undergraduate psychology professor for whom I had written my college autobiography, called me into his office one day to tell me that he thought I would make an excellent psychiatrist and I should consider going to medical school when I graduated. Barely able to contain my excitement, I raced to a pay phone and called my mother. Why was I so excited? Looking back, I think it was because his suggestion shifted my vision of myself not so much around gender as around class, and thereby also began to shift my vision of a possible future. Would I have been able to build such a future had I not met and married Daryl Bem within the next fourteen months? I'll never know the answer to that question. But I do know that just as Morgan's almost passing comment about psychiatry validated what was probably already a deep well of intellectual and professional desire, so Daryl's support for almost thirty years enabled me both to define and to actualize those desires.

As much as I wanted the opportunity to train at a top psychology department, my graduate education was not very helpful intellectually. How could it have been? I lived in Ann Arbor for only sixteen months, and, for ten of those months, my sister and all her difficulties were with me.

Looking back, I had only one truly valuable experience in graduate school. My adviser, David Birch, was an experimental psychologist who had done most of his prior research on motivation in rats, but now he had a grant to study motivation—more specifically, "verbal self-control"—in humans. For my first-year research project, he wanted me to do one of the studies he had already designed and included in his grant proposal. This is standard operating procedure in graduate departments of psychology, but the study didn't interest me, so Birch gave me until the following Tuesday to come up with a study of my own. I did have an idea, and I talked about it at length with Daryl. By the time Tuesday rolled around, the two of us had it in workable form. Birch approved it, and from that moment on, he acted as if I had creative research ideas. Like the undergraduate professor who suggested I go into psychiatry, he led me to see myself as having special potential.

Other than that, nothing in my graduate school experience was educationally memorable. I took the required courses covering ten areas of psychology and then chose to concentrate in developmental psychology because it had so few additional requirements that I would be able to return to Pittsburgh after only a year and a half in residence. In addition, David Birch could still be my adviser. I received my Ph.D. at the ripe age of twenty-three, just three years after I had graduated from college.

But even if I had not yet developed either a broad intellectual base or a serious intellectual project, I had done two empirical studies based on my own ideas, one for my first-year project and the other for my dissertation, and the first of these had already been published as a single-author article in a strongly refereed journal. When it came time to look for a job in the middle of my third year as a Ph.D. student, on paper at least, I was ahead of most of my peers, few of whom had published anything while in graduate school. That is no longer the case. Today, a psychology graduate student who hasn't at least coauthored one paper with a faculty member will have difficulty on the job market.

Another difference between then and now is that academic jobs were not openly advertised in the late 1960s. Instead, a faculty member in a department with an opening would call some colleagues he respected at other universities (and I say "he" here because it almost always was a he) and ask whether anyone noteworthy was graduating that year. No matter how good a student you were, the only way you could become an applicant was to be recommended by a faculty member who was himself someone people thought to call for a recommendation. This old-boy network enabled every sort of discrimination, which is why open advertising of academic jobs—and allowing applicants to apply for any job they wished—was finally instituted in the 1970s.

In early 1968, David Birch could think of at least three or four good departments that might want to hire me, so he was surprised when not even one department showed any interest. He never found out for certain what the problem was, but he had a hypothesis. At the end of his recommendation letter, he mentioned that I had a husband who was also an academic psychologist; perhaps, he said, none of the departments to which he had written wanted that strange new species known today as the dual-career couple.

At some point the possibility of a full-time tenure-track position emerged in the Carnegie Tech psychology department. So I gave a job talk in which I presented my two studies, I spent a day interviewing individually with all the faculty, and they hired me. First, of course, they had to make sure that Carnegie Tech had no anti-nepotism rule prohibiting the hiring of a married couple, which it didn't—perhaps, Daryl and I used to joke, because it never occurred to Andrew Carnegie that a woman would apply.

I spent two years as a full-time faculty member at Carnegie Tech, from September 1968 to August 1970. During those years, both the school and I went through our own respective identity crises. Carnegie Tech struggled with the question of whether to remain a technical college specializing in engineering and science or to become a university. It chose the latter course and changed its name in so doing to Carnegie-Mellon University. I struggled with the question of whether I really wanted to be a research psychologist.

Part of my problem was that although I thoroughly enjoyed teaching, I wasn't doing any research at all, and it wasn't because I didn't have time. I had so much time that Daryl and I would leave the office every day at 3:45 in order to catch the most convenient ramp onto the expressway before it closed at 4 P.M. No, the reason was that no research question interested me enough. So I went to my office every morning. I taught my classes. I advised my students. I gave public lectures with Daryl on the evils of gender stereotyping and the virtues of egalitarianism. And then when I went home, I talked a lot to Daryl about whether I shouldn't perhaps be working at a small liberal arts college where I wouldn't be expected to do research, like Chatham College, for example, only two or three miles away.

I never did explore the idea of teaching at Chatham College because, in my second year at Carnegie-Mellon, I found what would become my intellectual passion for years to come. I no longer remember the particular moment when I suddenly had the idea of doing research in the service of my feminist politics. But at some point I started to feel uncomfortable about the fact that Daryl and I had no empirical evidence, no *data,* to back up the claims we were making in our public lectures about how much better it would be for both women and men if society would stop stereotyping virtually all aspects of the human personality as either feminine or masculine; how much better, in other words, if everyone were free to be their own unique blending of temperament and behavior, if everyone could be "androgynous."

Then the idea occurred to me: I could gather the relevant data myself. I could do empirical research on the question of whether so-called androgynous people might be healthier in some way than more conventionally gendered people. And by doing this, I could also introduce the concept of androgyny into the psychological literature and thereby begin to challenge the traditional assumption of the mental health establishment that a mature, healthy identity necessarily requires women to be feminine and men to be masculine.

From that moment on, my political, personal, and professional passions fed one other during every moment of the day. I had not just a job; I had a mission. But it was a mission for which I had no formal training and little in the way of direct background knowledge. So I sequestered myself in the Carnegie-Mellon library and immersed myself in the psychological literature on gender.

Somewhere in the midst of my solitary conversion to feminist scholarship (a conversion which, unbeknown to me, was simultaneously taking hold of many other female scholars in many other fields), Daryl and I got a telephone call from social psychologist Phil Zimbardo at Stanford University inviting us to spend the 1970–71 academic year as visiting faculty there. We probably can, we said, but why are you asking? That is, are you folks interested only in having us visit, or is there a possibility of our being offered regular jobs at the end of the year? Yes, indeed, the possibility does exist, Phil replied, but we first need to see, among other things, what it feels like to have a married faculty couple in our midst.

Even during our first five years together at Michigan and Carnegie-Mellon, Daryl helped to make my career possible in many ways. First, he was willing to take a leave from CMU so that I could go to Michigan for graduate school, which provided structural support. As far back as my first-year research project, he was also willing (and even eager) to talk about my ideas with me, which provided substantive support. When I was having my first identity crisis about whether to remain a research psychologist or switch to a teaching career, he always listened to my concerns and made it clear that anything I wanted to do was fine with him, which provided emotional support. When I finally decided to do feminist research, he agreed that I should not worry about trying to maintain a sharp distinction between science and politics because no such distinction was viable anyway, which provided ideological support. And then, of course, there was the fact that my decision to do feminist research itself grew out of our joint lectures on egalitarianism, which in turn grew out of our lived experience together as an egalitarian couple, which means that he (or we as a unit) provided me with epistemological support. I haven't even mentioned yet how I got my jobs, not only at Carnegie-Mellon but later at Stanford, which brings me full circle to the kind of structural support I received from Daryl—or, more accurately in the job case, from being Daryl's wife.

All this was magnified a thousandfold during our eight years at Stanford. It turns out that Stanford, which has one of the top two or three psychology departments in the country, had discussed the possibility of hiring *Daryl* on several previous occasions but had passed over him every time. The first time was in 1964, when they preferred somebody else; the last time was in 1969, when they passed over him because it was known by then that, as an outspokenly egalitarian couple, we would move only if full-time positions were available for both of us. This was in sharp contrast to most other academic couples of the day.

A participant in these discussions about us was a new member of the Stanford faculty who had been a colleague of ours at Carnegie-Mellon, a psycholinguist named Herb Clark. Stanford had two openings that year, one in social psychology (Daryl's area) and the other in either developmental psychology or personality psychology. Herb Clark had argued from the start that I, too, was very good and that Stanford should therefore consider offering its two positions to the two of us. But both because of the couple problem and, I'm sure, because I was someone who would never have come to Stanford's attention *on my own*, they didn't take Herb's argument seriously. At least they didn't until the spring of that year, when their other attempts to find people for those positions had failed to yield candidates they wanted to hire, and Herb Clark again mentioned the Bems. This time the discussion led to the idea of inviting us to visit for a year so that the department could then make a more informed decision about whether to hire us.

Daryl and I joked a lot that year about the many irrational anxieties generated in the department by the prospect of hiring a couple. Would we make passionate love or bicker embarrassingly in public? Would we always vote together in faculty meetings and thus create a power bloc?

In part, I think these jokes were displacements of our own anxiety or, rather, of my anxiety, because when I entered the Stanford universe, I entered a fast-track, high-stakes game, the likes of which I never knew existed. I first realized it the moment I walked into the door of Jordan Hall and saw on the wall to my left a list of the Stanford faculty. With few exceptions, every name was famous. This was no accident, because, as I quickly learned, only two categories of psychologists were recognized here: those critical few who, in the judgment of the department, were the paradigm-setters defining the major theoretical concepts and questions for the field of psychology as a whole, and the many others who were merely tillers in the vineyard. In time I came to liken this dichotomy to a school with only two grades: A+ and F.

Years later I would realize that the problem here wasn't just the arrogance of this dichotomy. Even more problematic was the issue of who has the power to judge what the critical concepts and questions in psychology are and, even more important, what kinds of concepts and questions get excluded when almost all the judges are white heterosexual men trained in a scientific tradition that still does not understand the many complicated ways in which science and politics are intertwined. At the time, however, I just wanted to get an A+.

Looking back, it is clear to me that Stanford's valuing only the special few meshed all too well with a mindset I had already begun to develop before moving to California. I don't think it's entirely irrelevant that I had identified during my early college years with the individualistic and meritocratic philosophy of Ayn Rand. Even more to the point, however, I had already begun to be bothered by the gap between Daryl's stature in the field of psychology and my own lack of such stature.

Long ago I had a brief conversation with another female psychology professor who was married to a much better-known male psychology professor, and she amazed me by saying—with no indication of ambivalence—how much she appreciated the opportunity to participate in intellectual conversations with brilliant and famous people she would never have met if not for her husband. I just nodded politely and smiled.

But during this conversation I was thinking about a time I actually left a convention of the American Psychological Association early, and without Daryl, because I couldn't tolerate the experience of being present (but not present) while Daryl talked about psychology with other male psychologists he knew well. I'm not here accusing either Daryl or these other psychologists of being sexist; I was only a graduate student at the time, and they were all professors who had worked together and even published together. But unlike that other well-known psychologist's wife, not only could I not just sit there and soak up their brilliance, I couldn't even stay at the convention because the experience of being included in a professional discussion only by virtue of being Daryl's wife was too uncomfortable. I've asked myself over the years whether this reaction means that I have a small ego or a large ego. Probably, I've concluded, I have both. But in any case, even before we moved to California, some part of me already wanted to try to catch up with Daryl, or at least to close the gap by more than a bit, and Stanford's A+ or F mentality added fuel to that fire.

The Stanford mentality meshed with my own mentality in another way. By the time I moved to Stanford, I had found my calling. It was feminism, and, by God, I was going to help change the face of both psychology and society or die trying. So Stanford's clear message that there was no value in being anything other than a paradigm-setter was, in many ways, just the message I wanted to hear. At any other college or university, I might have been more conflicted about being so bold, thinking that if I proceeded more cautiously, if I followed up more on other people's work, if I did a few more well-designed studies, it might just get me tenure. But not at Stanford. And so, I concluded, I might as well go for the gold because nothing less would get me tenure.

But that doesn't mean I was adequately prepared for my role as a Stanford faculty member, either professionally or emotionally. And because I wasn't prepared, my eight years on the Stanford faculty were both the most intensive on-the-job training experience I can imagine and more anxiety-producing than I care to remember.

The first year, when Daryl and I were still visitors, I was slated to teach both a large undergraduate course on personality and an undergraduate seminar on gender. Never having taken a course in either subject, I was ill prepared, to say the least. But Daryl was a good resource for the personality course, and the reading I had been doing on gender got me through the seminar. There was one hitch, however. My seminar was so overcrowded that I ended up teaching a separate section to about eight graduate students, all of whom had far better training in psychology than I had. I think those eight students came away from the seminar respecting both me and what I seemed to know about gender, but I doubt that they knew how terrified I was when the evening for the seminar rolled around each week.

The lecture course on personality was scary, too, not so much because I didn't know the material (with Daryl's guidance, I had put together a good set of lectures), but because I didn't yet know how to interpret the subtle feedback students give off when they are sitting and taking notes as part of a large, and largely silent, audience. Or maybe I was too tense to see their reactions. In any case, on one occasion, I interpreted their lack of visible response to mean that I had been deadly dull; I went back to my office at the end of the lecture, put my head on my desk, and cried. Ironically, the course ended up with high student ratings, so I must not have done such a terrible job after all.

But except for the fact that I had no graduate training in any of the topics I was teaching, this is all garden-variety stress for a new assistant professor. However, I also had no training for the kind of research I was planning to do. And my job was not only to do research but also to train graduate students to do research by working with them in an apprentice-type relationship.

The research I wanted to do required that I be able to identify people ahead of time as either conventionally gendered or androgynous. For all practical purposes, this meant that I had to design a new measure of masculinity/femininity that I could give to a large group, score, and use as the basis for inviting particular people to participate in further research. Never having had a course on either personality testing or test construction, creating what one might think of as a new personality test was not something I knew how to do. But I never let on to anyone how tenuous my preparation was. I just read whatever seemed directly relevant, consulted with Daryl, did what seemed to make sense, and held my breath. Thus was born the Bem Sex Role Inventory (BSRI), which is still being used today by many investigators.

Then came the problem of designing and carrying out the "further research" that the conventionally gendered and androgynous people identified by the BSRI were supposed to participate in. Before I joined the Stanford faculty, not only did I have no experience or training in personality testing. I also had no experience or training in the kind of social-psychological laboratory research I was about to undertake. Yes, I had done two studies of my own when I was a graduate student, but both had involved my subtly trying to teach one nursery-school child at a time to solve an intellectual problem that a child of that age was thought by developmental psychologists to be unable to solve. In contrast, the kinds of studies I was now planning to do were carefully staged and choreographed extravaganzas requiring not only multiple assistants who had to be carefully trained themselves but also an elaborately constructed script that temporarily deceived the subject about some critical aspect of the research.

Why did I choose to do this kind of laboratory-based research rather than, say, going out into the real world and exploring the real lives of conventionally gendered and androgynous people? Well, if truth be told, I think it was because this was the kind of research the personality and social psychologists at Stanford seemed to be doing, and it meshed well enough with the kinds of empirical comparisons I wanted to make between androgynous and conventionally gendered people. So once again, I let on to no one how thin my ice was. I just read whatever seemed directly relevant, consulted with Daryl, and did what seemed to make sense.

And last but not least, what caused me anxiety was the fact that my research interests and goals did not fit into the Stanford psychology department's intellectual structure. When I began to do research on androgyny, I appropriated a traditional paradigm within the field of personality psychology known as the study of individual differences, in order to gather empirical data that would allow me to challenge the sexist assumptions (or what I would today call the gender polarization) of both psychology and society. But not only did I think the department would see my interest in exposing gender polarization as politics rather than science. I also knew that the department didn't even place much value on the individual-differences paradigm—which was supposed to be my passport to scientific legitimacy—because it doesn't seek to reveal the universal nature of the human organism.

Now I myself am far more interested in scholarship that reveals the human organism's potential for plasticity and diversity. But this interest of mine didn't make sense even to the one other woman on the psychology faculty. Despite her involvement in a massive literature review of sex differences, she thus couldn't understand why it would be valuable—or even how it would be possible—to demonstrate that so much diversity exists within each sex that some men, for example, might have as much so-called maternal instinct as the most maternal of women.

"What kind of study on men and/or fathers are you suggesting?" she once asked me incredulously in a research meeting where a group of faculty and graduate students were discussing an article on mother-child attachment. "That we leave a baby unattended in a buggy outside a supermarket and keep track of whether any men peer into the buggy and coo when no one seems to be watching them so the men don't have to worry about their masculinity being called into question?" You bet your boots, I wish I had said. Because we need to know a lot more than we do now about the kinds of cultural contexts that would allow women and men to be as diverse as they can be, both as individuals and as groups.

Two memories suggest the intensity of the anxiety I experienced during my eight years at Stanford. The first memory is of a particular question I asked and reasked in my daily conversations with Daryl: "Do you think it would feel different if I had tenure?" Daryl's optimistic answer once came in the form of a limerick:

> Maccoby, Bower, Bandura
> Their power you'll learn to endura
> Even H. Roydn [the dean]

Won't be such a boyden
If ever you get your tenura.

The second memory is best conveyed by a headline in the *Stanford Daily* that appeared a year before I was scheduled to come up for tenure: "Sandra Bem to Quit, Cites 'High Pressure.'" I had already turned in a letter of resignation to the chair of my department by the time this headline appeared, and I had also arranged to teach during the following year at a small women's college in the San Francisco Bay Area while Daryl and I looked elsewhere in the country to see if we could find a setting that was more congenial for both of us. My strongest memory here is of the euphoria I felt after placing my letter of resignation into my department chair's mailbox. But the euphoria was replaced within a week by the sense that my resignation had been a mistake, so I put my tail between my legs and asked the department to allow me to rescind it. How did I get myself into this embarrassing situation? All I can say is that, for me at least, some decisions are impossible to role-play.

I can't imagine how I would have survived in the Stanford environment without Daryl's continuous availability and support. With it, however, I think I was able to rise to the occasion pretty well. By 1971, for example, I had already developed the Bem Sex Role Inventory, which became so widely used so quickly that, only ten years later, the journal article in which I first wrote about it had already become a citation classic. By 1972, I had received my first research grant from the National Institute of Mental Health to study androgyny. By 1975, I was the keynote speaker at a conference on the research needs of women, sponsored jointly by the National Institute of Mental Health and the American Psychological Association. By 1976, I was the recipient of the American Psychological Association's Distinguished Scientific Award for an Early Career Contribution to Psychology, an award given only every third year for the subfield of personality psychology. By 1977, I was the recipient of a Distinguished Publication Award from the Association for Women in Psychology, and I was the subject of a ten-page profile in *Human Behavior* entitled "Professing Androgyny." And by 1980, I was the recipient of the Young Scholar Award given by the American Association of University Women.

Winning the Early Career Award from the American Psychological Association in 1976 was especially important to me because it seemed to validate not just my research on gender but the whole emerging enterprise of feminist scholarship. After all, I had not played it safe by minimizing the links between my scholarship and my feminism. Quite the contrary. And this is surely why it also pleased me so much when, in 1986, Roger Brown included a whole chapter on androgyny in his social psychology textbook and introduced it in the following way:

Sandra Bem must have been feeling exuberant on the day that she set down these words:

"I consider myself an empirical scientist, and yet my interest in sex roles is and has always been frankly political. My hypotheses have derived from no formal theory, but rather from a set of strong intuitions about the debilitating effects of sex-role stereotyping, and my major purpose has always been a feminist one: to help free the human personality from the restricting prison of sex-role stereotyping and to develop a conception of mental health which is free from culturally imposed definitions of masculinity and femininity.

"But political passion does not persuade and, unless one is a novelist or a poet, one's intuitions are not typically compelling to others. Thus, because I *am* an empirical scientist, I have chosen to utilize the only legitimated medium of persuasion which is available to me: the medium of empirical data...."

When Sandra Bem announced her intention of using empirical sci-

ence as a medium of persuasion for the political purposes of feminism, she did not mean that she was prepared to "cook" her data, but only that she would, and indeed had, picked her research problems with an eye to political relevance. *There is nothing unusual in that beyond the self-knowledge and the candor.* (Emphasis added)

But I've jumped too far ahead here. I need to return to 1976, when Daryl and I were anxiously awaiting not only the birth of Jeremy in December but also the outcome of three huge gambles related to my work: Would I get the APA Early Career Award, for which I knew I had been nominated? — Yes, I would. Would I get my second grant, this one from the National Science Foundation, which would fund my research for the next four years? — Yes, I would. But, most important, would I get tenure in the Stanford psychology department? — No, I would not. Although the vote of the department as a whole would ultimately be unanimously in my favor, for many members of the department individually, that public and formal unanimity would be layered on a deep ambivalence about my work. That ambivalence would later allow the department's positive decision to be overturned by the dean and the dean's negative ruling to be upheld on appeal by both the provost of the university and the president. Too bad I didn't have the tenure party the graduate students wanted to give me when the department first cast its unanimous vote. No, I said, let's wait to celebrate until all the formalities are over.

In the years that have passed since Stanford denied me tenure, I, like so many other feminist scholars, have developed a much more sophisticated understanding of what sex discrimination is and how it operates. When I looked back at the documents in my case in preparation for writing this chapter, what I saw there thus looked a lot more like sex discrimination than it had seemed at the time.

I had a phone conversation just after I came to Cornell with a woman who was then either Stanford's affirmative action officer or

perhaps an assistant to Stanford's president with special responsibility for affirmative action. This woman was someone I had long
known to be a committed feminist. Did I think, she asked me, that
what had happened to me at Stanford was sex discrimination? I said
that it probably wasn't sex discrimination, because a similarly situated man (i.e., a man who had done exactly the same research that
I did) probably wouldn't have gotten tenure either. She agreed.

Maybe the two of us misjudged. Maybe a man who had done
the same research would have gotten tenure. After all, *whatever*
men do is usually more valued than whatever women do. But the
more important point is that a man probably wouldn't have done
the same research I did. And this, in turn, brings me to one of the
things I now understand about discrimination against women (and
minority groups) that I didn't understand in the 1970s, which is that
the question of whether a similarly situated man would be treated
similarly is not a viable way to think about most of the discrimination against women that still exists in American society. The reason
for this is simple. As groups, women and men are not similarly situated in society; therefore, the harms that most women suffer tend to
be gender-specific injuries for which there are no similarly situated
men to serve as a standard of comparison.

The two gender-specific injuries we hear most about these days
are battering of women and sexual harassment, but consider even
that old standby: the difference between male and female earnings.
At best, the similarly situated man model offers the promise of equal
wages only to those relatively few women who are doing exactly the
same work that men do, under the now almost universally accepted
feminist concept of equal pay for equal work. But what about the
overwhelming majority of women who are concentrated in jobs that
men don't do and hence cannot claim that their puny wages represent unequal pay for equal work? It was for these women that feminists invented the concept of "equal pay for work of comparable

value." Judging comparable value is itself a tricky issue, however, because if that judgment is made from the same kind of androcentric perspective that generated the similarly situated male yardstick, then women as a group will still end up earning lower wages than men as a group because, no matter how comparable the two classes of work actually are, the male-centered perspective will still judge the women's work to be of less value than the men's work.

This matter of the male-centered perspective brings me to the second pattern that leapt out at me when I reread my tenure documents. Except for the one senior woman in my department, whom I've already mentioned, not only was every person at Stanford who judged my work from a position of any formal authority a male (not just the dean, the provost, and the president, but also every other member of my department, every member of the dean's appointments and promotions committee, and even every member of the president's advisory board). Even more important, the whole appeal process was dominated by the single question of whether the dean's decision to deny me tenure was one that a "person in the position of the decision-maker might reasonably have made."

In 1977, it never occurred to me to challenge this reasonable *person* criterion. Since then, however, feminist scholars (including feminist legal scholars) have put forth a sophisticated critique challenging the very possibility in our society of a perspective or position uninflected by such structural inequalities as sex, race, class, sexual orientation, and ethnicity. Where the drafters and supporters of reasonable-person standards thus see a perspective of neutrality and objectivity, we feminists usually see instead the false universalizing of a male perspective (and a rich, white, Christian, heterosexual male perspective at that). Nowhere can this false universalizing of the male perspective be seen more clearly than in rape law, where it was long treated as reasonable for a man to assume that a woman had consented to heterosexual intercourse unless she fought him off physically to her full capacity. The point here is that not only were all but one of the decision-makers in my tenure case male; the reasonable-person language of Stanford's appeal process enabled those males to hide their male-centered perspective behind a curtain of objectivity.

In addition to asking me whether I thought a similarly situated man would have gotten tenure, Stanford's affirmative-action officer asked me whether I thought what happened to me would have happened to anyone in a newly emerging field. In other words, wasn't it a new-field problem rather than a problem of discrimination against women?

Again, I said yes, that is what I thought. And consistent with that line of reasoning, I had already argued in my first appeal that, in contrast to most other assistant professors coming up for tenure, there was in my case no obvious group of relevant experts from whom to seek an evaluation of my work, no establishment figures who would see me as carrying on the tradition that they had been a part of and whose pride in that tradition would lead them to celebrate the kind of work I was doing, even if it didn't lead them to celebrate my work in particular. As a result, I wrote in my first appeal, my outside referees necessarily represented "a bewildering diversity of perspectives . . . [and] constituencies that need[ed] to be addressed and satisfied . . . simultaneously."

I still see this argument as relevant, but I would now add that feminist psychology (or feminist studies more generally) is not just any new field. It is a field that directly challenges not only the marginalization of women but the neutrality of allegedly objective knowledge and allegedly objective institutions—a field, in other words, that theorizes the interconnections of gender, knowledge, and power. Put somewhat differently, it is a field that would only have been invented by women, a field whose suppression is thus part and parcel of the process of discrimination against women. The same holds, I would argue, for analogous fields like black studies and lesbian, gay, and bisexual studies, and also for the whole multi-cultural debate now raging in American society.

Upon reopening the tenure appeal folder in my file cabinet for the first time in almost twenty years, the first thing I saw there was a 1977 article from the *Brown Alumni Monthly* with the following headline: "Civil Action No. 75-0140: Louise Lamphere vs. Brown University. Is Brown guilty of discrimination against women faculty?" Louise Lamphere is a feminist anthropologist who, like me, was denied tenure. Unlike me, however, she brought a class-action suit against her university, and she won an out-of-court settlement that benefited not only herself but other women faculty as well. I never considered suing Stanford—in part, but only in part, because I still had far too narrow a definition of discrimination against women. But there were other reasons as well, including, I am sure, that I just wanted to put the incident behind me.

Something that helped me move beyond the trauma was the birth of Jeremy, on December 9, 1976, just one month before the department's initial vote to grant me tenure. Before I became pregnant with Jeremy, Daryl and I had thought long and hard about whether it would be wise to have another baby at that point. We decided that, in the long run, it would be wise, and our reasoning was as follows: we want a second child, we said. The only question is whether to postpone my getting pregnant until after the tension of my tenure deliberations. If we postpone and Stanford then gives me tenure, postponing would have been a fine decision because I would just get pregnant at that point. But what if we postpone and Stanford doesn't give me tenure, and we then move to another part of the country and have to readjust to two new jobs? Chances are we will postpone yet again and end up never having our second baby after all. No way, we concluded. Stanford may have the power to deny me tenure, but it isn't going to have the power to indirectly deny us our second child.

As it turned out, it was a good thing we did reason that way because when Jeremy was just twenty-one months old, the four of us did indeed move, from Stanford to Ithaca, where I would begin my new job as both associate professor (with tenure) of psychology and women's studies and director of the women's studies program at Cornell University, and where Daryl would begin his new job as professor of psychology (also with tenure but only half-time, at least to start).

When we had moved to Stanford, eight years earlier, it was Daryl who had opened the door for me, Daryl who was initially sought by the Stanford psychology department. This time around, it was I who led the way. Or perhaps, I should say it was the Cornell women's studies program that opened the door for us both.

It began in March 1978 at the annual conference of the Association for Women in Psychology, where I received a Distinguished Publication Award for my work on androgyny and delivered the keynote address. Also present at the conference were at least two other distinguished feminist scholars who, like me, had just been denied tenure at their respective universities: Mary Brown Parlee, from the psychology department at Barnard (which had just lost its autonomy in tenure decisions to Columbia), and Judith Long Laws from the Cornell sociology department. So the mood was decidedly mixed. If the three of us couldn't get tenure as feminist scholars, who could? And what did that imply about the future of feminist scholarship in the social sciences?

On the last day of the conference, a Cornell social psychologist named John Condry approached me and asked if I would have any interest in a job as director of Cornell's women's studies program. I said I might, but only if it came with tenured jobs for both me and

Daryl. The directorship did indeed include tenure, he said, but a new tenured line would have to be created for Daryl, and he himself would be happy to get people working on it if we were interested.

Over the next two months, enough people from enough departments lobbied the dean and provost that a new half-time line for Daryl was created. The two of us then came to give job talks in the first week of May, we sold our house at Stanford and bought a new house in Ithaca in the middle of June, and we moved across the country in the beginning of August. Implicit in this brief history of our move is yet another example of Daryl's always providing me with whatever emotional and structural support I needed at the time, including leaving a full professorship in a top psychology department in sunny California.

Part of the reason we could move across the country so quickly is that the Cornell offers came at an opportune (if mournful) moment. All through my tenure decision year, we worried—on top of everything else—about how, given my mother's ongoing struggle with breast cancer, we could possibly move if I didn't get tenure. Would my parents move with us? Would they stay in California without us? Would I look for a job in the San Francisco Bay Area so we wouldn't have to move? As it turned out, my mother died even before my last tenure appeal was denied, and my father became engaged very soon thereafter. By the time we moved to Ithaca in August 1978, my father was already remarried.

In the beginning, my work as director of women's studies felt like alienated labor. I had no investment in Cornell as an institution, my professional socialization at Stanford had led me to devalue administrative work as compared to research, and, if truth be told, some smart-ass (and defensive) part of myself considered running the women's studies program an imposition on my valuable time as an award-winning scholar and researcher.

My outlook changed over time, however, and I soon became committed to hiring as many excellent female faculty as I could who were producing outstanding feminist scholarship on women and gender. I also committed myself to staying on as director until these women came up for tenure because I strongly believed that this would enhance their prospects. Given this mission, I am proud to report that during my two terms as director, women's studies was able to hire seven feminist scholars, all of whom ultimately got tenure.

These seven fully deserved tenure, but merit alone hadn't gotten me tenure as a feminist scholar, nor had it gotten tenure for many other feminist scholars of my generation, including Judith Long Laws, who was denied tenure at Cornell in the same year that I was denied tenure at Stanford. I bring up the Laws case again because part of the reason the next generation of feminist scholars got tenure at Cornell was the class-action suit a group of women faculty, including Laws, brought against Cornell in 1979. Although an official settlement was not reached until 1985, this lawsuit clearly motivated Cornell to think more seriously about its hiring and treatment of women faculty.

In my own mind, another major mission I had during my years as director of women's studies was to prevent the kind of split that had developed in some other women's studies programs between heterosexual feminists and lesbian feminists. And so I regularly argued that feminism is not only about challenging the marginalization of women; it is also about challenging the allegedly natural links that have long been thought to exist among sex, psyche, and sexuality—the cultural belief that men are naturally masculine, women are naturally feminine, and everyone is naturally heterosexual. Given how much I did not want a split to develop at Cornell around sexuality, I was very pleased indeed that lesbian, bisexual, and gay studies ultimately emerged so unproblematically as a part of the women's studies program.

During this same period, from 1978 to 1985, I extended my work on androgyny in new directions, published several major articles, and attained the rank of full professor in 1981. But the work I did at Cornell that truly satisfied me did not begin until after my terms as director of women's studies.

I had been wondering for a long time if, as I used to put it, I "had a book in my head." If so, I knew it would be a "big picture" book that would finally integrate my long-standing interest in gender with my long-standing interest in sex and sexual orientation (which, until that time, I had expressed primarily through my teaching and my child-rearing). I didn't yet know how to accomplish this integration, so during a sabbatical year at Harvard in 1987–88, I read voraciously on anything and everything even vaguely interesting to me. Of all the things I read, perhaps the most significant was Catherine Mac-Kinnon's essay "Difference and Dominance" because it enabled me to see that our social world is indeed an invisible affirmative action program for (rich, white, Christian, heterosexual) men. And with this realization, I was not only able to build a theory that tried to explain how both sexism and heterosexism are reproduced in U.S. society in generation after generation. I was also able to grasp the "whole" of what I had been teaching and theorizing, both at work and at home, for over twenty years.

But grasping that whole was not easy, nor was writing it down in a way that would be accessible to the nonspecialized reader. Which brings me back, as usual, to Daryl. Both when I was first struggling to produce the overall outline for *The Lenses of Gender* and, later, when I was trying to tame a whole menagerie of ideas on gender and sexuality from disciplines as diverse as anthropology, biology, history, philosophy, and law (to name but a few of the fields on which I poached), Daryl was once again always supportive of me. Yes, I did have a distinctive approach to gender and sexuality, he was always ready to reassure me one more time if I seemed to need it, and hence I ought to be writing this book. And, yes, he would be happy to be my sounding board—over breakfast or lunch or tea, at home or at a booth in our favorite gourmet bakery or wherever, and for as long as I would like.

A recurring scenario from this period is the two us sitting across from each other at a table, me reading from a collection of yellow pads full of notes and Daryl listening quietly. Then the intellectual (and sometimes emotional) fireworks begin. Daryl plays back to me, so to speak, what he understands me to have said, along with his own thoughts about how my ideas might be better organized. I get a little huffy because he hasn't gotten the central points quite right, but I quickly settle down and reclarify. He plays my ideas back again but with yet more repackaging. I see some possibilities for restructuring that I hadn't thought of before, so we talk for a bit about the implications of this restructuring. And then the conversation ends with my (usually) feeling I can now move further ahead in my thinking and writing.

In retrospect, I now realize I had been writing *The Lenses of Gender* in my mind for a good fifteen years before I finally started writing it on paper. No wonder, then, that I sometimes feel I was destined to write it. And no wonder as well that I am so proud of its having been selected as the recipient of four book awards.

I should probably add as a footnote that writing that book came with yet another fringe benefit. It freed me from any lingering desire for tenure at Stanford that might have been buried in my unconscious. Because I loved writing *The Lenses of Gender,* and I'm almost certain I would never have written it had I lived out my professional life in the Stanford psychology department. Nor, of course, would I have even contemplated writing anything so outrageous as this autobiography-of-a-family. True to form, Daryl supported this project, too, from the moment I mentioned it.

But as much as Daryl's ever-present and always-available supportiveness has meant to me over the years, it also has a downside, or an undertow, that I can best convey by describing the conflict I experienced when the time came to draft this chapter in particular. The seemingly innocuous question troubling me was: What narrative frame shall I use here?

The frame I had originally planned to use—Daryl as the wonderfully supportive facilitator of my work—was the one I ended up using because it is the only rational position I can take. But I have always been a little ambivalent about Daryl's support—in part because we were so asymmetrical in our need for such shoring up. That ambivalence came to the surface as I sat down to write, and it began to plague me with other narrative frames that have occasionally plagued me in the past. And it does not take a psychoanalyst to recognize that these other frames all reveal a deep inner conflict about my lack of self-sufficiency. One frame, for example, positions me as both so emotionally and intellectually needy, and also so dependent, that I can't even function as a professor, let alone as a creative scholar, without Daryl. Another frame casts me not by any means as Daryl's creation but, in that same vein, as someone who could not have become an influential feminist scholar without Daryl's help.

With these more nightmarish scenarios now circulating in my head, I began to go into an obsessive, high-anxiety spin, wondering not only if Daryl's supportiveness might have undermined my sense of authorship and agency, but also if I shouldn't think of myself as puny and small and my accomplishments as more Daryl's than mine.

As I obsessed about these matters, I became more and more anxious and depressed until, at some point, I got the idea of doing exactly what I have done at this kind of moment of being totally stuck in my writing for almost thirty years. I thought of calling Daryl. Only now Daryl is not exactly my husband any longer so the idea of still needing his help with my writing fills me with even more conflict than it did in the best of times. So I put the idea aside and played around instead with the possibility of organizing the chapter around my ambivalent relation to Daryl's supportiveness. But I know instinctively, that, as a feminist who believes in the value of *inter*dependency, I need to try to move beyond this rather than use it as the foundation of a whole chapter. So in the end I do call Daryl, with whom I am still on very friendly terms, and ask him if he would be willing to discuss my chapter with me over lunch. He is delighted, in part because it will allow us to share, if only for an hour, a kind of intimacy we haven't shared for several years.

So here we were again, sitting across from each other in a booth at Collegetown Bagels and Appetizers, me reading from my yellow pads and Daryl listening. And then he spoke.

"Sandy," he said, "here's what I think you should do. Talk first about the good stuff and then move into the undertow. And think about the undertow as a result of your growing into the profession in the particular way you did. In other words, think about it situationally instead of dispositionally. You were, after all, more or less sui generis. You had no mentor, no intellectual heritage, no research adviser whose research program you could simply extend in some new direction. Your ideas were all drawn from real life and from your own marginalized way of looking at life. They were and are creative, but you've always been a maverick, and that's part of why you've needed my support."

"And," he went on, "it's not as if other academics work alone. Most of them, especially in psychology, enter the profession through a mentoring relation with a research adviser whose work they later extend in some way, and they also talk a lot with colleagues and frequently even with coauthors, from whom they probably get at least as much intellectual (and perhaps even emotional) support as you have gotten over the years from me. They just take it for granted more than you do because they are following a more standardized script than you are."

I then added, "And not only that. My conflict about what I have gotten from you—and even my tendency to frame it as dependency rather than colleagueship—is surely related to the fact that you, Daryl, are so extreme on the dimension of self-sufficiency. And we haven't even mentioned yet that, as both a woman and a feminist psychologist, I was also dealing with a much more difficult professional environment than you were. At least I was until you started fooling around with research on ESP, but you were already a full professor with tenure by then so that doesn't really count."

"But most important," he said as we were getting up to leave, "your ideas were always your own. All I ever added was a bit of packaging."

As ambivalent as I had been about calling Daryl that day, I left our lunch with no ambivalence at all. Not only had our conversation cleared my head of the obsessive self-denigration I occasionally traumatize myself with. It had also allowed me to reexperience the support that had facilitated my work for twenty-eight years, and it thereby reaffirmed the argument I had wanted to make in this chapter from the moment I first conceived it. Just as my marriage to Daryl had enabled us to build a new community of family and to invent an egalitarian form of marriage and even to develop a gender-liberated, antihomophobic, and sex-positive form of child-rearing, so too it had enabled me to build a wonderfully unorthodox career.

PART 3

Evaluating Our Experiment

CHAPTER SEVEN

Egalitarian Partnering Revisited

When Daryl and I got married in 1965, we embarked on our own personal experiment in gender liberation, an experiment that ultimately came to have two sets of radical goals. In the language I would use today, our first goal was to build a relationship with each other that would be free of both gender polarization and male dominance; our second goal was to raise our children in a gender-liberated, antihomophobic, sex-positive way.

Like any retrospective review of an innovative experiment, in this chapter and the next I ask somewhat more analytically in what ways were we able to meet these goals and in what ways were we not. Stepping back even further, in these chapters I look at what our experience has to say about the viability and the value of trying to construct an alternative family form in accordance with feminist values.

These questions are hard for me to focus on now that Daryl and I have separated. I keep having the temptation to transform them into the rather different question of what went wrong that ultimately led to our separation. So I think it may be easier for me (and perhaps for the reader as well) if I set aside the fact of our separation and ask about the viability and value of our feminist experiment irrespective of the fact that it didn't last forever. Odd as this approach may seem at first glance, "till death do us part" is not the only—or even the best—criterion of whether and how we met our goals.

In his book *Gender and Power,* sociologist Robert Connell argues that a thorough analysis of the gender structure of any institution (including the family) must consider three separate arenas: labor, control, and cathexis. Labor refers to who does what kind of work and how it is valued. Control refers to who has authority or power and how it is expressed. Cathexis refers to who has responsibility for emotional connections and how they are kept both alive and in check. Although all three of these arenas are critical to the amount of gender polarization in a family, control—or power—is where male dominance can be seen most readily.

This framework has been used effectively by Barbara Risman in her 1998 book *Gender Vertigo* to analyze a small sample of heterosexual couples who tried, as Daryl and I did, to structure their lives in an egalitarian and gender-liberated way. This framework will also serve me well, I think, as I try to analyze in what ways Daryl and I really did manage to be egalitarian and gender-liberated as partners and parents and in what ways we did not. This analysis of our relationship is separate, of course, from an analysis of our child-rearing practices, which I will take up in the next chapter.

In chapter 4, I said that the ultimate criterion of an egalitarian relationship is that neither partner should have continuing precedence over the other for any reason. This goes to the heart of Connell's category of control or power, and, in traditional heterosexual families, it also goes to the heart of male dominance.

In our relationship as partners, Daryl and I did manage to be egalitarian—and thereby to avoid the traditional problem of male dominance—in almost all important areas of our lives. And where we didn't quite manage to be egalitarian, we tended to veer in the direction of female dominance, in part because I seemed to have more preferences than Daryl and perhaps more willingness to express those preferences. Although this pattern of slight female dominance in a fundamentally egalitarian relationship is not exactly what we had in mind when we first laid out our egalitarian principles more than thirty years ago—I think we were naively imagining a relationship that was more perfectly (and perhaps robotically) symmetrical—this pattern worked well for us, it fit our personalities, and it allowed us to have independent careers as well as separate identities. And even if a friend once joked—when we were all making lists of the ten most important things we wanted to do before we died—that the number one item on Daryl's list should be "to get to decide for himself what he wants on his list rather than having Sandy try to make this decision for him," the truth is that in real life, we both had enormous autonomy to be and do whatever we wanted; we were both willing to compromise; and we never got involved in power games or other subterranean agendas. Also—and this factor should not be underestimated—Daryl (like his father before him) was and is enormously accommodating.

In chapter 4, I also said that in an egalitarian marriage, labor would be divided much as it is between roommates: by preference, agreement, flipping a coin, given to hired help, or—as is perhaps most often the case—simply left undone. In other words, it would not be divided up, as in a traditional marriage, on the basis of gender. Putting aside for the moment our division of labor as parents, in this domain too, Daryl and I managed as partners to be as egalitarian as we had ever planned to be, and we did this with little struggle.

In other words, we both worked full-time outside the home, and we both did about half the work within the home that wasn't being done for pay by someone else.

By no stretch of the imagination, however, did we always do exactly the same work within the home. Thus, as someone who had grown up male, Daryl tended to know more about cars than I did, so he tended to take more responsibility in that area. Later he was also more interested in computers, so he became the technician on whom I relied whenever my computer wouldn't do what I wanted—which, in the beginning, was very frequently. And in a striking reversal of the "wife without whom" the husband's writings might never have been so elegant, Daryl was always and forever both my sounding board and my copy editor, a role he did not seem to need to have reciprocated, by me or anyone else. In contrast, I tend to like physical activities, so I was usually the one who mowed the lawn and raked the leaves and shoveled the snow. We divided other nonparenting labor in different ways at different times during our many years together, but we never struggled over this much or felt that either person was doing more than his or her fair share, never valued one kind of work more than another, and never were that gendered in what we did.

In all our theorizing about egalitarianism, Daryl and I never talked or thought much about Connell's third category of cathexis or emotional work, so we didn't recognize this arena as one that might be central to an egalitarian relationship, despite the fact that feminist theorists have been writing about it for quite a long time. Even here, however, our labor was divided in a more or less egalitarian way, if accidentally so. This unintentional egalitarianism came about, I think, because as partners we seemed to require different kinds of emotional work, and I did one kind while Daryl did another. I, like a traditionally gendered woman, mediated all the relationships in our nuclear family, including the relationship between me and Daryl. And Daryl, like the best nondirective therapist I could have found, listened endlessly and sympathetically to everything troubling me, calming my anxieties, assuaging my insecurities, nurturing my confidence.

As partners, Daryl and I thus escaped most of the problematic traps of a traditional male-dominated heterosexual marriage, including the many gendered guilts and gratitudes that can bedevil those who try to be egalitarian. I'm thinking here of the traditional woman's greater sense of responsibility for housekeeping and the traditional man's greater sense of responsibility for breadwinning. I'm thinking as well of the traditional woman's sense of gratitude to the man for helping with what, in Daryl's view and mine, is simply his housework as well as hers. Our task was surely made easier by the flexibility of our jobs and the politically liberal atmosphere of our university and our town, but I still think the principle of no one person's having continuing advantage over the other for any reason is one I would advocate for any couple, as much today as thirty years ago.

Many years ago, someone in a lecture audience commented derisively that our feminist egalitarianism might work all right while we had no children, but we would quickly become traditionally gendered once we had children. This critic was not exactly right, for Daryl was deeply and daily involved in our kids' lives when they were babies and young children; even when they were older, he was passionately involved in talking about math and science and computers with Jeremy and an avid enthusiast of Emily's interests in music, drama, and creative writing as well.

Daryl's commitment to the kids' activities notwithstanding, however, by the time they reached adolescence, our family had clearly split into three extraordinarily conventional gender groupings: the mother and the children; the husband and the wife; and the father and the son.

Given Daryl's extraordinary involvement with the kids at the beginning of their lives, how did our family structure ultimately become so gendered? The process began, I think, with small conflicts even during the children's babyhood about how to handle various issues of child-rearing. The issues had no special significance. Should the baby be left to cry herself to sleep? Should the toddler have to finish eating what was on his plate? Can Emily sleep in her clothes tonight instead of in her pajamas, and what about on the floor instead of in the bed? If Jeremy has been coughing for three or four days but has no fever, should we call the doctor now or wait a few days longer? And if one of the kids feels a little sick this morning, should we still make him or her go to school? This is the mundane stuff of life with children.

But mundane or not, Daryl's instincts and mine were often different, and rather than struggling to bring both our voices to the negotiating table, instead, over time, Daryl deferred to me. And in so doing, he (and I) gradually began to define the children as more within my domain than his.

Daryl deferred to me in this context for much the same reasons he deferred in other contexts. In stating my opinion, I would become insistent, intense, certain — and, perhaps thinking he couldn't win anyway and having little or no stomach for conflict, Daryl disengaged. He essentially said to himself: "This isn't worth fighting about, I probably am too rigid, you [Sandy] probably are more the expert, and in any case, it all obviously matters a whole lot more to you than it does to me." Did either of us realize at the time that this meant he was abandoning his claim to be a fully equal parent? I don't think so.

For thoroughly different reasons, the family grouping of mom and the kids that began to be established as early as babyhood became further entrenched during their middle childhood. When I was a child, I didn't have any of the middle-class enrichment opportunities that our children were given as a matter of course—like learning to ice-skate or to ski—and as an adult I had been too busy with work and family to explore these kinds of experiences on my own. To the extent that my schedule allowed it, I therefore took advantage of the kids' extracurricular activities to enrich myself as well. For example, when the elementary school offered a Wednesday afternoon learn-to-ski program and needed a few adults to go along, I signed myself up with the kids and all three of us learned to ski; I did the same when the Cornell figure skating club offered cheap lessons on Sunday nights—although, in that case, I dragged Daryl (and eventually a whole group of Cornell colleagues), too. None of these other folks lasted as long as the kids or I did, however.

My point is that during the kids' middle childhood I spent lots more time around them than Daryl did, and although this was never intended to distance Daryl from the center of the family, it did draw a circle around Emily and Jeremy and me.

At first, Daryl's outsider status derived primarily from his lack of knowledge about whatever mundane things were going on in the kids' daily lives. It was not uncommon, for example, for Daryl to shift into the TV room immediately after dinner to watch the news while one or both of the kids and I stayed at the table talking about whatever was on their minds. I'm not putting the blame entirely on Daryl, because my listening to the trivia of their lives and the lives of their friends—which I truly enjoyed—may well have reflected some need in my own life that I was using them to fill. But then came their adolescence, when Daryl's position as outsider was gradually cemented as first one child and then the other began to have semi-serious adolescent problems, like so many adolescents in this day and age, and the impact of these problems reverberated through our already gendered family structures.

In retrospect, the pattern of what happened during their adolescence was all too predictable from our earlier family dynamics. I was already far more involved in the kids' lives than Daryl was, and now I got even more involved, perhaps too much involved. And because my emotional engagement was now almost wholly with the kids, I became more distanced from Daryl emotionally. At the same time, Daryl, who had never developed a language for talking with the kids about what was going on in their interior lives, withdrew from them even further and rarely if ever had conversations with them about their problems. Even more than before, what he knew about their deepest thoughts and feelings he knew because they told me and I told him.

Over time, this interaction process transformed our family. No longer were we two reasonably happy and well-functioning, even if overly gendered, little subunits. Instead we were a mother-and-kids subunit struggling, sometimes well and sometimes not so well, with problems that required attention, and a husband-and-wife subunit still functioning adequately on the surface but with a new estrangement festering below.

How we functioned as parents does not stray far from the power-labor-cathexis model put forth by Connell. In terms of power, we gradually veered very far from egalitarianism and very near to female dominance. In terms of labor, we veered—as the kids got older—toward my doing far more than half of what needed to be done. And in terms of cathexis, we ultimately veered all too close to my being the only one who was deeply in touch with the kids' thoughts and feelings. Again, none of this is to say that Daryl was uninvolved with the kids because, even at the height of his outsiderness, he continued to talk math, science, and computers with Jeremy and to support Emily's activities, for example, by playing the piano while she practiced her solos for musical performances.

But even if I have explained the *how* of our having become so traditionally gendered as parents, the *why* remains. Was it, for example, because of something relatively unchangeable within our respective psyches, and if so, was that in turn based on our genders or on something more individualized—the emotional climate of our families of origin perhaps or even our individual biologies? Alternatively, might we have become so traditionally gendered as parents not because of anything deep within our psyches but because of something more situational in our adult lives and thus more subject to change, even within adulthood?

My answer is all of the above. Whether because of our biologies or because of the emotional climate of our families of origin *and whether male or female,* Bems and Lipsitzes have very different ways of being in the world: Bems are more autonomous, more orderly, more activity-centered, and more desirous of time alone; Lipsitzes more introspective, more emotional, and more enmeshed in their personal relationships. Even had we been the same gender, our family-of-origin differences would thus seem more than adequate to make my relationship with the kids more emotionally connected than Daryl's relationship with them. But we aren't the same gender, and thus our respective socialization as female or male meshed perfectly throughout our lives with this difference in our families of origin. In any case, by adulthood, these factors simply cannot be teased apart. Daryl and I are who we are both emotionally and relationally; we are also different in ways that mesh with the traditional roles of mother and father; and that difference—now deeply ingrained in our psyches—is the product of both gendered and nongendered forces.

Does any of this mean that men can't "mother"? After all, the argument might go, if even the Bems couldn't produce a male mother, who on earth can?

In retrospect, I think we might have done a lot better if we had realized that the advice we gave in our lectures back in the late 1960s and early 1970s applied as much to ourselves as to our audiences. Men can cook, clean, diaper, and so on, we said—and they can presumably talk to teenagers about their problems as well—but not if women do it before men notice it needs to be done, and not if women also look over men's shoulders while they do it. Had we realized any of this was happening in our own family, and had we also thought more about the parenting implications of the emotional differences between us, perhaps we could have changed the structure of our family functioning to offset those differences a bit. But we didn't realize any of this, and together, both the gendered and the nongendered aspects of our personalities, along with the family situations we unthinkingly constructed, led us to become much more gendered as parents than we had intended.

None of this means, however, that men in general can't be nurturing parents. I'm sure, for example, that Jeremy will find it a lot more natural to do so than Daryl did, and I'm also sure that some of the men in Barbara Risman's study of egalitarian couples are also finding it more natural. After intensive interviews with these couples, Risman categorized them into three groups. The first group reminded me of Daryl and me, with the mother classified by Risman as the emotional expert, especially in relation to the kids. In the other two groups, the mother and father seemed either to have divided up the emotional work with the kids or—in the more emotionally intense families—to have doubled the emotional work with the kids, with the result being that the mother was no more emotionally bound or connected to the kids than the father. Perhaps it is in feminist families like these, rather than in families like mine and Daryl's, that we should look for male mothers.

On the other hand (and in an evolving narrative, there is always another hand), perhaps this whole analysis confuses egalitarianism with sameness—and sameness defined from a Sandy-centered perspective. Worse than that, perhaps Daryl disengaged from parenting over the years as much as he did in part because his way of relating interpersonally did not enable him to have the kind of emotionally intense and intimate relationship with our kids that both of us then defined as the sine qua non of good parenting. All my talk about difference and diversity notwithstanding, perhaps both my narrative and my egalitarian relationship with Daryl thus too much required my partner to be the same kind of parent that I am.

CHAPTER EIGHT

Feminist Child-Rearing Revisited

I come finally to the question of what the consequences were for our children of our so consciously trying to raise them in a gender-liberated, antihomophobic, and sex-positive way. Were our voices ultimately so drowned out by the forces of the culture that our efforts made little difference in the kinds of people they became? Did our kids' unusual upbringing produce unanticipated—and perhaps insurmountable—difficulties and conflicts for them? Do they feel positive enough about their upbringing that they would choose to raise their own children (assuming they have children) in much the same way that we raised them? And, perhaps most important, did their upbringing accomplish the goals we had in mind with respect to gender and sexuality as they were growing up? These goals were more or less as follows:

First, in the language I would have used twenty years ago, we wanted our children to be androgynous or gender-aschematic; or, as I would be more likely to say it now, we wanted them (insofar as possible) not to look at themselves—or at others or at the world in general—through a gender-polarizing lens. That is, we wanted them to treat biological sex as irrelevant to the kind of person they (or anyone else) should try to be; we wanted them to organize neither their feelings about nor their vision of themselves around gender; we wanted them not to use cultural conventions of maleness or femaleness, masculinity or femininity, as the basis for their sense of self or identity; and we wanted them not to presume that a woman should be feminine or a man masculine, however those terms might be culturally defined. In other words, we wanted them to be as free as possible in our unfree world to be open with respect to gender.

Second, we wanted them (insofar as possible) not to be androcentric in their vision of themselves or others or the world in general. By this I mean that we wanted them neither to privilege males and male experience nor to marginalize females and female experience; we wanted them not to think of males as the main characters in the drama of social life and females as the supporting cast, and we wanted them to see our culture's privileging of males and marginalizing of females as the historical and social injustice it is.

Third, we wanted them not to be what we would today call heteronormative. That is, we wanted them not only to see same-sex love and sexuality as no more unnatural than cross-sex love and sexuality. We also wanted them to see American culture's demonizing of same-sex relations and privileging of cross-sex relations as just as immoral as our culture's record on race.

Fourth, we wanted them to appreciate the body, both their own and others', in more or less its natural state, by which I mean unstarved, unshaven, uncosmeticized, and unbuffed. We also wanted them to take pleasure in and responsibility for their bodily desires, including their sexual desires, and also to be able to communicate so openly about sex that they would be able to maximize both intimacy and pleasure while minimizing every kind of risk, both physical and psychological.

Finally, and more generally, we wanted them to be what we used to call deviants-with-strength, but what I might now call cultural critics from the left with the courage of their convictions. By this I mean that we wanted them both to see and to be disturbed by the intolerance and inequity of their society, and we also wanted them to have such a sense of rightness and morality about the unconventional beliefs we hoped they would share with their parents that they would not only feel good about themselves despite their differences from the norm but would also be willing and able, with like-minded others, to fight for a more tolerant and just society.

I can think of no better way to communicate the consequences of our feminist child-rearing practices than for Jeremy and Emily to speak for themselves. Accordingly, what follows is a pair of interviews that I conducted with them separately on December 23, 1996, when they were twenty and twenty-two years old, respectively. These interviews have been heavily edited, first by me to make them shorter and then by Jeremy and Emily to make them appropriate for public consumption. I learned a great deal from these interviews, both about my children and about the benefits and risks of raising other children in a similar way.

Jeremy

Jeremy, one of the major goals of our feminist child-rearing practices was to enable you (insofar as possible) to treat gender as irrelevant. Would you say that you have actually managed to transcend gender?

Yes and no. Yes in that my activities, aesthetics, beliefs, and ways of interacting don't especially tend to line up with my biological sex. If you catch me interacting in a typically masculine way, like talking to male friends

about the inner workings of our computers, you'll usually find a compensating moment when I'm interacting in a typically feminine way, like talking to female friends about the inner workings of our lives. If one day I'm wearing clothing that would typically be described as masculine, there will be another day when I'm wearing clothing that would typically be described as feminine. And so on. But even though being male or masculine is not a central part of my identity, I can't really say I've transcended gender, because being androgynous *is* a central part of my identity. If I had really transcended gender, it wouldn't bother me to notice that in any particular domain, I am more typically masculine than feminine; for example, I tend to be more sexually attracted to women than to men. But it does bother me.

Say more about the ways in which you are unconventionally gendered.

Almost everything I do is unconventionally gendered. My preferred mode of conversation is an emotionally intense discussion of the inner details of life. This is more typical of the girls I know than the boys, who feel more comfortable talking about the surface features of life—what they did that day, what music they like, what projects they're working on. Now I can do both kinds of conversation, and sometimes I find it a pleasure to relax into the more "guyish" kind, but it doesn't ultimately reflect what I am. And if it were all I had, I'd feel unsatisfied.

Not too long ago, for example, I sat down with a female friend who described to me, practically word for word, the fight she'd just had with her mother over the telephone. She mentioned one moment in which she'd gotten angry and expressed herself with unusual force, and she regretted having lost control. But then when we discussed how previously she'd been afraid to get angry with her mom, she was able to reinterpret the event as a healthy release. Moments like that capture for me what human interaction ought to be about: they make me understand why there's more than one human being in the universe. But my guess is that most males wouldn't enjoy engaging at that level of detail with someone else's emotional life.

What about your own emotional life? I'm wondering whether you're in touch with your own feelings and whether you share your feelings, because I don't think the stereotypical male is supposed to do either.

I don't have any stake in hiding my emotional self. Think about how you and I talk all the time. My most automatic way of being is to share everything I feel in a way that sons certainly don't ordinarily do with their mothers. I wish I could say I were someone who cries when I listen to Mozart, but I can't because I don't. But perhaps it's just as revealing that I wish I did. And I'm not embarrassed about moments when I'm emotionally needy. Once last year I was rejected by a girl I'd been very interested in, and I was feeling embarrassed and hurt. Rather than shut it all inside, I spent the day with a friend who took very good care of me and talked to me softly in Russian until I was okay. That was one of the nicest things that ever happened between the two of us. But it's not a coincidence that my first example involved my talking with someone else about their emotional life rather than the other way around. I don't tend to be in need very often. Maybe that's conventionally masculine, but if so, it's not a kind of conventionality that bothers me.

What might your friends say about ways in which you're unconventionally gendered in addition to what you've already said?

First, I hope they'd say even what I have said already. But in addition, I think they'd say—if they were feeling generous—that I'm free and loose in ways that appeal to them but which they don't let themselves be. That's not specifically about gender, but surely one of the things holding them back is their expectation about how people of their sex ought to behave. For example, one of my best friends reminds me of Dad in the way he socializes. He's very precise and formal, focused on conversation as a medium for the sharing of knowledge, comfortable in settings when it's clear what's expected of him but less so when the setting is open-ended. I think he likes me partly for my willingness or my ability to be a larger number of different things. I can be a serious mathematician like him, but I can also be a therapist, and I can dance crazily around the room, and I can jump up and down like a little kid.

What would your friends say, if anything, about your gender in particular?

I don't know. They might think I'm a freak. But the friends I care about, if they do think that, think it affectionately.

A freak. What do you mean?

I wear a skirt sometimes, and I'm "too" affectionate with guys. There was a party when I was dancing with my ex-roommate and then we were rolling around on the floor and we weren't especially worried about how much we were touching each other or where we were touching each other. My other friends were uncomfortable because there were people at the party they didn't know well and whose reactions they couldn't gauge.

Is this affection with guys part of being gay? Are you describing yourself as gay?

No, I'm not describing myself as being gay. I mentioned a girl earlier. You didn't ask then if I was describing myself as straight.

You're right.

184 EVALUATING OUR EXPERIMENT

184 EVALUATING OUR EXPERIMENT

So another way I'm freer than many of my peers is that to me gay and straight, hetero and homo, aren't just identities. They are also dynamics that are everywhere, so if I'm rolling around with my roommate on the floor, while I don't want to say this means I'm gay, I also don't want to say it has nothing to do with my sexuality.

Say more about your wearing a skirt. Why? Where?

Let me talk about the why first. There are at least two reasons, one being aesthetic. I think that both women's clothing and women's bodies are more natural, more graceful, more attractive, more interesting than men's clothing and bodies. Certainly women's clothing is less restrictive and more colorful. And I often find it fun to be wearing this nice loose thing, called a skirt, that doesn't have these two legs that wrap right around your legs. Instead there's this open space that you get to be in and, completely apart from any social connotations, I think that's neat aesthetically. But I won't deny that I also like to be a little bit shocking and to see people's reactions because, normally, everybody looks kind of blah in public places and you can't really make many distinctions about what kinds of people are out there. But as soon as you go out in a skirt, you can tell from people's facial reactions where they fall, whether you want to know or not.

On a college campus, there are usually lots of people who aren't conventionally gendered, who are gender-benders, and most of them didn't grow up in families like ours. Do you see yourself as different from them?

It's all new for them in a way it isn't for me. When I lived in a co-op, one of the things we liked to do was to skinny-dip in a kiddy pool we had outside. We would fill it with hot water from the bathtub and put up a screen so the police wouldn't bother us. For me it was fun and relaxing but not such a radical departure from what we were expected to do or what our parents would want us to do that it would entertain me in and of itself. So I would want to talk about something other than the observation that, hey look, we're all here naked together. But for my housemates, it was new and special and so it captured center stage.

Maybe it's time now to move on to the next major question: How are you still conventionally gendered despite your upbringing?

Not in any way whatsoever. Next topic. No, I'll admit it. My intellectual interests are obviously conventionally gendered. The primary ones are math and computer programming and physics. But I also love literature and languages, and those aren't considered masculine.

How do you feel about the genderedness of your primary intellectual interests? You sound a little embarrassed about it.

I am a little embarrassed about it. I would prefer if my intellectual passions and my gender didn't line up in the way they do. I think it would be incredibly fun to be a woman with the interests that I have. That is, if I were to change anything to make things not line up so stereotypically, I would change my gender, not my interests.

I'm wondering how you think about the contrast here between you and Emily. Your primary interests are math, science, and computers. Hers are music, drama, and creative writing. Surely someone could look at all this conventional genderedness from the outside and say, my goodness, this must be a failure of your family's gender-liberated child-rearing.

Let's be honest here. It's not as if Emily is or I am only vaguely talented with respect to our skills. I'm distinctly good at math, and Emily's distinctly good at writing, so these are not casually chosen or culturally determined passions. So no, there's no failure of anything here. On the other hand, I do think it would have been much harder to accomplish what I've accomplished in math if I were a girl, just because of differences in how the world would have reacted.

Any other ways in which you see yourself as conventionally gendered?

Yes. I'm mostly straight, which I find annoying. I'm also assertive, but that doesn't bother me at all because I think being assertive, like being nurturing, is a natural way of being, which some girls are denied because of societal conditioning.

The next major category is about any potential downside of your upbringing, any ways in which your upbringing with respect to gender and sexuality has been a problem for you, mainly as a young adult, though you can refer back to the past if you want to. So the basic question here is: What worries or conflicts or problems, if any, has your upbringing produced for you, either with respect to your peers or your parents or your sense of your self as a man or whatever?

Conflict with peers hasn't been an issue in this era. I was harassed in school when I was much younger, but who knows whether that was because I was wearing a pink backpack or just because I was generically nerdy. As often as not, I don't think even the picker-onners know why they choose someone to pick on. These days, the problem with peers is more a kind of alienation. I talked earlier about being somewhat alienated even from progressive people because they have to rebel so consciously against the sexual politics of the older generation or of their more conservative peers. But the point is a more general one. In almost all my everyday encounters, I tend to be a little withdrawn because my default assumption is that I'm ultimately not going to fit in politically.

So I'm automatically alienated until proven otherwise as a social way of being. I don't think that's a problem, I just think it's true. So in any given social context, the question of whether or not to express my true self is automatically there, however I end up resolving it, because I know I'm going to be politically different from whoever I'm with in general and also politically different with respect to sex and gender specifically.

Is it relevant that not only your upbringing will have made you different but also your excellence in math and science, so you're different on two counts?

Yeah, at least two and probably more.

I have a more specific downside question to ask you. Feminists tend to have a bias against men and masculinity. How has that affected you, and has it made it difficult for you to figure out what it means to be a man?

The phrase "to be a man" instantly reminds me of your friend's comment a couple weeks ago that I look so manly now that my neck has gotten thicker, and I sheepishly thought, "Oh great, just what I want, a thick neck, like Gaston [in *Beauty and the Beast*]." The point of this story is that I don't like self-identifying as a man, that being manly is the last thing I want to be, and thus the feminist opposition to the cultural admiration for a manly man is completely built into me.

Is that bad? Is it different from internalized homophobia, like a kind of internalized manophobia?

It definitely raises that question because there is a way in which I'm denied a sexual self-identity. So, for example, when I notice I have muscles, I do think it's kind of neat but in an ironic way, which is really the same way I feel about the thick manly neck I now appear to have. But there's a broader point here because I'm in an ambivalent relation to more than just my maleness. I don't realize it most of the time, but I notice it when I see people who don't have it, people like one of my closest friends, who's one of the sweetest boys in the world and not all that unlike me politically. But he grew up in a world that admires men and manly things, and so he doesn't have any of the irony, the distance, the ambivalence that I have. And this extends to his relation to other domains as well, including race, class, and country, because unlike me, he also likes the United States unambivalently and the political condition of things generally. His life is good, his situation is good, he has enough money, and so he confidently figures it's an okay place for everybody.

Are you saying that having grown up in such a skeptical critical context has meant there is nothing that you can just flag-wave about?

Flag-waving is a good word. In contrast to my friend, I'm all too aware that my perspective is just one perspective and a privileged perspective at that. And this means that my friend can have both the confidence and the delusion that his perspective on the world is true, and sometimes I wish I could have that confidence and that delusion.

A great many people discover in college that their perspective is just partial, but I'm wondering whether part of what you're saying is that you've always known that. So you've never gotten to believe that the tooth fairy brings money or that America is the best country in the world or gender is real or that heterosexuality is natural?

Well, it would be sort of comforting sometimes to have an unambivalent relation to gender, country, religion, etc. But on the other hand, I recognize that other people's unambivalent relation to these things is based on too partial a perspective. So even though I can't be as confident as they are, I can confidently criticize them for their confidence.

Still on the downside, is there any way your upbringing has been a problem for you in relation to your parents?

This is a bit facetious, but it might have been nice to have something to rebel against, to have something to complain about during all those years when my friends were battling with their parents. But no, on the whole it's been nice. So either you were really good or you were really lucky.

Any other downside stuff you can think of?

Well, if you were doing it all over again, I would advise you to make it clearer to me that it's okay to have conventional desires as well as unconventional ones. As it was, I didn't talk openly about my romantic interests in girls when I was younger because I didn't like the idea of being a boy talking about girls. And even though I've now outgrown that and am comfortable talking with you about my romantic interests in women, I can still detect resonances of my old discomfort when I'm talking about women with male friends. If I feel we're talking too much about women, and especially if we're talking about women in a way that's at all objectifying, then I'll be inclined to cut the conversation short. But I wouldn't describe that as a genuine problem any more. It's just a part of who I am.

What is a problem, however, though not a very serious one, is that because I'm so aware of the historical commonness and meaning of guys' pressuring girls into sex, anything in my social life that even suggests I might be pressuring anyone will cause me to instantly draw back. And so the bottom line is that being unconventionally gendered and not wanting to be manly makes it harder for me to get dates because it means I can't be very forward without violating my own standards even if not anybody else's.

Does that mean you haven't been able to get dates or have sex with women?

No. It just means that things happen slowly.

Let's move away from the downside now. In addition to the things you've said so far, are there any ways you think your upbringing with respect to gender and sexuality has enhanced your life?

I get to be a complete person. That's what it comes down to.

A subquestion: Are there any sex or gender problems you're not likely to have, compared to others your sex and age?

I know people for whom coming out has been a huge struggle. I think that if I had ever had to come out as gay or bisexual at some point, I would have had an easier time of it than anybody else I've ever met in my life. In fact, it wouldn't even have been "coming out," because our family never had a built-in assumption of heterosexuality to "come out" from.

Next question: In your parents' gender-liberated child-rearing, there was a strong emphasis on antihomophobia and sex-positivity. That's not always a part of gender-liberated child-rearing. How has that affected you? How do you feel about that?

Antihomophobia first. Unlike practically everyone I know, gayness has always seemed totally normal to me, even at a gut level, because it's been there ever since I was born. So even though most of my friends are comfortable with nonheterosexuality, there's a deliberateness to their stance which I cherish not having to have. All right, I have to qualify that a bit because I faintly remember a time when I could imagine what it meant to be grossed out by two guys kissing. I can't imagine it now, but the fact that I do have such a memory somewhere in me means that my non-homophobia hasn't been automatic at every single moment of my life, but it's been damn close, as close as I think it could be for anyone living in twentieth-century America.

And as for sex-positivity, again, my main comment is that I think it's great, not just for social reasons but also for health and safety reasons. I have seen so many people in dangerous situations with respect to sex and not realizing it or not knowing what to do about it. One of the neatest consequences of my being educated and comfortable with sex is that I've gotten to be a kind of resource to my friends. I know where they can get birth control, where they can get tested for STDs, what books are good to read.

This question has to be limited by the people you know well, but do you have anything to say about how your attitudes and experience of sex and the body are different from other people's?

For me (not that this is an original idea), sex isn't primarily an act. It's a mutual exploration of bodies that doesn't have some one path or end in particular. And a corollary of this is that sex is continuous with any kind of physicality. It isn't completely separate from the way people might horse around or wrestle with one another the way guys so often do. So I don't compartmentalize it.

On the whole, my friends are more like me than unlike me on these issues, so I'm surprised when I unexpectedly encounter what I think of as an antiquated attitude among them. So it totally startled me when I said to one of my friends that I wasn't sure whether I had had sex with somebody, that I didn't know whether that was the best way to describe what had happened between us physically, and his response was so simplistic—if I had orgasm, it was sex; if not, it wasn't—whereas I didn't see what that had to do with it. But the reason I remember this so well is that I don't encounter this kind of attitude very often among my friends.

What about pleasure in the body and in the body's being sexual? Do you know what other people are like compared to you and whether the way you were raised had an impact on that?

On the one hand, our family's sex-positivity taught me that sex is a perfectly acceptable way to seek a wonderful kind of pleasure in the world. So I've had very little sexual anxiety to overcome, compared to other people. On the other hand, our family's feminism taught me that there are problematic reasons why men have typically gotten more pleasure than their partners. So I tend sexually to be more focused on giving than on receiving pleasure. So I might be having less fun than other people. But I doubt it.

If you have kids, how would you raise them in terms of gender and sexuality? How like your parents? How different from your parents?

I do see some holes in the way I was brought up. For example, sex-positivity was not something you guys taught unambivalently and uniformly. It was great in theory, but it's not a coincidence that one of the things you neglected to tell us at first was that people have sex for pleasure, not just for making babies. In other words, I think you were so focused on the scientific side of things that I didn't always fully realize that sex was fun. So I don't remember growing up thinking sex was this neat thing adults did, although I do remember thinking that about Pepsi. I would try to raise my kids in a more holistically sex-positive way.

In general, though, I think that what you did was great, and I think I would use it as a model when raising my own kids, although it's hard to imagine actually going through and drawing breasts on all the police-people again. In fact, I don't know if I would try to "retard my kids' gender education." That's a strategic decision, not a philosophical one: it's not that you didn't want us ever to know about gender, it's that you wanted us to learn about it at the age of reason so that we could view it critically. But I don't know if I agree with that strategically. My instinct is to be as complete about everything as early as possible, to tell my kids that our culture has gendered expectations but to teach the criticism at the same time.

Do you want to have kids?

Yes. Wanting kids is so deep and real for me that I hardly know how to begin to talk about it. I can't imagine not wanting kids. There are a million specific reasons why. One is that I have a great deal of nurturing in me that I need an outlet for. Another is that I'm curious about what a person would become as a result of having me for a parent. But these reasons don't explain the depth of my desire. I've heard it said, "children are the only real things." That captures it better than anything else. But I don't know if it would make sense to anyone who hasn't felt the same way.

Not only do I want kids, I want to be pregnant. I have real womb envy. Having a baby is one of the most basic and fundamental things the human body does, like eating and breathing and having sex. So I'm not getting the full human experience. To me, it seems weird that men are the beings who have been considered more complete historically because they're the ones who are missing one of the most fundamental aspects of humanness. In fact, I think the argument could be made that that whole phenomenon of men's being considered the more complete beings emerged as compensation for the fact that they can't make babies. I don't believe that historically, but it makes sense to me symbolically. And partly I would like to be pregnant because I'm an experimentalist. I think physical experiences are cool. I can't resist them. As soon as I heard about sensory-deprivation tanks, I wanted to be in one. As soon as I heard about smoking pot, I wondered what that would be like. And here's a huge experience, much deeper than these others, that lasts nine full months, and I wish I could see what it's like.

Do you want to get married?

You mean actually get married? Or do I envision spending my life with one partner? I don't know. I haven't figured any of that out yet.

It sounds like you're surer about having kids.

Definitely. That's one of the few things I feel sure of. I don't have any one preconceived model of what a life is supposed to look like, so I can't really understand wanting to marry as a desire apart from wanting to marry some one particular person. So the question becomes, is there someone I want to share my life with? And I haven't found such a person.

Are you a political activist with respect to gender and sexuality?

I wish I were, but no, not really. Mostly because these issues haven't felt as urgent to me emotionally as I know them to be intellectually. This may be because I haven't been inspired by injustice in my own life. A lot of the energy that other people bring to their political activities comes from their parents' and their peers' having been awful to them, and it's hard to get the energy to be an activist when it would have to come from just my own rational awareness that these are urgent problems, and that's not such an easy energy source. So I haven't been very politically active to date, but I would like to be more so in the future.

Are you a feminist?

Yes.

What does that mean to you?

Can I start by saying what it means to be an anything-ist? It means that the corresponding anything-ism is one of the most basic things that makes you tick. There aren't very many "ists" I would claim to be or many "isms" I would claim to espouse. Empiricism is probably the only other one. So being a feminist means that one of the most basic ways I look at the world, one of my most basic epistemologies, is in terms of where advantage and disadvantage have resided historically, and how that makes much that looks equal and fair inherently twisted.

Emily

Emily, one of the major goals of our feminist child-rearing practices was to enable you (insofar as possible) to treat gender as irrelevant. Would you say that you have actually managed to transcend gender?

I think I transcend gender in my head all the time. I don't look at other people as boys or girls. I put myself in their shoes and consider what they're feeling or how they're thinking or why they're acting the way they are. As for what I'm like myself: from the outside, I look like a girl, but from the inside out, I feel like a person who has aspects of both masculine and feminine but subscribes to neither in particular.

Say more about the ways in which you are unconventionally gendered.

In terms of dating style, I have frequently been the aggressor. I often make the first move when I'm interested in someone, whether verbally or sexually or in any other way, always being very direct and in pursuit rather than being the object of somebody else's romantic fantasies. In other words, I go out and get whoever is the object of my desire rather than waiting around in a store window for them to come to me.

And how does that work out for you?

Well! It works out well! Sometimes it can be frustrating in the sense that I wonder, if I didn't go out looking for romantic entanglements, would they come to me? But over time I see that I've had a string of successful romances which tend, when they end, to end in very good friendships.

Are there other examples of your being unconventionally gendered?

I don't shave my body hair. And I'm so much hairier than most women that people notice it and many comment on it, either because they've never seen so much body hair on a woman or because they aren't used to see-ing women who aren't shaven or because they want to express affirma-tion for women who don't shave or because they're shocked. Everyone's reaction is different, but I do always tend to get some reaction.

You have body hair where?

All over my legs and under my arms. It's between the knee and the crotch that is most striking to people, though, because even unshaven hippie chicks tend to have hair only under their arms or on their calves, so people aren't used to seeing a woman pretty much as hairy as a man from the waist down, especially in a bikini. And that brings a lot of people into contact with their homophobia, people who find me an attractive woman and then see my legs, because it's easy to imagine that these are the legs of a boy and that takes some getting used to, especially for boys who don't think of themselves as attracted to male-looking legs.

What's gone into your decision to be unshaven?

Partly the logistic nightmare of being shaven—razor burn, shaving rash, the frequency necessary to maintain any kind of a smooth shave. And also because it's against my politics and nature to allow society to tell me there's anything wrong aesthetically with the way my body is natu-rally. And also as an example for other people. Because lots of women who do shave comment, when they see my unshaven legs, that they wish they could get over their self-consciousness but they feel too unattrac-tive when they don't shave. And these are often women who don't have nearly as much body hair as I have. So if they can look at me and think my legs look fine, maybe they can become more accepting of their own legs.

What was the process of your coming to be able to do this? Did you have to get over your own self-consciousness?

As a young adolescent, I was filled with a terrified ambivalence the first time I took an old battered razor of Dad's and tried to shave my armpits and my legs with it. Never mind that I used no shaving cream or even water and soap. I knew that what I was undertaking was treachery to my mother's doctrine.

By the time I got into high school, I wouldn't tend to shave at all in the winter, but then in the summer, I would either shave up to where my shorts ended or I would shave all the way up if I was wearing a bathing suit. But then I started saying to myself: "Today I will go out without shaving even though I'm wearing shorts." And then in college I took a massage class where people were massaging oil into my legs and that was really hard for me at first. But I took it as a goal to be able to do it. Even now, though, if I don't feel like dealing with people's reactions to my body hair, then I'll wear a short-sleeved shirt instead of a tank top, and pants instead of shorts, but that's temporary and then I just have to figure out how to feel comfortable. It's an ongoing process. But I haven't shaved for a couple of years now, and the longer I go and the more contexts in which I expose my unshavenness, the easier it is and the more my legs just look like my legs to me. So over time I've gotten desensitized.

And by now you can think of yourself as a totally sexy woman?

Absolutely. And I can certainly run around all summer wearing shorts and swimming in a bikini without shaving at all, and that may look wacky to lots of people, but to me it feels completely sexy.

Other areas where you feel unconventionally gendered?

Well, I'm not straight. Even though I do mostly date boys, I've definitely been aware of being attracted to women, too. Also, I'm not someone who falls easily into monogamy or who even believes in monogamy in the way that lots of people who get married seem to believe in it. I'm not saying I will never get married or have a monogamous relationship. That's in my future where all kinds of new things are possible. So even though, according to stereotype, it's fairly conventional for women to be the ones who want to settle down and get married and for men to find it hard to commit themselves, so far at least, that question about commitment has been much more for myself than for anyone I have dated.

On a college campus, there are lots of people who aren't conventionally gendered, and most of them didn't grow up in families like ours. Is there any way you see yourself as different even from them?

Yes. They have usually had to come to their identities and beliefs on their own, often finding revelatory what I have always taken for granted. In other words, they are still building and developing tools, frequently analytic tools, that I was handed directly. They had—and still have—a lot more to unlearn.

Maybe we should move on now to the next major question, which is: How have you not transcended gender? In what ways are you still conventionally gendered despite your upbringing?

Well, externally I definitely look like a girl. I have conventional signals that say I'm a girl. I wear makeup sometimes. I have long hair. I'm kind of little. I have breasts.

What about hobbies and passions and interests?

I have a serious doll and paper-doll collection. And a collection of teacups for tea parties. All very girly. I have always played with costumes and clothing—also very girly and/or theatrical. But I also played soccer, softball, and field hockey until my interest in theater finally took over.

Someone else could easily categorize your interests as feminine and Jeremy's as masculine. And they could even go further and say that this is an example of how your parents' gender-liberated child-rearing "failed" because it produced a boy with boy interests and a girl with girl interests. How would you respond to that?

Why bother classifying our interests this way? It's just so obvious who is talented where. If you listen to me sing, you can't help but say, "This girl has a great voice." And if you look at Jeremy when he's doing math, it's clear that he is a mathematical "genius." People just have talents where they have them, and you're not going to get a boy who hates math becoming a great mathematician any more than you're going to get a girl who has no voice taking opera seriously. We don't do what we do well because Jeremy's a boy and I'm a girl. Also I think it's absurd to talk about any kind of child-rearing failing when it produces children with interests and even passions that are guided by talent.

In any of the areas where you see yourself as conventionally gendered, do you have anything to say about how you feel about being conventionally gendered?

Sometimes I wish it weren't obvious that I am female. I'd like to see how that would change my reality, my identity.

The next major category is about any potential downside of your upbringing, any ways in which your upbringing with respect to gender and sexuality has been a problem for you, mainly as a young adult, though you can refer back to the past if you want to. So the basic question is: What worries or conflicts or problems, if any, has your upbringing produced for you?

It has taken me a long time to feel like a pretty girl, to feel attractive and sexy, and that was important to me. I had lots of inner confidence, but it didn't translate into feeling attractive. And this had lots to do, I think, with having it feel unnatural to be a girl.

What do you mean that it felt unnatural to be a girl?

To be raised gender-liberated means to question gender, to undermine gender, to deconstruct and devalue gender in certain ways. And yet you still have the physical reality of being gendered at birth, of being born a boy or a girl, and it's not as if you can say, well, yeah, the doctor said I was a girl, but what does the doctor know? So here are these gendered individuals trying to transcend gender as they're growing up, trying to not believe in gender, trying to believe in something other than conventional gender, and that is a hard line to walk. Because there I was, a struggling and fairly heterosexual young woman wanting to be romantically involved with men, but I was also an ugly-duckling gender nonconformist who had a problem with being a girl and a problem with femininity because I knew it was a conventional gender trap just waiting to eat me up and spit me out in a little pink bow.

And so you have to find people who love you as you are. But when you're talking about romantic sexual energy, you first have to love yourself as you are. You have to feel sexy. And that's where it's been important as I've been growing up to figure out how to stand on turf where I feel comfortable, where I feel like I am an attractive human being.

So the hard part, the downside here, was . . . ?

Coming to terms with my desire to be a pretty girl. Because it's hard for me to accept "pretty girl" as an ideal. It's such a shallow limited goal. But I've had to accept that I do want to be an attractive person and I am female.

Maybe we've covered this already, but one of the questions I had written down for you was: There's a feminist bias against femininity, and does that raise a question of how to be a woman?

That's where I have my own ideas about what a feminist utopia should look like. I think you have to indulge people's fantasies, not deny them. The constructs of masculinity and femininity, whatever feminist biases may arise against them, will never be done away with completely. Better to invite everyone to dabble in either or both—or to invent something new altogether. There is nothing intrinsically wrong with either, unless we are bound by our genitalia to one or the other.

Let's shift the topic a bit now while still staying on the downside. Are there any worries, conflicts, or problems that resulted from your upbringing with respect to either your peers or your parents?

It is sometimes difficult to have been born into a tradition of deconstructing the very thing that is at the heart of so many people's identities: their gender. It is very hard to convince people who believe that the gender of the body and the gender of the psyche are inherently and naturally linked to see things from my point of view, let alone to see me as I am.

As for conflicts with my parents, I would have to say that even during times when my life has felt desperately hard to live, the reasons were never ideological ones. So I've never once wished that my parents had raised me more conventionally. It just never felt as if it were my political beliefs or my beliefs around gender and sexuality that were making my life difficult. In fact, I've always felt privileged to have been raised by such visionaries. I don't agree with every little detail of my upbringing, with certain ways you might have represented certain things at certain moments, but I always felt it was the right upbringing for me.

Let's move away from the downside of your upbringing now. In addition to any of the things you've said so far, are there any ways you think your upbringing with respect to gender and sexuality has enhanced your life?

I think one of the most fabulous and successful things you and Dad did was to keep Jeremy and me in a very specific and cultivated state of ignorance when it came to the narrow-minded biases and beliefs of more conventional society. So, for example, I love the fact that I literally did not know that people discriminated between relationships involving same-sex and opposite-sex partners (let alone that they discriminated against same-sex partners) until I encountered homophobia myself in the out-side world at age five when someone's big brother called my best friend Sarah and me "lezzies" because we were holding hands.

If you have kids, how would you raise them in terms of gender and sexuality? How like your parents? How different from your parents?

I think I'm very different from either of my parents, but I think my beliefs still come directly from my parents. So it would manifest differently for me. For example, I wouldn't say that the lady wearing lots of makeup in the grocery store is trying to look like a clown. I don't think there's anything inherently wrong with saying that, but it's not what I would say. I would pass along the same ideas and ideals, but with different details.

Do you want to say any more?

The two of you gave me a huge range within which to play and to move beyond gender, and I really appreciate that. For instance, for some of my gender nonconformist peers, coming out to their parents is one of the most terrifying, sometimes tragic moments in their lives. I feel very lucky that I will never have to face something like this. If anything, my parents prepared me to come out to the world.

Do you want to have kids?

I think so. At least one. I think so. But I don't necessarily want to be in a conventional-looking nuclear family, partly because I don't know if I want to be monogamously mated. I do think it's important for kids to have some kind of stability, though, even if it's a fluid stability, so I don't know what I'm going to do about all that yet.

Would you describe yourself as a feminist, and what does that mean to you?

Yes. It means I stand for and stand up for women's rights, for equality between men and women, for education against and for the abolition of sexism, sexual discrimination, and so on.

It always astounds me when bright, liberated peers of mine are unwilling to label themselves feminists. Even in a women's studies class at Oberlin College a few years ago, most women in the class balked rather than answer yes to the question, "Are you a feminist?" Their reasons? Mostly that feminism has come to mean so many different things, how could they ally themselves with all of them? As far as I'm concerned, this is only a few steps away from identifying all feminists as "bra-burning lesbian dykes" and sidestepping commitment to the cause that earned us a place at Oberlin College in the first place.

Conclusion

Just as Daryl and I long ago embarked on our experiment in egalitarian partnering and parenting with the naive belief that we could easily eliminate all traces of gender from our family functioning, so too we embarked on our experiment in feminist child-rearing with the naive belief that gender would ultimately not figure in our children's psyches, that they would truly be able to transcend gender. Emily and Jeremy are less naive. They know from personal experience that when traditional gender categories are removed as a legitimate source of identity—but one still must live in a highly gendered culture—new identity issues emerge that they are working on in their own quite revolutionary ways. And some of the old identity issues hang around as well, if in a somewhat altered form. Thus, Emily, the girl, is still more tangled up in the body than is Jeremy, the boy.

But even if gender still lingers in our children's psyches, when all is said and done, I remain a total advocate for the kind of feminist partnering, parenting, and child-rearing that Daryl and I experimented with for almost thirty years, not only because I judge our experiment to have worked well for us and our children, but also because, from a broader perspective, I am even more worried today than I was when I was young about where our society is heading.

We are, after all, in the midst of a moral panic, with the religious right battling vigorously—and, all too often, successfully—against many of the gains that either have been made or are now being fought for in the domain of gender and sexuality, including abortion rights, access to birth control, sex education in the schools, AIDS education, custody rights for gay parents, antidiscrimination laws for gay men and lesbians, and so on. And whereas in the 1960s, the culture was just opening itself up to all kinds of gender border crossings, including, for example, having more male teachers in nursery schools, today there is so much hysteria about sex in general and the sexual abuse of children in particular that not only are males increasingly unwelcome in early childhood education but insurance policies for preschools are actually being written that require two adults to be present every time a baby's diaper is changed.

My students sometimes ask if the struggle is worth the bother because the system as a whole seems so intransigent. But think about the alternative, I say in reply. If people like us don't struggle individually and collectively to diversify our social institutions, to make them more open with respect to gender and sexuality, much of the openness and nontraditionality that we have come to take for granted could disappear because our culture's traditional social institutions have inertia on their side. Like the current in a stream, they are ready to carry us all to their own destination, and if we don't want to go there, either individually or collectively, then we have no choice but to struggle, no choice but to try as hard as we can to rechannel at least a part of that cultural stream.

It won't be easy, and the struggle will surely not end in our lifetime. But to borrow a phrase from the philosopher Judith Butler, what glorious "gender trouble" we will have made for society in the meantime.

Epilogue

Daryl and I talked many times during the writing of this memoir about whether and how his voice should be included, but we didn't resolve the matter until I had almost finished and the absence of his voice finally began to feel like a huge lurking presence. An interview of the sort I did with the kids didn't feel quite right, so we tried tape-recording and editing a conversation between us. In the end, however, we decided on an essay-style commentary by Daryl alone. What follows is Daryl's essay:

In Woody Allen's film *Manhattan,* a man's wife divorces him, enters a romantic relationship with another woman, and then writes an unflattering, tell-all book about her ex, played by Woody Allen, and their failed marriage. He did not get to write an epilogue.

I am more fortunate. After reading the manuscript of Sandy's memoir, I agreed with her that the absence of my voice hovered over it like an ambiguous presence, a Rorschach inkblot onto which readers could too easily project their own perceptions of how I must be reacting. At the least, they would be left wondering whether I am reenacting the anguished role of Woody Allen's character or chafing to tell "my side" of the story.

In fact, however, Sandy's memories, perceptions, and interpretations of our life together are quite similar to my own; for me, this memoir serves as a personal scrapbook or album which enables me to reminisce about a major part of my life that I will always cherish. Moreover, I have no ambivalence about its being published. After all, I encouraged us to go public with our marriage in the first place, and simple truth-in-advertising would seem to require that we update the story—especially considering that things didn't work out exactly as we had envisioned them thirty-three years ago.

Which raises the question that I believe readers are likely to have a legitimate curiosity about but which is left largely unanswered by the memoir: Why did Sandy and I separate after nearly thirty years of marriage?

In providing my own personal answer to this question, I would first like to underscore the point made by Sandy in the preface, that our separation was not precipitated by issues of sexual orientation. Because both Sandy and I have had same-sex relationships since we separated, it is particularly tempting to suppose (incorrectly) that our marriage was in some important way sexually incomplete or inauthentic. In particular, the belief that every gay man in a heterosexual marriage must necessarily be living a lie, enduring an unhappy suppressed sexuality, or leading a clandestine double life is so ingrained in the popular imagination that many people find it difficult to imagine that it might not be universally so. Our society has yet to learn that human sexuality is far more fluid than the current set of limited categories implies.

No, the reasons for our separation are both deeper and more

mundane than sexual orientation. In fact, I believe that our separation was precipitated by precisely the same complementary personality styles that drew us together and sustained us for nearly thirty years. As noted in the memoir, Sandy sought someone stable and solid to save her from the chaos of her earlier life, and I sought someone who could elicit my own emotionality and extricate me from what Sandy and I often called my "self-sufficiency run amuck." Sandy was the first person in my adult life on whom I could lean emotionally.

I believe that this began to shift quite subtly in the late seventies, when Sandy failed to gain tenure at Stanford. The denial of tenure, the unsuccessful appeals, our subsequent job search, and the birth of Jeremy all put her under a lot of stress, and I gladly stepped into the role of emotional nurturer. By itself, there was nothing wrong with that, but I began to consider my own stresses to be trivial compared with Sandy's "real" ones. As a result, I began increasingly to avoid "burdening" her with anything that was troubling me. My solicitous role easily masked the fact that this, too, is a form of emotional withdrawal. A perpetual therapist is not an optimal lover. Because I no longer relied on her to draw me out emotionally, I began to revert to my pre-Sandy, emotionally self-sufficient style, and this began to set the stage for increased distance between us in later years.

I also think that we were both victims of the naive view that one person can fulfill all of another person's needs. That is, I think we were too encapsulated a unit within our own lives and that of our children. It is true that I had a number of outside interests, such as my involvement with Planned Parenthood and additional activities that I could pursue on my own, such as playing the piano or giving magic shows. But Sandy did not. The children and I constituted virtually her entire nonprofessional life. More generally, I don't think we were creative enough in refreshing our marriage with both shared and independent activities outside the family unit. Here our shared introversion exacerbated the problem. I have always savored solitude and, hence, did little to push us out of our cocoon.

And finally, my avoidance of conflict—the same trait that made our egalitarian relationship so easy to sustain over the years—became an increasingly important factor in distancing us from one another. As the complexities of our children's adolescences and their developmental issues became more prominent, my willingness—even eagerness—to defer to Sandy's "obvious" expertise led to the fragmenting of our family into the mom-and-kids unit and the dad unit. Sandy's plaint that she often felt like a single parent was the inevitable sign that something had broken and—according to my personal understanding of events—ultimately led her to initiate our separation. How ironic that our egalitarian relationship should founder on such a gender cliché.

But there is a second, more upbeat irony that emerges from our separation. I believe that we have been better and more equal parents since we separated. We are now more willing to accept different models of what constitutes good parenting, and I am freer to play a parental role that is more consonant with my personal style without feeling that I am failing to live up to some uniform, Sandy-defined standard. A final irony here is that I think the kids themselves have always been more accepting of our different parenting styles than we were. Sandy may have felt like a single parent at times, but I don't think the kids ever felt that they had only a single parent. I wish we could have learned this elementary lesson at lesser cost.

Which leads to the question: Knowing what I know now, would I do it all over again? Yes. Would I do some things differently? Of course. But even if it still ended in separation, I would do it all over again. The four of us are still family. Sandy and I are still kin.

Open the temple gates unto my love,
Open them wide that she may enter in,
And all the posts adorn as doth behove,
And all the pillars deck with garlands trim,
For to receive this saint with honour due,
That cometh in to you . . .

Bring her up to the high altar, that she may
The sacred ceremonies there partake,
The which do endless matrimony make;
And let the roaring organ loudly play
The praises of the Lord in lively notes;
The whiles, with hollow throats,
The choristers the joyous anthem sing,
That all the woods may answer, and their echoes ring. . . .

Sing, ye sweet angels, Alleluia sing,
That all the woods may answer and your echo ring.

EDMUND SPENSER, from "Epithalamion"

Hear the mellow wedding bells,—
Golden bells!
What a world of happiness their harmony foretells!
Through the balmy air of night
How they ring out their delight!
From the molten golden notes,
What a liquid ditty floats
To the turtle-dove that listens, while she gloats
On the moon!
Oh, from out the sounding cells,
What a gush of euphony voluminously wells!
How it swells!
How it dwells

On the Future! How it tells
Of the rapture that impels
To the swinging and the ringing
Of the bells, bells, bells,
Of the bells, bells, bells, bells,
Bells, bells, bells,—
To the rhyming and the chiming of the bells!

EDGAR ALLAN POE, from "The Bells"

When our two souls stand up erect and strong,
Face to face, silent, drawing nigh and nigher,
Until the lengthening wings break into fire
At either curved point,—what bitter wrong
Can the earth do us, that we should not long
Be here contented! Think. In mounting higher,
The angels would press on us and aspire
To drop some golden orb of perfect song
Into our deep, dear silence. Let us stay
Rather on earth, Beloved—where the unfit
Contrarious moods of men recoil away
And isolate pure spirits, and permit
A place to stand and love in for a day . . .

ELIZABETH BARRETT BROWNING, from Sonnet XXII
from Sonnets from the Portuguese

That I may come near to her, draw me nearer to thee than to her; that I may know her, make me to know thee more than her; that I may love her with the perfect love of a perfectly whole heart, cause me to love thee more than her and most of all.   Amen. Amen.

That nothing may be between me and her, be thou between us, every moment. That we may be constantly togther, draw us into separate loneliness with thyself. And when we meet breast to breast, my God, let it be on thine own.   Amen. Amen.

TEMPLE GAIRDNER, prayer before his marriage

He is here, Urania's son,
Hymen come, from helicon;
God that glads the lover's heart,
He is here to join and part.
So the groomsman quits your side
And the bridegroom seeks the bride:
Friend and comrade yield you o'er
To her that hardly loves you more.

Now the sun his skyward beam
Hast tilted from the Ocean stream.
Light the Indies, laggard sun:
Happy bridegroom, day is done,
And the star from Oeta's steep
Calls to bed but not to sleep.

Happy bridegroom, Hesper brings
All desired and timely things.
All whom morning sends to roam,
Hesper loves to lead them home.
Home return who him behold,
Child to mother, sheep to fold,
Bird to nest from wandering wide:
Happy bridegroom, seek your bride.

Pour it out, the golden cup
Given and guarded, brimming up,
Safe through jostling markets borne
And the thicket of the thorn;
Folly spured and danger past,
Pour it to the god at last.

Now, to smother noise and light,
Is stolen abroad the wildering night,
And the blotting shades confuse
Path and meadow full of dews;
And the high heavens, that all control,
Turn in silence round the pole.
Catch the starry beams they shed
Prospering the marriage bed.

. . . All is quiet, no alarms;
Nothing fear of nightly harms.
Safe you sleep on guarded ground,
And in silent circle round
The thoughts of friends keep watch and ward,
Harnessed angels, hand on sword.

A. E. HOUSMAN, from "Epithalamium"

". . . I hereby give myself. I love you. You are the only being whom I can love absolutely with my complete self, with all my flesh and mind and heart. You are my mate, my perfect partner, and I am yours. You must *feel* this now, as I do. . . . It was a marvel that we ever met. It is some kind of divine luck that we are together now. We must never, never part again. We are, here in this, *necessary* beings, like gods. As we look at each other we verify, we *know*, the perfection of our love, we *recognise* each other. *Here* is my life, here if need be is my death. It's life and death, as if they were to destroy Israel—if I forget thee, O Jerusalem—"

IRIS MURDOCH, from *The Book and the Brotherhood*

. . . may her bridegroom bring her to a house
Where all's accustomed, ceremonious;
For arrogance and hatred are the wares
Peddled in the thoroughfares.
How but in custom and in ceremony
Are innocence and beauty born?
Ceremony's a name for the rich horn,
And custom for the spreading laurel tree.

WILLIAM BUTLER YEATS,
from "A Prayer for My Daughter"

To the wife of my bosom
All happiness from everything
And her husband.
May he be good and considerate
Gay and cheerful and restful.
And make her the best wife
In the world
The happiest and the most content
With reason.
To the wife of my bosom
Whose transcendent virtues
Are those to be most admired
Loved and adored and indeed
Her virtues are all inclusive

Eternal Vows in Sacred Space · 113

Her virtues her beauty and her beauties
Her charms her qualities her joyous nature
All of it makes of her husband
A proud and happy man . . .

GERTRUDE STEIN, from "Patriarchal Poetry"

V

*The Miracle of
the Body*

I'm the one who has the body,
you're the one who holds the breath.

You know the secret of my body,
I know the secret of your breath.

That's why your body
is in mine.

You know
and I know, Ramanatha,

the miracle

of your breath
in my body.

DEVARA DASIMAYYA,
poem to Lord Siva (Ramanatha),
translation by A. K. Ramanujan

The sexual revolution and the development of birth control have changed the pattern of life for many couples in the Western world, but wedding ceremonies still contain veiled celebrations of the act of sexual initiation.

Some passages in the section that follows may be inappropriate for reading aloud in a formal setting. But wise men and women, as all soon-to-be-married couples must be, know we live in this life in our bodies, which inspire in us the love we may later on choose to celebrate in its transcendent aspects. We go as desire moves us: the poet Denise Levertov calls it "the ache of marriage . . . the ark of the ache of it."

Hail to Priapus, father of us all, hail!
Grant me eternally flowering virility
So I may charm both men and beautiful girls.
Keep me from being worn out by tedious
dinner parties and festivals,
And don't send me old age, decrepitude, or some unhappy death
Which will drag me off to the land
from where no one returns.
Hail to holy Priapus, father Priapus, hail!
Up and away, O joyous throng,
However many you are,
Up and away, run!
Run to the sacred wood,
You maidens who worship the sacred waters,
Run, all of you, to friendly Priapus,
And say in your charming voices:
Hail, O holy Priapus, father of us all, hail!
In fact, it is he who bids us sport in the woods,
Frolic in the water as we like.
He keeps bothersome people at a distance,
Those who irreverently pollute the streams.
So now say to him:
O Priapus, O divine one, be good to us!
O Priapus, powerful friend, hail,
And may it please you to be called

Progenitor of the whole world,
Yes, even of the Universe itself, even of Pan!
For in truth, earth, air, and sea were conceived
Out of your virility, your vigorous lust.
Jove himself lays down his thunderbolts when you speak,
While lovely Venus honors you, and Cupid does too,
And Grace, with her dancing sisters,
Bringers of joy, while
Virgins call on you to prepare them for marriage and
The bride calls on you to make sure
Her husband's manhood will stand shining forever.
Hail, O sacred father Priapus, hail!

Greek Prayer to Priapus

O Bride brimful of
rosy little loves!

O brightest jewel of
the Queen of Paphos!

Come now
            to your
bedroom to your
bed
        and play there
sweetly   gently
with your bridegroom

And may Hesperus
lead you not at all
unwilling
                until

you stand wondering
before the silver

Throne of Hera
Queen of Marriage

SAPPHO, translation
by Mary Barnard

249

Wild Nights - Wild Nights!
Were I with thee
Wild Nights should be
Our luxury!

Futile - the Winds -
To a Heart in port -
Done with the Compass -
Done with the Chart!

Rowing in Eden -
Ah, the Sea!
Might I but moor - Tonight -
In Thee!

EMILY DICKINSON,
from *The Complete Poems*,
edited by Thomas H. Johnson

I know not whether thou has been absent:
I lie down with thee, I rise up with thee,
In my dreams thou art with me.
If my eardrops tremble in my ears,
I know it is thou moving within my heart.

Aztec love song

The Song of
Solomon

Characters:

KING SOLOMON
THE SHULAMITE
THE BROTHERS
CHORUS OF THE DAUGHTERS OF JERUSALEM

Scene I

THE SHULAMITE (the bride)

Let him kiss me with the kisses of his mouth:
For thy love is better than wine.

The king hath brought me into his chambers.

THE DAUGHTERS OF JERUSALEM

We will be glad and rejoice in thee,
We will make mention of thy love more than of wine:
Rightly do they love thee.

THE SHULAMITE

I am black, but comely,
O ye daughters of Jerusalem,
As the tents of Kedar,
As the curtains of Solomon.

Look not upon me, because I am swarthy,
Because the sun hath scorched me.

Tell me, O thou whom my soul loveth,
Where thou feedest thy flock, where thou makest it to rest at
    noon:
For why should I be as one that is veiled
Beside the flocks of thy companions?

KING SOLOMON

If thou know not, O thou fairest among women,
Go thy way forth by the footsteps of the flock,
And feed thy kids beside the shepherds' tents.

I have compared thee, O my love,
To a steed in Pharaoh's chariots.
Thy cheeks are comely with plaits of hair,
Thy neck with strings of jewels.
We will make thee plaits of gold
With studs of silver.

THE SHULAMITE

While the king sat at his table,
My spikenard sent forth its fragrance.
My beloved is unto me as a bundle of myrrh,
That lieth betwixt my breasts.
My beloved is unto me as a cluster of henna-flowers
In the vineyards of En-gedi.

KING SOLOMON

Behold, thou art fair, my love; behold, thou art fair;
Thine eyes are as doves.

THE SHULAMITE

Behold, thou art fair, my beloved, yea, pleasant:
Also our couch is green.
The beams of our house are cedars,
And our rafters are firs.

I am a rose of Sharon,
A lily of the valleys.

KING SOLOMON

As a lily among thorns,
So is my love among the daughters.

THE SHULAMITE

As the apple tree among the trees of the wood,
So is my beloved among the sons.
I sat down under his shadow with great delight,
And his fruit was sweet to my taste.

He brought me to the banqueting house,
And his banner over me was love.
Stay ye me with raisins, comfort me with apples:
For I am sick of love.
His left hand is under my head,
And his right hand doth embrace me.
I adjure you, O daughters of Jerusalem,
By the roes, and by the hinds of the field,
That ye stir not up, nor awaken love,
Until it please.

Scene II

The voice of my beloved! behold, he cometh,
Leaping upon the mountains, skipping upon the hills.
My beloved is like a roe or a young hart:
Behold, he standeth behind our wall,
He looketh in at the windows,
He showeth himself through the lattice.
My beloved spoke, and said unto me,
"Rise up, my love, my fair one, and come away.
For, lo, the winter is past,
The rain is over and gone;
The flowers appear on the earth;
The time of the singing of birds is come,
And the voice of the turtle is heard in our land;
The fig tree ripeneth her green figs,
And the vines are in blossom,
They give forth their fragrance.
Arise, my love, my fair one, and come away.
O my dove, that art in the clefts of the rock, in the covert of
    the steep place,
Let me see thy countenance, let me hear thy voice;
For sweet is thy voice, and thy countenance is comely.

THE BROTHERS

Take us the foxes, the little foxes, that spoil the vineyards;
For our vineyards are in blossom.

THE SHULAMITE

My beloved is mine, and I am his:
He feedeth his flock among the lilies.

Until the day be cool, and the shadows flee away,
Turn, my beloved, and be thou like a roe or a young hart
Upon the mountains of Bether.
By night on my bed I sought him whom my soul loveth:
I sought him, but I found him not.
I said, "I will rise now, and go about the city,
In the streets and in the broad ways,
I will seek him whom my soul loveth":
I sought him, but I found him not.
The watchmen that go about the city found me:
To whom I said, "Saw ye him whom my soul loveth?"
It was but a little that I passed from them,
When I found him whom my soul loveth:
I held him, and would not let him go,
Until I had brought him into my mother's house,
And into the chamber of her that conceived me.

I adjure you, O daughters of Jerusalem,
By the roes, and by the hinds of the field,
That ye stir not up, nor awaken love,
Until it please.

Scene III

THE DAUGHTERS OF JERUSALEM

Who is this that cometh up out of the wilderness like pillars of
    smoke,
Perfumed with myrrh and frankincense,
With all powders of the merchant?

Behold, it is the litter of Solomon;
Threescore mighty men are about it,
Of the mighty men of Israel.

They all handle the sword, and are expert in war:
Every man hath his sword upon his thigh,
Because of fear in the night.

King Solomon made himself a palanquin
Of the wood of Lebanon.
He made the pillars thereof of silver,
The bottom thereof of gold, the seat of it of purple,
The midst thereof being paved with love,
From the daughters of Jerusalem.

Go forth, O ye daughters of Zion, and behold King Solomon,
With the crown wherewith his mother hath crowned him in the
    day of his espousals,
And in the day of the gladness of his heart.

KING SOLOMON

Behold, thou art fair, my love; behold, thou art fair;
Thine eyes are as doves behind thy veil:
Thy hair is as a flock of goats,
That lie along the side of Mount Gilead.
Thy teeth are like a flock of ewes that are newly shorn,
Which are come up from the washing;
Whereof every one hath twins,
And none is bereaved among them.

Thy lips are like a thread of scarlet,
And thy mouth is comely:
Thy temples are like a piece of a pomegranate
Behind thy veil.
Thy two breasts are like two fawns that are twins of a roe,
Which feed among the lilies.

Until the day be cool, and the shadows flee away,
I will get me to the mountain of myrrh,
And to the hill of frankincense.

Thou art all fair, my love;
And there is no spot in thee.
Come with me from Lebanon, my bride,
With me from Lebanon:
Look from the top of Amana,
From the top of Senir and Hermon,
From the lions' dens,
From the mountains of the leopards.
Thou hast ravished my heart, my sister, my bride;
Thou hast ravished my heart with one of thine eyes.
With one chain of thy neck.
How fair is thy love, my sister, my bride!
How much better is thy love than wine!
And the smell of thine ointments than all manner of spices!
Thy lips, O my bride, drop as the honeycomb:
Honey and milk are under thy tongue;
And the smell of thy garments is like the smell of Lebanon.

A garden shut up is my sister, my bride;
A spring shut up, a fountain sealed.
Thy shoots are an orchard of pomegranates, with precious fruits;
Henna with spikenard plants,
Spikenard and saffron,
Calamus and cinnamon, with all trees of frankincense;
Myrrh and aloes, with all the chief spices.
Thou art a fountain of gardens,
A well of living waters,
And flowing streams from Lebanon.

THE SHULAMITE

Awake, O north wind; and come, thou south;
Blow upon my garden, that the spices thereof may flow out.
Let my beloved come into his garden,
And eat his precious fruits.

KING SOLOMON

I am come into my garden, my sister, my bride:
I have gathered my myrrh with my spice;
I have eaten my honeycomb with my honey;
I have drunk my wine with my milk.
Eat, O friends;
Drink, yea, drink abundantly, O beloved.

Scene IV

THE SHULAMITE

I was asleep, but my heart waked:
It is the voice of my beloved that knocketh, saying,
"Open to me, my sister, my love, my dove, my undefiled:
For my head is filled with dew,
My locks with the drops of the night."
I have put off my coat; how shall I put it on?
I have washed my feet; how shall I defile them?
My beloved put in his hand by the hole of the door,
And my heart was moved for him.
I rose up to open to my beloved;
And my hands dropped with myrrh,
And my fingers with liquid myrrh,
Upon the handles of the bolt.

I opened to my beloved;
But my beloved had withdrawn himself, and was gone.
My soul had failed me when he spoke:
I sought him, but I could not find him;
I called him, but he gave me no answer.
The watchmen that go about the city found me,
They smote me, they wounded me;
The keepers of the walls took away my mantle from me.

I adjure you, O daughters of Jerusalem, if ye find my beloved,
That ye tell him, that I am sick of love.

THE DAUGHTERS OF JERUSALEM

What is thy beloved more than another beloved,
O thou fairest among women?
What is thy beloved more than another beloved,
That thou dost so adjure us?

THE SHULAMITE

My beloved is white and ruddy,
The chiefest among ten thousand.
His head is as the most fine gold,
His locks are bushy, and black as a raven.
His eyes are like doves beside the water brooks;
Washed with milk, and fitly set.
His cheeks are as a bed of spices, as banks of sweet herbs:

His lips are as lilies, dropping liquid myrrh.
His hands are as rings of gold set with beryl:
His body is as ivory work overlaid with sapphires.
His legs are as pillars of marble, set upon sockets of fine gold:
His aspect is like Lebanon, excellent as the cedars.

His mouth is most sweet: yea, he is altogether lovely.
This is my beloved, and this is my friend,
O daughters of Jerusalem.

THE DAUGHTERS OF JERUSALEM

Whither is thy beloved gone,
O thou fairest among women?
Whither hath thy beloved turned him,
That we may seek him with thee?

THE SHULAMITE

My beloved is gone to his garden, to the beds of spices,
To feed in the gardens, and to gather lilies.
I am my beloved's, and my beloved is mine:
He feedeth his flock among the lilies.

Scene V

KING SOLOMON

Thou art beautiful, O my love, as Tirzah,
Comely as Jerusalem,
Terrible as an army with banners.
Turn away thine eyes from me,
For they have overcome me.
Thy hair is as a flock of goats,
That lie along the side of Gilead.

Thy teeth are like a flock of ewes,
Which are come up from the washing;
Whereof every one hath twins,
And none is bereaved among them.

Thy temples are like a piece of pomegranate
Behind thy veil.

THE DAUGHTERS OF JERUSALEM

Who is she that looketh forth as the morning,
Fair as the moon,
Clear as the sun,
Terrible as an army with banners?

THE SHULAMITE

I went down into the garden of nuts,
To see the green plants of the valley,
To see whether the vine budded,
And the pomegranates were in flower.

THE DAUGHTERS OF JERUSALEM

Return, return, O Shulamite;
Return, return, that we may look upon thee.

KING SOLOMON

How beautiful are thy feet in sandals, O prince's daughter!
The joints of thy thighs are like jewels,
The work of the hands of a cunning workman.
Thy navel is like a round goblet,
Wherein no mingled wine is wanting:
Thy belly is like a heap of wheat
Set about with lilies.

Thy two breasts are like two fawns
That are twins of a roe.
Thy neck is like the tower of ivory;
Thine eyes as the pools in Heshbon, by the gate of Bathrabbim;

Thy nose is like the tower of Lebanon
Which looketh toward Damascus.

Thine head upon thee is like Carmel,
And the hair of thine head like purple;
The king is held captive in the tresses thereof.
How fair and how pleasant art thou,
O love, for delights!
This thy stature is like to a palm tree,
And thy breasts to clusters of grapes.
I said, "I will climb up into the palm tree,
I will take hold of the branches thereof":
Let thy breasts be as clusters of the vine,
And the smell of thy breath like apples;
And thy mouth like the best wine,
That goeth down smoothly for my beloved,
Gliding through the lips of those that are asleep.

THE SHULAMITE

I am my beloved's,
And his desire is toward me.
Come, my beloved, let us go forth into the field;
Let us lodge in the villages.
Let us get up early to the vineyards;
Let us see whether the vine hath budded, and its blossom be
    open,
And the pomegranates be in flower:

There will I give thee my love.
The mandrakes give forth fragrance,
And at our doors are all manner of precious fruits, new and
    old.
Which I have laid up for thee, O my beloved.

Oh that thou wert as my brother,
That sucked the breasts of my mother!
When I should find thee without, I would kiss thee;
Yea, and none would despise me.
I would lead thee, and bring thee into my mother's house
Who would instruct me;
I would cause thee to drink of spiced wine,
Of the juice of my pomegranate.
His left hand should be under my head,
And his right hand should embrace me.

I adjure you, O daughters of Jerusalem,
That ye stir not up, nor awaken love,
Until it please.

Scene VI

THE DAUGHTERS OF JERUSALEM

Who is this that cometh up from the wilderness,
Leaning upon her beloved?

KING SOLOMON

Under the apple tree I awakened thee:
There thy mother was in travail with thee,
There was she in travail that brought thee forth.

THE SHULAMITE

Set me as a seal upon thine heart, as a seal upon thine arm:
For love is strong as death;
Jealousy is cruel as the grave:
The flashes thereof are flashes of fire,

A very flame of the Lord.
Many waters cannot quench love,
Neither can the floods drown it:
If a man would give all the substance of his house for love
He would utterly be contemned.

THE BROTHERS

We have a little sister,
And she hath no breasts:
What shall we do for our sister
In the day when she shall be spoken for?
If she be a wall,
We will build upon her a turret of silver:
And if she be a door,
We will inclose her with boards of cedar.

THE SHULAMITE

I am a wall, and my breasts like the towers thereof:
Then was I in his eyes as one that found peace.
Solomon had a vineyard at Baal-hamon;
He let out the vineyard unto keepers;
Every one for the fruit thereof was to bring a thousand pieces
    of silver.
My vineyard, which is mine, is before me:
Thou, O Solomon, shalt have the thousand,
And those that keep the fruit thereof two hundred.

KING SOLOMON

Thou that dwellest in the gardens,
The companions hearken for thy voice:
Cause me to hear it.

Make haste, my beloved,
And be thou like to a roe or to a young hart
Upon the mountains of spices.

The Song of Solomon (King James Version)
set as a play by Ernest Sutherland Bates

My body, the horn,
The Boat of Heaven,
Is full of eagerness like the young moon.
My untilled land lies fallow.

Who will plow my body?
Who will plow my high field?
Who will plow my wet ground?

Who will station the ox there?
Who will plow my body?

Great Lady, the King will plow your body.
I the King will plow your body.

Then plow my body, man of my heart!
Plow my body! . . .

He has sprouted; he has burgeoned!
He is lettuce planted by the water.
He is the one my womb loves best . . .

My honey-man, my honey-man sweetens me always.
My lord, the honey-man of the gods . . .

Let the bed that rejoices the heart be prepared!
Let the bed that sweetens the loins be prepared!
Let the royal bed be prepared!

The bed is ready!
The bed is waiting!

The king went with lifted head to the holy loins.
He went to the queen with lifted head.
He opened wide his arms to the holy priestess of heaven.

from an ancient Sumerian sacred-wedding poem,
adapted from the translation by
Diane Wolkstein and Samuel Noah Kramer

As the mirror to my hand,
the flowers to my hair,
kohl to my eyes,
tambul to my mouth
musk to my breast
necklace to my throat,
ecstasy to my flesh,
heart to my home—

as wing to bird,
water to fish,
life to the living—
so you to me.

But tell me,
Madhava, beloved,
who are you?
Who are you really?

Vidyapati says, they are one another.

VIDYAPATI, Hindu love poem,
translation by Edward C. Dimock, Jr.,
and Denise Levertov

Let the earth of my body be mixed with the earth
my beloved walks on.
Let the fire of my body be the brightness
in the mirror that reflects his face.
Let the water of my body join the waters
of the lotus pool he bathes in.
Let the breath of my body be air
lapping his tired limbs.
Let me be sky, and moving through me
that cloud-dark Shyama, my beloved.

Hindu love poem,
translation by Edward C. Dimock, Jr.,
and Denise Levertov

. . . It is said by some that there is no fixed time or order
between the kiss and the pressing or scratching with the nails
or fingers, but that all these things should be done generally
before sexual union takes place, while striking and making the
various sounds generally takes place at the time of the union.
Vatsyayana, however, thinks that anything may take place at
any time, for love does not care for time or order. . . .

The following are the places for kissing, viz., the forehead, the eyes, the cheeks, the throat, the bosom, the breasts, the lips, and the interior of the mouth. Moreover the people of the Lat country kiss also the following places, viz., the joints of the thighs, the arms and the navel. But Vatsyayana thinks that though kissing is practiced by these people in the above places on account of the intensity of their love, and the customs of their country, it is not fit to be practiced by all.

Now in a case of a young girl there are three sorts of kisses, viz.:

> The nominal kiss.
> The throbbing kiss.
> The touching kiss.

1. When a girl only touches the mouth of her lover with her own, but does not herself do anything, it is called the "nominal kiss."

2. When a girl, setting aside her bashfulness a little, wishes to touch the lip that is pressed into her mouth, and with that object moves her lower lip, but not the upper one, it is called the "throbbing kiss."

3. When a girl touches her lover's lip with her tongue, and having shut her eyes, places her hands on those of her lover, it is called the "touching kiss."

Others authors describe four other kinds of kisses, viz.:

> The straight kiss.
> The bent kiss.
> The turned kiss.
> The pressed kiss.

1. When the lips of two lovers are brought into direct contact with each other, it is called a "straight kiss."

2. When the heads of two lovers are bent toward each other, and when so bent, kissing takes place, it is called a "bent kiss."

3. When one of them turns up the face of the other by holding the head and chin, and then kissing, it is called a "turned kiss."

4. Lastly, when the lower lip is pressed with much force, it is called a "pressed kiss."

There is also a fifth kind of kiss called the "greatly pressed kiss," which is effected by taking hold of the lower lip between two fingers, and then after touching it with the tongue, pressing it with great force with the lip.

When a man kisses the upper lip of a woman, while she in return kisses his lower lip, it is called the "kiss of the upper lip."

When one of them takes both the lips of the other between his or her own, it is called "a clasping kiss." A woman, however, only takes this kind of kiss from a man who has no moustache. And on the occasion of this kiss, if one of them touches the teeth, the tongue, and the palate of the other, with his or her tongue, it is called the "fighting of the tongue." In the same way, the pressing of the teeth of the one against the mouth of the other is to be practiced.

Kissing is of four kinds, viz., moderate, contracted, pressed, and soft, according to the different parts of the body which are kissed, for different kinds of kisses are appropriate for different parts of the body.

When a woman looks at the face of her lover while he is asleep, and kisses it to show her intention or desire, it is called a "kiss that kindles love."

When a woman kisses her lover while he is engaged in business, or while he is quarreling with her, or while he is looking at something else, so that his mind may be turned away, it is called a "kiss that turns away."

When a lover coming home late at night kisses his beloved who is asleep on her bed in order to show her his desire, it is called a "kiss that awakens." On such an occasion the woman may pretend to be asleep at the time of her lover's arrival, so that she may know his intention and obtain respect from him.

When a person kisses the reflection of the person he loves in a mirror, in water, or on a wall, it is called a "kiss showing the intention."

When a person kisses a child sitting on his lap, or a picture, or an image, or figure, in the presence of the person beloved by him, it is called a "transferred kiss."

When at night at a theatre, or in an assembly, a man coming up to a woman kisses a finger of her hand if she standing, or a toe of her foot if she be sitting, or when a woman in shampooing her lover's body, places her face in his thigh (as if she were sleepy) so as to inflame his passion, and kisses his thigh or great toe, it is called a "demonstrative kiss."

There is also a verse on this subject as follows:

"Whatever things may be done by one of the lovers to the other, the same should be returned by the other, i.e., if the woman kisses him he should kiss her in return; if she strikes him he should also strike her in return."

"On Kissing," from *The Kama Sutra of Vatsyayana:*
The celebrated Hindu Treatise on Love

Married men ought never to attempt or hurry their initial enterprise if they do not find themselves ready for it. If a man discovers himself to be agitated and on edge, it is better to give up outright any attempt at marital commerce and await a further occasion when he is less upset. . . . Women are to blame who receive us with that disdainful, squeamish and outraged air which, while it kindles us, snuffs us out. The daughter-in-law of Pythagoras rightly said that a woman who goes to bed with a man ought to take off her modesty along with her petticoat. . . .

Till possession be taken, our husband should leisurely and

by degrees make several little trials and light offers, without obstinately committing himself to an immediate conquest. Those who know their members to be naturally obedient need only guard themselves against an overwrought imagination.

We are right in remarking the untamed liberty of this member. He puffs himself up most importunately when we do not need him, and swoons away when our need is greatest. . . . Is there any member more rowdy and indiscreet?

When it comes to examples, I myself know one so rude and ungoverned that for forty years it has led its master in one continuous explosion, and is like to do so until he die of it. . . .

But let us proceed.

. . . A man, says Aristotle, must handle his wife with prudence, lest in tickling her too lasciviously, extreme pleasure makes her exceed the bounds of reason. What he says upon the account of conscience, physicians say for the sake of health: a pleasure excessively hot, voluptuous and frequent spoils the seed and hinders conceptions. . . . I for my part always went the plain way to work. . . .

Our poet, Virgil, describes a marriage blessed with concord and contentment and yet not over-loyal. . . . Let us confess the truth: there is hardly one of us who is not more afraid of being shamed by his wife's lapses than his own. . . . What an unjust scale of vices! . . . Lucullus, Caesar, Pompey, Antony, Cato and other good men were cuckolds and knew it, without making a fuss. In those days there was only one idiot, Lepidus, who died of grief from it. . . .

I see no marriages fail sooner than those based on beauty and amorous desires. More solid and durable foundations are necessary, and greater precautions. A boiling dashing ardor is worthless. Love and marriage are two goals approached by different and distinct paths. . . . Marriage has utility, justice, honor and constancy for its share. . . . Love builds itself wholly upon pleasure. . . . Marriage is a solemn and religious tie; and therefore the pleasure we take from it should be restrained, serious and seasoned with a certain gravity. . . . A good marriage—if there be any—rejects the company and conditions of love and seeks to reproduce those of friendship. It is a sweet companionship of life, full of trust and an infinite number of useful and solid services and mutual obligations. . . .

That few are observed to be happy is a token of its value and price. If well-formed and rightly taken, there is not a finer estate in human society. Though we cannot live without it, yet we do nothing but decry it. We see the same with bird-cages: the birds outside despair to get in and those within despair to get out.

MICHEL DE MONTAIGNE, from *The Autobiography*,
translation by Marvin Lowenthal

Abstinence sows sand all over
The ruddy limbs & flaming hair,
But Desire Gratified
Plants fruits of life & beauty there.

WILLIAM BLAKE,
from *The Notebook*

"I have no name" . . .
  What shall I call thee?
"I happy am,
  Joy is my name."
Sweet joy befall thee!

Pretty joy! . . .
Sweet joy I call thee:

Thou dost smile,
I sing the while,
Sweet joy befall thee!

WILLIAM BLAKE,
from "Infant Joy"

When you came, you were like red wine and honey,
And the taste of you burnt my mouth with its sweetness.
Now you are like morning bread,
Smooth and pleasant.
I hardly taste you at all, for I know your savor;
But I am completely nourished.

AMY LOWELL, "A Decade"

I first tasted under Apollo's lips,
love and love sweetness,
I, Evadne;
my hair is made of crisp violets

or hyacinth which the wind combs back
across some rock shelf;
I, Evadne,
was made of the god of light.

His hair was crisp to my mouth,
as the flower of the crocus,
across my cheek,
cool as the silver-cress

on Erotos bank;
between my chin and throat,
his mouth slipped over and over.

Still between my arm and shoulder,
I feel the brush of his hair,
and my hands keep the gold they took,
as they wandered over and over,
that great arm-full of yellow flowers.

H.D., "Evadne"

Waking alone in a multitude of loves when morning's light
Surprised in the opening of her nightlong eyes
His golden yesterday asleep upon the iris
And this day's sun leapt up the sky out of her thighs
Was miraculous virginity old as loaves and fishes,
Though the moment of a miracle is unending lightning
And the shipyards of Galilee's footprints hide a navy of doves.

No longer will the vibrations of the sun desire on
Her deepsea pillow where once she married alone,
Her heart all ears and eyes, lips catching the avalanche
Of the golden ghost who ringed with his streams her mercury
    bone,
Who under the lids of her windows hoisted his golden luggage,
For a man sleeps where fire leapt down and she learns through
    his arm
That other sun, the jealous coursing of the unrivalled blood.

DYLAN THOMAS, "On the Marriage of a Virgin"

E. E. Cummings

II

there is a
moon sole
in the blue
night

       amorous of waters
tremulous,
blinded with silence the
undulous heaven yearns where

in tense starlessness
anoint with ardor
the yellow lover

stands in the dumb dark
svelte
and
urgent

      (again
love i slowly
gather
of thy languorous mouth the

thrilling
flower)

III

as is the sea marvelous
from god's

hands which sent her forth
to sleep upon the world

and the earth withers
the moon crumbles
one by one
stars flutter into dust

but the sea
does not change
and she goes forth out of hands and
she returns into hands

and is with sleep. . . .

love,
          the breaking

of your
                soul
                upon
my lips

                        from "Amores"

somewhere i have never travelled,gladly beyond
any experience,your eyes have their silence:
in your most frail gesture are things which enclose me,
or which i cannot touch because they are too near

your slightest look easily will unclose me
though i have closed myself as fingers,
you open always petal by petal myself as Spring opens
(touching skilfully, mysteriously)her first rose

or if your wish be to close me,i and
my life will shut very beautifully,suddenly,
as when the heart of this flower imagines
the snow carefully everywhere descending;

nothing which we are to perceive in this world equals
the power of your intense fragility:whose texture
compels me with the colour of its countries,
rendering death and forever with each breathing

(i do not know what it is about you that closes
and opens;only something in me understands
the voice of your eyes is deeper than all roses)
nobody,not even the rain, has such small hands

"somewhere i have never travelled"

. . . because two bodies, naked and entwined,
leap over time, they are invulnerable,
nothing can touch them, they return to the
        source,
there is no you, no I, no tomorrow,
no yesterday, no names, the truth of two
in a single body, a single soul,
oh total being . . .

OCTAVIO PAZ, from "Sunstone"

Denise Levertov

The ache of marriage:

thigh and tongue, beloved,
are heavy with it,
it throbs in the teeth

We look for communion
and are turned away, beloved,
each and each

It is leviathan and we
in its belly
looking for joy, some joy
not to be known outside it

two by two in the ark of
the ache of it.

"The Ache of Marriage"

My great brother
          Lord of the Song
wears the ruff of
          forest bear.

Husband, thy fleece of silk is black,
          a black adornment;
lies so close to the turns of the flesh,
burns my palm-stroke.

My great brother
          Lord of the Song
wears the ruff of
          forest bear . . .

Hair of man, man-hair, hair of
breast and groin, marking contour as
          silverpoint marks in cross-
          hatching, as river-
          grass on the woven current
          indicates ripple,
praise.

"A Psalm Praising
the Hair of Man's Body"

My black sun, my
Odessa sunflower,
spurs of Tartar gold
ring at your ankles,
you stand taller before me than the ten
towers of Jerusalem.

Your tongue has found
my tongue, peonies
turn their profusion towards
the lamp, it is you that burn there,
the Black Sea sings you awake.

Wake the violoncellos of Lebanon,
rub the bows with cedar resin,
wake the Tundra horsemen
to hunt tigers.
                    Your skin
tastes of the salt of Marmora,
the hair of your body casts
its net over me.

               To my closed eyes
    appears a curved
    horizon where darkness
    dazzles in your light. Your arms
    hold me from falling.

                    "Song for a Dark Voice"

    expectation is our time
    and waiting for you is best
    so many evenings
    flowered on the laughing sky

    we are so alone
    we hold hands
    and even a cat is silent under a stove
    and listens to how the rain falls

    drops splash—those your feet
    you are coming to me across gold puddles
    your face is wet—I will kiss away the rain
    come come

    into my warm hands
    into my waiting hands
    into my greedy mouth
        like rain

                        HALINA POŚWIATOWSKA

There is nothing false in thee.
In thy heat the youngest body
Has warmth and light.
In thee the quills of the sun
Find adornment.
What does not die
Is with thee.

Thou art clothed in robes of music.
Thy voice awakens wings.

And still more with thee
Are the flowers of earth made bright.

Upon thy deeps the fiery sails
Of heaven glide.

Thou art the radiance and the joy.
Thy heart shall only fail
When all else has fallen.

What does not perish
Lives in thee.

KENNETH PATCHEN,
"There Is Nothing False in Thee"

I was wrapped in black
fur and white fur and
you undid me and then
you placed me in gold light
and then you crowned me,
while snow fell outside
the door in diagonal darts.

While a ten-inch snow
came down like stars
in small calcium fragments,
we were in our own bodies . . .
and you were in my body . . .
and at first I rubbed your
feet dry with a towel
because I was your slave
and then you called me princess.
Princess!

Oh then
I stood up in my gold skin
and I beat down the psalms
and I beat down the clothes
and you undid the bridle
and you undid the reins
and I undid the buttons,
the bones, the confusions,
the New England postcards,
the January ten o'clock night,

and we rose up like wheat,
acre after acre of gold,
and we harvested,
we harvested.

ANNE SEXTON, from "Us"

The wind blew all my wedding day,
And my wedding-night was the night of the high wind;
And a stable door was banging, again and again,
That he must go and shut it, leaving me

Stupid in the candlelight, hearing rain,
Seeing my face in the twisted candlestick,
Yet seeing nothing. When he came back
He said the horses were restless, and I was sad
That any man or beast that night should lack
The happiness I had.

Now in the day
All's ravelled under the sun by the wind's blowing.
He has gone to look at the floods, and I
Carry a chipped pail to the chicken-run,
Set it down, and stare. All is the wind
Hunting through clouds and forests, thrashing
My apron and the hanging cloths on the line.
Can it be borne, this bodying-forth by wind
Of joy my actions turn on, like a thread
Carrying beads? Shall I be let to sleep
Now this perpetual morning shares my bed?
Can even death dry up
These new delighted lakes, conclude
Our kneeling as cattle by all-generous waters?

PHILIP LARKIN, "Wedding Wind"

Lay your sleeping head, my love,
Human on my faithless arm;
. . . in my arms till break of day
Let the living creature lie,
Mortal, guilty, but to me,
The entirely beautiful.

Soul and body have no bounds:
To lovers as they lie upon

Her tolerant enchanted slope
In their ordinary swoon,
Grave the vision Venus sends
Of supernatural sympathy,
Universal love and hope . . .

W. H. AUDEN, from
"Lay Your Sleeping Head"

Body of my woman, I will live on through your
    marvelousness.
My thirst, my desire without end, my wavering road!
Dark river beds down which the eternal thirst is flowing,
and the fatigue is flowing, and the grief without shore.

PABLO NERUDA

I love it when you roll over and
lie on me in the dark, your weight
steady on me as tons of water, my
lungs like a little shut box, it
almost makes me faint to feel the
dry barbed surface of your legs
opening my legs, my heart swells like a
soft purple boxing glove and
then I love to lie there doing
nothing, my powerful arms thrown-down
bolts of muslin rippling at the selvage, your
pubic bone a pyramid laid
point-down on the point of another—
dazzling fulcrum! Then in the stillness and
night I love to feel you grow between my legs like a plant in fast motion, the

way in the auditorium in the
dark near the beginning of our lives we
sat by the hundreds and over our heads on the
bright screen the enormous flowers
unfolded in silence.

Sharon Olds, "I Love It When"

O when the world's at peace
and every man is free
then will I go down unto my love.

O and I may go down
several times before that.

Wendell Berry,
"The Mad Farmer's Love Song"

You, because you love me, hold
Fast to me, caress me, be
Quiet and kind, comfort me
With stillness, say nothing at all.
You, because I love you, I
Am strong for you, I uphold
You. The water is alive
Around us. Living water
Runs in the cut earth between
Us. You, my bride, your voice speaks
Over the water to me.
Your hands, your solemn arms,
Cross the water and hold me.
Your body is beautiful.
It speaks across the water.
Bride, sweeter than honey, glad

Of heart, our hearts beat across
The bridge of our arms. Our speech
Is speech of the joy in the night
Of gladness. Our words live.
Our words are children dancing
Forth from us like stars on water.
My bride, my well beloved,
Sweeter than honey, than ripe fruit,
Solemn, grave, a flying bird,
Hold me. Be quiet and kind.
I love you. Be good to me.
I am strong for you. I uphold
You. The dawn of ten thousand
Dawns is afire in the sky.
The water flows in the earth.
The children laugh in the air.

KENNETH REXROTH,
"The Old Song and Dance"

The Country of Marriage

"She's my girl. . . . She's my blue sky. After sixteen years, I still bite her shoulders. She makes me feel like Hannibal crossing the Alps."

JOHN CHEEVER, from "The Country Husband"

When the vows are said, the ring or rings exchanged, and the symbolizing embrace shared, the now-married couple breaks out of the magic circle, turning their backs on the heavy baggage of ceremony. As they turn, they smile, and their happiness sheds light across the whole assembly of guests. For the couple, there now begins the time of adjustment and resolution, of learning one's capacity for shared labor in the new country, but quite as important for each individual, of exploring what poet Archibald MacLeish refers to as "the greatest and richest good—my own life to live."

I will reveal to you a love potion, without medicine, without herbs, without any witch's magic; if you want to be loved, then Love.

HECATON OF RHODES

There are three sights which warm my heart and are beautiful in the eyes of the Lord and of men: concord among brothers, friendship among neighbors, and a man and wife who are inseparable.

from The Wisdom of Ben Sira, Chapter 25, Verse 1

Come along! today is a festival!
Clap your hands and say, "This is a day of happiness!"
Who in the world is like this bridal pair?
The earth and the sky are full of sugar. Sugar cane is sprouting all around!
We can hear the roar of the pearly ocean. The whole world is full of waves!
The voices of Love are approaching from all sides. We are on our way to heaven!
Once upon a time we played with angels. Let's all go back up there again.

Heaven is our home! Yes, we are even higher up than heaven, higher than the angels!

My dear, it's true that spiritual beauty is wonderful. But your loveliness in this world is even more so!

JALAL AL-DIN RUMI, Persian love poem,
adapted from the translation by A. J. Arberry

> The moon shall be a darkness,
> The stars give no light,
> If ever I prove false
> To my heart's delight;
> In the middle of the ocean
> Green grow the myrtle tree,
> If ever I prove false
> To my Love that loves me.

ANONYMOUS

My true love hath my heart and I have his,
By just exchange one for another given;
I hold his dear and mine he cannot miss;
There never was a better bargain driven:
My true love hath my heart and I have his.

My heart in me keeps him and me in one;
My heart in him his thoughts and senses guides;
He loves my heart for once it was his own;
I cherish his because in me it bides:
My true love hath my heart and I have his.

SIR PHILIP SIDNEY, "My True Love Hath My Heart"

Sappho

Safe now. I've flown to you
like a child to its mother.

Is there in any land
any man whom you love
more than you love me?

I would go anywhere
to take you in my arms
again, my darling.

Translations by
Willis Barnstone

As the ant brought to Solomon the King
The thigh of a grass-hopper as an offering,
So do I bring my soul, beloved, to thee.

I have placed my head and my heart
On the sill of the door of my love.
Step gently, child!

Turkoman love song

My grief has ended. Comes now the season of joy.
For the flowers of Spring are jeweling my green garden.
Let us make ready to walk through its paths.
Go! Tell the nightingale that Spring is here.

And tell the minstrel to come with his lute.
Let him sing us a ballad of the flowers of Spring.
Do not listen to the parrot whispering to the rose
That Autumn will soon be here.

With spring my love returned to me,
And again I behold the moon of my delight.
Let others have their various festivals.
My only festival is when, in Spring,
I see my love's narrow feet
Step through the garden like lisping twin flowers.
Then Khushal Khan puts on his brightest robes
And enters the bazaar of his love's soft arms.

Afghan love song

My boat is of ebony,
the holes in my flute are golden.

As a plant takes out stains from silk
so wine takes sadness from the heart.

When one has good wine,
a graceful boat,
and a maiden's love,
why envy the immortal gods?

LI TAI PO, "Song on the River"

My boat glides swiftly
beneath the wide cloud-ridden sky,
and as I look into the river
I can see the clouds drift by the moon;
my boat seems floating
on the sky.

And thus I dream
my beloved is mirrored
on my heart.

TU FU, "On the River Tchou"

Take a lump of clay, wet it, pat it,
And make an image of me, and an image of you.
Then smash them, crash them, and add a little water.
Break them and remake them into an image of you
And an image of me.
Then in my clay, there's a little of you.
And in your clay, there's a little of me.
And nothing ever shall us sever;
Living, we'll sleep in the same quilt,
And dead, we'll be buried together.

MADAME KUAN

'Tis the gift to be simple
'Tis the gift to be free
'Tis the gift to come down
Where we ought to be

And when we find ourselves
In the place just right
It will be in the valley
Of love and delight.

"Simple Gifts," a Shaker hymn

Love me little, love me long
Is the burden of my song;
Love that is too hot and strong, burneth all to waste;
Still I would not have thee cold,
Or backward or too bold,
For love that lasteth till 'tis old
Fadeth not in haste . . .

ANONYMOUS

Who shall have my fair lady!
Who but I, who but I, who but I?
Under the green leaves!
The fairest man
That best love can,
Under the green leaves!

ANONYMOUS

. . . Here upon earth, we'are Kings, and none but wee
Can be such Kings, nor of such subjects bee.
Who is so safe as wee? where none can doe

Treason to us, except one of us two.
    True and false feares let us refraine,
Let us love nobly, and live, and adde againe
Yeares and yeares unto yeares, till we attaine
To write threescore . . .

JOHN DONNE, from "The Anniversarie"

I wonder by my troth, what thou, and I
Did, till we lov'd? were we not wean'd till then?
But suck'd on countrey pleasures, childishly?
Or snorted we in the seaven sleepers den?
T'was so; But this, all pleasures fancies bee.
If ever any beauty I did see,
Which I desir'd, and got, t'was but a dreame of thee.

And now good morrow to our waking soules,
Which watch not one another out of feare;
For love, all love of other sights controules,
And makes one little roome, an every where.
Let sea-discoverers to new worlds have gone,
Let Maps to other, worlds on worlds have showne,
Let us possesse one world, each hath one, and is one.

My face in thine eye, thine in mine appeares,
And true plaine hearts doe in the faces rest,
Where can we finde two better hemispheares
Without sharpe North, without declining West?
What ever dyes, was not mixt equally;
If our two loves be one, or, thou and I
Love so alike, that none doe slacken, none can die.

JOHN DONNE, "The Good-Morrow"

Marriage is a sweet state,
I can affirm it by my own experience,
In very truth, I who have a good and wise husband
Whom God helped me to find.
I give thanks to him who will save him for me,
For I can truly feel his great goodness
And for sure the sweet man loves me well.

Throughout that first night in our home,
I could well feel his great goodness,
For he did me no excess
That could hurt me.
But, before it was time to get up,
He kissed me 100 times, this I affirm,
Without exacting further outrage,
And yet for sure the sweet man loves me well.

He used to say to me in his soft language:
"God brought you to me,
Sweet lover, and I think he raised me
To be of use to you."
And then he did not cease to dream
All night, his conduct was so perfect,
Without seeking other excesses.
And yet for sure the sweet man loves me well.

O Princes, yet he drives me mad
When he tells me he is all mine;
He will destroy me with his gentle ways,
And yet for sure the sweet man loves me well.

CHRISTINE DE PISAN, "In Praise of Marriage,"
translation by C. Meredith Jones

A wreathed garland of deserved praise,
Of praise deserved, unto thee I give,
I give to thee, who knowest all my wayes,
My crooked winding wayes, wherein I live,
Wherein I die, not live: for life is straight,
Straight as a line, and ever tends to thee,
To thee, who art more farre above deceit,
Then deceit seems above simplicitie.
Give me simplicitie that I may live,
So live and like, that I may know thy wayes,
Know them and practise them: then shall I give
For this poore wreath, give thee a crown of praise.

GEORGE HERBERT, "A Wreath"

She is gentle and also wise;
Of all other she beareth the prize,
    That ever I saw.

To hear her sing, to see her dance!
She will the best herself advance,
    That ever I saw.

To see her fingers that be so small!
In my conceit she passeth all
    That ever I saw.

Nature in her hath wonderly wrought.
Christ, never such another bought
    That ever I saw.

I have seen many that have beauty
Yet is there none like to my lady
    That ever I saw.

Therefore I dare boldly say,
I shall have the best and fairest may
That ever I saw.

ANONYMOUS

My love to my husband was not only a matrimonial love, as betwixt man and wife, but a natural love, as the love of brethren, parents, and children, also a sympathetical love, as the love of friends, likewise a customary love, as the love of acquaintances, a loyal love, as the love of a subject, an obedient love, as the love to virtue, an uniting love, as the love of soul and body, a pious love, as the love to heaven, all which several loves did meet and intermix, making one mass of love.

ANONYMOUS

If ever two were one, then surely we.
If ever man were lov'd by wife, then thee;
If ever wife was happy in a man,
Compare with me ye women if you can.
I prize thy love more than whole Mines of gold,
Or all the riches that the East doth hold.
My love is such that Rivers cannot quench,
Nor ought but love from thee, give recompence.
Thy love is such I can no way repay,
The heavens reward thee manifold I pray.
Then while we live, in love let's so persever,
That when we live no more, we may live ever.

ANNE BRADSTREET, "To my Dear and loving Husband"

Come live with me and be my love,
And we will all the pleasures prove
That hills and valleys, dales and fields
And all the craggy mountains yields.

There we will sit upon the rocks
And see the shepherds feed their flocks,
By shallow rivers to whose falls
Melodious birds sing madrigals.

And I will make thee beds of roses
With a thousand fragrant posies,
A cap of flowers and a kirtle
Embroidered all with leaves of myrtle.

A gown made of the finest wool
Which from our pretty lambs we pull;
Fair lined slippers for the cold,
With buckles of the purest gold;

A belt of straw and ivy buds,
With coral clasps and amber studs:
And if these pleasures may thee move,
Come live with me and be my love.

The shepherds' swains shall dance and sing
For thy delight each May morning:
If these delights thy mind may move,
Then live with me and be my love.

CHRISTOPHER MARLOWE,
"The Passionate Shepherd to His Love"

I did not live until this time
    Crown'd my felicity,
When I could say without a crime,
    I am not thine, but thee.

This carcass breath'd, and walkt, and slept,
    So that the world believ'd
There was a soul the motions kept;
    But they were all deceiv'd.

For as a watch by art is wound
    To motion, such was mine:
But never had Orinda found
    A soul till she found thine;

Which now inspires, cures and supplies,
    And guides my darkned breast:
For thou art all that I can prize,
    My joy, my life, my rest. . . .

KATHERINE PHILIPS, from
"To My Excellent Lucasia, on Our Friendship"

O my heart's heart, and you who are to me
    More than myself myself, God be with you,
    Keep you in strong obedience leal and true
To Him whose noble service setteth free;
Give you all good we see or can foresee,
    Make your joys many and your sorrows few,
    Bless you in what you bear and what you do,
Yea, perfect you as He would have you be. . . .

CHRISTINA ROSSETTI, from
"Monna Innominata: A Sonnet of Sonnets"

. . . Your hands lie open in the long fresh grass,
The finger-points look through like rosy blooms:
Your eyes smile peace. The pasture gleams and glooms
'Neath billowing skies that scatter and amass.
All round our nest, far as the eye can pass,
Are golden kingcup-fields with silver edge
Where the cow-parsley skirts the hawthorn-hedge.
'Tis visible silence, still as the hour-glass.
Deep in the sun-searched growths the dragon-fly
Hangs like a blue thread loosened from the sky:—
So this winged hour is dropped to us from above.
Oh! clasp we to our hearts, for deathless dower,
This close-companioned inarticulate hour
When twofold silence was the song of love. . . .

DANTE GABRIEL ROSSETTI, from "The House of Life"

. . . The mairie was a mile and a half from the farm, and they went thither on foot, returning in the same way after the ceremony in the church. The procession, first united like one long coloured scarf that undulated across the fields, along the narrow path winding amid the green corn, soon lengthened out, and broke up into different groups that loitered to talk. The fiddler walked in front with his violin, gay with ribbons at its pegs. Then came the married pair, the relations, the friends, all following pell-mell; the children stayed behind amusing themselves plucking the bellflowers from oat-ears, or playing amongst themselves unseen. Emma's dress, too long, trailed a little on the ground; delicately, with her gloved hands, she picked off the coarse grass and the thistledowns. . . .

The table was laid under the cart-shed. On it were four sirloins, six chicken fricassées, stewed veal, three legs of mutton, and in the middle a fine roast sucking-pig, flanked by four chitterlings with sorrel. At the corners were decanters of brandy. Sweet bottled-cider frothed round the corks, and all the glasses had been filled to the brim with wine beforehand. Large dishes of yellow cream, that trembled with the least shake of the table, had designed on their smooth surface the initials of the newly wedded pair in nonpareil arabesques. A confectioner of Yvetot had been intrusted with the tarts and sweets. As he had only just set up in the place, he had taken a lot of trouble, and at dessert he himself brought in a set dish that evoked loud cries of wonderment. To begin with, at its base there was a square of blue cardboard, representing a temple with porticoes, colonnades, and stucco statuettes all round, and in the niches constellations of gilt paper stars; then on the second stage was a dungeon of Savoy cake, surrounded by many fortifications in candied angelica, almonds, raisins and quarters of oranges; and finally, on the upper platform a green field with rocks set in lakes of jam, nutshell boats, and a small Cupid balancing himself in a chocolate swing whose two uprights ended in real roses for balls at the top.

Until night they ate. When any of them were too tired of sitting, they went out for a stroll in the yard, or for a game with corks in the granary, and then returned to table. Some towards the finish went to sleep and snored. But with the coffee every one woke up. Then they began songs, showed off tricks, raised heavy weights, performed feats with their fingers, then tried lifting carts on their shoulders, made broad jokes, kissed the women. At night when they left, the horses, stuffed up to the nostrils with oats, could hardly be got into the shafts; they kicked, reared, the harness broke, their masters laughed or swore; and all night in the light of the moon along country roads there were runaway carts at full gallop plunging into the ditches, jumping over yard after yard of stones, clambering up the hills, with women leaning out from the tilt to catch hold of the reins.

Those who stayed at the Bertaux spent the night drinking in the kitchen. The children had fallen asleep under the seats.

The bride had begged her father to be spared the usual marriage pleasantries. However, a fishmonger, one of their cousins (who had even brought a pair of soles for his wedding present), began to squirt water from his mouth through the keyhole, when old Rouault came up just in time to stop him, and explain to him that the distinguished position of his son-in-law would not allow of such liberties. . . .

GUSTAVE FLAUBERT, from *Madame Bovary*,
translation by Eleanor Marx

SONNET XIV

If thou must love me, let it be for nought
Except for love's sake only. Do not say,
"I love her for her smile—her look—her way
Of speaking gently,—for a trick of thought
That falls in well with mine, and certes brought
A sense of pleasant ease on such a day"—
For these things in themselves, Beloved, may
Be changed, or change for thee,—and love, so wrought,
May be unwrought so. Neither love me for
Thine own dear pity's wiping my cheeks dry,—
A creature might forget to weep, who bore
Thy comfort long, and lose thy love thereby!
But love me for love's sake, that evermore
Thou mayest love on, through love's eternity.

ELIZABETH BARRETT BROWNING, from *Sonnets from the Portuguese*

How do I love thee? Let me count the ways.
I love thee to the depth and breadth and height
My soul can reach, when feeling out of sight
For the ends of Being and ideal Grace.
I love thee to the level of everyday's
Most quiet need, by sun and candle-light.
I love thee freely, as men strive for Right;
I love thee purely, as they turn from Praise.
I love thee with the passion put to use
In my old griefs, and with my childhood's faith.
I love thee with a love I seemed to lose
With my lost saints,—I love thee with the breath,
Smiles, tears, of all my life!—and, if God choose,
I shall but love thee better after death.

ELIZABETH BARRETT BROWNING, from *Sonnets from the Portuguese*

What greater thing is there for two human souls than to feel that they are joined . . . to strengthen each other . . . to be at one with each other in silent unspeakable memories.

GEORGE ELIOT

Marriage is terrifying, but so is a cold and forlorn old age. . . . marriage, if comfortable, is not at all heroic. It certainly narrows and damps the spirits of generous men. In marriage, a man becomes slack and selfish and undergoes a fatty degeneration of his moral being . . . the air of the fireside withers out all the fine wildings of the husband's heart. He is so comfortable and happy that he begins to prefer comfort and happiness to everything else on earth, his wife included. . . . Twenty years ago, this man was equally capable of crime or heroism; now he is fit for neither. His soul is asleep, and you may speak without constraint; you will not wake him. . . . For women there is less of this danger. Marriage is of so much use to a woman, opens out to her so much more of life, and puts her in the way of so much more freedom and usefulness, that, whether she marry ill or well, she can hardly miss some benefit. It is true, however, that some of the merriest and most genuine of woman are old maids. . . .

A certain sort of talent is almost indispensable for people who would spend years together and not bore themselves to death. . . . to dwell happily together, they should be versed in the niceties of the heart, and born with a faculty for willing compromise . . . should laugh over the same sort of jests and have many . . . an old joke between them which time cannot wither nor custom stale. . . . You could read Kant by yourself if you wanted, but you must share a joke with someone else. You can forgive people who do not follow you through a philosophical disquisition; but to find your wife laughing when you had tears in your eyes, or staring when you were in a fit of laughter, would go some way towards a dissolution of the marriage. . . . Certainly, if I could help it, I would never marry a wife who wrote.

[For a woman] a ship captain is a good man to marry . . . for absences are a good influence in love. . . . It is to be noticed that those who have loved once or twice already are so much the better educated to a woman's hand. . . . Lastly, no woman should marry a teetotaller, or a man who does not smoke. . . .

A man expects an angel for a wife; [yet] he knows that she is like himself—erring, thoughtless and untrue; but like himself also, filled with a struggling radiancy of better things. . . . You may safely go to school with hope; but ere you marry, should have learned the mingled lesson of the world: that hope and love address themselves to a perfection never realised, and yet, firmly held, become the salt and staff of life; that you yourself are compacted of infirmities . . . and yet you have a something in you lovable and worth preserving; and that, while the mass of mankind lies under this scurvy condemnation, you will scarce find one but, by some generous reading, will become to you a lesson, a model and a noble spouse through life. So thinking, you will constantly support your own unworthiness and easily forgive the failings of your friend. Nay, you will be wisely glad that you retain the . . . blemishes; for the faults of married people continually spur up each of them, hour by hour, to do better and to meet and love upon a higher ground.

Robert Louis Stevenson, from *Virginibus Puerisque*

> When you are old and gray and full of sleep,
> And nodding by the fire, take down this book,
> And slowly read, and dream of the soft look
> Your eyes had once, and of their shadows deep;
>
> How many loved your moments of glad grace,
> And loved your beauty with love false or true;
> But one man loved the pilgrim soul in you,
> And loved the sorrows of your changing face . . .

William Butler Yeats,
from "When You Are Old"

I propose to speak . . . of a troth that is observed *by virtue of the absurd*—that is to say, simply because it has been pledged—and by virtue of being an absolute which will uphold husband and wife as persons. Fidelity, it must be admitted, stands emphatically athwart the stream of values nowadays admired by nearly every one. Fidelity is extremely *unconventional*. It contradicts the general belief in the revelatory value of both spontaneity and manifold experiences. It denies that in order to remain lovable a beloved must display the greatest possible *number* of qualities. It denies that its own goal is happiness. It offensively asserts first, that its aim is obedience to a Truth that is believed in, and secondly, that it is the expression of a wish to be constructive. For fidelity is not in the least a sort of conservatism, but rather a construction. An "absurdity" quite as much as passion, it is to be distinguished from passion by its persistent refusal to submit to its own dream, by its persistent need of acting in behalf of the beloved, by its being persistently in contact with a reality which it seeks to control, not to flee.

I maintain that fidelity thus understood sets up the person. For the person is manifested like something made, in the widest sense of making. It is built up as a thing is made, thanks to a making, and in the same conditions as we make things, its first condition being a fidelity to something that before was not, but now is in process of being created. Person, made thing, fidelity— the three terms are neither separable nor separately intelligible. All three presuppose that a stand has been taken, and that we have adopted what is fundamentally the attitude of creators. Hence in the humblest lives the plighting of a troth introduces the opportunity of making and of rising to the plane of the person—on condition, of course, that the pledge has not been for "reasons" in the giving of which there is a reservation which will allow those reasons to be repudiated some day when they have ceased to appear "reasonable"! The pledge exchanged in marriage is the very type of a *serious* act, because it is a pledge given once and for all. The irrevocable alone is serious. Every life, even the most disinherited one, has some immediate potentiality of dignity, and it is in an 'absurd' fidelity that this dignity may be attained—in a readiness to say "No" to a dazzling passion, when there is every earthly reason for saying "Yes." . . .

In marriage the loving husband or wife vows fidelity first of all to *the other* at the same time as to his or her true self . . . the fidelity of the married couple is acceptance of one's fellow-creature, a willingness to take the other as he or she is in his or her intimate particularity. Let me insist that fidelity in marriage cannot be merely that negative attitude so frequently imagined; it must be active. To be content not to deceive one's wife or husband would be an indication of indigence, not one of love. Fidelity demands far more: it wants the good of the beloved, and when it acts in behalf of that good it is creating in its own presence the neighbour. And it is by this roundabout way through the other that the self rises into being a person—beyond its own happiness. Thus as persons a married couple are a mutual creation, and to become persons is the double achievement of "active love." What denies both the individual and his natural egotism is what constructs a person. At this point faithfulness in marriage is discovered to be the law of a new life. . . .

DENIS DE ROUGEMONT, from *Love in the Western World*

The essence of a good marriage is respect for each other's personality combined with that deep intimacy, physical, mental, and spiritual, which makes a serious love between man and woman the most fructifying of all human experiences. Such love, like everything that is great and precious, demands its own morality, and frequently entails a sacrifice of the less to the greater; but such sacrifice must be voluntary, for, where it is not, it will destroy the very basis of the love for the sake of which it is made.

BERTRAND RUSSELL, from *Marriage and Morals*

. . . man, like woman, is flesh, therefore passive, the plaything of his hormones and of the species, the restless prey of his desires. And she, like him, in the midst of the carnal fever, is a consenting, a voluntary gift, an activity; they live out in their several fashions the strange ambiguity of existence made body. In those combats where they think they confront one another, it is really against the self that each one struggles, projecting into the partner that part of the self which is repudiated; instead of living out the ambiguities of their situation, each tries to make the other bear the abjection and tries to reserve the honor for the self. If, however, both should assume the ambiguity with a clear-sighted modesty, correlative of an authentic pride, they would see each other as equals and would live out their erotic drama in amity. The fact that we are human beings is infinitely more important than all the peculiarities that distinguish human beings from one another. . . .

It is nonsense to assert that revelry, vice, ecstasy, passion, would become impossible if man and woman were equal in concrete matters; the contradictions that put the flesh in opposition to the spirit, the instant to time, the swoon of immanence to the challenge of transcendence, the absolute of pleasure to the nothingness of forgetting, will never be resolved; in sexuality will always be materialized the tension, the anguish, the joy, the frustration, and the triumph of existence. To emancipate woman is to refuse to confine her to the relations she bears to man, not to deny them to her; let her have her independent existence and she will continue none the less to exist for him *also*: mutually recognizing each other as subject, each will yet remain for the other an *other*. The reciprocity of their relations will not do away with the miracles—desire, possession, love, dream, adventure—worked by the division of human beings into two separate categories; and the words that move us—giving, conquering, uniting—will not lose their meaning. On the contrary, when we abolish the slavery of half of humanity, together with the whole system of hyprocrisy that it implies, then the 'division' of humanity will reveal its genuine significance and the human couple will find its true form.

Simone de Beauvoir, from *The Second Sex*,
translation by H. M. Parshley

No wandering any more where the feet stumble
Upon a sudden rise, or sink in damp
Marsh grasses. No uncertain following on
With nothing there to follow—a sure bird,
A fence, a farmhouse. No adventuring now
Where motion that is yet not motion dies.
Circles have lost their magic, and the voice
Comes back upon itself. . . . The road is firm.
It runs, and the dust is not too deep, and the end
Never can heave in sight—though one is there.
It runs in a straight silence, till a word
Turns it; then a sentence, and evening falls
At an expected inn, whose barest room
Cannot be lonely if a hand is reached
To touch another hand, the walls forgotten. . . .
Laughter is morning, and the road resumes;
Adventurous, it never will return.

Mark Van Doren, "Marriage"

Slowly, slowly wisdom gathers:
Golden dust in the afternoon,
Somewhere between the sun and me,
Sometimes so near that I can see,
Yet never settling, late or soon.

Would that it did, and a rug of gold
Spread west of me a mile or more:
Not large, but so that I might lie
Face up, between the earth and sky,
And know what none has known before.

Then I would tell as best I could
The secrets of that shining place:
The web of the world, how thick, how thin,
How firm, with all things folded in;
How ancient, and how full of grace.

MARK VAN DOREN, "Slowly, Slowly Wisdom Gathers"

Like everything which is not the involuntary result of fleeting
emotion, but the creation of time and will, any marriage, happy
or unhappy, is infinitely more interesting and significant than
any romance, however passionate.

W. H. AUDEN

When women as well as men emerge from biological living to
realize their human selves, [their later] halves of life may become
their years of greatest fulfillment. . . . when women do not need
to live through their husbands and children, men will not fear
the love and strength of women, nor need another's weakness
to prove their own masculinity. They can finally see each other

as they are. And this may be the next step in human evolution.

Who knows what women can be when they are finally free to become themselves? Who knows what women's intelligence will contribute when it can be nourished without denying love? Who knows of the possibilities of love when men and women share not only children, home, and garden, not only the ful-fillment of their biological roles, but the responsibilities and passions of the work that creates the human future and the full human knowledge of who they are? It has barely begun, the search of women for themselves. But the time is at hand. . . .

BETTY FRIEDAN, from The Feminine Mystique

Here are a man and a woman, being married.
The entire world of summer lawns
holds its breath for the event. The trees
around them are lovely, displaying the small
breath and motions of August. The couple glance
at one another. Where has the moon gone,
the requisite moon? Nearby, a mother
begs her child, "Try to remember;
when did you have it last?" Oh,
impossible mystery. Where is joy
when it is not here? Time says nothing.
These things can happen, and will,
while children at the yard's border play
among grown-ups tasting the summer's wine.

Memory looks at its watch, smiling.
The moon will begin to come round
the way it always did but we'd forgotten.

The lovers touch hands and think of
some place they want to be, and go there.
The child, happy at last,
has remembered where its lost ball is.
In the garden the pink phlox and the lilies
show off, between the old moon
here in the hot sky and the one to come.
Everyone hugs or shakes hands
and walks off toward the future, waving.
The man and woman look at each other.
They know it means happiness, this year. They do.

DAVID KELLER, from "Afternoon,
in a Back Yard on Chestnut Street"

The truth has never been of any real value to any human being.
It is a symbol for mathematicians and philosophers to pursue.
In human relations, kindness and lies are worth a thousand
truths.

GRAHAM GREENE, from *The Heart of the Matter*

Though you know it anyhow
Listen to me, darling, now,

Proving what I need not prove
How I know I love you, love.

Near and far, near and far,
I am happy where you are;

Likewise I have never learnt
How to be it where you aren't.

Far and wide, far and wide,
I can walk with you beside;

Furthermore, I tell you what,
I sit and sulk where you are not.

Visitors remark my frown
When you're upstairs and I am down,

Yes, and I'm afraid I pout
When I'm indoors and you are out;

But how contentedly I view
Any room containing you.

In fact I care not where you be,
Just as long as it's with me.

In all your absences I glimpse
Fire and flood and trolls and imps.

Is your train a minute slothful?
I goad the stationmaster wrothful.

When with friends to bridge you drive
I never know if you're alive,

And when you linger late in shops
I long to telephone the cops.

Yet how worth the waiting for,
To see you coming through the door.

Somehow, I can be complacent
Never but with you adjacent.

Near and far, near and far,
I am happy where you are;

Likewise, I have never learnt
How to be it where you aren't.

Then grudge me not my fond endeavor,
To hold you in my sight forever;

Let none, not even you, disparage
Such valid reason for a marriage.

Ogden Nash, "Tin Wedding Whistle"

—Muses, whose worship I may never leave
but for this pensive woman, now I dare,
teach me her praise! with her my praise receive.—

Three years already of the round world's war
had rolled by stoned & disappointed eyes
when she and I came where we were made for.

Pale as a star lost in returning skies,
more beautiful than midnight stars more frail
she moved towards me like chords, a sacrifice;

entombed in body trembling through the veil
arm upon arm, learning our ancient wound,
we see our one soul heal, recovering pale.

Then priestly sanction, then the drop of sound.
Quickly part to the cavern ever warm
deep from the march, body to body bound,

descend (my soul) out of dismantling storm
into the darkness where the world is made.
Come back to the bright air. Love is multiform.

Heartmating hesitating unafraid
although incredulous, she seemed to fill
the lilac shadow with light wherein she played,

whom sorry childhood had made sit quite still,
an orphan silence, unregarded sheen,
listening for any small soft note, not hopeful:

caricature: as once a maiden Queen,
flowering power comeliness kindness grace,
shattered her mirror, wept, would not be seen.

These pities moved. Also above her face
serious or flushed, swayed her fire-gold
not earthly hair, now moonless to unlace,

resistless flame, now in a sun more cold
great shells to whorl about each secret ear,
mysterious histories, strange shores, unfold.

New musics! One the music that we hear
this is the music which the masters make
out of their minds, profound solemn & clear.

And then the other music, in whose sake
all men perceive a gladness but we are drawn
less for that joy than utterly to take

our trial, naked in the music's vision,
the flowing ceremony of trouble and light,
all Loves becoming, none to rest upon.

Such Mozart made,—an ear so delicate
he fainted at a trumpet-call, a child
so delicate. So merciful that sight,

so stern, we follow rapt who ran awild.
Marriage is the second music, and thereof
we hear what we can bear, faithful & mild. . . .

JOHN BERRYMAN, from "Canto Amor"

March 22: On Sunday evening with the children in bed and
Pauline writing letters I talked to K [the author's husband]:
". . . I'm learning to milk the cow. I'm going to take over your
afternoon's work sometimes and you can have the time for
more study. I can chop wood and feed the fowls. We'll share
the time."

"I can't possibly allow you to do rough work, chop wood
and do the fowls. Not when you have the desire and the ability
and the opportunity to do what you do."

I was surprised to hear this.

He continued, " . . . People who can do the work you do
should be allowed to do it and those who can't should hew the
wood and draw the water, feed the fowls, chop and wood and
milk Susie."

This distressed me.

He went on, "There's no need for you to take on my afternoon work."

"But my work loses its value unless you are happy. Everything loses its value. Your contentment comes before my work."

"I'm happy."

"No you're not."

He looked at me with interest. I went on, "You're not getting
as much time for study as I am. You're the real mother of this
family; I'm just one of the children. We must share the time."

He pushed the kettle over the flames. "But your study means more to you than mine does to me."

"I question it. But in any case that's not my point. Your work means more to me than my own does to me because your work involves your contentment and that comes before my work with me."

He was interested but looked doubtful.

"It's the truth," I added. "Unless you are happy in your work mine is valueless to me."

K examined my face as though he was seeing it for the first time.

"It may not be apparent," I said, "but I love you and you come first in the world with me, before everything, before any-body. You and the children. My family and home are more to me than my work. If it came to the choice it would be my work that went overboard. No doubt I've appeared to be a failure in the home but that is not indicative. Do you feel I've failed you in the home?" I called on all my courage to ask this question which could draw a devastating answer.

He put out two cups and saucers. "Well, it has crossed my mind that you shouldn't have married."

Catastrophe! "But I've been a good mother! Look at me all through my babies. How I stuck to them . . ."

"Yes. But, what I mean is that a person, any person, with your inclinations should not marry. You should have gone on with your work. Marriage has sidetracked you."

Desperately on the defensive, "I wash and dress the little boys in the morning, and Jonquil. I feed them."

"I know. What I mean is that people like you with talents and ideas should be undisturbed by marriage."

"Ah . . . but you see! I wouldn't have had these desires at all if I hadn't married. When I didn't teach and had no babies I hardly lifted a brush. Hardly did a thing. The *need* to study, to do, to make, to think, *arises* from being married. I need to be married to work."

He poured the boiling water on the tea. "I still think that you should be allowed your work in preference to my being allowed mine. Your desire is stronger than mine."

"That's quite possible. But I'm still going to hurry up and learn to milk Susie."

We had tea, ran off the dishes and went to bed. Neither of us lowered the flag, neither won, and we haven't talked about that since, but the part about his coming before my work must have registered and held for there's been a tenderness in his manner toward me like the reappearance of the sun. . . .

November 12: Hurrying up the road in the rain I reflected on my position in my small vital circle and my influence on them: . . . When I'm unhappy my sorrow and violence cast all about me and everybody pays, right down to the baby, whereas now with my impulses back in their normal channel, now that I am happy . . . our home—at least my home—is incredibly joyful.

I am aware of how much I mean to each one. . . . For some reason that is obscure to me they all turn to me and seek my love and I pour on them *thousands* of kisses. . . . My mouth, my face, my waist, my breasts, my hands . . . sheer common property. . . . I'm the one without whose goodnight kiss no one will go to bed. At this time I'm first with them all. Why does each need my love so much? You'd think my elusiveness in continual slipping away would lessen their call on me. . . .

How long will this last? I wonder. It was not always like this in the past . . . so shy in my adolescence, so apart in my childhood . . . and cannot always be. Some day I may be looking back on these days when arms were endlessly round my neck, my body seldom my own; some day I may find myself sitting at a table with all the silence I want, possibly more than I want. There may be large echoing rooms and corridors, and stairs and stunning views, none of which would put its arms round my neck and want to make love to me, call to me in the night. . . .

Now that I feel better, temporarily, I must honor all this love by trying to be gentler and kinder, by forgiving more readily and teaching more sensitively. Love has the quality of informing almost everything—even one's work.

SYLVIA ASHTON-WARNER, from Myself

You learned from me that commitment, love, loyalty, "being there" are at the center of everything. I taught you, by example, that life is very complex, that there are no final solutions, there is only the commitment to the search for quality and genuineness. I taught you to treasure the real and to shun the plastic. I taught you to value human relationships, to run away from bigotry and to expose it when you find it. I taught you to believe in the value of books, to respect education and learning, to admire goodness and integrity and wisdom. Let's not forget humor. Above all, perhaps, I taught you by example that a thoughtful and examined life requires difficult choices; that there are, for such a life, no instant fixes. We live in a society which sells trivial answers for every complex human dilemma. In our household, from our example, you were able to draw on a different set of strengths, not available in the ambient society of your growing up. I see all of these strengths in your life now. You have become the kind of woman I dreamed of raising.

RENÉE HAENEL LEVINE, letter to her daughter

The darkness lifts, imagine, in your lifetime.
There you are—cased in clean bark you drift
through weaving rushes, fields flooded with cotton.

Beautiful, pass and be
Less than the guiltless shade
To which our vows were said;

Less than the sound of the oar
To which our vows were made,—
Less than the sound of its blade
Dipping the stream once more.

Louise Bogan, "To be Sung on the Water"

All has been translated into treasure:
Weightless as amber,
Translucent as the currant on the branch,
Dark as the rose's thorn.

Where is the shimmer of evil?
This is the shell's iridescence
And the wild bird's wing.

Ignorant, I took up my burden in the wilderness.
Wise with great wisdom, I shall lay it down upon flowers.

Louise Bogan, from "After the Persian"

This institution,
perhaps one should say enterprise
out of respect for which
one says one need not change one's mind
about a thing one has believed in,
requiring public promises

of one's intention
to fulfil a private obligation:
I wonder what Adam and Eve
think of it by this time,
this fire-gilt steel
alive with goldenness;
how bright it shows— . . .

Below the incandescent stars
below the incandescent fruit,
the strange experience of beauty;
its existence is too much . . .

"Everything to do with love is mystery;
it is more than a day's work
to investigate this science."
One sees that it is rare—
that striking grasp of opposites
opposed each to the other, not to unity,
which in cycloid inclusiveness
has dwarfed the demonstration
of Columbus with the egg— . . .

MARIANNE MOORE, from "Marriage"

This poem is for my wife
I have made it plainly and honestly
The mark is on it
Like the burl on the knife

I have not made it for praise
She has no more need for praise
Than summer has
On the bright days

In all that becomes a woman
Her words and her ways are beautiful
Love's lovely duty
The well-swept room

Wherever she is there is sun
And time and a sweet air
Peace is there
Work done

There are always curtains and flowers
And candles and baked bread
And a cloth spread
And a clean house

Her voice when she sings is a voice
At dawn by a freshening sea
Where the wave leaps in the
Wind and rejoices

Wherever she is it is now
It is here where the apples are
Here in the stars
In the quick hour

The greatest and richest good—
My own life to live—
This she has given me

If giver could

ARCHIBALD MacLEISH, "Poem in Prose"

Samuel Menashe

You whose name I know
As well as my own
You whose name I know
But not to tell
You whose name I know
Yet do not say
Even to myself—
You whose name I know
Know that I came
Here to name you
Whose name I know

"Whose Name I Know"

O Many Named Beloved
Listen to my praise
Various as the seasons
Different as the days
All my treasons cease
When I see your face

"Many Named"

A-
round
my neck
an amu-
let
Be-
tween

my eyes
a star
A
ring
in my
nose
and a
gold
chain
to
Keep me
where
You
are

"A-"

Having come unto
the tall house of our habit
where it settles rump downward
on its stone foundations
in the manner of a homely brood mare
who throws good colts

and having entered
where sunlight is pasted on the windows
ozone rises from the mullions
dust motes pollinate the hallway
and spiders remembering a golden age
sit one in each drain

we will hang up our clothes and our vegetables
we will decorate the rafters with mushrooms
on our hearth we will burn splits of silver popple
we will stand up to our knees in their flicker
the soup kettle will clang five notes of pleasure
and love will take up quarters.

MAXINE KUMIN, "Homecoming"

We have come in the winter
To this warm country room,
The family and friends
Of the bride and the groom,
To bring them our blessing,
To share in their joy,
And to hope that years passing
The best measures employ
To protect their small clearing,
And their love be enduring.

May the hawk that flies over
These thick-wooded hills,
Where through tangled ground cover
With its cushion of quills
The plump porcupine ambles
And the deer come to browse
While through birches and brambles
Clear cold water flows,
Protect their small clearing,
And their love be enduring.

May the green leaves returning
To rock maples in spring
Catch fire, and, still burning,
Their flaming coat fling
On the lovers when sleeping
To contain the first chill
Of crisp autumn weather
With log-fires that will
Protect their small clearing,
And their love be enduring.

May the air that grows colder
Where the glacier has left
Its erratic boulder
Mountain water has cleft,
And the snow then descending
No less clear than their love
Be a white quilt depending
From sheer whiteness above
To protect their small clearing,
And their love be enduring.

WILLIAM JAY SMITH,
"Song for a Country Wedding"
For Deborah and Marc

I believe that living is an act of creativity and that, at certain moments in our lives, our creative imaginations are more conspicuously demanded than at others. At certain moments, the need to decide upon the story of our own lives becomes particularly pressing—when we choose a mate, for example . . .

... every marriage [is] a narrative construct—or two narrative constructs. In unhappy marriages, I see two versions of reality rather than two people in conflict. I see a struggle for imaginative dominance going on. Happy marriages seem to me those in which the two partners agree on the scenario they are enacting. ... marriage seems to me a subjectivist fiction with two points of view often deeply in conflict, sometimes fortuituously congruent.

Marriages go bad not when love fades—love can modulate into affection without driving two people apart—but when this understanding about the balance of power breaks down. ...

PHYLLIS ROSE, from *Parallel Lives: Five Victorian Marriages*

Funny the way the healing comes
in a northeaster, rain sliding
sideways across the glass, the waves
beaching themselves, rolling home
across the gray water, running before the wind
boxing the spruce and cedars fat with resistance.

Russian olives and beach plum,
stripped to their bird-bone branches
blackened with rain against the still
green lawn, jerk and twitch, stiff
with cold; offering so little
to the blow, they bend, barely.

Even from the bay window, clouds
are near, putting a ceiling on the sky
trying to slip off the water through a slit

of dove-gray on the horizon. Only
gulls are nervy enough to fly
in this weather. They, too, slide

sideways, behind the rain, wings
spread wide, grabbing the currents
and sledding across the wind, as if
they were made for a northeaster, designed
all gray with flashes of white
to match its color. Banking,

they turn into the wind and wobble,
their backsides to us, heading away, small,
unsteady as a child learning to walk
the hard way. Inside, all the things God gives
that were always there, all that's man-made
keeping us, the light bulbs glowing

through yellowed parchment shades
shedding seventeenth-century light, filling in
the shadow of our daughter, the fire
toasting the room, Gershwin and Porter
coming from Public Radio in a braid
of complicated notes, a music written

before we were born, surviving in a changed
world, and this good man holding me, I
holding him, as we glide in Top-Siders
across the rug, seeing each other return
sliding sideways into our eyes
this side of the glass.

MARY STEWART HAMMOND,
"Slow Dancing in the Living Room: Thanksgiving"

Wendell Berry

How hard it is for me, who live
in the excitement of women
and have the desire for them
in my mouth like salt. Yet
you have taken me and quieted me.
You have been such light to me
that other women have been
your shadows. You come near me
with the nearness of sleep.
And yet I am not quiet.
It is to be broken. It is to be
torn open. It is not to be
reached and come to rest in
ever. I turn against you,
I break from you, I turn to you.
We hurt, and are hurt,
and have each other for healing.
It is healing. It is never whole.

"Marriage"

One faith is bondage. Two
are free. In the trust
of old love, cultivation shows
a dark graceful wilderness
at its heart. Wild
in that wilderness, we roam
the distances of our faith,
safe beyond the bounds

of what we know. O love,
open. Show me
my country. Take me home.

1.
I dream of you walking at night along the streams
of the country of my birth, warm blooms and the nightsongs
of birds opening around you as you walk.
You are holding in your body the dark seed of my sleep.

2.
This comes after silence. Was it something I said
that bound me to you, some mere promise
or, worse, the fear of loneliness and death?
A man lost in the woods in the dark, I stood
still and said nothing. And then there rose in me,
like the earth's empowering brew rising
in root and branch, the words of a dream of you
I did not know I had dreamed. I was a wanderer
who feels the solace of his native land
under his feet again and moving in his blood.
I went on, blind and faithful. Where I stepped
my track was there to steady me. It was no abyss
that lay before me, but only the level ground.

3.
Sometimes our life reminds me
of a forest in which there is a graceful clearing
and in that opening a house,
an orchard and garden,
comfortable shades, and flowers
red and yellow in the sun, a pattern

The Country of Marriage · *207*

made in the light for the light to return to.
The forest is mostly dark, its ways
to be made anew day after day, the dark
richer than the light and more blessed,
provided we stay brave
enough to keep on going in.

4.

How many times have I come to you out of my head
with joy, if ever a man was,
for to approach you I have given up the light
and all directions. I come to you
lost, wholly trusting as a man who goes
into the forest unarmed. It is as though I descend
slowly earthward out of the air. I rest in peace
in you, when I arrive at last.

5.

. . . You are the known way leading always to the unknown,
and you are the known place to which the unknown is always
leading me back. More blessed in you than I know,
I possess nothing worthy to give you, nothing
not belittled by my saying that I possess it.
Even an hour of love is a moral predicament, a blessing
a man may be hard up to be worthy of. He can only
accept it, as a plant accepts from all the bounty of the light
enough to live, and then accepts the dark,
passing unencumbered back to the earth, as I
have fallen time and again from the great strength
of my desire, helpless, into your arms.

6.

What I am learning to give you is my death
to set you free of me, and me from myself
into the dark and the new light. Like the water

of a deep stream, love is always too much. We
did not make it. Though we drink till we burst
we cannot have it all, or want it all.
In its abundance it survives our thirst.
In the evening we come down to the shore
to drink our fill, and sleep, while it
flows through the regions of the dark.
It does not hold us, except we keep returning
to its rich waters thirsty. We enter,
willing to die, into the commonwealth of its joy.

7.
I give you what is unbounded, passing from dark to dark,
containing darkness: a night of rain, an early morning.
I give you the life I have let live for love of you:
a clump of orange-blooming weeds beside the road,
the young orchard waiting in the snow, our own life
that we have planted in this ground, as I
have planted mine in you. I give you my love for all
beautiful and honest women that you gather to yourself
again and again, and satisfy—and this poem,
no more mine than any man's who has loved a woman.

from "The Country of Marriage"

Morning in Eternal Space

Here I must say, a little anyhow: what I can hardly hope to bear out in the record: that a house of simple people which stands empty and silent in the vast Southern country morning sunlight, and everything which on this morning in eternal space it by chance contains . . . shines quietly forth such grandeur, such sorrowful holiness of its exactitudes in existence: as no human consciousness shall ever rightly perceive . . . : that there can be more beauty and more deep wonder in the standings and spacings of mute furnishings on a bare floor between the squaring bourns of walls than in any music ever made: that this square home, as it stands in unshadowed earth between the winding years of heaven, is, not to me but of itself, one among the serene and final, uncapturable beauties of existence: that this beauty is made between hurt but invincible nature and the plainest cruelties and needs of human existence in this uncured time, and is inextricable among these and as impossible without them as a saint born in paradise.

JAMES AGEE, from *Let Us Now Praise Famous Men*

*T*he wedding ceremony per se is over. For a few moments, the couple may wish to gather their thoughts in privacy: Jewish tradition makes a point of that need, specifying a short retreat for the two alone before the festivities begin. Then the guests and wedding party gather to exchange toasts to the new family, to beloved forebears and absent friends and relatives.

In many parts of the world, however, the wedding cycle carries on with libations to the earth—gifts of corn, rice, oil, wine, spilled on the ground as invitation to the spirits to join the party. These joyous but serious rituals of integration of the newly married couple into the cycles of nature shed their power over projected time to come, even to the time, long in the future, of inevitable separation and loss. Thoughts of that order are not inappropriate to a wedding. The house of which James Agee speaks, which we call the house of marriage, stands under "the winding years of heaven" and is both lived in and vacated according to their measure. But it stands in ring upon ring of fields, hills, horizon, sky, and stars, whose embrace never falters, in which the love passed down human generations seems to our questing minds even to live on in the mode we call eternity.

The following prayers and blessings from many lands and ages lift the curtain, as I said before, on that vast landscape which can be for a courageous couple their true country. It may seem strange to find invocations to and praises of the sun, wind, thunder, and other natural powers in a book on weddings. But we are born out of and return to *their order of being, and our state of "marriage" in the largest sense must be to them.*

So . . . libations to all gods!

Libations, then dancing!

And then to sleep, in a place only the Wintu Indian knows.

The Fountains mingle with the River
    And the Rivers with the Ocean,
The winds of Heaven mix for ever
    With a sweet emotion;
Nothing in the world is single;
    All things by a law divine
In one spirit meet and mingle.
    Why not I with thine?—

See the mountains kiss high Heaven
    And the waves clasp one another;
No sister-flower would be forgiven
    If it disdained its brother,
And the sunlight clasps the earth
    And the moonbeams kiss the sea:
What is all this sweet work worth
    If thou kiss not me?

PERCY BYSSHE SHELLEY, "Love's Philosophy"

. . . Therefore, on every morrow, are we wreathing
A flowery band to bind us to the earth.
Spite of despondence, of the inhuman dearth
Of noble natures, of the gloomy days,
Of all the unhealthy and o'erdarkened ways

Made for our searching: yes, in spite of all,
Some shape of beauty moves away the pall
From our dark spirits . . .

JOHN KEATS, from "Endymion"

Live you by love confined,
There is no nearer nearness;
Break not his light bounds,
The stars' and seas' harness:
There is nothing beyond,
We have found the land's end.
We'll take no mortal wound
Who felt him in the furnace,
Drowned in his fierceness,
By his midsummer browned:
Nor ever lose awareness
Of nearness and farness
Who've stood at earth's heart careless
Of suns and storms around,
Who have leant on the hedge of the wind,
On the last ledge of darkness . . .

C. DAY LEWIS, from "Live You by Love"

When the white fog burns off,
the abyss of everlasting light
is revealed. The last cobwebs
of fog in the
black firtrees are flakes
of white ash in the world's hearth.

Cold of the sea is counterpart
to this great fire. Plunging
out of the burning cold of ocean
we enter an ocean of intense
noon. Sacred salt
sparkles on our bodies.

After mist has wrapped us again
in fine wool, may the taste of salt
recall to us the great depths about us.

DENISE LEVERTOV, "The Depths"

Now that I have your face by heart, I look
Less at its features than its darkening frame
Where quince and melon, yellow as young flame,
Lie with quilled dahlias and the shepherd's crook.
Beyond, a garden. There, in insolent ease
The lead and marble figures watch the show
Of yet another summer loathe to go
Although the scythes hang in the apple trees.

Now that I have your face by heart, I look.

Now that I have your voice by heart, I read
In the black chords upon a dulling page
Music that is not meant for music's cage,
Whose emblems mix with words that shake and bleed.
The staves are shuttled over with a stark
Unprinted silence. In a double dream
I must spell out the storm, the running stream.
The beat's too swift. The notes shift in the dark.

Now that I have your voice by heart, I read.

Now that I have your heart by heart, I see
The wharves with their great ships and architraves;
The rigging and the cargo and the slaves
On a strange beach under a broken sky.
O not departure, but a voyage done!
The bales stand on the stone; the anchor weeps
Its red rust downward, and the long vine creeps
Beside the salt herb, in the lengthening sun.

Now that I have your heart by heart, I see.

Louise Bogan, "Song for the Last Act"

I will woo her, I will go with her into the wilderness and comfort her: there I will restore her vineyards, turning the Vale of Trouble into the Gate of Hope, and there she will answer as in her youth, when she came up out of Egypt. On that day she shall call me, "My husband . . ."

Then I will make a covenant on behalf of Israel with the wild beasts, the birds of the air, and the things that creep on the earth, and I will break bow and sword and weapon of war and sweep them off the earth, so that all living creatures may lie down without fear. I will betroth you to myself forever, betroth you in lawful wedlock with unfailing devotion and love; I will betroth you to myself to have and to hold, . . . I will answer for the heavens, and they will answer for the earth, and the earth will answer for the corn, the new wine and the oil.

Hosea 2:14–15; 18–23 (New English Bible)

I invoke thee, who art the greatest of all, who created all, who generated it from thyself, who sees all and is never seen. Thou hast given to the sun its glory and its power, to the moon hast thou granted the right to wax and wane and follow a regular course, without having robbed anything from other regions, but having been equal with all. For at thy appearance the world came into being and there was light. All things bowed down before thee, whom no one can contemplate in thy true form, who changes form, who remains the invisible Ayion of the Ayion.

Greek prayer to the god Ayion

O Morning Star! when you look down upon us, give us peace and refreshing sleep. Great Spirit! bless our children, friends, and visitors through a happy life. May our trails lie straight and level before us. Let us live to be old. We are all your children and ask these things with good hearts.

Hymn of the Great Plains Indians to the sun

O Spirit, grant us a calm lake, little wind, little rain, so that the canoes may proceed well, so that they may proceed speedily.

Tanganyikan fishermen's prayer

May you be for us a moon of joy and happiness. Let the young become strong and the grown man maintain his strength, the pregnant woman be delivered and the woman who has given birth, suckle her child. Let the stranger come to the end of his journey and those who remain at home dwell safely in their houses. Let the flocks that go to feed in the pastures return happily. May you be a moon of harvest and of calves. May you be a moon of restoration and of good health.

African prayer to the new moon

The year is abundant, with much millet and rice;
And we have our high granaries,
With myriads, and hundreds of thousands, and millions of
    measures in them
For spirits and sweet spirits,
To present to our ancestors, male and female,
And to supply all our ceremonies.
The blessings sent down on us are of every kind.

Chinese prayer of thanksgiving

I humbly ask that this Palace, as far downward as the lowermost rock-roots, suffer no harm from reptiles among its bottom-ropes; as far upward as the blue clouds are diffused in the Plain of High Heaven, suffer no harm from flying birds in the celestial smoke-hole; that the joinings of the firmly planted pillars, and of the crossbeams, rafters, doors, and windows may not move or make a noise, that there may be no slackening of the tied rope-knots and no dishevelment of the roof-thatch, no creaking of the floor-joints or alarms by night.

I humbly ask that the gods guard the great eight road-forks like a mighty assemblage of rocks. . . .

Whenever, from the Root-country, the Bottom-country, there come savage and unfriendly beings, consort not and parley not with them; but if they go below, keep watch below; if they go above, keep watch above, protecting us against pollution with a night guarding and with a day guarding. The offerings I furnish in your honor are bright cloth, shining cloth, soft cloth, and rough cloth. Of *sake* I fill the bellies of the jars. Grain I offer you. Of things that dwell in the mountains and on the moors I offer the soft of hair and the coarse of hair. Of things

that dwell in the blue sea-plain, the broad of fin and the narrow
of fin, even to the weeds of the shallows and the weeds of the
shore.

Japanese invocation to the spirits to protect the Palace

Fly ahead of me.
Open the way,
Prepare the path.
O spirit of the sun
That dwells in the jungle-south,
O mother of light
Who are jealous.
I turn to thee, imploring
Keep your shadows high, very high!
And you who dwell in the west on the mountaintop,
O my lordly forebear of the great strength,
The powerful hill.
Come to me!
And you, venerable charmer of the flames,
With the gray beard.
I implore thee!
Give approval to all my thoughts
And to all my desires.
Listen to me,
Listen to all my prayers, all my prayers!

· · ·

All together let us smoke tobacco,
Let us all drink wine.
All together let us ride a horse.

Morning in Eternal Space · 221

Let us all wear furs.
We shall not keep hidden
What we have learned.
We shall preserve
What we have found.

. . .

We have decided here and now to marry our son and daughter.
Therefore, O goddess of Fire, hearken and be witness. Protect
this pair from every illness; watch over them so that they may
grow old.

Three Turko-Mongolian prayers

You are my [husband/wife]
My feet shall run because of you.
My feet, dance because of you.
My heart shall beat because of you.
My eyes, see because of you.
My mind, think because of you.
And I shall love because of you.

Eskimo love song

O, You who dwell in Tsegihi,
In the house made of dawn,
In the house made of evening twilight,
In the house made of dark cloud,
In the house made of the he-rain, of the dark mist,
In the house made of the she-rain, of pollen, of grasshoppers,
Where the dark mist curtains the doorway,
The path to which is the rainbow,

Where the zigzag lightning stands high on top,
Oh, divinity!
With your moccasins of dark cloud, come to us,
With your leggings and shirt and headdress of dark cloud, come
    to us,
With your head enveloped in dark cloud, come to us,
With the dark thunder above you, come to us, soaring,
With the shapen cloud at your feet, come to us, soaring,
With the far darkness made of the dark cloud over your head,
    come to us, soaring.
With the far darkness made of the rain and the mist over your
    head, come to us, soaring.
With the zigzag lightning flung out on high over your head,
With the rainbow hanging high over your head, come to us,
    soaring.
With the far darkness made of the dark cloud on the ends of
    your wings,
With the far darkness made of the rain and the mist on the ends
    of your wings, come to us, soaring.
With the zigzag lightning, with the rainbow hanging high on
    the ends of your wings, come to us, soaring.
With the near darkness made of the dark cloud of the he-rain
    and the she-rain, come to us,
With the darkness on the earth, come to us.
With these I wish the foam floating on the flowing water over
    the roots of the great corn.
I have made your sacrifice,
I have prepared a smoke for you,
My feet restore for me.
My limbs restore, my body restore, my mind restore, my voice
    restore for me.
Today, take out your spell for me,
Today, take away your spell for me,

Away from me you have taken it,
Far off from me it is taken,
Far off you have done it.
Happily I recover,
Happily I become cool,
My eyes regain their power, my head cools, my limbs regain
   the strength, I hear again.
Happily I walk; impervious to pain, I walk; light within, I walk;
   joyous, I walk.
Abundant dark clouds I desire,
An abundance of vegetation I desire,
An abundance of pollen, abundant dew, I desire.
Happily may fair white corn, to the ends of the earth, come
   with you.
Happily may fair yellow corn, fair blue corn, fair corn of all
   kinds, plants of all kinds, goods of all kinds, jewels of all
   kinds, to the ends of the earth, come with you.
With these before you, happily may they come with you,
With these behind, below, above, around you, happily may
   they come with you,
Thus you accomplish your tasks.
Happily, the old men will regard you,
Happily, the old women will regard you,
The young men and the young women will regard you,
The children will regard you,
The chiefs will regard you,
Happily, as they scatter in all directions, they will regard you.
Happily, as they approach their homes, they will regard you.
May their roads home be on the trail of peace,
Happily may they all get back.
In beauty I walk,
With beauty before me, I walk,
With beauty behind me, I walk,

With beauty below and above me, in the beauty about me, I
  walk.
It is finished in beauty.
It is finished in beauty.
It is finished in beauty.

Navajo hymn to the Thunderbird,
translation by Washington Matthews

To the West:
  Over there are the mountains. May you see them as long as
you live, for from them you receive sweet pine for incense.

To the North:
  Strength will come from the North. May you look for many
years upon the Star that never moves.

To the East:
  Old age will come from below, from where comes the light
of the Sun.

To the South:
  May warm winds of the South bring you food.

Blackfoot prayer to the four directions

To the Mound of the East: Spring

Under the influence of the vernal yang, the vegetation is reborn.
The time of fertilizing rains, the time of love.

The thunder sounds and wakes the hibernating creatures.
That which seemed dead revives, and pursues its destiny.

May the innumerable new beings live their life to its end.
May the crowd of the living fully enjoy the happiness of the
  vernal spring.

To the Mound of the South: Summer

The red light grows, heat increases,
The flowering trees are in full splendor.

After the flowers will come fruits, plentiful and savory . . .

To the Mound of the West: Autumn

The West is the region of white light.
Autumn wind gently kills the vegetation.
But the seeds of the plants are preserved.
They contain the germ of the spring to come.

To the Mound of the North: Winter

Somber is the region of the North. All beings which hibernate
    have gone into the earth.
Vegetables have lose their leaves, and frost freezes the land . . .
May the people, remembering their origin, retain love for
    simplicity. . . .
May they make offerings, may they prepare the lands, in order
    that their next harvest may be abundant.

Chinese prayer to the four directions

Ten thousand things bright
Ten thousand miles, no dust
Water and sky one color
Houses shining along your road.

Chinese blessing

The life in us is like the water in the river. It may rise this year higher than man has ever known it, and flood the parched uplands; even this may be the eventful year, which will drown out all our muskrats. It was not always dry land where we dwell. I see far inland the banks which the stream anciently washed, before science began to record its freshets. Every one has heard the story which has gone the rounds of New England, of a strong and beautiful bug which came out of the dry leaf of an old table of apple-tree wood, which had stood in a farmer's kitchen for sixty years, first in Connecticut, and afterward in Massachusetts,—from an egg deposited in the living tree many years earlier still, as appeared by counting the annual layers beyond it; which was heard gnawing out for several weeks, hatched perchance by the heat of an urn. . . . Who knows what beautiful and winged life, whose egg has been buried for ages under many concentric layers of woodenness in the dead dry life of society, deposited at first in the alburnum of the green and living tree, which has been gradually converted into the semblance of its well-seasoned tomb,—heard perchance gnawing out now for years by the astonished family of man, as they sat round the festive board,—may unexpectedly come forth from amidst society's most trivial and handselled furniture, to enjoy its perfect summer life at last!

. . . such is the character of that morrow which mere lapse of time can never make to dawn. The light which puts out our eyes is darkness to us. Only that day dawns to which we are awake. There is more day to dawn. The sun is but a morning star.

Henry David Thoreau, from Walden

How enduring are our bodies, after all! The forms of our brothers and sisters, our parents and children and wives, lie still in the hills and fields around us.

HENRY DAVID THOREAU, from The Journal

To the dim light and the large circle of shade
I have clomb, and to the whitening of the hills,
There where we see no color in the grass.
Natheless my longing loses not its green,
It has so taken root in the hard stone
Which talks and hears as though it were a lady.

Utterly frozen is this youthful lady,
Even as the snow that lies within the shade;
For she is no more moved than is the stone
By the sweet season which makes warm the hills
And alters them afresh from white to green
Covering their sides again with flowers and grass.

When on her hair she sets a crown of grass
The thought has no more room for other lady,
Because she weaves the yellow with the green
So well that Love sits down there in the shade,—
Love who has shut me in among low hills
Faster than between walls of granite-stone.

She is more bright than is a precious stone;
The wound she gives may not be healed with grass:
I therefore have fled far o'er plains and hills
For refuge from so dangerous a lady;
But from her sunshine nothing can give shade,—
Not any hill, nor wall, nor summer-green.

A while ago, I saw her dressed in green,—
So fair, she might have wakened in a stone
This love which I do feel even for her shade;
And therefore, as one woos a graceful lady,
I wooed her in a field that was all grass
Girdled about with very lofty hills.

Yet shall the streams turn back and climb the hills
Before Love's flame in this damp wood and green
Burn, as it burns within a youthful lady,
For my sake, who would sleep away in stone
My life, or feed like beasts upon the grass,
Only to see her garments cast a shade.

How dark soe'er the hills throw out their shade,
Under her summer-green the beautiful lady
Covers it, like a stone cover'd in grass.

Cino Da Pistoia, "Sestina of the Lady Pietra
degli Scrovigni," translation by Dante Gabriel Rossetti

I found her out there
On a slope few see,
That falls westwardly
To the salt-edged air,
Where the ocean breaks
On the purple strand,
And the hurricane shakes
The solid land.

I brought her here,
And have laid her to rest
In a noiseless nest
No sea beats near.

She will never be stirred
In her loamy cell
By the waves long heard
And loved so well.

So she does not sleep
By those haunted heights
The Atlantic smites
And the blind gales sweep,
Whence she often would gaze
At Dundagel's famed head,
While the dipping blaze
Dyed her face fire-red;

And would sigh at the tale
Of sunk Lyonnesse,
As a wind-tugged tress
Flapped her cheek like a flail;
Or listen at whiles
With a thought-bound brow
To the murmuring miles
She is far from now.

Yet her shade, maybe,
Will creep underground
Till it catch the sound
Of that western sea
As it swells and sobs
Where she once domiciled,
And joy in its throbs
With the heart of a child.

THOMAS HARDY,
"I Found Her Out There"

I want to paint men and women with that something of the eternal which the halo used to symbolize . . . to express the love of two lovers by a wedding of two complementary colors, their mingling and opposition, the mysterious vibration of kindred tones. To express the thought of a brow by the radiance of a light tone against a somber background.

To express hope by some star, the eagerness of a soul by a sunset radiance.

VINCENT VAN GOGH, from a letter to his brother, Theo

This we know, all things are connected, like the blood which unites one family. All things are connected. Whatever befalls the earth, befalls the sons of the earth. Man did not weave the web of life; he is merely a strand in it. Whatever he does to the web, he does to himself.

CHIEF SEATTLE OF THE DWAMISH TRIBE

Blessed is the light that turns to fire, and blessed the
    flames that fire makes of what it burns.
Blessed the inexhaustible sun, for it feeds the moon that
    shines but does not burn.
Praised be hot vapors in earth's crust, for they force up
    mountains that explode as molten rock and cool, like
    love remembered.
Holy is the sun that strikes sea, for surely as water
    burns life and death are one. . . .

GRACE SCHULMAN, from "Blessed Is the Light"

They lived long, and were faithful
to the good in each other.
They suffered as their faith required.

The Country of Marriage · 231

Now their union is consummate
in earth, and the earth
is their communion. They enter
the serene gravity of the rain,
the hill's passage to the sea.
After long striving, perfect ease.

WENDELL BERRY,
"A Marriage, an Elegy"

May the wind be always at your back.
May the road rise up to meet you.
May the sun shine warm on your face,
The rains fall soft on your fields.
Until we meet again, may the Lord
Hold you in the hollow of his hand.

Irish blessing

God banish from your house
The fly, the roach, the mouse

That riots in the walls
Until the plaster falls;

Admonish from your door
The hypocrite and liar;

No shy, soft, tigrish fear
Permit upon your stair,

Nor agents of your doubt.
God drive them whistling out.

Let nothing touched with evil,
Let nothing that can shrivel

Heart's tenderest frond, intrude
Upon your still, deep blood.

Against the drip of night
God keep all windows tight,

Protect your mirrors from
Surprise, delirium,

Admit no trailing wind
Into your shuttered mind

To plume the lake of sleep
With dreams. If you must weep

God give you tears, but leave
Your secrecy to grieve,

And islands for your pride,
And love to nest in your side.

STANLEY KUNITZ, "Benediction"

Beautiful is thy rising upon the horizon of heaven, when the
     living Disk hangs vibrant.
Thou it is that shineth upon the Eastern horizon, and every
     land is filled with thy beauty.
It is thy beauty, the greatness, and thy splendor that cause
     praises to thee from every land when thy rays embrace
     their lands.
Thou compellest their love of thee, for though thou art far
     distant, yet do thy rays illumine the earth.
When thou takest thy rest in the Western Horizon, the land is
     in darkness, with thoughts of death. . . .

The Country of Marriage ·

Day breaks at thy appearance upon the Horizon, when thou
    givest light by means of the Disk by day; yea, darkness
    flees when thou sendest forth thy beams . . .
Thou makest man to unite with woman, thou hast put a life-
    giving seed into humankind, making live a child within the
    womb of its mother . . .
If there is a chicken within the egg, thou givest it breath within
    its shell, so that it lives. Thou makest it to unite all its
    strength, so that it breaketh the egg, cometh forth from
    the shell and calleth for its mother. . . . It walketh upon
    its two feet.
Thou hast created the earth by thy mere wish when thou wast
    the only one: all men and animals, all that goeth upon
    their feet upon the earth, and all that fly on high . . .

AMENOPHIS IV (IKHNATON), hymn to the sun

Every day is a god, each day is a god, and
holiness holds forth in time. I worship each
god, I praise each day splintered down,
splintered down and wrapped in time like a
husk, a husk of many colors spreading, at dawn
fast over the mountains split.

   I wake in a god. I wake in arms holding my
quilt, holding me as best they can inside my
quilt.

   Someone is kissing me—already. I wake, I
cry, "Oh," I rise from the pillow. Why should
I open my eyes?

   I open my eyes. The god lifts from the water.
His head fills the bay. He is Puget Sound, the

Pacific; his breast rises from pastures; his
fingers are firs; islands slide wet down his
shoulders. Islands slip blue from his shoulders
and glide over the water, the empty, lighted
water like a stage.

Today's god rises, his long eyes flecked in
clouds. He flings his arms, spreading colors; he
arches, cupping sky in his belly; he vaults,
vaulting and spread, holding all and spread
on me like skin. . . .

The day is real. . . .

The day is real. . . . I stand and smooth the
quilt.

"Oh," I cry, "Oh!"

ANNIE DILLARD, from *Holy the Firm*

Libations! Libations!
To the protective spirits on high!
To the wandering spirits below!
To the spirits of the mountains,
To the spirits of the valleys,
To the spirits of the East,
To the spirits of the West,
To the spirits of the North,
To the spirits of the South,
To the bride and groom, together, libation!
May the spirits on high, as well as the spirits below, fill you
    with grace!

Divine helpers, come! Keep watch all night! Rather than see
the bridegroom so much as damage his toenail, may the good
spirits go ahead of him. May the bride not so much as damage

her fingernail! The good spirits will be their cushions so that not a hair of their heads shall be harmed.

And you, all you good wedding guests waiting in the shadows, come out into the light! May the light follow you!

African wedding benediction

. . . hand in hand, on the edge of the sand,

They danced by the light of the moon,
     The moon,
     The moon,
They danced by the light of the moon.

EDWARD LEAR, from "The Owl and the Pussycat"

Where will you and I sleep?
At the down-turned jagged rim of the sky, you and I will sleep.

Wintu tribe "Dream Song"

Suggested Readings for Various Members of the Wedding Party

The Bride

The Bridegroom

The Bride and Bridegroom Singly or Together

Father of the Bride

Mother of the Bride

Father of the Bridegroom

Mother of the Bridegroom

Parents, Brothers, Sisters, and Others of the Immediate Families

Close Friends

In addition to the above, many scriptural and liturgical passages throughout are appropriate for reading by all members of the wedding party. Officiants may wish to enlarge on their normal liturgical and scriptural readings with selections from "Eternal Vows in Sacred Space" and "Morning in Eternal Space."

Index

Credits

Grateful acknowledgment is made for permission to reprint the following copyrighted material:

FOR THE BEST IN PAPERBACKS, LOOK FOR THE

In every corner of the world, on every subject under the sun, Penguin represents quality and variety—the very best in publishing today.

For complete information about books available from Penguin—including Puffins, Penguin Classics, and Arkana—and how to order them, write to us at the appropriate address below. Please note that for copyright reasons the selection of books varies from country to country.

In the United Kingdom: Please write to *Dept. JC, Penguin Books Ltd, FREEPOST, West Drayton, Middlesex UB7 0BR.*

If you have any difficulty in obtaining a title, please send your order with the correct money, plus ten percent for postage and packaging, to *P.O. Box No. 11, West Drayton, Middlesex UB7 0BR*

In the United States: Please write to *Consumer Sales, Penguin USA, P.O. Box 999, Dept. 17109, Bergenfield, New Jersey 07621-0120.* Visa and MasterCard holders call 1-800-253-6476 to order all Penguin titles

In Canada: Please write to *Penguin Books Canada Ltd, 10 Alcorn Avenue, Suite 300, Toronto, Ontario M4V 3B2*

In Australia: Please write to *Penguin Books Australia Ltd, P.O. Box 257, Ringwood, Victoria 3134*

In New Zealand: Please write to *Penguin Books (NZ) Ltd, Private Bag 102902, North Shore Mail Centre, Auckland 10*

In India: Please write to *Penguin Books India Pvt Ltd, 706 Eros Apartments, 56 Nehru Place, New Delhi 110 019*

In the Netherlands: Please write to *Penguin Books Netherlands bv, Postbus 3507, NL-1001 AH Amsterdam*

In Germany: Please write to *Penguin Books Deutschland GmbH, Metzlerstrasse 26, 60594 Frankfurt am Main*

In Spain: Please write to *Penguin Books S. A., Bravo Murillo 19, 1° B, 28015 Madrid*

In Italy: Please write to *Penguin Italia s.r.l., Via Felice Casati 20, I-20124 Milano*

In France: Please write to *Penguin France S. A., 17 rue Lejeune, F-31000 Toulouse*

In Japan: Please write to *Penguin Books Japan, Ishikiribashi Building, 2-5-4, Suido, Bunkyo-ku, Tokyo 112*

In Greece: Please write to *Penguin Hellas Ltd, Dimocritou 3, GR-106 71 Athens*

In South Africa: Please write to *Longman Penguin Southern Africa (Pty) Ltd, Private Bag X08, Bertsham 2013*